MAGIC FOR MARIGOLD
&
JANE OF LANTERN HILL

BY

L. M. MONTGOMERY

Author of
"Anne of Green Gables,"
"Anne of Avonlea,"
"Kilmeny of the Orchard," etc.

The Story Girl first published 1911
The Golden Road first published 1913
This edition published by Read Books Ltd.
Copyright © 2017 Read Books Ltd.
This book is copyright and may not be
reproduced or copied in any way without
the express permission of the publisher in writing

British Library Cataloguing-in-Publication Data
A catalogue record for this book is available
from the British Library

CONTENTS

Lucy Maud Montgomery

Lucy Maud Montgomery was born on 30th November 1874, on Prince Edward Island, Canada. Her mother, Clara Woolner (Macneil), died before Lucy reached the age of two and so she was raised by her maternal grandparents in a family of wealthy Scottish immigrants. The Family were deeply rooted in the development of the island, having arrived there in the 1770's, and both Lucy's grandfather and great grandfather had been figures in the province's governance.

As a young girl, Montgomery had a very privileged upbringing. Due to the families wealth, she had access to a greater number of books than was usual in this era. These resources, coupled with the family's Scottish traditions of oral storytelling, gave her a taste for literature.

Montgomery took a teacher's degree at Charlottetown's Prince of Wales College before beginning work at a rural school to raise funds for and additional year at Dalhousie University. She continued to teach for a couple of years until her income from writing enabled her to become a full-time author. She then moved back home to live with her grandmother. In 1908, Montgomery produced her first full-length novel, titled *Anne of Green Gables*. It was an instant success and, following it up with several sequels, Montgomery became a regular on the best-seller list and an international household name.

In 1911 she married Ewan Macdonald, a Presbyterian minister, following the death of her grandmother. They had two sons together but the marriage was fraught with difficulties. Ewan had a severe mental disorder that frequently left him incapacitated, seriously hampering his career and eventually forcing him to resign from the ministry in 1935. The couple retired to Toronto and resided there together until Montgomery's death on 24th April 1942.

MAGIC FOR MARIGOLD

First published in 1929

CHAPTER I

What's in a Name?

1

Once upon a time—which, when you come to think of it, is really the only proper way to begin a story—the only way that really smacks of romance and fairyland—all the Harmony members of the Lesley clan had assembled at Cloud of Spruce to celebrate Old Grandmother's birthday as usual. Also to name Lorraine's baby. It was a crying shame, as Aunt Nina pathetically said, that the little darling had been in the world four whole months without a name. But what could you do, with poor dear Leander dying in that terribly sudden way just two weeks before his daughter was born and poor Lorraine being so desperately ill for weeks and weeks afterwards? Not very strong yet, for that matter. And there was tuberculosis in her family, you know.

Aunt Nina was not really an aunt at all—at least, not of any Lesley. She was just a cousin. It was the custom of the Lesley caste to call every one "Uncle" or "Aunt" as soon as he or she had become too old to be fitly called by a first name among the young fry. There will be no end of these "aunts" and "uncles" bobbing in and out of this story—as well as several genuine ones. I shall not stop to explain which kind they were. It doesn't matter. They were all Lesleys or married to Lesleys. *That* was all that mattered. You were born to the purple if you were a Lesley. Even the pedigrees of their cats were known.

All the Lesleys adored Lorraine's baby. They had all agreed in loving Leander—about the only thing they had ever been known to agree on. And it was thirty years since there had been a baby at Cloud of Spruce. Old Grandmother had more than once said gloomily that the good old stock was running out. So this small lady's advent would have been hailed with delirious delight if it hadn't been for Leanders death and Lorraine's long illness. Now that Old Grandmother's birthday had come, the Lesleys had an excuse for their long-deferred jollification. As for the name, no Lesley baby was ever named until every relative within get-at-able distance had had his or her say in the matter. The selection of a suitable name was, in their eyes, a much more important thing than the mere christening. And how much more in the case of a fatherless baby whose mother was a sweet soul enough—but—you know—a Winthrop!

Cloud of Spruce, the original Lesley homestead, where Old Grandmother and Young Grandmother and Mrs. Leander and the baby and Salome Silversides lived, was on the harbour shore, far enough out of Harmony village to be in the real country; a cream brick house—a nice chubby old house—so covered with vines that it looked more like a heap of ivy than a house; a house that had folded its hands and said, "I will rest." Before it was the beautiful Harmony Harbour; with its purring waves, so close that in autumnal storms the spray dashed over the very doorsteps and encrusted the windows. Behind it was an orchard that climbed the slope. And about it always the soft sighing of the big spruce wood on the hill.

The birthday dinner was eaten in Old Grandmother's room—which had been the "orchard room" until Old Grandmother, two years back, had cheerfully and calmly announced that she was tired of getting up before breakfast and working between meals.

"I'm going to spend the rest of my life being waited on," she said. "I've had ninety years of slaving for other people—" and bossing them, the Lesleys said in their hearts. But not out loud, for it did really seem at times as if Old Grandmother's ears could hear for miles. Uncle Ebenezer said something once about Old

Grandmother, to himself, in his cellar at midnight, when he knew he was the only human being in the house. Next Sunday afternoon Old Grandmother cast it up to him. She said Lucifer had told her. Lucifer was her cat. And Uncle Ebenezer suddenly remembered that *his* cat had been sitting on the edge of the potato bin when he said that.

It was safest not to say things about Old Grandmother.

Old Grandmother's room was a long, dim-green apartment running across the south end of the house, with a glass door opening right into the orchard. Its walls were hung with photographs of Lesley brides for sixty years back, most of them with enormous bouquets and wonderful veils and trains. Clementine's photograph was among them—Clementine, Leander's first wife, who had died six years ago with *her* little unnamed daughter. Old Grandmother had it hanging on the wall at the foot of her bed so that she could see it all the time. Old Grandmother had been very fond of Clementine. At least, she always gave Lorraine that impression.

The picture was good to look at—Clementine Lesley had been very beautiful. She was not dressed as a bride—in fact the picture had been taken just before her marriage and had a clan fame as "Clementine with the lily." She was posed standing with her beautiful arms resting on a pedestal and in one slender, perfect hand—Clementine's hands had become a tradition of loveliness—she held a lily, at which she was gazing earnestly. Old Grandmother had told Lorraine once that a distinguished guest at Cloud of Spruce, an artist of international fame, had exclaimed on seeing that picture,

"Exquisite hands! Hands into which a man might fearlessly put his soul!"

Lorraine had sighed and looked at her rather thin little hands. Not beautiful—scarcely even pretty; yet Leander had once kissed their finger-tips and said—but Lorraine did not tell Old Grandmother what Leander had said. Perhaps Old Grandmother might have liked her better if she had.

11

Old Grandmother had her clock in the corner by the bed—a clock that had struck for the funerals and weddings and goings and comings and meetings and partings of five generations; the grandfather clock her husband's father had brought out from Scotland a hundred and forty years ago; the Lesleys plumed themselves on being Prince Edward Island pioneer stock. It was still keeping excellent time and Old Grandmother got out of bed every night to wind it. She would have done that if she had been dying.

Her other great treasure was in the opposite corner. A big glass case with Alicia, the famous Skinner doll, in it. Old Grandmother's mother had been a Skinner and the doll had no part in Lesley traditions, but every Lesley child had been brought up in the fear and awe of it and knew its story. Old Grandmother's mother's sister had lost her only little daughter of three years and had never been "quite right" afterwards. She had had a waxen image of her baby made and kept it beside her always and talked to it as if it had been alive. It was dressed in a wonderful embroidered dress that had belonged to the dead baby, and wore one of her slippers. The other slipper was held in one waxen hand ready for the small bare foot that peeped out under the muslin flounces. The doll was so lifelike that Lorraine always shuddered when she passed it, and Salome Silversides was very doubtful of the propriety of having such a thing in the house at all, especially as she knew that Lazarre, the French hired man, thought and told that it was the Old Lady's "Saint" and believed she prayed before it regularly. But all the Lesleys had a certain pride in it. No other Prince Edward Island family could boast a doll like that. It conferred a certain distinction upon them and tourists wrote it up in their local papers when they went back home.

Of course the cats were present at the festivity also. Lucifer and the Witch of Endor. Both of black velvet with great round eyes. Cloud of Spruce was noted for its breed of black cats with topaz-hued eyes. Its kittens were not scattered broadcast but given away with due discrimination.

Lucifer was Old Grandmother's favourite. A remote, subtle cat. An inscrutable cat so full of mystery that it fairly oozed out of him. The Witch of Endor became her name but compared to Lucifer she was commonplace. Salome wondered secretly that Old Grandmother wasn't afraid of a judgment for calling a cat after the Old Harry. Salome "liked cats in their place" but she was furious when Uncle Klon said to her once,

"Salome Silversides! Why, you ought to be a cat yourself with a name like that. A sleek, purring plushy Maltese."

"I'm sure I don't look like a cat," said Salome, highly insulted. And Uncle Klon agreed that she did not.

Old Grandmother was a gnomish dame of ninety-two who meant to live to be a hundred. A tiny, shrunken, wrinkled thing with flashing black eyes. There was a Puckish hint of malice in most things she said or did. She ruled the whole Lesley clan and knew everything that was said and done in it. If she had given up "slaving" she certainly had not given up "bossing." To-day she was propped up on crimson cushions, with a fresh, frilled, white cap tied around her face, eating her dinner heartily and thinking things not lawful to be uttered about her daughters-in-law and her granddaughters-in-law and her great-grand-daughters-in-law.

2

Young Grandmother, a mere lass of sixty-five, sat at the head of the long table—a tall, handsome lady with bright, steel-blue eyes and white hair, whom Old Grandmother thought a somewhat pert young thing. There was nothing of the traditional grandmother of caps and knitting about *her*. She was like a stately old princess in her purple velvet gown with its wonderful lace collar. The gown had been made eight years before, but when Young Grandmother wore anything it seemed at once in the height of the fashion. Most of the Lesleys present thought she

13

should not have laid aside her black even for a birthday dinner. But Young Grandmother did not care what they thought any more than Old Grandmother did. She had been a Blaisdell—one of "the stubborn Blaisdells"—and the Blaisdell traditions were as good as the Lesley traditions any day.

Lorraine sat on the right of Young Grandmother at the table, with the baby in her cradle beside her. Because of the baby she had a certain undeniable importance never before conceded her. All the Lesleys had been more or less opposed to Leander's "second choice." Only the fact that she was a minister's daughter appeased them. She was a shy, timid, pretty creature—quite insignificant except for her enormous masses of lustrous, pale gold hair. Her small face was sweet and flower-like and she had peculiarly soft grey-blue eyes with long lashes. She looked very young and fragile in her black dress. But she was beginning to be a little happy once more. Her arms, that had reached out so emptily in the silence of the night, were filled again. The fields and hills around Cloud of Spruce that had been so stark and bare and chill when her little lady came were green and golden now, spilled over with blossoms, and the orchard was an exquisite perfumed world by itself. One could not be altogether unhappy, in springtime, with such a wonderful, unbelievable baby.

The baby lay in the old Heppelwhite cradle where her father and grandfather had lain before her—a quite adorable baby, with a saucy little chin, tiny hands as exquisite as the apple-blossoms, eyes of fairy blue, and the arrogant, superior smile of babies before they have forgotten all the marvellous things they know at first. Lorraine could hardly eat her dinner for gazing at her baby—and wondering. Would this tiny thing ever be a dancing, starry-eyed girl—a white bride—a mother? Lorraine shivered. It did not do to look so far ahead. Aunt Anne got up, brought a shawl, and tenderly put it around Lorraine's shoulders. Lorraine was almost melted, for the June day was hot, but she wore the shawl all through dinner rather than hurt Aunt Anne's feelings. That one fact described Lorraine.

On Young Grandmother's left sat Uncle Klondike, the one handsome, mysterious, unaccountable member of the Lesley clan, with his straight, heavy eyebrows, his flashing blue eyes, his mane of tawny hair and the red-gold beard which had caused a sentimental Harmony lady of uncertain years to say that he made her think of those splendid old Vikings.

Uncle Klondike's real name was Horace, but ever since he had come back from the Yukon with gold dropping out of his pockets he had been known as Klondike Lesley. His deity was the God of All Wanderers and in his service Horace Lesley had spent wild, splendid, adventurous years.

When Klondike had been a boy at school he had a habit of looking at certain places on the map and saying, "I'll go there." Go he did. He had stood on the southernmost boulder of Ceylon and sat on Buddhist cairns at the edge of Thibet. The Southern Cross was a pal and he had heard the songs of nightingales in the gardens of the Alhambra. India and the China seas were to him as a tale that is told, and he had walked alone in great Arctic spaces under northern lights. He had lived in many places but he had never thought of any of them as home. That name had all unconsciously been kept sacred to the long, green, seaward-looking glen where he had been born.

And finally he had come home, sated, to live the rest of his life a decent law-abiding clansman, whereof the conclusive sign and token was that he had trimmed his moustache and beard into decency. The moustache had been particularly atrocious. Its ends hung down nearly as far as his beard did. When Aunt Anne asked him despairingly why upon earth he wore a moustache like that he retorted that he wrapped it round his ears to keep them warm. The clan were horribly afraid he meant to go on wearing them—for Uncle Klon was both Lesley *and* Blaisdell. He finally had them clipped, though he could never be induced to go the length of a clean-shaven face, fashion or no fashion. But, though he went to bed early at least once a week, he still savoured life with gusto and the clan were always secretly much afraid of him and his satiric winks and cynical speeches. Aunt Nina, in particular, had held him in terror ever since the day she had told him proudly that her husband had *never* lied to her.

"Oh, you poor woman," said Uncle Klon, with real sympathy in his tone.

Nina supposed there was a joke somewhere but she could never find it. She was a W. C. T. U. and an I. O. D. E. and most of the other letters of the alphabet—but somehow she found it hard to get the hang of Klondike's jokes.

Klondike Lesley was known to be a woman-hater. He scoffed openly at all love, more especially the supreme absurdity of love at first sight. This did not prevent his clan from trying for years to marry him off. It would be the making of Klondike if he had a good wife who would stand no nonsense. They were very obvious about it, and with the renowned Lesley frankness, recommended several excellent brides to him. But Klondike Lesley was notoriously hard to please.

"Katherine Nichols?"

"But look at the thick ankles of her."

"Emma Goodfellow?"

"Her mother used to call out 'meow' in church whenever the minister said something she didn't like. Can't risk heredity."

"Rose Osborn?"

"I can't stand a woman with pudgy hands."

"Sara Jennet?"

"An egg without salt."

"Lottie Parks?"

"I'd like her as a flavouring, not as a dish."

"Ruth Russell?"—triumphantly, as having at last hit on a woman with whom no reasonable man could find fault.

"Too peculiar. When she has nothing to say she doesn't talk. That's really too uncanny in a woman, you know."

"Dorothy Porter?"

"Ornamental by candlelight. But I don't believe she'd look so well at breakfast."

"Amy Ray?"

"Always purring, blinking, sidling, clawing. Nice small pussy-cat but I'm no mouse."

"Agnes Barr?"

"A woman who says Coué's formula instead of her prayers!"

"Olive Purdy?"

"Tongue—temper—and tears. Go sparingly, thank you."

Even Old Grandmother took a hand and met with no better success. She was wiser than to throw any one girl at his head—the men of the Lesley clan never had married the women picked out for them. But she had her own way of managing things.

"'He travels the fastest who travels alone,'" was all she could get out of Klondike.

"Very clever of you," said Old Grandmother, "if travelling fast is all there is to life."

"Not clever of *me*. Don't you know your Kipling, Grandmother?"

"What is a Kipling?" said Old Grandmother.

Uncle Klondike did not tell her. He merely said he was doomed to die a bachelor—and could not escape his kismet.

Old Grandmother was not a stupid woman even if she didn't know what a Kipling was.

"You've waited too long—you've lost your appetite," she said shrewdly.

The Lesleys gave it up. No use trying to fit this exasperating relative with a wife. A bachelor Klon remained, with an awful habit of wiring "sincere sympathy" when any of his friends got married. Perhaps it was just as well. His nephews and nieces might benefit, especially Lorraine's baby whom he evidently worshipped. So here he was, unwedded, light-hearted and content, watching them all with his amused smile.

Lucifer had leaped on his knee as soon as he had sat down. Lucifer condescended to very few but, as he told the Witch of Endor, Klondike Lesley had a way with him. Uncle Klon fed Lucifer with bits from his own plate and Salome, who ate with the family because she was a fourth cousin of Jane Lyle, who had married the stepbrother of a Lesley, thought it ghastly.

3

The baby had to be talked all over again and Uncle William-over-the-bay covered himself with indelible disgrace by saying dubiously,

"She is not—ahem—really a pretty child, do you think?"

"All the better for her future looks," said Old Grandmother tartly. She had been biding her moment, like a watchful cat, to give a timely dig. "*You*," she added maliciously, "were a very pretty baby—though you did not have any more hair on your head than you have now."

"Beauty is a fatal gift. She will be better without it," sighed Aunt Nina.

"Then why do you cold-cream your face every night and eat raw carrots for your complexion and dye your hair?" asked Old Grandmother.

Aunt Nina couldn't imagine how Old Grandmother knew about the carrots. *She* had no cat to tattle to Lucifer.

"We are all as God made us," said Uncle Ebenezer piously.

"Then God botched some of us," snapped Old Grandmother, looking significantly at Uncle Ebenezer's enormous ears and the frill of white whisker around his throat that made him look oddly like a sheep. But then, reflected Old Grandmother, whoever might be responsible for the nose, it was hardly fair to blame God for Ebenezer's whiskers.

"She has a peculiarly shaped hand, hasn't she?" persisted Uncle William-over-the-bay.

Aunt Anne bent over and kissed one of the little hands.

"The hand of an artist," she said.

Lorraine looked at her gratefully and hated Uncle William-over-the-bay bitterly for ten minutes under her golden hair.

"Handsome is as handsome does," said Uncle Archibald, who rarely opened his mouth save to emit a proverb.

"Would you mind telling me, Archibald," said Old Grandmother pleasantly, "if you really look that solemn when you're asleep."

No one answered her. Aunt Mary Martha-over-the-bay, the only one who could have answered, had been dead for ten years.

"Whether she's pretty or not, she's going to have very long lashes," said Aunt Anne, reverting to the baby as a safer subject of conversation. There was no sense in letting Old Grandmother start a family row for her own amusement so soon after poor Leander's passing away.

"God help the men then," said Uncle Klon gravely.

Aunt Anne wondered why Old Grandmother was laughing to herself until the bed shook. Aunt Anne reflected that it would have been just as well if Klondike with his untimely sense of humour had not been present in a serious assemblage like this.

"Well, we must give her a pretty name, anyhow," said Aunt Flora briskly. "It's simply a shame that it's been left as long as this. No Lesley ever was before. Come, Grandmother, you ought to name her. What do you suggest?"

Old Grandmother affected the indifferent. She had three namesakes already so she knew Leander's baby wouldn't be named after *her*.

"Call it what you like," she said. "I'm too old to bother about it. Fight it out among yourselves."

"But we'd like your advice, Grandmother," unfortunately said Aunt Leah, whom Old Grandmother was just detesting because she had noticed the minute Leah shook hands with her that she had had her nails manicured.

"I have no advice to give. I have nothing but a little wisdom and I cannot give you *that*. Neither can I help it if a woman has a bargain-counter nose."

"Are you referring to *my* nose," inquired Aunt Leah with spirit. She often said she was the only one in the clan who wasn't afraid of Old Grandmother.

"The pig that's bit squeals," retorted Old Grandmother. She leaned back on her pillows disdainfully and sipped her tea with a vengeance. She had got square with Leah for manicuring her nails.

She had insisted on having her dinner first so that she might watch the others eating theirs. She knew it made them all more or less uncomfortable. Oh, but it was fine to be able to be disagreeable again. She had had to be so good and considerate for four months. Four months was long enough to mourn for anybody. Four months of not daring to give anybody a wigging. They had seemed like four centuries.

Lorraine sighed. She knew what *she* wanted to call her baby. But she knew that she would never have the courage to say it. And if she did she knew they would never consent to it. When you married into a family like the Lesleys you had to take the consequences. It was very hard when you couldn't name your own baby—when you were not even asked what you'd *like* it named. If Lee had only lived it would have been different. Lee, who was not a bit like the other Lesleys—except Uncle Klon, a little—Lee, who loved wonder and beauty and laughter—laughter that had been hushed so suddenly. Surely the jests of Heaven must have had more spice since he had joined in them. How he would have howled at this august conclave over the naming of his baby! How he would have brushed them aside! Lorraine felt sure he would have let her call her baby—

"*I* think," said Mrs. David Lesley, throwing her bombshell gravely and sadly, "that it would only be graceful and fitting that she should be called after Leander's first wife."

Mrs. David and Clementine had been very intimate friends. But Clementine! Lorraine shivered again and wished she hadn't, for Aunt Anne's eye looked like another shawl.

Everybody looked at Clementine's picture.

"Poor little Clementine," sighed Aunt Stasia in a tone that made Lorraine feel she should never have taken poor little

Clementine's place.

"Do you remember what lovely jet black hair she had?" asked Aunt Marcia.

"And what lovely hands?" said Great-Aunt Matilda.

"She was so young to die," sighed Aunt Josephine.

"She was *such* a sweet girl," said Great-Aunt Elizabeth.

"A sweet girl all right," agreed Uncle Klon, "but why condemn an innocent child to carry a name like that all her life? That would really be a sin."

The clan, with the exception of Mrs. David, felt grateful to him and looked it, especially Young Grandmother. The name simply wouldn't have done, no matter how sweet Clementine was. That horrid old song, for instance—*Oh, my darling Clementine,* that boys used to howl along the road at nights. No, no, not for a Lesley. But Mrs. David was furious. Not only because Klondike disagreed with her but because he was imitating her old lisp, so long outgrown that it really was mean of him to drag it up again like this.

"Will you have some more dressing?" inquired Young Grandmother graciously.

"No, thank you." Mrs. David was not going to have any more, by way of signifying displeasure. Later on she took a still more terrible revenge by leaving two-thirds of her pudding uneaten, knowing that Young Grandmother had concocted it. Young Grandmother woke up in the night and wondered if anything could really have been the matter with the pudding. The others *might* have eaten it out of politeness.

"If Leander's name had been almost anything else she might have been named for her father," said Great-Uncle Walter. "Roberta—Georgina—Johanna—Andrea—Stephanie—Wilhelmina—"

"Or Davidena," said Uncle Klon. But Great-Uncle Walter ignored him.

"You can't make anything out of a name like *Leander.* Whatever did you call him that for, Marian?"

"His grandfather named him after him who swam the Hellespont," said Young Grandmother as rebukingly as if she had not, thirty-five years before, cried all one night because Old Grandfather had given her baby such a horrid name.

"She might be called Hero," said Uncle Klon.

"We had a dog called that once," said Old Grandmother.

"Leander didn't tell you before he died that he wanted any special name, did he, Lorraine?" inquired Aunt Nina.

"No," faltered Lorraine. "He—he had so little time to tell me—anything."

The clan frowned at Nina as a unit. They thought she was very tactless. But what could you expect of a woman who wrote poetry and peddled it about the country? *Writing* it might have been condoned—and concealed. After all, the Lesleys were not intolerant and everybody had some shortcomings. But *selling* it openly!

"I should like baby to be called Gabriella," persisted Nina.

"There has never been such a name among the Lesleys," said Old Grandmother. And that was *that*.

"I think it's time we had some new names," said the poetess rebelliously. But every one looked stony, and Nina began to cry. She cried upon the slightest provocation. Lorraine remembered that Leander had always called her Mrs. Gummidge.

"Come, come," said Old Grandmother, "surely we can name this baby as well comfortably as uncomfortably. Don't make the mistake, Nina, of thinking that you are helping things along by making a martyr of yourself."

"What do *you* think, Miss Silversides?" inquired Uncle Charlie, who thought Salome was being entirely ignored and didn't like it.

"Oh, it doesn't matter what *I* think. *I* am of no consequence," said Salome, ostentatiously helping herself to the pickles.

"Come, come, now, you're one of the family," coaxed Uncle Charlie, who knew—so he said—how to handle women.

"Well"—Salome relaxed because she was really dying to have

22

her say in it—"I've always thought names that ended in 'ine' were so elegant. *My* choice would be Rosaline."

"Or Evangeline," said Great-Uncle Walter.

"Or Eglantine," said Aunt Marcia eagerly.

"Or Gelatine," said Uncle Klon.

There was a pause.

"Juno would be such a nice name," said Cousin Teresa.

"But we are Presbyterians," said Old Grandmother.

"Or Robinette," suggested Uncle Charlie.

"We are English," said Young Grandmother.

"I think Yvonne is such a romantic name," said Aunt Flora.

"Names have really nothing to do with romance," said Uncle Klon. "The most thrilling and tragic love affair I ever knew was between a man named Silas Twingletoe and a woman named Kezia Birtwhistle. It's my opinion children shouldn't be named at all. They should be numbered until they're grown up, then choose their own names."

"But then you are not a mother, my dear Horace," said Young Grandmother tolerantly.

"Besides, there's an Yvonne Clubine keeping a lingerie shop in Charlottetown," said Aunt Josephine.

"Lingerie? If you mean underclothes for heaven's sake say so," snapped Old Grandmother.

"Juanita is a rather nice uncommon name," suggested John Eddy Lesley-over-the-bay. "J-u-a-n-i-t-a."

"Nobody would know how to spell it or pronounce it," said Aunt Marcia.

"I think," began Uncle Klon—but Aunt Josephine took the road.

"*I* think—"

"*Place aux dames*," murmured Uncle Klon. Aunt Josephine thought he was swearing but ignored him.

"*I* think the baby should be called after one of our missionaries. It's a shame that we have three foreign missionaries in the connection and not one of them has a namesake—even if they are only fourth cousins. *I* suggest we call her Harriet after the oldest one."

"But," said Aunt Anne, "that would be slighting Ellen and Louise."

"Well," said Young Grandmother haughtily—Young Grandmother was haughty because nobody had suggested naming the baby after *her*—"call her the whole three names, Harriet Ellen Louise Lesley. Then no fourth cousin need feel slighted."

The suggestion seemed to find favour. Lorraine caught her breath anxiously and looked at Uncle Klon. But rescue came from another quarter.

"Have you ever," said Old Grandmother with a wicked chuckle, "thought what the initials spell?"

They hadn't. They did. Nothing more was said about missionaries.

4

"Sylvia is a beautiful name," ventured Uncle Howard, whose first sweetheart had been a Sylvia.

"You couldn't call her that," said Aunt Millicent in a shocked tone. "Don't you remember Great-Uncle Marshall's Sylvia went insane? She died filling the air with shrieks. *I* think Bertha would be more suitable."

"Why, there's a Bertha in John C. Lesley's family-over-the-bay," said Young Grandmother.

John C. was a distant relative who was "at outs" with his clan. So Bertha would never do.

"Wouldn't it be nice to name her Adela?" said Aunt Anne. "You know Adela is the only really distinguished person the connection has ever produced. A famous authoress—"

"*I* should like the mystery of her husband's death to be cleared up before any grandchild of mine is called after her," said Young

Grandmother austerely.

"Nonsense, Mother! You surely don't suspect Adela."

"There *was* arsenic in the porridge," said Young Grandmother darkly.

"I'll tell you what the child should be called," said Aunt Sybilla, who had been waiting for the psychic moment. "Theodora! It was revealed to me in a vision of the night. I was awakened by a feeling of icy coldness on my face. I came all out in goose flesh. And I heard a voice distinctly pronounce the name—*Theodora*. I wrote it down in my diary as soon as I arose."

John Eddy Lesley-over-the-bay laughed. Sybilla hated him for weeks for it.

"I wish," said sweet old Great-Aunt Matilda, "that she could be called after my little girl who died."

Aunt Matilda's voice trembled. Her little girl had been dead for fifty years but she was still unforgotten. Lorraine loved Aunt Matilda. She wanted to please her. But she couldn't—she *couldn't*—call her dear baby Emmalinza.

"It's unlucky to call a child after a dead person," said Aunt Anne positively.

"Why not call the baby Jane," said Uncle Peter briskly. "My mother's name—a good, plain, sensible name that'll wear. Nickname it to suit any age. Jenny—Janie—Janet—Jeannette— Jean—and Jane for the seventies."

"Oh, wait till I'm dead—*please*," wailed Old Grandmother. "It would always make me think of Jane Putkammer."

Nobody knew who Jane Putkammer was or why Old Grandmother didn't want to think of her. As nobody asked why—the dessert having just been begun—Old Grandmother told them.

"When my husband died she sent me a letter of condolence written in red ink. Jane, indeed!"

So the baby escaped being Jane. Lorraine felt really grateful to Old Grandmother. She had been afraid Jane might carry the day. And how fortunate there was such a thing as red ink in the world.

"Funny about nicknames," said Uncle Klon. "I wonder did they have nicknames in Biblical times. Was Jonathan ever shortened into Jo? Was King David ever called Dave? And fancy Melchizedek's mother always calling him that."

"Melchizedek hadn't a mother," said Mrs. David triumphantly—and forgave Uncle Klon. But not Young Grandmother. The pudding remained uneaten.

"Twenty years ago Jonathan Lesley gave me a book on 'The Hereafter,'" said Old Grandmother reminiscently. "And he's been in the Hereafter eighteen years and I am still in the Here."

"Any one would think you expected to live forever," said Uncle Jarvis, speaking for the first time. He had been sitting in silence, hoping gloomily that Leander's baby was an elect infant. What mattered a name compared to that?

"I do," said Old Grandmother, chuckling. That was one for Jarvis, the solemn old ass.

"We're not really getting anywhere about the baby's name, you know," said Uncle Paul desperately.

"Why not let Lorraine name her own baby?" said Uncle Klon suddenly. "Have you any name you'd like her called, dear?"

Again Lorraine caught her breath. Oh, hadn't she! She wanted to call her baby Marigold. In her girlhood she had had a dear friend named Marigold. The only girl-friend she ever had. Such a dear, wonderful, bewitching, lovable creature. She had filled Lorraine's starved childhood with beauty and mystery and affection. And she had died. If only she might call her baby Marigold! But she knew the horror of the clan over such a silly, fanciful, outlandish name. Old Grandmother—Young Grandmother—no, they would never consent. She knew it. All her courage exhaled from her in a sigh of surrender.

"No-o-o," she said in a small, hopeless voice. Oh, if she were only not such a miserable coward.

And that terrible Old Grandmother knew it.

"She's fibbing," she thought. "She has a name but she's too

scared to tell it. Clementine, now—she would have stood on her own feet and told them what was what."

Old Grandmother looked at Clementine, forever gazing at her lily, and forgot that the said Clementine's ability to stand on her own feet and tell people—even Old Grandmother—what was what had not especially commended her to Old Grandmother at one time. But Old Grandmother liked people with a mind of their own—when they were dead.

Old Grandmother was beginning to feel bored with the whole matter. What a fuss over a name. As if it really mattered what that mite in the cradle, with the golden fuzz on her head, was called. Old Grandmother looked at the tiny sleeping face curiously. Lorraine's hair but Leander's chin and brow and nose. A fatherless baby with only that foolish Winthrop girl for a mother.

"I *must* live long enough for her to remember me," thought Old Grandmother. "It's only a question of keeping on at it. Marian has no imagination and Lorraine has too much. Somebody must give that child a few hints to live by, whether she's to be minx or madonna."

"If it was only a boy it would be so easy to name it," said Uncle Paul.

Then for ten minutes they wrangled over what they would have called it if it had been a boy. They were beginning to get quite warm over it when Aunt Myra took a throbbing in the back of her neck.

"I'm afraid one of my terrible headaches is coming on," she said faintly.

"What would women do if headaches had never been invented?" asked Old Grandmother. "It's the most convenient disease in the world. It can come on so suddenly—go so conveniently. And nobody can prove we haven't got it."

"I'm sure no one has ever suffered as I do," sighed Myra.

"We all think that," said Old Grandmother, seeing a chance to shoot another poisoned arrow. "I'll tell you what's the matter with you. Eye strain. You should really wear glasses at your age, Myra."

"Why can't those headaches be cured?" said Uncle Paul. "Why don't you try a new doctor?"

"Who is there to try now that poor Leander is in his grave?" wailed Myra. "I don't know what we Lesleys are ever going to do without him. We'll just have to *die*. Dr. Moorhouse drinks and Dr. Stackley is an evolutionist. And you wouldn't have me go to that woman-doctor, would you?"

No, of course not. No Lesley would go to that woman-doctor. Dr. M. Woodruff Richards had been practising in Harmony for two years, but no Lesley would have called in a woman-doctor if he had been dying. One might as well commit suicide. Besides, a woman-doctor was an outrageous portent, not to be tolerated or recognised at all. As Great-Uncle Robert said indignantly, "The weemen are gittin' entirely too intelligent."

Klondike Lesley was especially sarcastic about her. "An unsexed creature," he called her. Klondike had no use for unfeminine women who aped men. "Neither fish nor flesh nor good red herring," as Young Grandfather had been wont to say. But they talked of her through their coffee and did not again revert to the subject of the baby's name. They were all feeling a trifle sore over *that*. It seemed to them all that neither Old Grandmother nor Young Grandmother nor Lorraine had backed them up properly. With the result that all the guests went home with the great question yet unsettled.

"Just as I expected. All squawks—nothing but squawks as usual," said Old Grandmother.

"We might have known what would happen when we had this on Friday," said Salome, as she washed up the dishes.

"Well, the great affair is over," said Lucifer to the Witch of Endor as they discussed a plate of chicken bones and Pope's noses on the back veranda, "and that baby hasn't got a name yet. But these celebrations are red-letter days for *us*. Listen to me purr."

CHAPTER II

Sealed of the Tribe

1

Things were rather edgy in the Lesley clan for a few weeks. As Uncle Charlie said, they had their tails up. Cousin Sybilla was reported to have gone on a hunger strike—which she called a fast—about it. Stasia and Teresa, two affectionate sisters, quarrelled over it and wouldn't speak to each other. There was a connubial rupture between Uncle Thomas and Aunt Katherine because she wanted to consult Ouija about a name. Obadiah Lesley, who in thirty years had never spoken a cross word to his wife, rated her so bitterly for wanting to call the baby Consuela that she went home to her mother for three days. An engagement trembled in the balance. Myra's throbbings in the neck became more frequent than ever. Uncle William-over-the-bay vowed he wouldn't play checkers until the child was named. Aunt Josephine was known to be praying about it at a particular hour every day. Nina cried almost ceaselessly over it and gave up peddling poetry for the time being, which led Uncle Paul to remark that it was an ill wind which blew no good. Young Grandmother preserved an offended silence. Old Grandmother laughed to herself until the bed shook. Salome and the cats held their peace, though Lucifer carefully kept his tail at half-mast. Everybody was more or less cool to Lorraine because she had not taken his or her choice. It really looked as if Leander's baby was never going to get a name.

Then—the shadow fell. One day the little lady of Cloud of

Spruce seemed fretful and feverish. The next day more so. The third day Dr. Moorhouse was called—the first time for years that a Lesley had to call in an outside doctor. For three generations there had been a Dr. Lesley at Cloud of Spruce. Now that Leander was gone they were all at sea. Dr. Moorhouse was brisk and cheerful. Pooh—pooh! No need to worry—not the slightest. The child would be all right in a day or two.

She wasn't. At the end of a week the Lesley clan were thoroughly alarmed. Dr. Moorhouse had ceased to pooh-pooh. He came anxiously twice a day. And day by day the shadow deepened. The baby was wasting away to skin and bone. Anguished Lorraine hung over the cradle with eyes that nobody could bear to look at. Everybody proposed a different remedy but nobody was offended if it wasn't used. Things were too serious for that. Only Nina was almost sent to Coventry because she asked Lorraine one day if infantile paralysis began like that, and Aunt Marcia was frozen out because she heard a dog howling one night. Also, when Flora said she had found a diamond-shaped crease in a clean tablecloth—a sure sign of death in the year—Klondike insulted her. But Klondike was forgiven because he was nearly beside himself over the baby's condition.

Dr. Moorhouse called in Dr. Stackley, who might be an evolutionist but had a reputation of being good with children. After a long consultation they changed the treatment; but there was no change in the little patient. Klondike brought a specialist from Charlottetown who looked wise and rubbed his hands and said Dr. Moorhouse was doing all that could be done and that while there was life there was always hope, especially in the case of children.

"Whose vitality is sometimes quite extraordinary," he said gravely, as if enunciating some profound discovery of his own.

It was at this juncture that Great-Uncle Walter, who hadn't gone to church for thirty years, made a bargain with God that he would go if the child's life was spared, and that Great-Uncle William-over-the-bay recklessly began playing checkers again.

Better break a vow before a death than after it. Teresa and Stasia had made up as soon as the baby took ill, but it was only now that the coolness between Thomas and Katherine totally vanished. Thomas told her for goodness' sake to try Ouija or any darned thing that might help. Even Old Cousin James T., who was a black sheep and never called "Uncle" even by the most tolerant, came to Salome one evening.

"Do you believe in prayer?" he asked fiercely.

"Of course I do," said Salome indignantly.

"Then *pray. I* don't—so it's no use for me to pray. But you pray your darnedest."

2

A terrible day came when Dr. Moorhouse told Lorraine gently that he could do nothing more. After he had gone Young Grandmother looked at Old Grandmother.

"I suppose," she said in a low voice, "we had better take the cradle into the spare room."

Lorraine gave a bitter cry. This was equivalent to a death sentence. At Cloud of Spruce, just as with the Murrays down at Blair Water, it was a tradition that dying people must be taken into the spare room.

"You'll do one thing before you take her into the spare room," said Old Grandmother fiercely. "Moorhouse and Stackley have given up the case. They've only half a brain between them anyhow. Send for that woman-doctor."

Young Grandmother looked thunderstruck. She turned to Uncle Klon, who was sitting by the baby's cradle, his haggard face buried in his hands.

"Do you suppose—I've *heard* she was very clever—they say she was offered a splendid post in a children's hospital in Montreal but preferred general practice—"

"Oh, get her, get her," said Klondike—savage from the bitter business of hoping against hope. "Any port in a storm. She can't do any harm now."

"Will *you* go for her, Horace," said Young Grandmother quite humbly.

Klondike Lesley uncoiled himself and went. He had never seen Dr. Richards before—save at a distance, or spinning past him in her smart little runabout. She was in her office and came forward to meet him gravely sweet.

She had a little, square, wide-lipped, straight-browed face like a boy's. Not pretty but haunting. Wavy brown hair with one teasing, unruly little curl that *would* fall down on her forehead, giving her a youthful look in spite of her thirty-five years. What a dear face! So wide at the cheekbones—so deep grey-eyed. With such a lovely, smiling, generous mouth. Some old text of Sunday-school days suddenly flitted through Klondike Lesley's dazed brain:

"She will do him good and not evil all the days of her life."

For just a second their eyes met and locked. Only a second. But it did the work of years. The irresistible woman had met the immovable man and the inevitable had happened. She might have had thick ankles—only she hadn't; her mother might have meowed all over the church. Nothing would have mattered to Klondike Lesley. She made him think of all sorts of lovely things, such as sympathy, kindness, generosity, and women who were not afraid to grow old. He had the most extraordinary feeling that he would like to lay his head on her breast and cry, like a little boy who had got hurt, and have her stroke his head and say,

"Never mind—be brave—you'll soon feel better, dear."

"Will you come to see my little niece?" he heard himself pleading. "Dr. Moorhouse has given her up. We are all very fond of her. Her mother will die if she cannot be saved. Won't you come?"

"Of course I will," said Dr. Richards.

She came. She said little, but she did some drastic things about diet and sleeping. Old and Young Grandmothers gasped when she ordered the child's cradle moved out on the veranda. Every day for two weeks her light, steady footsteps came and went about Cloud of Spruce. Lorraine and Salome and Young Grandmother hung breathlessly on her briefest word.

Old Grandmother saw her once. She had told Salome to bring "the woman-doctor in," and they had looked at each other for a few minutes in silence. The steady, sweet, grey eyes had gazed unquailingly into the piercing black ones.

"If a son of mine had met you I would have ordered him to marry you," Old Grandmother said at last with a chuckle.

The little humorous quirk in Dr. Richards's mouth widened to a smile. She looked around her at all the laughing brides of long ago in their billows of tulle.

"But I would not have married him unless I wanted to," she said.

Old Grandmother chuckled again.

"Trust you for that." But she never called her "the woman-doctor" again. She spoke with her own dignity of "Dr. Richards"—for a short time.

Klondike brought Dr. Richards to Cloud of Spruce and took her away. Her own car was laid up for repairs. But nobody was paying much attention to Klondike just then.

At the end of the two weeks it seemed to Lorraine that the shadow had ceased to deepen on the little wasted face.

A few more days—was it not lightening—lifting? At the end of three more weeks Dr. Richards told them that the baby was out of danger. Lorraine fainted and Young Grandmother shook and Klondike broke down and cried unashamedly like a schoolboy.

3

A few days later the clan had another conclave—a smaller and informal one. The aunts and uncles present were all genuine ones. And it was not, as Salome thankfully reflected, on a Friday.

"This child must be named at once," said Young Grandmother authoritatively. "Do you realize that she might have died without a name?"

The horror of this kept the Lesleys silent for a few minutes. Besides, every one dreaded starting up another argument so soon after those dreadful weeks. Who knew but what it had been a judgment on them for quarrelling over it?

"But *what* shall we call her?" said Aunt Anne timidly.

"There is only one name you can give her," said Old Grandmother, "and it would be the blackest ingratitude if you didn't. Call her after the woman who has saved her life, of course."

The Lesleys looked at each other. A simple, graceful, natural solution of the problem—if only—

"But *Woodruff!*" sighed Aunt Marcia.

"She's got another name, hasn't she?" snapped Old Grandmother. "Ask Horace there what M stands for? *He* can tell you, or I'm much mistaken."

Every one looked at Klondike. In the anxiety of the past weeks everybody in the clan had been blind to Klondike's goings-on—except perhaps Old Grandmother.

Klondike straightened his shoulders and tossed back his mane. It was as good a time as any to tell something that would soon have to be told.

"Her full name," he said, "is now Marigold Woodruff Richards, but in a few weeks' time it will be Marigold Woodruff Lesley."

"And that," remarked Lucifer to the Witch of Endor under the milk bench at sunset, with the air of a cat making up his mind to the inevitable, "is that."

"What do you think of her?" asked the Witch, a little superciliously.

"Oh, she has points," conceded Lucifer. "Kissable enough."

The Witch of Endor, being wise in her generation, licked her black paws and said no more, but continued to have her own opinion.

CHAPTER III

April Promise

1

On the evening of Old Grandmother's ninety-eighth birthday there was a sound of laughter on the dark staircase—which meant that Marigold Lesley, who had lived six years and thought the world a very charming place, was dancing downstairs. You generally heard Marigold before you saw her. She seldom walked. A creature of joy, she ran or danced. "The child of the singing heart," Aunt Marigold called her. Her laughter always seemed to go before her. Both Young Grandmother and Mother, to say nothing of Salome and Lazarre, thought that golden trill of laughter echoing through the somewhat prim and stately rooms of Cloud of Spruce the loveliest sound in the world. Mother often said this. Young Grandmother never said it. That was the difference between Young Grandmother and Mother.

Marigold squatted down on the broad, shallow, uneven sandstone steps at the front door and proceeded to think things over—or, as Aunt Marigold, who was a very dear, delightful woman, phrased it, "make magic for herself." Marigold was always making magic of some kind.

Already, even at six, Marigold found this an entrancing occupation—"int'resting," to use her own pet word. She had picked it up from Aunt Marigold and from then to the end of life things would be for Marigold interesting or uninteresting. Some people might demand of life that it be happy or untroubled or successful. Marigold Lesley would only ask that it be interesting. Already she was looking with avid eyes on all the exits and entrances of the drama of life.

There had been a birthday party for Old Grandmother that day, and Marigold had enjoyed it—especially that part in the pantry about which nobody save she and Salome knew. Young Grandmother would have died of horror if she had known how many of the whipped cream tarts Marigold had actually eaten.

But she was glad to be alone now and think things over. In Young Grandmother's opinion Marigold did entirely too much thinking for so small a creature. Even Mother, who generally understood, sometimes thought so too. It couldn't be good for a child to have its mind prowling in all sorts of corners. But everybody was too tired after the party to bother about Marigold and her thoughts just now, so she was free to indulge in a long delightful reverie. Marigold was, she would have solemnly told you, "thinking over the past." Surely a most fitting thing to do on a birthday, even if it wasn't your own. Whether all her thoughts would have pleased Young Grandmother, or even Mother, if they had known them, there is no saying. But then they did not know them. Long, long ago—when she was only five and a half—Marigold had horrified her family—at least the Grandmotherly part of it—by saying in her nightly prayer, "Thank you, dear God, for 'ranging it so that nobody knows what I think." Since then Marigold had learned worldly wisdom and did not say things like that out loud—in her prayers. But she continued to think privately that God was very wise and good in making thoughts exclusively your own. Marigold hated to have people barging in, as Uncle Klon would have said, on her little soul.

But then, as Young Grandmother would have said and did say, Marigold always had ways no orthodox Lesley baby ever thought of having—"the Winthrop coming out in her," Young Grandmother muttered to herself. All that was good in Marigold was Lesley and Blaisdell. All that was bad or puzzling was Winthrop. For instance, that habit of hers of staring into space with a look of rapture. *What* did she see? And what right had she to see it? And when you asked her what she was thinking of she stared at you and said, "Nothing." Or else propounded some weird, unanswerable problem such as, "Where was I before I was me?"

The sky above her was a wonderful soft deep violet. A wind that had lately blown over clover-meadows came around the ivied shoulder of the house in the little purring puffs that Marigold loved. To her every wind in the world was a friend—even those wild winter ones that blew so fiercely up the harbour. The row of lightning-rod balls along the top of Mr. Donkin's barn across the road seemed like silver fairy worlds floating in the afterlight against the dark trees behind them. The lights across the harbour were twinkling out along the shadowy shore. Marigold loved to watch the harbour lights. They fed some secret spring of delight in her being. The big spireas that flanked the steps—Old Grandmother always called them Bridal Wreaths, with a sniff for meaningless catalogue names—were like twin snowdrifts in the dusk. The old thorn hedge back of the apple-barn, the roots of which had been brought out from Scotland in some past that was to Marigold of immemorial antiquity, was as white as the spireas, and scented the air all around it. Cloud of Spruce was such a place always inside and out for sweet, wholesome smells. People found out there that there was such a thing as honeysuckle left in the world. There was the entrancing pale gold of lemon lilies in the shadows under the lilac-trees, and the proud white iris was blooming all along the old brick walk worn smooth by the passing of many feet. Away far down Marigold knew the misty sea was lapping gladly on the windy sands of the dunes. Mr. Donkin's dear little pasture-field, full of blue-eyed grass, with the birches all around it, was such a *contented* field. She had always envied Mr. Donkin that field. It looked, thought Marigold, as if it just loved being a field and wouldn't be anything else for the world. Right over it was the dearest little grey cloud that was slowly turning to rose like a Quaker lady blushing. And all the trees in sight were whispering in the dusk like old friends—all but the lonely, unsociable Lombardies.

Salome was singing lustily in the pantry, where she was washing dishes. Salome couldn't sing, but she always sang and Marigold liked to hear her, especially at twilight. "Shall we ga-a-a-ther at the ri-ver. The *bew*-tiful-the *bew*-tiful river?" warbled Salome. And Marigold *saw* the beautiful river, looking like the harbour below Cloud of Spruce. Lazarre was playing his fiddle behind the copse of young spruces back of the apple-barn— the old brown fiddle that his great-great-great-grandfather had brought from Grand Pré. Perhaps Evangeline had danced to it. Aunt Marigold had told Marigold the story of Evangeline. Young Grandmother and Mother and Aunt Marigold and Uncle Klon were in Old Grandmother's room talking over clan chit-chat together. A bit of gossip, Old Grandmother always averred, was an aid to digestion. Everybody Marigold loved was near her. She hugged her brown knees with delight, and thought with a vengeance.

2

Marigold had lived her six years, knowing no world but Harmony Harbour and Cloud of Spruce. All her clan loved her and petted her, though some of them occasionally squashed her for her own good. And Marigold loved them all—even those she hated she loved as part of her clan. And she loved Cloud of Spruce. How lucky she had happened to be born there. She loved everything and everybody about it. To-night everything seemed to drift through her consciousness in a dreamy, jumbled procession of delight, big and little things, past and present, all tangled up together.

The pigeons circling over the old apple-barn; the apple-barn itself—such an odd old barn with a tower and oriel window like a church—and the row of funny little hemlocks beyond it.

"Look at those hemlocks," Uncle Klon had said once. "Don't they look like a row of old-maid schoolteachers with their fingers up admonishing a class of naughty little boys." Marigold always thought of them so after that and walked past them in real half-delicious fear. What if they should suddenly shake their fingers so at *her*? She would die of it, she knew. But it *would* be int'resting.

The hemlocks were not the only mysterious trees about Cloud of Spruce. That lilac-bush behind the well, for example. Sometimes it was just lilac-bush. And sometimes, especially in the twilight or early dawn, it was a nodding old woman knitting. It *was*. And the spruce-tree down at the shore which in twilight or on stormy winter days looked just like a witch leaning out from the bank, her hair streaming wildly behind her. Then there were trees that talked—Marigold heard them. "Come, come," the pines at the right of the orchard were always calling. "We have something to tell you," whispered the maples at the gate. "Isn't it enough to look at us?" crooned the white birches along the road side of the garden, which Young Grandmother had planted when she came to Cloud of Spruce as a bride. And those Lombardies that kept such stately watch about the old house. At night the wind wandered through them like a grieving spirit. Elfin laughter and fitful moans sounded in their boughs. You might say what you liked but Marigold would never believe that those Lombardies were just *trees*.

The old garden that faced the fair blue harbour, with its white gate set midway, where darling flowers grew and kittens ran beautiful brief little pilgrimages before they were given away—or vanished mysteriously. It had all the beauty of old gardens where sweet women have aforetime laughed and wept. Some bit of old clan history was bound up with almost every clump and walk in it, and already Marigold knew most of it. The things that Young Grandmother and Mother would not tell her Salome would, and the things that Salome would not Lazarre would.

The road outside the gate—one of the pleasant red roads of "the Island." To Marigold, a long red road of mystery. On the right hand it ran down to the windy seafields at the harbour's mouth and stopped there—as if, thought Marigold, the sea had bitten it off. On the left it ran through a fern valley, up to the shadowy crest of a steep hill with eager little spruce-trees running up the side of it as if trying to catch up with the big ones at the top. And over it to a new world beyond where there was a church and a school and the village of Harmony. Marigold loved that hill road because it was full of rabbits. You could never go up it without seeing some of the darlings. There was room in Marigold's heart for all the rabbits of the world. She had horrible suspicions that Lucifer caught baby rabbits—and *ate them*. Lazarre had as good as given that dark secret away in his rage over some ruined cabbages in the kitchen-garden. "Dem devil rabbit," he had stormed. "I wish dat Lucifer, he eat dem *all*." Marigold *couldn't* feel the same to Lucifer after that, though she kept on loving him, of course. Marigold always kept on loving—and hating—when she had once begun. "She's got *that* much Lesley in her anyhow," said Uncle Klon.

The harbour, with its silent mysterious ships that came and went; Marigold loved it the best of all the outward facts of her life—better, as yet, than even the wonderful green cloud of spruce on the hill eastward that gave her home its name. She loved it when it was covered with little dancing ripples like songs. She loved it when its water was smooth as blue silk; she loved it when summer showers spun shining threads of rain below its western clouds; she loved it when its lights blossomed out in the blue of summer dusks and the bell of the Anglican Church over the bay rang faint and sweet. She loved it when the mist mirages changed it to some strange enchanted haven of "fairylands forlorn"; she loved it when it was ruffled in rich dark crimson under autumn sunsets; she loved it when silver sails went out of it in the strange white wonder of dawn; but she loved it best on late still afternoons, when it lay like a great gleaming mirror, all faint, prismatic colours like the world in a soap-bubble. It was so nice and thrilly to stand down on the wharf and see the trees upside down in the water and a great blue sky underneath you. And what if you couldn't stick on but fell down into that sky? *Would you fall through it?*

And she loved the purple-hooded hills that cradled it—those long dark hills that laughed to you and beckoned—but always kept some secret they would never tell.

"What is over the hills, Mother?" she had asked Mother once.

"Many things—wonderful things—heart-breaking things," Mother had answered with a sigh.

"I'll go and find them all sometime," Marigold had said confidently.

And then Mother had sighed again.

But the other side of the harbour—"over the bay"—continued to hold a lure for Marigold. Everything, she felt sure, would be different over there. Even the people who lived there had a fascinating name—"over-the-bay-ers"—which when Marigold had been *very* young, she thought was "over-the-bears."

Marigold had been down to the gulf shore on the other side of the dreamy dunes once, with Uncle Klon and Aunt Marigold. They had lingered there until the sunken sun had sucked all the rosy light out of the great blue bowl of the sky and twilight came down over the crash and the white turmoil of the breakers. For the tide was high and the winds were out and the sea was thundering its mighty march of victory. Marigold would have been terrified if she had not had Uncle Klon's lean brown hand to hold. But with him to take the edge off those terrible thrills it had been all pure rapture.

Next to the harbour Marigold loved the big spruce wood on the hill—though she had been up there only twice in her life.

As far back as she could remember that spruce hill had held an irresistible charm for her. She would sit on the steps of Old Grandmother's room and look up it by the hour so long and so steadily that Young Grandmother would wonder uneasily if the child were just "right." There had been a half-wit two generations back in the Winthrops.

The hill was so high. Long ago she had used to think that if she could get up on that hill she could touch the sky. Even yet she thought if she were there and gave a little spring she *might* land right in heaven. Nothing lived there except rabbits and squirrels—and perhaps "de leetle green folk," of whom Lazarre had told her. But beyond it—ah, beyond it—was the *Hidden Land*. It seemed to Marigold she had always called it that— always known about it. The beautiful, wonderful Hidden Land. Oh, to see it, just to climb up that hill to the very top and gaze upon it. And yet when Mother asked her one day if she would like a walk up the hill Marigold had shrunk back and exclaimed,

"Oh, Mother, the hill is so high. If we got to the top we'd be above *everything*. I'd rather stay down here with things."

Mother had laughed and humoured her. But one evening, only two months later, Marigold had daringly done it alone. The lure suddenly proved stronger than the dread. Nobody was around to forbid her or call her back. She walked boldly up the long flight of flat sandstone steps that led right up the middle of the orchard, set into the grass. She paused at the first step to kiss a young daffodil goodnight—for there were daffodils all about that orchard. Away beyond, the loveliest rose-hued clouds were hanging over the spruces. They had caught the reflection of the west, but Marigold thought they shone so because they looked on the Hidden Land—the land she would see in a moment if her courage only held out. She could be brave so long as it was not dark. She must get up the hill—and back—before it was dark. The gallant small figure ran up the steps to the old lichen-covered fence and sagging green gate where seven slim poplars grew. But she did not open it. Somehow she could not go right into that spruce wood. Lazarre had told her a story of that spruce wood—or some other spruce wood. Old Fidèle the caulker had been cutting down a tree there and his axe was dull and he swore, "Devil take me," he said, "if I don't t'row dis dam axe in de pond." *"An' de devil took heem."* Lazarre was dreadfully in earnest.

"Did any one see it?" asked Marigold, round-eyed.

"No; but dey see de hoof-prints," said Lazarre conclusively. "And stomp in de groun' roun' de tree. An' you leesten now—where did Fidèle go if de devil didn't take heem? Nobody never see heem again roun' dese parts."

So no spruce wood for Marigold. In daylight she never really believed the devil had carried off Fidèle, but one is not so incredulous after the sun goes down. And Marigold did not really want to see the devil, though she thought to herself that it *would* be int'resting.

She ran along the fence to the corner of the orchard where the spruces stopped. How cool and velvety the young grass felt. It *felt* green. But in the Hidden Land it would be ever so much greener—"living green," as one of Salome's hymns said. She scrambled through a lucky hole in the fence, ran out into Mr. Donkin's wheat-stubble and looked eagerly—confidently for the Hidden Land.

For a moment she looked—tears welled up in her eyes—her lips trembled—she almost cried aloud in bitterness of soul.

There was no Hidden Land!

Nothing before her but fields and farmhouses and barns and groves—just the same as along the road to Harmony. Nothing of the wonderful secret land of her dreams. Marigold turned; she must rush home and find Mother and cry—cry—cry! But she stopped, gazing with a suddenly transfigured face at the sunset over Harmony Harbour.

She had never seen the whole harbour at one time before; and the sunset was a rare one even in that island of wonderful sunsets. Marigold plunged her eyes into those lakes of living gold and supernal crimson and heavenly apple-green—into those rose-coloured waters—those far-off purple seas—and felt as if she were drowning ecstatically in loveliness. Oh, *there* was the Hidden Land—there beyond those shining hills—beyond that great headland that cut the radiant sea at the harbours mouth—there in that dream city of towers and spires whose gates were of pearl. It was not lost to her. How foolish she had been to fancy it just over the hill. Of course it couldn't be there—so near home. But she knew where it was now. The horrible disappointment and the sense of bitter loss that was far worse than the disappointment, had all vanished in that moment of sheer ecstasy above the world. She *knew.*

It was growing dark. She could see the lights of Cloud of Spruce blooming out in the dusk below her. And the night was creeping out of the spruces at her. She looked once timidly in that direction—and there, just over a little bay of bracken at the edge of the wood, beckoning to her from a copse—a Little White Girl. Marigold waved back before she saw it was only a branch of wild, white plum-blossom, wind-shaken. She ran back to the orchard and down the steps to meet Mother at the door of Old Grandmother's room.

"Oh, Mother, it's so nice to come home at bedtime," she whispered, clutching the dear warm hand.

"Where have you been, child?" ask Young Grandmother rather sternly.

"Up on the hill."

"You must not go there alone at this time of night," said Young Grandmother.

Oh, but she had been there once. And she had seen the Hidden Land.

Then she had gone up the hill with Mother this spring—only a few weeks ago—to pick arbutus. They had had a lovely time and found a spring there, with ferns thick around its untrampled edges—a delicate dim thing, half shadow, all loveliness. Marigold had pulled the ferns aside and peeped into it—had seen her own face looking up at her. No, not her own face. The Little Girl who lived in the spring, of course, and came out on moonlit nights to dance around it. Marigold knew naught of Grecian myth or Anglo-Saxon folk-lore but the heart of childhood has its own lovely interpretation of nature in every age and clime, and Marigold was born knowing those things that are hidden forever from the wise and prudent and sceptical.

She and Mother had wandered along dear little paths over gnarled roots. They had found a beautiful smooth-trunked beech or two. They had walked on sheets of green moss velvety enough for the feet of queens. Later on, Mother told her, there would be June-bells and trilliums and wild orchids and lady's slippers there for the seeking. Later still, strawberries out in the clearings at the back.

"When I get big I'm coming here every day," said Marigold. She thought of the evening so long ago—a whole year—when she had seen for a moment the Little White Girl. It *couldn't* have been a plum-bough. Perhaps some day she would see her again.

3

Lucifer was prowling about the bed of striped ribbon-grass, giving occasional mysterious pounces into it. The Witch of Endor was making some dark magic of her own on the white gate-post. They were both older than Marigold, who felt therefore that they were uncannily aged. Lazarre had confided to her his belief that they would live as long as the Old Lady did. "Dey tells her everyt'ing—everyt'ing," Lazarre had said. "Haven' I seen dem, sittin' dare on her bed, wi' deir tail hangin' down, a-talkin' to her lak dey was Chreestian? An' every tam dat Weetch she catch a mouse, don' she go for carry it to de Old Lady to see? You take care what you do 'fore dose cats. I wouldn't lak to be de chap dat would hurt one of dem. What dem fellers don' know ain't wort' knowin'." Marigold loved them but held them in awe. Their unfailing progeny gave her more delight. Little furry creatures were always lying asleep on the sunwarm grasses or frisking in yard and orchard. Ebon balls of fluff. Though not all ebon, alas. The number of spotted and striped kittens around led Uncle Klon to have his serious doubts about the Witch's morals. But he had the decency to keep his doubts to himself, and Marigold liked the striped kittens best—undisturbed by any thought of bends sinister. Creatures with such sweet little faces could have no dealings with the devil she felt quiet sure, whatever their parents might be up to.

Lazarre had given over fiddling and was going home—his little cottage down in "the hollow," where he had a black-eyed wife and half a dozen black-eyed children. Marigold watched him crossing the field, carrying something tied up in a red hanky, whistling gaily, as he was always doing when not fiddling, his head and shoulders stooped because he was continually in such a hurry that they were always several inches in advance of his feet. Marigold was very fond of Lazarre, who had been choreman at Cloud of Spruce before she was born and so was part of the things that always had been and always would be. She liked the quick, cordial twinkle in his black eyes and the gleam of his white teeth in his brown face. He was very different from Phidime Gautier, the big blacksmith in the Hollow, of whom Marigold went in positive dread, with his fierce black moustaches you could hang your hat on. There was an unproved legend that he ate a baby every other day. But Lazarre wasn't like that. He was kind and gentle and gay.

She was sure Lazarre couldn't hurt anything. To be sure there was that horrible tale of his killing pigs. But Marigold never believed it. She knew Lazarre couldn't kill pigs—at least, not pigs he was acquainted with.

He could carve wonderful baskets out of plum-stones and make fairy horns out of birch-bark, and he always knew the right time of the moon to do anything. She loved to talk with him, though if Mother and the Grandmothers had known what they talked about sometimes they would have put a sharp and sudden stop to it. For Lazarre, who firmly believed in fairies and witches and "ghostises" of all kinds, lived therefore in a world of romance, and made Marigold's flesh creep deliciously with his yarns. She didn't believe them all, but you *had* to believe what had happened to Lazarre himself. He had seen his grandmother in the middle of the night standing by his bed when she was forty

46

miles away. And next day word had come that the old lady had "gone daid."

That night Marigold had cried out in terror, when Mother was taking the lamp out of her room, "Oh, Mother, don't let the dark in—don't let the dark in. Oh, Mother, I'm so afraid of the big dark."

She had never been afraid to go to sleep in the dark before, and Mother and Young Grandmother could not understand what had got into her. Finally they compromised by leaving the light in Mother's room with the door open. You had to go through Mother's room to get to Marigold's. The dusky, golden half-light was a comfort. If people came and stood by your bed in the middle of the night—people who were forty miles away—you could at least *see* them.

Sometimes Lazarre played his fiddle in the orchard on moonlight nights and Marigold danced to it. Nobody could play the fiddle like Lazarre. Even Salome grudgingly admitted that.

"It's angelic, ma'am, that's what it is," she said with solemn reluctance as she listened to the bewitching lilts of the unseen musician up in the orchard. "And to think that easygoing French boy can make it. My good, hardworking brother tried all his life to learn to play the fiddle and never could. And this Lazarre can do it without trying. Why he can almost make *me* dance."

"That would be a miracle indeed," said Uncle Klon.

And Young Grandmother did tell Marigold she spent too much time with Lazarre.

"But I like him so much, and I want to see as much of him as I can in this world," explained Marigold. "Salome says he can't go to heaven because he's a Frenchman."

"Salome is very wicked and foolish to say such a thing," said Young Grandmother sternly. "Of course, Frenchmen go to heaven if they behave themselves"—not as if she were any too sure of it herself, however.

4

Salome went through the hall and into the orchard room with a cup of tea for Old Grandmother. As the door opened Marigold heard Aunt Marigold say,

"We'd better go to the graveyard next Sunday."

Marigold hugged herself with delight. One Sunday in every spring the Cloud of Spruce folks made a special visit to the little burying-ground on a western hill with flowers for their graves. Nobody went with them except Uncle Klon and Aunt Marigold. And Marigold loved a visit to the graveyard and particularly to Father's grave. She had an uneasy conviction that she ought to feel sad, as Mother and Young Grandmother did, but she never could manage it.

It was really such a charming spot. That smooth grey stone between the two dear young firs all greened over with their new spring tips, and the big spirea-bush almost hiding the grave and waving a hundred white hands to you in the wind that rippled the long grasses. The graveyard was full of spirea. Salome liked this. "Makes it more cheerful-like," she was wont to say. Marigold didn't know whether the graveyard was cheerful or not, but she knew she loved it. Especially when Uncle Klon was with her. Marigold was very fond of Uncle Klon. There was such fun in him. His sayings were so int'resting. He had such a delightful way of saying, "When I was in Ceylon," or "When I was in Borneo," as another might say, "When I was in Charlottetown" or "When I was over the bay." And he occasionally swore such fascinating oaths—at least Salome said they were oaths, though they didn't sound like it. "By the three wise monkeys," was one of them. So mysterious. *What* were the three wise monkeys? Nobody ever talked to her as he did. He told her splendid stories of the brave days of old, and wonderful yarns of his own adventures. For instance, that thrilling tale of the night he was lost on the divide between Gold Run and Sulphur Valleys in the Klondike. And that one about the ivory island in the far northern seas—

an island covered with walrus tusks heaped like driftwood, as if all the walruses went there to die. He told her jokes. He always made her laugh—even in the graveyard, because he told her such funny stories about the names on the tombstones and altogether made her feel that these folks were really all alive somewhere. Father and all, just as nice and funny as they were in the world. So why grieve about them? Why sigh as Salome always did when she paused by Mrs. Amos Reekie's grave and said,

"Ah, many's the cup of tea I've drunk with *her!*"

"Won't you drink lots more with her in heaven?" demanded Marigold once, rather recklessly, after some of Uncle Klon's yarns.

"Good gracious, no, child." Salome was dreadfully shocked. Though in her secret soul she thought heaven would be a much more cheerful place if one *could* have a good cup of tea with an old crony.

"They drink wine there, don't they?" persisted Marigold. "The Bible says so. Don't you think a cup of tea would be more *respectable* than wine?"

Salome *did* think so, but she would have died the death before she would have corrupted Marigold's youthful mind by saying so.

"There are mysteries too deep for us poor mortals to understand," she said solemnly.

Uncle Klon was third in Marigold's young affections. Mother of course came first; and then Aunt Marigold, with her dear wide mouth quirked up at the corners, so that she always seemed to be laughing even when very sad. These three were in the inner sanctum of Marigold's heart, a very exclusive little sanctum out of which were shut many who thought they had a perfect right to be there.

Marigold sometimes wondered whom she wanted to be like when she grew up. In some moods she wanted to be like Mother. But Mother was "put upon." Generally she thought she wanted to be like Aunt Marigold—who had a little way of saying things.

Nobody else could have said them. Marigold always felt she would recognise one of Aunt Marigold's sayings if she met it in her porridge. And when she said only, "It's a fine day," her voice had a nice confidential tone that made you feel nobody else knew it was a fine day—that it was a lovely secret shared between you. And when you had supper at Aunt Marigold's she *made* you take a third helping.

5

Marigold hardly knew where the grandmothers came in. She knew she ought to love them, but did she? Even at six Marigold had discovered that you cannot love by rule o' thumb.

Young Grandmother was not so bad. She was old, of course, with that frost-fine, serene old age that is in its way as beautiful as youth. Marigold felt this long before she could define it, and was disposed to admire Young Grandmother.

But Old Grandmother. To Marigold, Old Grandmother, so incredibly old, had never seemed like anything human. She could never have been born; it was equally unthinkable that she could ever die. Marigold was thankful she did not have to go into Old Grandmother's room very often. Old Grandmother could not be bothered with children—"unspanked nuisances," she called them.

But she had to go sometimes. When she had been naughty she was occasionally sent to sit on a little stool on the floor of Old Grandmother's room as a punishment. And a very dreadful punishment it was—much worse than Mother and Young Grandmother, who thought they were being lenient, realised. There she sat for what seemed like hours, and Old Grandmother sat up against her pillows and stared at her unwinkingly. Never speaking. *That* was what made it so ghastly.

Though when she did speak it was not very pleasant, either. How contemptuous Old Grandmother could be. Once when she had made Marigold angry, "Hoity toity, a little pot is soon hot!" Marigold winched under the humiliation of it for days. A little pot indeed!

It was no use trying to keep anything from this terrible old lady who saw through everything. Once Marigold had tried to hoodwink her with a small half-fib.

"You are not a true Lesley. The Lesleys never lie," said Old Grandmother.

"Oh, don't they!" cried Marigold, who already knew better.

Suddenly Old Grandmother laughed. Old Grandmother was surprising sometimes. After Marigold had gone into the spare room one day and tried on the hats of several guests, there was a council in the orchard room that evening. Mother and Young Grandmother were horrified. But Old Grandmother would not allow Marigold to be punished.

"I did that myself once," she said. "But I wasn't found out," she whispered to Marigold with a chuckle. She chuckled again on the day when Young Grandmother had asked Marigold a foolish, unanswerable question. "*Why* are you so bad?" But Marigold had answered it—sulkily. "It's more *int'resting* than being good."

Old Grandmother called her back as she was following outraged Young Grandmother out of the room, and put a tiny blue-veined hand on her shoulder.

"It may be more interesting," she whispered, "but *you* can't keep it up because you're a Lesley. The Lesleys never *could* be bad with any comfort to themselves. Too much conscience. No use making yourself miserable just for the sake of being bad."

Marigold always went into the orchard room on Sunday mornings to recite her golden text and catechism questions to Old Grandmother. Woe betide her if she missed a word. And in her nervousness she always did miss, no matter how perfectly she could say them before she went in. And she always was sent in there to take pills. Nobody at Cloud of Spruce could make Marigold take pills except Old Grandmother. *She* had no trouble. "Don't screw up your face like that. I hate ugly children.

Open your mouth." Marigold opened it. "Pop it in." Popped in it was. "Swallow it." It was swallowed—somehow. And then Old Grandmother would put her hand somewhere about the bed and produce a handful of big fat juicy blue raisins.

For she was not always unamiable. And sometimes she showed Marigold the big family Bible—a sort of Golden Book where all the clan names were written, and where all sorts of yellowed old clippings were kept. And sometimes she told her stories about the brides on the walls and the hair wreaths where the brown and gold and black locks of innumerable dead and gone Lesleys bloomed in weird, unfading buds and blossoms.

Old Grandmother was always saying things, too—queer, odd speeches with a tang in them Marigold somehow liked. They generally shocked Young Grandmother and Mother, but Marigold remembered and pondered over them though she seldom understood them fully. They did not seem related to anything in her small experience. In after life they were to come back to her. In many a crisis some speech of Old Grandmother's suddenly popped into mind and saved her from making a mistake.

But on the whole Marigold always breathed a sigh of relief when the door of the orchard room closed behind her.

6

Marigold at six had already experienced most of the passions that make life vivid and dreadful and wonderful—none the less vivid and dreadful at six than at sixteen or sixty. Probably she was born knowing that you were born to the purple if you were a Lesley. But pride of race blossomed to full stature in her the day she talked with little May Kemp from the Hollow.

"Do you wash your face *every* day?" asked May incredulously.

"Yes," said Marigold.

"Whether it needs it or not?"

"Of course. Don't you?"

"Not me," said May contemptuously. "I just wash mine when its dirty."

Then Marigold realised the difference between the Lesley caste and outsiders as all Young Grandmother's homilies had not been able to make her.

Shame? Oh, she had known it to the full—drunk its cup to the dregs. Would she ever forget that terrible supper-table when she had slipped, red and breathless, into her seat, apologising for being late? An inexcusable thing when there were company to tea—two ministers and two ministers' wives.

"I couldn't help it, Mother. I went to help Kate Blacquierre drive Mr. Donkin's cows to water and we had such a time chasing that bloody heifer."

At once Marigold knew she had said something dreadful. The frozen horror on the faces of her family told her that. One minister looked aghast, one hid a grin.

What had she said?

"Marigold, you may leave the table and go to your room," said Mother, who seemed almost on the point of tears. Marigold obeyed wretchedly, having no idea in the world what it was all about. Later on she found out.

"But Kate said it," she wailed. "Kate said she'd like to break every bloody bone in that bloody heifer's body. I never thought 'bloody' was swearing, though it's an ugly word."

She had *sworn* before the minister—before two ministers. And their wives! Marigold did not think she could ever live it down. A hot wave of shame ran over her whenever she thought about it. It did not matter that she was never allowed to go with Kate again; she had not cared much for Kate anyhow. But to have disgraced herself and Mother and the Lesley name! She had thought it bad enough when she had asked Mr. Lord of Charlottetown, with awe and reverence, "Please, *are you God?*" She had been laughed at so for that and had suffered keen humiliation. But this! And yet she could not understand why "bloody" was swearing. Even Old

Grandmother—who had laughed herself sick over the incident—couldn't explain that.

The spirit of jealousy had claimed her, too. She was secretly jealous of Clementine, the girl who had once been Father's wife—whose grave was beside his on the hill under the spireas—jealous for her mother. Father had belonged to Clementine once. Perhaps he belonged to her again now. There were times when Marigold was absolutely possessed with this absurd jealousy. When she went into Old Grandmother's room and saw Clementine's beautiful picture on the wall, she hated it. She wanted to go up and tear it down and trample on it. Lorraine would have been horrified if she had dreamed of Marigold's feelings in this respect. But Marigold kept her secret fiercely and went on hating Clementine—especially her beautiful hands. Marigold thought her mother quite as beautiful as Clementine. She always felt so sorry for little girls whose mothers were not beautiful. And Mother had the loveliest feet. Uncle Klon had said more than once that Lorraine had the daintiest little foot and ankle he had ever seen in a woman. This did not count for much among the Lesleys. Ankles were better not spoken of, even if the present-day fashion of skirts did show them shamelessly. But Mother's hands weren't pretty; they were too thin—too small; and Marigold felt sometimes she just couldn't *bear* Clementine's hands. Especially when some of the clan praised them. Old Grandmother referred to them constantly; it really did seem as if Old Grandmother sensed Marigold's jealousy and liked to tease her.

"I don't think she was so pretty," Marigold had been tortured into saying once.

Old Grandmother smiled.

"Clementine Lawrence was a beauty, my dear. Not an insignificant little thing like—like her sister up there in Harmony."

But Marigold felt sure Old Grandmother had started to say "like your mother," and she hated Clementine and her hands and her fadeless white lily more poisonously than ever.

54

Grief? Sorrow? Why, her heart nearly broke when her dear grey kitten had died. She had never known before that anything *she* loved could die. "Has yesterday gone to heaven, Mother?" she had sobbed the next day.

"I—I suppose so," said Mother.

"Then I don't want to go to heaven," Marigold had cried stormily. "I never want to meet that dreadful day again."

"You'll probably have to meet far harder days than that," had been Young Grandmother's comforting remark.

As for fear, had she not always known it? One of her very earliest memories was of being shut up in the dim shuttered parlor because she had spilled some of her jam pudding on Young Grandmother's best tablecloth. How such a little bit of pudding could have spread itself over so much territory she could not understand. But into the parlour she went—a terrible room with its queer streaky lights and shadows. And as she huddled against the door in the gloom she saw a dreadful thing. To the day of her death Marigold believed it happened. All the chairs in the room suddenly began dancing around the table in a circle headed by the big horsehair rocking-chair. And every time the rocking-chair galloped past her it bowed to her with awful, exaggerated politeness. Marigold screamed so wildly that they came and took her out—disgusted that she could not endure so easy a punishment.

"That's the Winthrop coming out in her," said Young Grandmother nastily.

The Lesleys and Blaisdells had more pluck. Marigold never told what had frightened her. She knew they would not believe her. But it was to be years before she could go into the parlour without a shudder, and she would have died rather than sit in that horsehair rocking-chair.

She had never been quite so vindictive over anything as over the affair of the Skinner doll. That had happened last August. May Kemp's mother had come up to clean the apple-barn, and May had come with her. May and Marigold had played happily for awhile in the playhouse in the square of currant-bushes—a beautiful playhouse in that you could sit in it and eat ruby-hued fruit off your own walls—and then May had said she would give one of her eyes to see the famous Skinner doll. Marigold had gone bravely into the orchard room to ask Old Grandmother if May might come in and see it. She found Old Grandmother asleep— really asleep, not pretending as she sometimes did. Marigold was turning away when her eyes fell on Alicia. Somehow Alicia looked so lovely and appealing—as if she were *asking* for a little fun. Impulsively Marigold ran to the glass case, opened the door and took Alicia out. She even slipped the shoe out of the hand that had held it for years, and put it on the waiting foot.

"Ain't you the bold one?" said May admiringly, when Marigold appeared among the red currants with Alicia in her arms.

But Marigold did not feel so bold when Salome, terrible and regal in her new plum-coloured drugget and starched white apron, had appeared before them and haled her into Old Grandmother's room.

"I should have known she was too quiet," said Salome. "There was the two of 'em—with HER on a chair for a throne, offering HER red currants on lettuce leaves and kissing HER hands. And a crown of flowers on HER head. And both HER boots on. You could 'a' knocked me down with a feather. HER, that's never been out o' that glass case since I came to Cloud o' Spruce."

"Why did you do such a naughty thing?" said Old Grandmother snappily.

"She—she wanted to be loved so much," sobbed Marigold. "Nobody has loved her for so long."

"You might wait till I'm dead before meddling with her. She will be yours then to 'love' all you want to."

"But you will live forever," cried Marigold. "Lazarre says so. And I didn't hurt her one bit."

"You might have broken her to fragments."

"Oh, no, no, I couldn't hurt her by loving her."

"I'm not so sure of that," muttered Old Grandmother, who

was constantly saying things Marigold was to understand twenty years later.

But Old Grandmother was very angry, and she decreed that Marigold was to have her meals alone in the kitchen for three days. Marigold resented this bitterly. There seemed to be something especially degrading about it. This was one of the times when it was just as well God had arranged it so that nobody knew what you thought.

That night when Marigold went to bed she was determined she would not say all her prayers. Not the part about blessing Old Grandmother. "Bless Mother and Young Grandmother and Salome." Marigold got up then and got into bed, having carefully placed her two shoes close together under the bed so that they wouldn't be lonesome. She did that every night. She couldn't have slept a wink if those shoes had been far apart, missing each other all night.

But she couldn't sleep to-night. In vain she tried to. In vain she counted sheep jumping over a wall. They *wouldn't* jump. They turned back at the wall and made faces at her—a bad girl who wouldn't pray for her old grandmother. Marigold stubbornly fought her Lesley conscience for an hour; then she got out of bed, knelt down and said, "Please bless Mother and Young Grandmother and Salome and everybody who needs a blessing."

Surely that took in Old Grandmother. Surely she could go to sleep now. But just as surely she couldn't. This time she surrendered after half an hour's fight. "Please bless Mother and Young Grandmother and Salome—and you can bless Old Grandmother if you like."

There now. She wouldn't yield another inch.

Fifteen minutes later Marigold was out of bed again.

"Please bless Mother and Young Grandmother and Salome and Old Grandmother for Jesus' sake, amen."

The sheep jumped now. Faster and faster and faster—they were like a long flowing white stream—Marigold was asleep.

7

The stars were coming out. Marigold loved to watch them—though the first time she had seen stars to realise them she had been terribly frightened. She had wakened up as Mother stepped out of Uncle Klon's car when he had brought them home from a visit in South Harmony. She had looked up through the darkness and shrieked.

"Oh, Mother, the sky has burned up and nothing but the sparks are left."

How they had all laughed and how ashamed she had been. But now Uncle Klon had taught her things about them and she knew the names of Betelguese and Rigel, Saiph and Alnita better than she could pronounce them. Oh, spring was a lovely time, when the harbour was a quivering, shimmering reach of blue and the orchard was sprinkled with violets and the nights were like a web of starlight.

But all the seasons were lovely. Summer, when strawberries were red on the hill-field and the rain was so sweet in the wild rose cups, and the faint sweetness of new-mown hay was everywhere, and the full moon made such pretty dapples under the orchard trees, and the great fields of daisies across the harbour were white as snow.

Of all the seasons Marigold loved autumn best. Then the Gaffer Wind of her favourite fairy-tale blew his trumpet over the harbour and the glossy black crows sat in rows on the fences, and the yellow leaves began to fall from the aspens at the green gate, and there was the silk of frost on the orchard grass in the mornings. In the evenings there was a nice reek of burning leaves from Lazarre's bonfires and the ploughed fields on the hill gleamed redly against the dark spruces. And some night you went to bed in a drab dull world and wakened up to see a white miraculous one. Winter had touched it in the darkness and transformed it.

Marigold loved winter, too, with the mysterious silence of its moonlit snow-fields and the spell of its stormy skies. And the big black cats creeping mysteriously through the twilit glades where the shadows of the trees were lovelier than the trees themselves, while the haystacks in Mr. Donkin's yard looked like a group of humpy old men with white hair. The pasture-fields which had been green and gold in June were cold and white, with ghost-flowers sticking up above the snow. Marigold always felt so sorry for those dead flowerstalks. She wanted to whisper to them, "Spring will come."

The winter mornings were int'resting because they had breakfast by candlelight. The winter evenings were dear when the wind howled outside, determined to get into Cloud of Spruce. It clawed at the doors—shrieked at the windows—gave Marigold delicious little thrills. But it never got in. It was so nice to sit in the warm bright room with the cats toasting their furry flanks before the fire and the pleasant purr of Salome's spinning-wheel in the kitchen. And then to bed in the little room off Mother's, with sweet, sleepy kisses, to snuggle down in soft, creamy blankets and hear the storm outside. Yes, the world *was* a lovely place to be alive in, even if the devil did occasionally carry off people who swore.

CHAPTER IV

Marigold Goes A-visiting

1

Marigold, for the first time in her small life, was going on what she called a "real" visit. That is, she was going to Uncle Paul's to stay all night, without Mother or Young Grandmother. In this fact its "realness" consisted for Marigold. Visiting with Grandmother was int'resting and visiting with Mother int'resting *and* pleasant, but to go somewhere on your own like this made you feel old and adventurous.

Besides, she had never been at Uncle Paul's, and there were things there she wanted to see. There was a "water-garden," which was a hobby of Uncle Paul's and much talked of in the clan. Marigold hadn't the least idea what a "water-garden" was. There was a case of stuffed hummingbirds. And, more int'resting than all else, there was a skeleton in the closet. She had heard Uncle Paul speak of it and hoped madly that she might get a glimpse of it.

Uncle Paul was not an over-the-bear, so was not invested with such romance as they, who lived so near the Hidden Land, were. He lived only at the head of the Bay, but that was six miles away, so it was really "travelling" to go there. She liked Uncle Paul, though she was a little in awe of Aunt Flora; and she liked Frank.

Frank was Uncle Paul's young half-brother. He had curly black hair and "romantic" grey eyes. So Marigold had heard Aunt Nina say. She didn't know what romantic meant, but she liked Frank's eyes. He had a nice, slow smile and a nice, soft drawling voice. Marigold had heard he was going to marry Hilda Wright. Then that he wasn't. Then that he had sold his farm and was going to some mysterious region called "the West." Lazarre told Salome it was because Hilda had jilted him. Marigold didn't know what jilted was, but whatever it was she hated Hilda for doing it to Frank. She had never liked Hilda much anyway, even if she were some distant kind of a cousin by reason of her great-grandmother being a Blaisdell. She was a pale pretty girl with russet hair and a mouth that never pleased Marigold. A stubborn mouth and a bitter mouth. Yet very pleasant when she laughed. Marigold almost liked Hilda when she laughed.

"Dey're too stubborn, dat pair," Lazarre told Salome. "Hilda say Frank he mus' spik first an' Frank he say he be dam if he do."

Marigold was sorry Frank was going West, which, as far as she was concerned, was something "beyond the bourne of time and space," but she looked forward to this visit with him. He would show her the humming-birds and the water-garden, and she believed she could coax him to let her have a peep at the skeleton. And he would take her on his knee and tell her funny stories; perhaps he might even take her for a drive in his new buggy behind his little black mare Jenny. Marigold thought this ever so much more fun than riding in a car.

Of course she was sorry to leave Mother even for a night, and sorry to leave her new kitten. But to go for a real visit! Marigold spent a raptured week looking forward to it and living it in imagination.

2

And it was horrid—horrid. There was nothing nice about it from the very beginning, except the drive to the Head with Uncle Klon and Aunt Marigold, over wood-roads spicy with the fern scent of the warm summer afternoon. As soon as they left her there the horridness began. Marigold did not know that she was homesick, but she knew she was unhappy from her head to her toes and that everything was disappointing. What good was a case of humming-birds if there were no one to talk them over with? Even the water-garden did not interest her, and there were no signs of a skeleton anywhere. As for Frank, he was the worst disappointment of all. He hardly took any notice of her at all. And he was so changed—so gruff and smileless, with a horrible little moustache which looked just like a dab of soot on his upper lip. It was the moustache over which he and Hilda had quarrelled, though nobody knew about it but themselves.

Marigold ate very little supper. She thought every mouthful would choke her. She took only two bites of Aunt Flora's nut cake with whipped cream on top, and Aunt Flora, who had made it on purpose for her, never really forgave her. After supper she went out and leaned forlornly against the gate, looking wistfully up the long red road of mystery that led back home. Oh, if she were only home—with Mother. The west wind stirring in the grasses—the robin-vesper calls—the long tree shadows across a field of wheaten gold—all hurt her now because Mother wasn't here.

"Nothing is ever like what you think it's going to be," she thought dismally.

It was after supper at home now, too. Grandmother would be weaving in the garret—and Salome would be giving the cats their milk—and Mother—Marigold ran in to Aunt Flora.

"Aunt Flora, I must go home right away—please—*please.*"

"Nonsense, child," said Aunt Flora stiffly. "Don't take a fit of the fidgets now."

Marigold wondered why she had never noticed before what a great beaky nose Aunt Flora had.

"Oh, *please* take me home," she begged desperately.

"You can't go home to-night," said Aunt Flora impatiently. The car isn't working right. Don't get lonesome now. I guess you're tired. You'd better go to bed. Frank'll drive you home to-morrow if it doesn't rain. Come now, seven's your bedtime at home, isn't it?"

"Seven's your bedtime at home." At *home*—lying in her own bed, with the light shining from Mother's room—with a delicious golden ball of fluff that curled and purred all over your bed and finally went to sleep on your legs. Marigold couldn't bear it.

"Oh, I want to go home. I want to go home," she sobbed.

"I can't have any nonsense now," said Aunt Flora firmly. Aunt Flora was noted for her admirable firmness with children. "Surely you're not going to be a crybaby. I'll take you up and help you undress."

3

Marigold was lying alone in a huge room in a huge bed that was miles from the floor. She was suddenly half wild with terror and altogether wild with unendurable homesickness. It was dark with a darkness that could be felt. She had never gone to bed in the dark before. Always that friendly light in Mother's room— and sometimes Mother stayed with her till she went to sleep, though Young Grandmother disapproved of that. Marigold had been afraid to ask Aunt Flora to leave the light. Aunt Flora had tucked her in and told her to be a good girl.

"Shut your eyes and go right to sleep, and it will be morning before you know it—and you can go home."

Then she had gone out and shut the door. Aunt Flora flattered herself she knew how to deal with children.

Marigold *couldn't* go to sleep in the dark. And it would be years and *years* before morning came—if it ever did.

"There's nobody here who loves me," she thought passionately.

The black endless hours dragged on. They really were hours, though to Marigold they seemed like centuries. It must surely be nearly morning.

How the wind was wailing round the house! Marigold loved

the wind at home, especially at this time of the year when it made her cosy little bed seem cosier. But was this some terrible wind that Lazarre called "de ghos' wind"?

"It blows at de tam of de year when de dead peop' get out of dare grave for a lil' while," he told her.

Was this the time of year? And that man-hole she had seen in the ceiling before Aunt Flora took the light out? Lazarre had told her a dreadful story about seeing a horrible face "wit long hairy ear" looking down at him from a man-hole.

There was a closet in the room. *Was that the closet where the skeleton was?* Suppose the door opened and it fell out. Or walked out. Suppose its bones rattled—Uncle Paul said they did sometimes. What was it she had heard about Uncle Paul keeping a pet rat in the barn? Suppose he brought it into the house at night! Suppose it wandered about! Wasn't that a rat gnawing somewhere?

Would she ever see home again? Suppose mother died before morning. Suppose it rained—rained for a week—and they wouldn't take her home. She knew how Aunt Flora hated to get mud on the new car. And wasn't that thunder?

It was only wagons rumbling across the long bridge over the East River below the house, but Marigold did not know that. She did know she was going to scream—she knew she couldn't live another minute in that strange bed in that dark, haunted room. *What was that?* Queer scratches on the window. Oh—Lazarre's story of the devil coming to carry off a bad child and scratching on the window to get in. Because she hadn't said her prayers. Marigold hadn't said hers. She had been too homesick and miserable to think of them. She couldn't say them now—but she could sit up in bed and scream like a thing demented. And she did.

4

Uncle Paul and Aunt Flora, wakened out of their first sound sleep after a hard day's work, came running in. Marigold stopped screaming when she saw them.

"The child's trembling—she must be cold," said Uncle Paul.

"I'm not cold," said Marigold through her chattering teeth, "but I must go home."

"Now, Marigold, you must be a reasonable little girl," soothed Aunt Flora firmly. "It's eleven o'clock. You can't get home to-night. Would you like some raisins?"

"I want to go home," repeated Marigold.

"Who's raising the Old Harry here?" said Frank, coming in. He had heard Marigold's shrieks when he was getting ready for bed. "Here, sis, is a chocolate mouse for you. Eat it and shut your little trap."

It was a lovely, brown chocolate mouse with soft, creamy insides—the kind of confection the soul of the normal Marigold loved. But now it only suggested Uncle Paul's mythical rat.

"I don't want it—I want to go home."

"Perhaps if you bring her up a kitten," suggested Uncle Paul in desperation.

"I don't want a kitten," wailed Marigold. "I want to go home."

"I'll give you my coloured egg-dish if you'll stay quietly till morning," implored Aunt Flora, casting firmness to the winds.

"I don't want the coloured egg-dish. I want to go home."

"Well, go," said Uncle Paul, finally losing his patience with this exasperating child. "There's plenty of good road."

But Aunt Flora had realised that Marigold was on the verge of hysterics, and to have a hysterical child on her hands was a prospect that made even her firmness quail. She had never approved of Paul's whim of bringing the child here anyhow. This was a Winthrop trick if ever there was one.

"I think Frank had better hitch up and take her home. She may cry herself sick."

"She's a great big baby and I'm ashamed of her," said Uncle Paul crushingly. That speech was to rankle in Marigold's soul for many a day, but at the moment she was only concerned with the fact that Uncle Paul told Frank to go out and hitch up.

"Well, this *is* the limit," said Frank grouchily.

Aunt Flora helped the sobbing Marigold to dress. Uncle Paul was so annoyed that he wouldn't even say good-bye to her. Aunt Flora said it very stiffly. When Mother had kissed Marigold good-bye she had whispered, "When you come home be sure to thank Aunt Flora for the lovely time she has given you." But it did not seem just the right thing to say, so Marigold said nothing.

"Cut out the weeps," ordered Frank as he lifted her into the buggy. "Upon my word, I admire Herod."

Frank was abominably cross. He had had a hard day's work in the harvest-field and was in no mood for a twelve-mile ride, all for the whim of a silly kid. Lord, what nuisances kids were. He was glad he would never have any. Marigold conquered her sobs with an effort. She was going home. Nothing else mattered. Frank sent his black mare spinning along the road and never spoke a word, but Marigold didn't care. She was going home.

Half-way home they turned the corner at the school, and Martin Richard's house was just beyond—a little, old-fashioned white house with a tall Lombardy standing sentinel at either corner, and a tangle of rose-bushes fringing its short lane.

"Why, Frank," cried Marigold, "what's the matter with the house?"

Frank looked—shouted, "My Golly!"—stopped the mare—sprang out of the buggy—tore into the yard—hammered on the door. A window over the door opened—Marigold saw a girl lean out. It was Hilda Wright, who must have been staying all night with her cousin, Jean Richards. Frank saw her, too.

"The house is on fire," he shouted. "Get them up—quick. There's no time to lose."

A wild half-hour followed—a most int'resting half-hour. Luckily Frank's mare had been trained to stand without hitching, and Marigold sat there watching greedily. The house suddenly sparkled with lights. Men rushed out for buckets and ladders. Gigantic grotesque shadows went hurtling over the barns in the lantern-light. Dogs barked their heads off. It was very satisfying while it lasted. The fire was soon put out. The kitchen roof had caught from a spark. But after it was out, Marigold could see Frank and Hilda standing very close together by one of the Lombardies.

Marigold sat in the buggy and enjoyed the sudden swoops of wind. It was not a stormy night after all—it was a windy, starry night. How thick the stars were. Marigold would have liked to count them but she did not dare. Lazarre had told her that if you tried to count the stars you would drop down dead. Suppose—somewhere—a star fell down at your feet. Suppose a lot of them did. Suppose you were chasing stars all over the meadows—over the hills—over the dunes. Till you picked up handfuls of them.

Frank and Hilda came out to the buggy together. Hilda was carrying a little lantern, and the red silk scarf around her head fluttered about her face like a scarlet flame. The bitterness had gone out of her mouth and she was smiling. So was Frank.

"And you've sat here all this time alone without a word. And Jenny not even hitched. Well, you're a plucky little kid after all. I don't wonder you were homesick and scared in that big barn Flora calls a spare room. I'll get you home now in two shakes. Nighty-night, honey."

The "honey" was not for Marigold but for Hilda, who after being kissed, leaned forward and squeezed Marigold's hand.

"I'm *glad* you were homesick," she whispered. "But I hope you won't ever be homesick again."

"I guess Frank won't go West now," whispered Marigold.

"If he does I'll go with him," whispered Hilda. "I'll go to the ends of the earth with him."

"Look here, darling, you'll catch cold," interrupted Frank considerately. "Hop in and finish your beauty sleep. I'll be up to-morrow night. Just now I've got to get this little poppet home.

67

She saved your uncle's house to-night with her monkey didoes, anyway."

Frank was so nice and jolly and funny all the rest of the way home that Marigold was almost sorry when they got there. Every one at Cloud of Spruce was in bed, but Mother was not asleep. She came down at once and hugged Marigold when she heard Frank's story—at least as much as he chose to tell. He said nothing about Hilda, but he gave Marigold a fierce parting hug and put two chocolate mice in her hand.

"Guess you can eat these fellows now without choking," he said.

Marigold, safe in her own dear bed, with her kitten at her feet, ate her mice and fell asleep wondering if Frank were "dam" because he had, after all, spoken first.

CHAPTER V

The Door That Men Call Death

1

After all Old Grandmother did not live out her hundred years—much to the disappointment of the clan, who all wanted to be able to brag that one of them had "attained the century mark." The McAllisters over-the-bay had a centenarian aunt and put on airs about it. It was intolerable that they should go the Lesleys one better in anything when they were comparative newcomers, only three generations out from Scotland, when the Lesleys were five.

But Death was not concerned about clan rivalry and somehow even Old Grandmother's "will to live" could not carry her so far. She failed rapidly after that ninety-eighth birthday-party and nobody expected her to get through the next winter—except Marigold, to whom it had never occurred that Old Grandmother would not go on living forever. But in the spring Old Grandmother rallied amazingly.

"Mebbe she'll make it yet," said Mrs. Kemp to Salome. Salome shook her head.

"No; she's done. It's the last flicker of the candle. I wish she *could* live out the century. It's disgusting to think of old Christine McAllister, who's been deaf and blind and with no more mind than a baby for ten years, living to be a hundred and Lesley with all her faculties dying at only ninety-nine."

Marigold in the wash-house doorway caught her breath. Was

Old Grandmother going to *die*—could such a thing happen? Oh, it couldn't. It *couldn't*. The bottom seemed to have dropped out of everything for Marigold. Not that she was conscious of any particular love for Old Grandmother. But she was one of The Things That Always Have Been. And when one of The Things That Always Have Been disappear, it is a shock. It makes you feel as if *nothing* could be depended on.

She had got a little used to the idea by next Saturday, when she went in to say her verses to Old Grandmother. Old Grandmother was propped up on her rosy pillows, knitting furiously on a blue jacket for a new great-grandson at the Coast. Her eyes were as bright and boring as ever.

"Sit down. I can't hear your verses till I've finished counting."

Marigold sat down and looked at the brides. She did not want to look at Clementine's picture but she had to. She couldn't keep her eyes from it. She clenched her small hands and set her teeth. Hateful, hateful Clementine, who had more beautiful hands than Mother. And that endless dreamy smile at the lily—as if nothing else mattered. If she had only had the self-conscious smirk of the other brides, Marigold might not have hated her so much. *They* cared what people thought about them. Clementine didn't. She was so sure of herself—so sure of having Father—so sure of being flawlessly beautiful, she never thought for a moment of anybody's opinion. She *knew* that people couldn't help looking at her and admiring her even though they hated her. Marigold wrenched her eyes away and fastened them on the picture of an angel over Old Grandmother's bed—a radiant being with long white wings and halo of golden curls, soaring easily through sunset skies. *Was* Old Grandmother going to die? And if she did, would she be like that? Marigold had a daring little imagination but it faltered before such a conception.

"What are you thinking of?" demanded Old Grandmother so suddenly and sharply that Marigold spoke out the question in her mind before she could prevent herself.

"Will you be an angel when you die, ma'am?"

Old Granny sighed. "I suppose so. How it will bore me. Who's been telling you I was going to die?"

"Nobody," faltered Marigold, alive to what she had done. "Only—only—"

"Out with it," ordered Old Grandmother.

"Mrs. Kemp said it was a pity you couldn't live to be the hundred when old Chris McAllister did."

"Since when," demanded Old Grandmother in an awful tone, "have the Lesleys been the rivals of the McAllisters? *The McAllisters!* And does anybody suppose that Chris McAllister has been *living* for the last ten years? Why, she's been deader than I'll be when I've been under the sod for a century! For that matter she never *was* alive. As for dying, I'm not going to die till I get good and ready. For one thing, I'm going to finish this jacket first. What else did Mrs. Kemp say? Not that I care. I'm done with curiosity about life. I'm only curious now about death. Still, she was always an amusing old devil."

"She didn't say much more—only that the Lawson baby couldn't live and Mrs. Gray-over-the-bay had a cancer and Young Sam Marr had appendicitis."

"Cheerful little budget. I dreamed last night I went to heaven and saw Old Sam Marr there and it made me so mad I woke up. The idea of Old Sam Marr in heaven."

Old Grandmother shook her knitting-needle ferociously at a shrinking little bride who seemed utterly lost in the clouds of tulle and satin that swirled around her.

"Why don't you want him in heaven?" asked Marigold.

"If it comes to that I don't know. I never disliked Old Sam. It's only—he couldn't *belong* in heaven. No business there at all."

Marigold had some difficulty in imagining Old Grandmother "belonging" in heaven either.

"You wouldn't want him in—the other place."

"Of course not. Poor old harmless, doddering Sam. Always spewing tobacco-juice over everything. The only thing he had to be proud of was the way he could spit. There really ought to be a betwixt-and-between place. Only," added Granny with a grin, "if there were, most of us would be in it."

She knitted a round of her jacket sleeve before she spoke again. Marigold put in the time hating Clementine.

"I was sorry when Old Sam Marr died, though," said Granny abruptly. "Do you know why? He was the last person alive who could remember me when I was young and handsome."

Marigold looked at Old Grandmother. Could this ugly little old woman ever have been young and pretty? Old Grandmother caught the scepticism in her eyes.

"You don't believe I ever was. Why, child, my hair was red-gold and my arms were the boast of the clan. No Lesley man ever married an ugly woman. Some of us were fools and some shrews, but we never shirked a woman's first duty—to please a man's eyes. To be sure, the Lesley men knew how to pick wives. Come here and let me have a look at you."

Marigold went and stood by the bed. Old Grandmother put a skinny hand under her chin, tilted up her face and looked very searchingly at her.

"Hmm. The Winthrop hair—too pale a gold, but it may darken—the Lesley blue eyes—the Blaisdell ears—too early to say whose nose you have—*my* complexion. Well, thank goodness, I don't think you'll be hard to look at."

Old Grandmother chuckled as she always did when achieving a bit of modern slang. Marigold went out feeling more cheerful. She didn't believe Old Grandmother had any idea of dying.

2

Granny continued to improve. She sat up in bed and knit. She saw everybody who came and chattered to them. She held long pow-wows with Lucifer. She wouldn't let Young Grandmother have her new silk dress made without a high collar. She had Lazarre in and hauled him over the coals because he was said to have been drunk and given his wife a black eye.

"She won't die dese twenty year," said the aggrieved Lazarre. "Dere's only room for wan of dem down dare."

Then Aunt Harriet in Charlottetown gave a party in honour of her husband's sister, and Young Grandmother and Mother were going in Uncle Klon's car. They would not be back before three o'clock that night, but Salome would be there and Old Grandmother was amazingly well and brisk. And then at the last moment Salome was summoned to the deathbed of an aunt in South Harmony. Young Grandmother in her silken magnificence and Mother looking like a slender lily in her green crêpe, with the blossom of her face atop of it, came to the orchard room.

"Of course we can't go now," said Young Grandmother regretfully. She had wanted to go—the said husbands sister had been a girlhood friend of hers.

"Why can't you go?" snapped Old Grandmother. "I've finished my jacket and I'm going to die at three o'clock tonight, but that isn't any reason why you shouldn't go to the party, is it? Of course you'll go. Don't dare stay home on my account."

Young Grandmother was not much worried over Old Grandmother's prediction. That was just one of her characteristic remarks.

"Do you feel any worse?" she asked perfunctorily.

"When I'm perfectly well there's not much the matter with me," said Old Grandmother cryptically. "There's no earthly sense in your staying home on my account. If I need anything Marigold can get it for me. I hope you ate a good supper. You won't get much at Harriet's. She thinks starving her guests is living the simple life. And she always fills the cups too full on purpose—so there'll be no room for cream. Harriet can make a pitcher of cream go farther than any woman I know."

"*We* are not going there for what we will get to eat," said Young Grandmother majestically.

Old Grandmother chuckled.

"Of course not. Anyhow, you'll *go*. I want to hear all about that party. It'll be amusing. I'd rather be amused than loved now. You take notice whether Grace and Marjory are speaking to each other yet or not. And whether Kathleen Lesley has had her eyebrows plucked. I heard she was going to when she went to New York. And if Louisa has on that awful pink georgette dress with green worms on it—try to see if you can't spill some coffee over it."

"If you think we'd better not go—" began Young Grandmother.

"Marian Blaisdell, if you don't get out of this room instantly I'll throw something at you. There's Klon honking now. You know he doesn't like to wait. Be off, both of you, and send Marigold in. She can sit here and keep me company till her bedtime."

Old Grandmother watched Young Grandmother and Mother out with a curious expression in her old black eyes.

"She hates to think of me dying because she won't be *Young* Grandmother any longer. It's a promotion she's not anxious for," she told Marigold, who had come reluctantly in. "Get your picture book and sit down, child. I want to think for awhile. Later on I've got some things to say to you."

"Yes, ma'am." Marigold always said "Yes, ma'am" to Old Grandmother and "Yes, Grandmother" to Young Grandmother. She sat down obediently but unwillingly. It was a lovely spring evening and Sylvia would be waiting at the Green Gate. They had planned to make a special new kind of magic by the White Fountain that night. And now she would have to spend the whole evening sitting here with Old Grandmother, who wouldn't even talk but lay there with her eyes closed. Was she asleep? If she were, couldn't she, Marigold, run up through the orchard to the Green Gate for a moment to tell Sylvia why she couldn't come. Sylvia mightn't understand otherwise. The Magic Door was open right beside her chair—she could slip through it—be back in a minute.

"Are you asleep, ma'am?" she whispered cautiously.

"Shut up. Of course I'm asleep," snapped Old Grandmother.

Marigold sighed and resigned herself. Dear knows what

Sylvia would do. Never come again perhaps. Marigold had never broken tryst with her before. She turned her chair softly around so that her back would be toward Clementine, and looked at the other brides in the crinolines and flower-lined poke bonnets of the sixties, the bustles and polonaises of the eighties, the balloon sleeves and bell skirts of the nineties, the hobbles and huge hats of the tens. Marigold knew nothing of their respective dates, of course. They all belonged to that legendary time before she was born, when people wore all kinds of absurd dresses. The only one who didn't look funny was Clementine, in her lace-shrouded shoulders, her sleek cap of hair and her fadeless, fashionless lily. She came back to Clementine every time—somehow she couldn't help it. It was like a sore tooth you *had* to bite on. But she would not turn round to look at her. She *would* not.

3

"What are you staring at Clementine like that for?" Old Grandmother was sitting erectly up in bed. "Handsome, wasn't she? The handsomest of all the Lesley brides. Such colour—such expression—and the charming gestures of her wonderful hands. It was such a pity—" Old Grandmother stopped abruptly. Marigold felt sure she had meant to say, "It was such a pity she died."

Old Grandmother threw back the blankets and slipped two tiny feet over the edge of the bed.

"Get me my clothes and stockings," she ordered. "There in the top bureau drawer. And the black silk dress hanging in the closet. And the prunella shoes in the blue box. Quick, now."

"You're not going to get up?" gasped Marigold in amazement. She had never seen Old Grandmother up in her life. She hadn't supposed Old Grandmother could get up.

"I'm going to get up and I'm going to take a walk in the orchard," said Old Grandmother. "You just do as I tell you and no back talk. I did what I pleased before you were born or thought of, and I'll do what I please to-night. That's why I made them go to the party. Hop."

Marigold hopped. She brought the clothes and the black dress and the prunella boots and helped Old Grandmother put them on. Not that Old Grandmother required much assistance. She stood up triumphantly, holding to the bed post.

"Bring me my black silk scarf and one of the canes in the old clock. I've walked about this room every night after the rest were in bed—to keep my legs in working order—but I haven't been out of doors for nine years."

Marigold, feeling as if she must be in a dream, brought the cane, and followed Old Grandmother out of The Magic Door and down the shallow steps. Old Grandmother paused and looked around her. The moon was not yet up, though there was silvery brightness behind the spruces on the hill. To the west there was a little streak of soft, dear gold behind the birches. There was a cold clear dew on the grass. The Witch of Endor was shrieking insults at somebody out behind the apple-barn.

Old Grandmother sniffed.

"Oh, the salt tang of the sea! It's good to smell it again. And the apple-blossoms. I had forgotten what spring was like. Is that old stone bench still in the orchard under the cedar-tree? Take me there. I want to see one more moon rise over that cloud of spruce."

Marigold took hold of Old Grandmother's hand and they went into the orchard—a spot Marigold was very fond of. It was such a very delightful and extraordinary old orchard where apple-trees and fir-trees and pine-trees were deliciously mixed up together. Between the trees in the open spaces were flower-beds. Thickets of sweet clover, white and fragrant; clumps of Canterbury-bells, pink and purple. Plots of mint and southernwood. Big blush roses. Perfumed winds blew there. Elves dwelt in the currant bushes. Little Green Folk lived up in the old beech-tree.

There was a queer sort of expectant hush over the orchard as

Marigold and Old Grandmother went through it to where the great spreading cedar rose out of a drift of blooming spirea-bushes. Marigold thought it must be because the flowers were watching for the moon to rise.

4

Old Grandmother sank down on the stone bench with a grunt. She sat there silent and motionless for what seemed to Marigold a very long time. The moon rose over the cloud of spruce and the orchard became transfigured. A garden of flowers in moonlight is a strange, enchanted thing with a touch of diablerie, and Marigold, sensitive to every influence, felt its charm long years before she could define it. Nothing was the same as in daylight. She had never been out in the orchard so late as this before. The June lilies held up their cups of snow; the moonlight lay silver white on the stone steps. The perfume of the lilacs came in little puffs on the crystal air; beyond the orchard lay old fields she knew and loved, mysterious misty spaces of moonshine now. Far, far away was the murmur of the sea.

And still Old Grandmother dreamed on. Did she see faces long under the mould bright and vivid again? Were there flying feet, summoning voices, that only she could hear in that old moonlit orchard? What voices were calling to her out of the firs? Marigold felt a funny little prickling along her spine. She was perfectly sure that she and Old Grandmother were not alone in the orchard.

"Well, how have you been since we came out here?" demanded Old Grandmother at last.

"Pretty comf'able," said Marigold, rather startled.

"Good," said Old Grandmother. "It's a good test—the test of silence. If you can sit in silence with any one for half an hour and feel 'comfortable,' you and that person can be friends. If not, friends you'll never be and you needn't waste time trying. I've brought you out here to-night for two reasons, Marigold. The first is to give you some hints about living, which may do you some good and may not. The second was to keep a tryst with the years. We haven't been alone here, child."

No; Marigold had known that. She drew a little closer to Old Grandmother.

"Don't be frightened, child. The ghosts that walk here are friendly, homey ghosts. They wouldn't hurt you. They are of your race and blood. Do you know you look strangely like a child who died seventy years before you were born? My husband's niece. Not a living soul remembers that little creature but me—her beauty—her charm—her wonder. But I remember her. You have her eyes and mouth—and that same air of listening to voices only she could hear. Is that a curse or a blessing I wonder? My children played in this orchard—and then my grandchildren—- and my great-grandchildren. Such a lot of small ghosts! To think that in a house where there were once fourteen children there is now nobody but you."

"That isn't my fault," said Marigold, who felt as if Old Grandmother were blaming her.

"It's nobody's fault, just as it was nobody's fault that your father died of pneumonia before you were born. Cloud of Spruce will be yours some day, Marigold."

"Will it?" Marigold was startled. Such a thing had never occurred to her.

"And you must always love it. Places know when they're loved—just the same as people. I've seen houses whose hearts were actually broken. This house and I have always been good friends. I've always loved it from the day I came here as a bride. I planted most of those trees. You must marry some day, Marigold, and fill those old rooms again. But not too young— not too young. I married at seventeen and I was a grandmother at thirty-six. It was awful. Sometimes it seems to me that I've *always* been a grandmother.

"I *could* have been married at sixteen. But I was determined

I wouldn't be married till I had finished knitting my apple-leaf bedspread. Your great-grandfather went off in such a rage I didn't know if he'd ever come back. But he did. He was only a boy himself. Two children—that's what we were. Two young fools. That's what everybody called us. And yet we were wiser then than I am now. We knew things then I don't know now. I've stayed up too late. Don't do that, Marigold—don't live till there's nothing left of life but the Pope's nose. Nobody will be sorry when I die."

Suddenly Marigold gasped.

"*I* will be sorry," she cried—and meant it. Why, it would be terrible. No Old Grandmother at Cloud of Spruce. How could the world go on at all?

"I don't mean that kind of sorriness," said Old Grandmother. "And even you won't be sorry long. Isn't it strange? I was once afraid of Death. He was a foe then—now he is a lover. Do you know, Marigold, it is thirty years since any one called me by my name? Do you know what my name is?"

"No-o," admitted Marigold. It was the first time she had ever realised that Old Grandmother must have a name.

"My name is Edith. Do you know I have an odd fancy I want to hear some one call me that again. Just once. Call me by my name, Marigold."

Marigold gasped again. This was terrible. It was sacrilege. Why, one might almost as well be expected to call God by His name to His face.

"Say anything—anything—with my name in it," said Old Grandmother impatiently.

"I—I don't know what to say,—Edith," stammered Marigold. It sounded dreadful when she had said it. Old Grandmother sighed.

"It's no use. *That* isn't my name—not as you say it. Of course it couldn't be. I should have known better." Suddenly she laughed.

"Marigold, I wish I could be present at my own funeral. Oh, wouldn't it be fun! The whole clan will be here to the last sixth cousin. They'll sit around and say all the usual kind, good, dull things about me instead of the interesting truth. The only true thing they'll say will be that I had a wonderful constitution. That's always said of any Lesley who lives to be over eighty. Marigold—" Old Grandmother's habit of swinging a conversation around by its ears was always startling, "what do you really think about the world?"

Marigold, though taken by surprise, knew exactly what she thought about the world.

"It think it's very int'resting," she said.

Old Grandmother stared at her, then laughed.

"You've hit it. 'Whether there be tongues they shall fail—whether there be prophecies they shall vanish away'—but the pageant of human life goes on. I've never tired watching it. I've lived nearly a century—and when all's said and done there's nothing I'm more thankful for than that I've always found the world and the people in it interesting. Yes, life's been worth living. Marigold, how many little boys are sweet on you?"

"Sweet on me." Marigold didn't understand.

"Haven't you any little beau?" explained Old Grandmother.

Marigold was quite shocked. "Of course not. I'm too small."

"Oh, are you? I had *two* beaux when I was your age. Can you imagine *me* being seven years old and having two little boys sweet on me?"

Marigold looked at Old Grandmother's laughter-filled and moonlight-softened black eyes and for the first time realised that Old Grandmother had not always been old. Why, she might even have been Edith.

"For that matter I had a beau when I was six," said Old Grandmother triumphantly. "Girls were *born* having beaux in my day. Little Jim Somebody—I've forgotten his last name if I ever knew it—walked three miles to buy a stick of candy for me. I was only six, but I knew what that meant. He has been dead for eighty years. And there was Charlie Snaith. He was nine. We always called him Froggy-face. I'll never forget his huge round eyes staring at me as he asked, 'Can I be your beau?' Or how he looked when I giggled and said 'no.' There were a good many 'no's' before I finally said 'yes.'" Old Grandmother laughed reminiscently, with all the delight of a girl in her teens.

"It was Great-Grandfather you first said 'yes' to, wasn't it?" asked Marigold.

Old Grandmother nodded.

"But I had some narrow escapes. I was crazy about Frank Lister when I was fifteen. My folks wouldn't let me have him. He wanted me to run away with him. I've always been sorry I didn't. But then if I had I'd have been sorry for that, too. I was very near taking Bob Clancy—and now all I can remember about him was that he got drunk once and varnished his mother's kitchen with maple-syrup. Joe Benson was in love with me. I had told him I thought he was magnificent. If you tell a certain kind of man he's magnificent you can have him—if you really want that kind of a man. Peter March was a nice fellow. He was thought to be dying of consumption, and he pleaded with me to marry him and give him a year of happiness. Just suppose I had. He got better and lived to be seventy. Never take a risk like that with a live man, Marigold. He married Hilda Stuart. A pretty girl but too self-conscious. And every time Hilda spent more than five cents a week Peter took neuralgia. He always sat ahead of me in church, and I was always tormented with a desire to slap a spot on his bald head that looked like a fly."

"Was Great-Grandfather a handsome man?" asked Marigold.

"Handsome? Handsome? Every one was handsome a hundred years ago. I don't know if he was handsome or not. I only know he was my man from the moment I first set eyes on him. It was at a dinner-party. He was there with Janet Churchill. She thought she had him hooked. She always hated me. I had gold slippers on that night that were too tight for me. I kicked them off under the table for a bit of ease. Never found one of them again. I knew Janet was responsible for it. But I got even with her. I took her beau. It wasn't hard. She was a black velvet beauty of a girl—far prettier than I was—but she kept all her goods in the show-window. Where there is no mystery there is no romance. Remember that, Marigold."

"Did you and Great-Grandfather live here when you were married?"

"Yes. He built Cloud of Spruce and brought me here. We were quite happy. Of course we quarrelled now and then. And once he swore at me. I just swore back at him. It horrified him so he never set me such a bad example again. The worst quarrel we ever had was when he spilled soup over my purple silk dress. I always believed he did it on purpose because he didn't like the dress. He has been dead up there in South Harmony graveyard for forty years, but if he were here now I'd like to slap his face for that dress."

"How did you get even with him?" asked Marigold, knowing very well Old Grandmother *had* got even.

Old Grandmother laughed until she had hardly enough breath left to speak.

"I told him that since he had ruined my dress I'd go to church next Sunday in my petticoat. And I *did*."

"Oh, Grandmother." Marigold thought this was going too far.

"Oh, I wore a long silk coat over it. He never knew till we were in our pew. When I sat down the coat fell open in front and he saw the petticoat—a bright Paddy-green it was. Oh, his face—I can see it yet."

Old Grandmother rocked herself to and fro on the stone bench in a convulsion of mirth.

"I pulled the coat together. But I don't think your great-grandfather got much good of *that* sermon. When it was over he took me by the arm and marched me down the aisle and out to our buggy. No hanging round to talk gossip that day. He never spoke all the way home—sat there with his mouth primmed up. In fact he never said a word about it at all—but he never could bear green the rest of his life. And it was my color. But the next time I got a green dress he gave our fat old washerwoman a dress off the same piece. So of course I couldn't wear the dress, and I never dared get green again. After all, it took a clever person to get the better of your great-grandfather in the long run. But that was the only serious quarrel we ever had, though we used to squabble for a few years over the bread. He wanted the slices cut thick and I wanted them thin. It spoiled a lot of meals for us."

"Why couldn't you have each cut them to suit yourselves?"

Old Grandmother chuckled.

"No, no. That would have been giving in on a trifle. It's harder to do that than give in on something big. Of course we worked it out like that after we had so many children the question was to get enough bread for the family, thick or thin. But to the end of his life there were times when he would snort when I cut a lovely thin paper-like slice, and times when I honestly couldn't help sniffing when he carved off one an inch thick."

"*I* like bread thin," said Marigold, sympathising with Old Grandmother.

"But if you marry a man who likes it thick—and I know now that every proper man does—let him have it thick from the start. Don't stick on trifles, Marigold. The slices of bread didn't worry me when your great-grandfather fell in love with his second cousin, Mary Lesley. She always tried to flirt with every male creature in sight. Simply couldn't leave the men alone. She wasn't handsome but she carried herself like a queen, so people thought she was one. It's a useful trick, Marigold. You might remember it. But don't flirt. Either you hurt yourself or you hurt some one else."

"Didn't *you* flirt?" asked Marigold slyly.

"Yes. That's why I'm telling you not to. For the rest—take what God sends you. That was a bad time while it lasted. But he came back. They generally come back if you have sense enough to keep still and wait—as I had, glory be. The only time I broke loose was the night of Charlie Blaisdell's wedding. Alec sat in a corner and talked to Mary all the evening. I flew out of the house and walked the six miles home in a thin evening dress and satin shoes. It was in March. It should have killed me, of course—but here I am at ninety-nine tough and tasty. And Alec never missed me! Thought I'd gone home with Abe Lesley's crowd. Oh, well, he came to his senses when Mary dropped him for something fresher. But I can't say I was ever very fond of Mary Lesley after that. She was a mischief-maker, anyhow, always blowing old jealousies into a flame for the fun of it.

"I got on very well with the rest of the clan, though the in-laws were mostly very stupid, poor things. Alec's mother didn't approve of us having such a big family. She said it kept Alec's nose to the grindstone. I had twins twice just to spite her, but we got on very well for all that. And Alec's brother Sam was a terrible bore. Nothing ever happened to him. He never even fell in love. Died when he was sixty, in his sleep. It used to make me mad to see any one wasting life like that. Paul was a black sheep. Always got drunk on every solemn or awful occasion. Got drunk at Ruth Lesley's wedding—she was married from here—and upset two stands of bees over there by the apple-barn just as the bridal party came out here to the orchard to be married. That was the liveliest wedding I was ever at. Never shall I forget old Minister Wood flying up those steps pursued by bees. Talk about ghosts!"

Old Grandmother laughed until she had to wipe the tears from her eyes.

"Poor Ruth. She was so stung up she looked like a bride with the smallpox. Oh, well, she had only about half a brain, anyway. She always threw her arms about her husband in public when she wanted to ask him some small favor. How red and furious he got! And he always refused. You'd have thought she'd have learned sense in time. Some women never do. Be sure you have some sense, Marigold, when it comes to handling the men."

"Tell me some more stories, Grandmother," entreated Marigold.

"Child, I could tell you stories all night. This orchard is full of them. Up there by the scabby apple-tree Bess Lesley swooned because Alexander McKay asked her to marry him too suddenly. People 'swooned' in my day—'fainted' in your grandmother's. Now they don't do either. But what a lot of fun they miss. Alexander thought Bess was dead—that he'd killed her with his abruptness. We found him on his knees by her, tearing his hair and shrieking blue murder. He thought I was a brute because I threw a dipperful of water over her. She came to very quickly— her curls were only paper ones—and such a looking creature as she was, with them hanging limp about her face and a complexion like a tallow candle. But she had a wonderful figure. It seems to me the girls look like sticks nowadays. Alexander clasped her in his arms and implored her to forgive him. She forgave him—and married him—but she never forgave me. Talking of ghosts—they had a haunted door in their house. Always found open no matter how it was shut and locked."

"Do you really believe that, Grandmother?"

"Of course. Always believe things like that. If you don't believe things you'll never have any fun. The more things you can believe the more interesting life is, as you say yourself. Too much incredulity makes it a poor thing. As for the ghosts, we had another haunted house in the clan—Garth Lesley's-over-the-bay. It was haunted by a white cat!"

"Why?"

"Nobody knew. But there it was. The Garth Lesleys were rather proud of it. Lots of people saw it. *I* saw it. At least, I saw a white cat washing its face on the stairs."

"But was it the ghost cat?"

"Oh, there you go again. I prefer to believe it was. Otherwise I could never say I'd seen a real ghost. Over there in that corner where the three pines are, Hilary and Kate Lesley agreed to tell each other what they really thought of each other. They thought it would be fun—but they never 'spoke' again. Kate was engaged at one time to her third cousin, Ben Lesley-over-the-bay. It was broken off and later she found her photograph in his mother's album adorned with horns and a moustache. There was a terrible family row over that. In the tail of the day she married Dave Ridley. A harmless creature—only he *would* eat the icing off his wife's piece of cake whenever they went anywhere to tea. Kate didn't seem to mind—she hated icing—but I always wanted to choke him with gobs of icing until he had enough of it for once. Ben's sister Laura was jilted by Turner Reed. He married Josie Lesley and when they appeared out in church the first Sunday Laura Lesley went too, in the dress that was to have been her wedding one, and sat down on the other side of Ben. Alec said she should have been tarred and feathered, but I tell you I liked her spunk. There's a piece of that very dress in my silk log-cabin quilt in the green chest in the garret. You are to have it—and my pearl ring. Your great-grandfather found the pearl in an oyster the day we were engaged and had it set for me. It was reckoned worth five hundred dollars. I've left it to you in my will so none of the others can raise a rumpus or do you out of it. Edith-over-the-bay has had her eye on it for years. Thinks she should have it because she was my first namesake. She owes me more than her name if she but knew it. She wouldn't exist at all if it hadn't been for me. *I* made the match between her father and mother. I was quite a matchmaker in my time. They really didn't want to marry each other a bit but they were just as happy as if they had. All the same, Marigold, don't ever let any one make a match for *you*."

Old Grandmother was silent for a few moments, thinking over, maybe, more old, forgotten loves of the clan. The wind swayed the trees and the shadows danced madly. *Were* they only shadows—?

"Annabel Lesley and I used to sit under the syrup apple-tree over there and talk," said Old Grandmother—in a different voice. A gentle, tender voice. "I loved Annabel. She was the only one of the Lesley clan I really loved. A sweet woman. The only woman I ever knew who would keep secrets. A woman who would really burn a letter if you asked her to. It was safe to empty your soul out to her. Learn to keep a secret, Marigold. And she was just. Learn to be just, Marigold. The hardest thing in the world is to be just. I never was just. It was so much easier to be generous."

"I could sit here all night and hear you tell about those people," whispered Marigold.

Old Grandmother sighed. "Once I could have stayed up all night—talking—dancing—and then laugh in the sunrise. But you can't do those things at ninety-nine. I must leave my ghosts and go in. After all they were a pretty decent lot. We've never had a real scandal in the clan. Unless that old affair about Adela's husband and the arsenic could be called one. You'll notice when Adela's books are spoken of, she's 'our cousin.' But when the porridge mystery comes up she's 'a third cousin.' Not that I ever believed she did it. Marigold, will you forgive me for all the pills I've made you take?"

"Oh, they were good for me," protested Marigold.

Old Grandmother chuckled.

"Those are the things we have to be forgiven for. But I don't ask you to forgive me for all the Bible verses I made you learn. You'll be grateful to me for them some day. It's amazing what beautiful things there are in the Bible. 'When all the morning stars sang together.' And that speech of Ruth's to Naomi. Only it always enraged me, too, because no daughter-in-law of mine would ever have said the like to *me*. Ah, well, they're all gone now except Marian. It's time—it's high time for me to go, too."

Marigold felt it was such a pity Old Grandmother had to die just when she had got really acquainted with her. And besides Marigold had something on her conscience.

"Grandmother," she whispered, "I—I've made faces at you when you weren't looking."

Old Grandmother touched Marigold's little round cheek with the tip of her finger.

"Are you so sure I didn't see your faces? I did—often. They weren't quite as impish as the ones I made at your age. I'm glad I've lived long enough for you to remember me, little Marigold. I'm leaving off—you're beginning. Live joyously, little child. Never mind the old traditions. Traditions don't matter in a day when queens have their pictures in magazine advertisements. But play the game of life according to the rules. You might as well, because you can't cheat life in the end.

"And don't think too much about what people will say. For years I wanted to do something but I was prevented by the thought of what my cousin Evelina would say. At last I did it. And she said, 'I really didn't think Edith had so much spunk in her.' Do anything you want to, Marigold—as long as you can go to your looking-glass afterwards and look yourself in the face. The oracle has spoken. And after all, is it any use? You'll make your own mistakes and learn from them as we all do. Hand me my cane, child. I'm glad I came out. I haven't had a laugh for years till to-night when I thought of poor Minister Wood and the bees."

"Why, I've heard you laugh often, Grandmother," said Marigold, wonderingly.

"Cackling over the mistakes of poor humanity isn't laughing," said Old Grandmother. She rose easily to her feet and walked through the orchard, leaning very lightly on her cane. At the gate she paused and looked back, waving a kiss to the invisible presences behind her. The moonlight made jewels of her eyes. The black scarf wound tightly round her head looked like a cap of sleek black hair. Suddenly the years were bridged. She was Edith—Edith of the gold slippers and the Paddy-green petticoat. Before she thought, Marigold cried out,

"Oh—Edith—I know what you looked like now."

"That had the right sound," said Old Grandmother. "You've given me a moment of youth, Marigold. And now I'm old again and tired—very tired. Help me up the steps."

5

"Can I help you undress?"

"No, I'm not going to die in a nightdress." Old Grandmother

climbed on the bed and pulled the puff over her. "And I'm going to smash one tradition to bits. I'm not going to die in the spare room. But I'm hungry. I think I'd like an egg fried in butter. But you can't do it. Isn't that pathetic? Me wanting a fried egg on my very deathbed and not able to get it."

Old Grandmother chuckled again—her old satiric chuckle. The Edith of the orchard had gone back to the shadows of a lost century.

"Go and bring me a glass of milk and a roll—one of Salome's rolls. She makes the best rolls in the world. You can tell her so after I'm gone. I wouldn't give her the satisfaction of telling it as long as I am alive."

Marigold flew to the kitchen, elate with a secret purpose. She was going to fry Old Grandmother an egg. She had never fried an egg, but she had watched Salome do it for Lazarre a hundred times. And she did it—beautifully. When she went back to the orchard room she carried the gold-and-white circle on Old Grandmother's own particular plate, with one of Salome's crisp golden-brown rolls.

"Well, of all the children!" said Old Grandmother. She sat up against her pillows and ate her egg with a relish. "It's got just the flavour it should have. You have the real Lesley touch. We always know by grace and not by law just how big a pinch to put in. Now bring Lucifer to me. I have things to tell that cat. And you must go to bed. It's twelve o'clock."

"Should I leave you, ma'am?"

Marigold took no stock in Old Grandmother's remarks about dying. That was just Old Grandmother's way of talking. Dying people didn't go roaming in orchards or eat eggs fried in butter. But perhaps she ought to stay with her till Mother and Young Grandmother came home.

"Of course you must leave me. I'm all right—and will be all right. There's no earthly reason why you should stay here. Turn the light low and leave the water on the table here."

Marigold brought Lucifer, warm and black from his nest in

the woodshed, and filled Old Grandmother's glass.

"Would you like anything more?"

"Nothing you can get me. I'd like a drink of the dandelion wine Alec's sister Eliza used to make. Nobody could make wine like her. Dead these sixty years—but I can taste it yet—like liquid sunlight. Off with you, now."

Marigold left Old Grandmother sipping ghostly dandelion wine of the vintage of the sixties, with Lucifer purring blackly beside her. Young Grandmother and Mother found her there when they came in at three o'clock. Lucifer was asleep, but Old Grandmother lay very still with a strange, wise little smile on her face, as if she had attained to the ultimate wisdom and was laughing still but in no unkindly fashion at all blind suppositions and perplexities.

"I shall never forgive myself," cried Young Grandmother— *Young* Grandmother no longer.

6

The blinds were drawn. The doors were purple-bowed. The Lesleys came and went decorously. A terrible, abysmal loneliness engulfed Marigold.

And then she suddenly ceased to believe Old Grandmother was dead. That was not Old Grandmother—that little ivory-white creature in the big flower-banked casket. *That* was not the Edith of the old orchard. *She* was living and laughing still—if not in the orchard then somewhere else. Even in heaven—which must and would become an entirely different place the moment Old Grandmother arrived there.

CHAPTER VI

The Power of the Dog

1

Marigold wakened one September morning earlier than her wont, when all the eastern sky was abloom with the sunrise, because she was going to school that day. She did not know whether she was glad or sorry, but she did know she was very much interested—and a little frightened. And she was determined she would not show she was frightened. For one thing she was sure Old Grandmother would have scorned her for being frightened; and Old Grandmother dead had somehow become a more potent influence in Marigold's life than Old Grandmother living. For another thing, Marigold had always felt that Mother was a little bit disappointed in her that night at Uncle Paul's. Of course that was ages ago when she was a mere child of six. She was seven now, and it would never do to show you were frightened.

She lay happily in her bed, her two little silver-golden braids with their curling ends lying over her pillows, looking out of the window beside her. She loved that window because she could see the orchard from it and the cloud of spruce. She could lie in bed and watch the tops of the spruces tossing in the morning wind. Always when she wakened up, there they were dark against the blue. Always when she went to sleep they were weaving magic with the moonlight or the stars. And she loved the other window of her room because she could see the harbour from it and across the harbour to a misty blue cloud behind which was her dear

Hidden Land.

Marigold was sure nobody in the world had such a dear little room as hers—a room, too, that could only be entered through Mother's. That made her feel so safe always. Because night, even when you were seven, was a strange though beautiful thing. Who knew what went on outside in the darkness? Strange uncanny beasts were abroad, as Marigold had good reason to know, having seen them. Perhaps the trees moved about and talked to one another. That pine which was always stretching out its arms to the maple might go across the orchard and put them around her. Those two old spruce crones, with the apple-barn between them in daytime, got their heads together at night. The little row of birches along Mr. Donkin's line-fence danced in and out everywhere. Perhaps that slim little beech in the spruce copse behind the barn, who kept herself to herself and was considered very stuck-up by the spruces, escaped from them for awhile and forgot her airs and graces in a romp with her own kind. And the hemlock schoolma'ams, with a final grim fingershake at terrified little boys, stalked at large, shaking their fingers at everything. Oh, the things they did were int'resting beyond any doubt, but Marigold was just as glad none of them could come walking up the stairs into her room without Mother catching them.

The air was tremulous with elfin music. Oh, it was certainly a lovely world—especially that part of it which you entered through The Magic Door and the Green Gate. To other people this part of the world was only the orchard and the "big spruce-bush" on the hill. They knew nothing of the wonderful things there. But you could find those wonderful things only if you went through The Magic Door and the Green Gate. And said The Rhyme. The Rhyme was a very important part of the magic, too. Sylvia would not come unless you said The Rhyme.

Grandmother—who was neither Young nor Old now but just Grandmother—did not approve of Sylvia. She could not understand why Mother permitted Sylvia at all. It was absurd and outrageous and unchristian.

"I could understand such devotion to a flesh-and-blood playmate," said Grandmother coldly. "But this nonsensical imaginary creature is beyond me. It's worse than nonsense. It is positively wicked."

"Almost all lonely children have these imaginary playmates," pleaded Lorraine. "I had. And Leander had. He often told me about them. He had three chums when he was a little boy. He called them Mr. Ponk and Mr. Urt and Mr. Jiggles. Mr. Ponk lived in the well and Mr. Urt in the old hollow poplar-tree and Mr. Jiggles 'just roamed round!'"

"Leander never told *me* about them," said Grandmother, almost unbelievingly.

"I've often heard you tell as a joke that one day when he was six he came running in out of breath and exclaimed, 'Oh Mother, I was chased up the road by a *pretending bull* and I ran without hope.'"

"Yes; and I scolded him well for it and sent him to bed without his supper," said Grandmother righteously. "For one thing he had been told not to run like that on a hot day and for another I had no more use for pretendings then than I have now."

"I don't wonder he never told you about Mr. Ponk & Co.," thought Lorraine. But she did not say it. One did not say those things to Grandmother.

"It is not so much Sylvia herself I object to," went on Grandmother, "as all the things Marigold tells us about their adventures. She seems actually to believe in them. That 'dance of fairies' they saw. Fairies! That's why she's afraid to sleep in the dark. Mark well my words, Lorraine, it will teach her to lie and deceive. You should put your foot down on this at once and tell her plainly there is no such a creature as this Sylvia and that you will not allow this self-deception to go on."

"I *can't* tell her that," protested Lorraine. "You remember how she fretted when her Sunday-school teacher told her that her dead kitten had no soul. Why, she made herself ill for a week."

"I was almost ill for a week after that fright she gave me the

93

morning she slipped out of bed and went off up the hill to play with Sylvia at sunrise, when you were in town," said Grandmother severely. "Never shall I forget my feelings when I went into her room in the morning and found her bed empty. And just after that kidnapping case in New Brunswick, too."

"Of course she shouldn't have done that," admitted Lorraine. "She and Sylvia had made a plan to go across to the big hill and 'catch the sun' when it came up behind it."

Grandmother sniffed.

"You talk as if you believed in Sylvia's existence yourself, Lorraine. The whole thing is unnatural. There's something wrong about a child who wants to be alone so much. Really, I think she is bewitched. Remember the day of the Sunday-school picnic? Marigold didn't want to go to it. Said she'd rather play with Sylvia. *That* was unnatural. And the other night when she said her prayers she asked God to bless Mother and Grandmother and Sylvia. I was shocked. And that story she came home with last week—how they had seen three enormous elephants marching along the spruce hill and drinking by moonlight at the White Fountain—by which I suppose she meant the spring."

"But that *may* have been true," protested Lorraine timidly. "You know that was the very time the elephants escaped from the circus in Charlottetown and were found in South Harmony."

"If three elephants paraded through Harmony somebody would likely have seen them besides Marigold. No; she made the whole thing up. And the long and short of it is, Lorraine, I tell you plainly that if you let your child go on like this people will think she is not all there."

This was very terrible—to Mother as well as Grandmother. It was a very disgraceful thing to have a child who was not all there. But still Mother was unwilling to destroy Marigold's beautiful dream-world.

"She told us the other day," continued Grandmother, "that Sylvia told her 'God was a very nice-looking old gentleman.' Fancy your child learning things like that from a playmate."

"*You* talk now as if *you* thought Sylvia was real," said Lorraine mischievously. But Grandmother ignored her.

"It is a good thing Marigold will soon be going to school. She will forget this Sylvia riff-raff when it opens."

The school was half a mile away and Grandmother was to drive Marigold there the first day. It seemed to Marigold that they never would get off, but Cloud of Spruce was never in a hurry. At last they really were on the road. Marigold had on her new blue dress, and her lunch was packed in a little basket. Salome had filled it generously with lovely heart-shaped sandwiches and cookies cut in animal shapes, and Mother had slipped in some of her favourite jelly in a little broken-handled cream jug of robins-egg blue, which Marigold had always loved in spite of its broken handle—or because of it. She was sure it felt it.

It was September and the day was true September. Marigold enjoyed the drive, in spite of certain queer feelings born of the suspicion that Mother was crying behind the waxberry-bush back at Cloud of Spruce,—until she saw The Dog. After that she enjoyed it no more. The Dog was sitting on the steps of old Mr. Plaxton's little house and when he saw them he tore down to the gate and along the fields inside the fence, barking madly. He was a fairly large dog, with short, tawny hair, ears that stuck straight up, and a tail with a black spot on the end of it. Marigold was sure he would tear her limb from limb if he could catch her. And she would have to go to school alone in the future.

She rather enjoyed the day in school, however, in spite of some alarming, sniggering small boys whom Marigold decidedly did not like. It was quite delightful to be made a fuss over, and the big girls made such a fuss over her. They quarrelled as to whom she would sit with and finally settled the matter by drawing straws. Lazarre called and took her home when school came out, and there was no sign of The Dog. So Marigold felt quite happy and thought school was very nice.

2

The next day it was not quite so nice. This time Mother walked to school with her and at first it was lovely. There was no dog at Mr. Plaxton's gate but on the other side of the road was the Widow Turner's great flock of geese and goslings with a huge gander who ran to the road and hissed at them through the fence. Marigold would not tell Mother that the geese frightened her and very soon she forgot about them. After all, a gander was not a dog; and it was delightful to be walking along that beautiful road with Mother. Marigold probably forgot everything she learned in school that day, but she never forgot the tricks of the winding road, the gay companies of goldenrod in the field corners, the way the fir-trees hung over the bend, the long waves going over Mr. Donkin's field of wheat, and the white young clouds sailing adventurously over the harbour. The road ran up the red hill, and the rain in the night had washed all the dust from the rounded clumps of spice fern along the edges.

Then they crossed a brook, not on the plank bridge but on a dear little bridge of stones, where they could see the pearl-crested eddies around the dripping grasses; and then came a dear bit of wood where balsam boughs made music and all the little violet-shadows were stippled with sunlight, and they walked on a fairy path near the fence, over sheets of lovely moss, almost up to the green corner where the white schoolhouse stood. Marigold would have been perfectly happy if she could have forgotten The Dog and the gander.

No, school wasn't quite so nice that day. The big girls did not take much notice of her. There was another new pupil, with amazing red-gold, bobbed curls, and they were all agog over her.

The teacher made Marigold sit with a little girl named Sarah Miller, whom she did not know and did not like; and a hateful boy across the aisle chewed gum and grinned at her alternately. When he chewed his ears waggled, and when he grinned at her his face was that of an unholy imp. He came up to her at recess, and Marigold turned her back upon him. Plainly this Lesley puss must have her claws clipped at once.

"You'd better get your mammy to bring you to school every day," he jeered. "If she don't, old Plaxton's dog'll eat you. That dog has et three people."

"Et them!" In spite of herself Marigold could not help turning round. The Dog had such a terrible fascination for her.

"Body and bones, I'll tell the world. One of them was a little girl about your age. Dogs always know when folks are afraid of them."

Marigold had a queer, sick, cold feeling. But she thought Old Grandmother would have made short work of this impudent boy.

"Do you suppose," she said cuttingly, "that *I* am afraid of a thousand dogs?"

"You talk big like all the Lesleys," retorted her tormentor. "But just you wait till that dog gets his teeth in your shin and you'll sing a different tune, Miss High-and-Mighty."

Marigold did not feel very high-and-mighty. And when she asked Sarah Miller if geese ever bit and Sarah said,

"Yes. Our old gander flew at me and knocked me down one day and bit me," Marigold felt that life was really too difficult. How was she ever to get home? There were no other children going her way. Mr. Donkin had no children nor Mr. Plaxton nor Mr. Ross nor the Widow Turner. Lazarre's children and Phidime's went to the French School "over east," where Marigold had so long ago dreamed the Hidden Land was.

Then Uncle Klon came along and took her home in the car. The gander hissed at them and The Dog flew down to the gate and howled his head off at them. He was really a very noisy Dog. Marigold did not say a word of her fears to Uncle Klon. She couldn't bear that he should think her a coward either. She talked the matter over with Lucifer, who had no opinion of dogs at all.

"Not that I have ever had anything to do with them," he admitted. "But I've heard that a dog insulted one of my ancestors."

When Marigold said her prayers that night she prayed most earnestly that The Dog might not be there the next morning.

3

Mother wanted to take her to school again but Grandmother said,

"There is no use in pampering her like that. She may as well get used to going alone, first as last. There's nothing on the road to hurt her."

"There are motor-cars."

"There are very seldom motor-cars on this road so early in the morning. Besides, they'll be there to-morrow just the same as to-day. Marigold must learn to walk on the side of the road and never cross it."

Marigold was not afraid of motor-cars. She loved to see them go purring past in the violet dusk, with their great golden moons of eyes, and sometimes turning in at the gate, making strange magic with their shifting light on trees and flowers. Even in daylight they were int'resting. But tawny dogs as big as lions and enormous hissing ganders were quite another thing. She had not slept all night for thinking of them. Suppose there wasn't any God! Old Cousin Malcolm-over-the-bay said there wasn't. *Suppose* The Dog should be there? *Suppose* the gate should be open. *Suppose* he could jump over the fence. *Suppose* he "et" her up, body and bones. Nobody would ever know what became of her. She remembered a horrible tale Lazarre had told her of a dog that flew at some one's throat and tore out the "juggler" vein. *Suppose* he tore out her "juggler" vein.

She said her prayers that morning very earnestly. And in spite of her terror she did not forget to put on her green dress, though she didn't like it, because it was its turn and mustn't feel neglected. She tried to eat some breakfast. She went out to the road, that had suddenly stretched to miles and miles, all filled with terror for her, with her lunch-basket and her little quaking heart.

"You're not frightened to go alone, darling?" said Mother, kissing her good-bye.

"Oh, no," lied Marigold gallantly. Mother must not know— must not even suspect.

"And I won't—I *won't* be frightened," she whispered defiantly to the world. "I'll *make* it true. I'm *sure* God will not let The Dog be there. I'm *quite* sure."

"Cheer up," said Lucifer on the gate post, blinking his topaz eyes at her. "A dog is only a dog. Bristle up your tail and spit at him. Any one can bark through a fence."

There was no delight in the road that day for Marigold, though the fir-trees blew gaily together on the windy hill and Mr. Donkin's calves stood in a ferny corner and looked at her with elfin mischief in their soft dark eyes. As she drew near Mr. Plaxton's house she could see The Dog sitting on the steps. Marigold grew cold all over, but she came on. Old Grandmother, she was sure, would have gone on. The Dog rushed down to the gate and tore along the fence and barked. Most furiously. *Did he know she was afraid of him?* It seemed a year to Marigold before she left him behind. She felt rather sickish all day in school and couldn't eat her lunch. And her spirit was bitter within her. God hadn't answered her prayer. Very likely old Cousin Malcolm was right. Of course he was right. Marigold went home past The Dog in a godless world, where only Terror reigned supreme.

4

For a week Marigold lived in that world and tasted its horror to the full. But she would have died before she admitted her cowardice to Mother or Grandmother. She might have told it to Aunt Marigold, but Aunt Marigold was away. She could not play with Sylvia, and a new batch of kittens left her cold. And every day that Dog rushed down to the gate and pursued her beside the fence with Barks. Marigold saw everything connected with The Dog in capitals. Some day—Marigold knew it—he would jump the fence.

One rainy day she felt sure he would not be there, but he was. Noisier than ever.

"I wish you were dead," Marigold whispered passionately. But she could not pray that he would die, though once she tried to. Even a dog has some rights, she felt. She still prayed—though she did not think it a bit of use.

And then one day The Dog did jump the fence.

5

"The child is getting frightfully thin and pale," worried Mother. "She hardly eats any breakfast. I'm sure that long walk to school is too much for her."

"I walked two and a half miles to school when I was her age," said Grandmother, who was worried, too, but wouldn't give in. "How is she to get to school if she doesn't walk? She can't be taken every day."

"She has nightmares—something Marigold never had before," persisted Mother. "Last night she screamed dreadfully that 'it' had caught her. And do you notice how little she laughs?"

"I notice she doesn't go traipsing up the hill after Sylvia any more and that's so much to the good," said Grandmother in a tone of satisfaction. "I'll tell her she mustn't go tearing round with the children at school, tiring herself out. That's what's the matter with her."

There was no need of such a command. Marigold was so quiet at school that the other children thought her stupid and the teacher thought her a model—though a little dull. She couldn't seem to remember half she was told. How could she when she didn't hear it, being wrapped up in dread of the walk home past The Dog? The terrible thing was that it wasn't getting any easier—harder if anything. Marigold felt that she couldn't go on being brave forever. Some day she would break down and confess everything, and everybody would know what a coward she was.

The Dog was at the steps as usual and as usual ran and barked. But Marigold was suddenly confronted with a new terror. The Widow Turner's geese were out on the road! They spread all over the road, and as she drew near, the big gander flew at her with huge outstretched wings, hissing furiously. Marigold dropped book and lunch-box, and screamed.

At that The Dog jumped the fence. He appeared to fly over it without effort. And just when Marigold expected to be devoured at a gulp or feel his teeth at her "juggler" vein, she saw him hurl himself at the gander. The outraged gander turned tail and ran as never gander ran before, towards the hole in the fence where he had escaped. The Dog chivied all the rest of the flock through after him and then leaped victoriously back to Marigold. His impact nearly knocked her off her feet, but the next moment she knew she was not a bit afraid. The Dog was capering around her in an ecstasy of friendliness, stopping every moment or so to yap out his good intentions. Why, he was really only an overgrown pup. And all his barking and tearing had just been sheer neighbourliness. No wonder God hadn't answered her prayer.

As Marigold walked on The Dog trotted cockily along beside her, occasionally licking her hand or lifting his adoring dog face with a delighted yelp. He seemed to be the happiest Dog in the world just to be with her. He went right to the school with her and that night when she went home, no longer a bit afraid, she went right up to the gate and kissed him through the bars.

"I'm so sorry I hated you and prayed that you wouldn't be here," she told him.

"What's a little hatred between friends?" said The Dog. "That gander shan't give you any more sass. I'll see to that, Lovely."

Marigold's laughter rang again through Cloud of Spruce that evening. The world was once more a nice, smiling place where everybody was happy. She ate a hearty supper and then she was off up the hill to Sylvia—which didn't please Grandmother so well. After that she scurried off to school early in the morning so that she could have a little time to play with The Dog, who having found he could jump the fence when he had to, jumped it every morning and evening just to be petted by Marigold and fed little snacks from her basket.

Marigold felt a certain sweetness of victory because she had never told any one how frightened she was. It seemed to her that she had redeemed herself from some taint of disgrace that had clung to her ever since the night at Uncle Paul's. But now that she was frightened no longer she told Mother, because she couldn't bear to have secrets from Mother. Lorraine was secretly horror-stricken when she realised what a long-drawn-out agony this small creature had been enduring in silence and solitude.

"I don't think you were a coward at all, dearest. You were very brave to go right on when you were so afraid—and keep going on."

"If I could have picked my mother I'd have picked you," whispered Marigold. Everything was beautiful again and every wind of the world was a friend.

"Didn't I tell you," purred Lucifer.

"I shall always like cats a *little* better than dogs," said Marigold, "but Mr. Plaxton's Dog is a Beautiful Dog."

"There ain't no such animal," Lucifer had the last word.

CHAPTER VII

Lost Laughter

1

Marigold woke up on a Saturday morning in June with stars of delight in her eyes. She thought it the loveliest thing that Sylvia's birthday should be in June. And they were going to have a birthday-picnic in the spruce-bush by the little spring with its untrampled edges—in a banquet-hall with tall spruces for columns. With little frosted cakes—some with "M" on them in pink icing and some with "S." And one gorgeous big cake with both "M" and "S" on it, intertwined, with a drift of cocoanut over everything. Mother had made it specially for Sylvia's birthday. Mother was such a brick. Grandmother, now—but Marigold was not going to think of Grandmother and her attitude in regard to Sylvia, on this wonderful morning of dawn-rosy meadows and sky-ey lures, of white young cherry-trees and winds dancing over the hills.

"Spring is *such* an exciting time," thought Marigold blissfully, as she sprang out of bed and began to dress.

Grandmother and Mother had already begun breakfast— Grandmother, very stately and dignified as usual, with silvery hair and sharp steel-blue eyes, was looking displeased. She disapproved of this birthday picnic as much as she disapproved of Sylvia. She had so confidently expected that Marigold would get over this Sylvia-nonsense when she went to school. But Marigold had been going to school for a year and seemed more besotted on Sylvia than ever.

"We'll have to tell her to-day that you're going to the sanitarium to-morrow," said Grandmother.

"Oh, not to-day," implored Lorraine. "Let her have one more happy day. Not till the morning."

Lorraine had taken a bad cold in March and it "hung on." Aunt Marigold said there was nothing serious as yet but advised a couple of months in the sanitarium. She frightened Grandmother and Lorraine a good deal more than the latter's condition justified, but Aunt Marigold was wise in her day and generation. She knew Lorraine was tired out and run down. She knew she needed a real rest and that she would never get it at Cloud of Spruce or visiting among her relatives. And she knew she would never leave Marigold unless she were thoroughly frightened. So Aunt Marigold did it thoroughly.

"You are going in the afternoon to-morrow. That will give her very little time to get used to it."

"Oh, but not to-day," pleaded Mother. Grandmother yielded. You couldn't refuse the request of a woman who was going to the sanitarium next day, even if you did think it remarkably silly. And then Marigold came running in with her little wild-rose face all alight, and began to eat her porridge out of the dear little blue bowl she loved. Real porridge. Grandmother insisted on that. No imaginary porridges called "cereals" for Grandmother.

"Isn't it lovely that Sylvia's birthday is in June?" she said. "And she's just eight years old, too. Isn't that 'strornary? Why, it makes us pretty near twins, doesn't it, Mother? We're going to have such an elegant time to-day. After the picnic we're going to find that echo that lives 'way, 'way back in the hilly land."

"Don't you go so far away that you can't get back in time for dinner," said Grandmother. "You were late last Saturday."

Marigold looked rather scornfully at Grandmother. Didn't Grandmother understand that when you went through The Magic Door you stepped straight into fairyland, where there was no such thing as time?

"I think I'll be a little scared to go so far back," said Marigold confidentially to Mother. Marigold never minded admitting she was scared since the day of The Dog—The Dog that now, alas, belonged only to the beautiful far-off past. In the winter Mr. Plaxton had sold him to a man who lived over the bay. And Marigold, who had once wished he was dead, walked past Mr. Plaxton's door every school morning with an aching lump in her throat, hating Mr. Plaxton and missing woefully that friendly eager catapult of barks that had always hurled itself over the fence at her. God had answered her prayer after all—rather late, she thought very bitterly.

"I see one has to be careful what one prays for," was her opinion.

"But Sylvia won't be scared. Sylvia isn't afraid of anything. Why—" Marigold cast about for some statement to show how very brave Sylvia was—"why, she'd just as soon call the minister John as not, if she wanted to."

"You see," telegraphed Grandmother's steel-blue eyes. But Mother only laughed.

"What jam do you want in your tarts, dear? Plum or gooseberry?"

Marigold liked gooseberry best, but—"Oh, plum, Mother. Sylvia likes plum."

The lunch-basket was made up and Marigold trotted happily into the orchard room—and trotted back again.

"Please, where is the key of the orchard door?" she said.

"It's upstairs on my bureau," said Grandmother. "Go out of the side door."

Marigold looked reproachfully at Grandmother, wondering if when *she* got to be over seventy years old she would be so stupid.

"You know I *have* to go through the orchard door, Grandmother. It's a Magic Door. None of the others are."

"Run upstairs and get the key for yourself, dear," said mother gently.

Grandmother sniffed, but looked rather pleased. An idea had

just come to her.

Marigold, happily unconscious of Grandmother's idea, got the key and went through The Magic Door into The Land Where Wishes Come True—which unimaginative people called the old orchard. You went through the orchard and up the stone steps until you came to the Green Gate, about which grew the seven slim poplars that always turned into nymphs when she and Sylvia played there. Marigold opened the gate—shut her eyes—said The Rhyme—opened them. Yes, there was Sylvia with her floating dark hair and her dreamy eyes, her snow-white hands and feet among the fine, fair shadows of the poplars. Marigold sprang forward with a cry of joy.

"To think I once thought you were a plum-blossom bough!" she laughed.

2

Grandmother did not carry out her idea as soon as Mother had gone away. That would have been cruel and Grandmother was never cruel—intentionally. She must wait until Marigold recovered from the grief of Mother's going. At first Marigold thought she could never get over it. She was shocked the first day she laughed. She had not expected to be able to laugh again until Mother came home. But Sylvia did say such funny things. And a letter came from Mother every day—such a dear, jolly, understanding letter. Then—

"Grandmother, please, can I have the key of The Magic Door?" asked Marigold one morning.

Grandmother looked at her with cold eyes.

"I have locked that door and it is to remain locked," she said deliberately. "I find that I often forget to lock it at night, and that is very dangerous."

"But, Grandmother," exclaimed Marigold, "I *must* have the key. You *know* I can't see Sylvia unless I go that way."

"Then you must get along without seeing her," said Grandmother immovably.

Marigold did not plead or coax. She knew quite well that no pleading would avail with Grandmother—who had been "one of the stubborn Blaisdells," as Salome said, before she married into the Lesley clan. But she went away with eyes that were stripped of laughter. Grandmother gazed after her triumphantly. This would put an end to all nonsense.

It did. Marigold made one effort to find Sylvia. She went out through the hall door, up the orchard and through the Green Gate. She shut her eyes—said The Rhyme—opened them.

There was no Sylvia.

Marigold crept back to the house—a pathetic, defeated little figure.

For a week Marigold moped—so Grandmother termed it. Grandmother was very good to her. She let her help cook—Salome being away on one of her rare vacations—shell lovely walnuts with kinkly meats, seed raisins, slice citron peel; even—oh, bliss of happier days!—beat eggs. But Marigold seemed interested in nothing. She sat about a great deal in a big chair on the veranda, looking out on the harbour, with a smileless little face.

One night Grandmother discovered that Marigold had gone to bed without saying her prayers. Horrified, Grandmother made Marigold get right up and say them. But when Marigold got into bed again she looked at Grandmother with sad, defiant eyes.

"My soul didn't pray a bit," she said.

When another week had passed, Grandmother began to worry about Marigold. All was not well with the child. She was growing thin and pale.

"It's the heat," said Grandmother. "If it would only get cooler she would be all right."

Grandmother would not even let herself look at the idea that Marigold was fretting for Sylvia. It was absurd to suppose that a child would become ill because of the imaginary loss of an imaginary playmate.

She went into Harmony and bought Marigold a magnificent doll—almost as big and beautiful as Alicia. Marigold thanked her, played with it a little, then laid it aside.

"Why don't you like your doll?" asked Grandmother severely.

"It's a very nice doll," said Marigold listlessly. "But it isn't alive. Sylvia was."

It was the first time she had spoken of Sylvia. Grandmother's brow grew dark.

"You are a very ungrateful little girl," said Grandmother.

Marigold sighed. She was sorry Grandmother thought her ungrateful. But she did not really care very much. When you are horribly tired you can't care very much about anything. There was no joy in waking up any longer. The bluebells in the orchard had no message for her and she had forgotten the language of the roses. The days seemed endless and the nights—the lonely, black, dreadful nights when the windows rattled so terribly and the wind sang and sobbed so lonesomely in the tree-tops around Cloud of Spruce—worse than endless. There was nothing then but a great, empty, aching loneliness. No sweet medicine of Mother's kisses. No Sylvia. But one night Marigold heard distant music.

"I think it is Sylvia singing on the hill," she said, when Grandmother asked her sharply what she was listening to.

Grandmother was vexed with herself that she couldn't help recalling that silly old superstition of Salome's that angels sing to children about to die. But Grandmother was really alarmed by now. The child was going to skin and bone. She hadn't laughed for a month. The house seemed haunted by her sad little face. What was to be done? Lorraine must not be worried.

Grandmother got Marigold a lovely new dress of silvery silk and a necklace of beautiful pale green beads. Nobody in the whole Lesley clan had such a beautiful necklace. Marigold put it on and thanked Grandmother dutifully, and went away and sat on her chair on the veranda. Grandmother gave Marigold her own way about everything—except the one thing that really mattered. But Grandmother did not for a moment suppose *that* mattered at all. And she certainly wasn't going to give in about a thing that didn't matter.

Marigold pined and paled more visibly every day. Grandmother was at her wit's end.

"If only Horace's wife was home," she said helplessly.

But Uncle Klon and Aunt Marigold were far away at the Coast, so Dr. Moorhouse was called in—very secretly so that no rumour of it might reach Lorraine—and Dr. Moorhouse couldn't find anything wrong with the child. A little run down. The weather was hot. Plenty of sleep, food and fresh air. He left some pills for her: Marigold took them as obediently for Grandmother as for Old Grandmother, but she grew no better.

"I'll soon be sleeping in the spare room, won't I, Grandmother?" she said one night.

Grandmother's old face grew suddenly older. The spare room!

"Don't be foolish, dear," she said very gently. "You are not going to die. You'll soon be all right."

"I don't want to be all right," said Marigold. "When I die I can go through The Magic Door without any key."

Grandmother could not sleep that night. She recalled what Great-Aunt Elizabeth had once said of Marigold.

"She is too glad to live. Such gladness is not of earth."

But then, Aunt Elizabeth had always been an old pessimist. Always predicting somebody's death. Of course she hit it once in a while, but not a tenth of her predictions ever came true. There was no need to worry over Marigold. The child had always been perfectly healthy. Though not exactly robust. Rather too sensitive—like Lorraine. The weather was so hot. As soon as it cooled, her appetite would come back. But still Grandmother could not sleep. She decided that if Marigold did not soon begin to improve, Lorraine would have to be sent for.

3

Dr. Adam Clow, professor of psychology in a famous university, was talking over family folk-lore with Grandmother, on the veranda of Cloud of Spruce, looking out into a blue dimness that was the harbour but which to him, just now, was a fair, uncharted land where he might find all his lost Aprils. Only the loveliest of muted sounds were heard—the faint whisper of friendly trees, the half-heard, half-felt moan of the surf, the airiest sigh of wind. Down the road the witching lilt of some invisible musician who was playing a fiddle at Lazarre's.

And the purr of black cats humped up on the steps—cats who must have been at Cloud of Spruce forever and would be there forever, changeless, ageless creatures that they were. What did the world look like to a cat, speculated Dr. Clow? Know what he might about psychology he did not know that.

Dr. Clow was a very old friend of Grandmother's, and this visit was a great event to her. There was nobody on earth for whose opinion she had such respect as she had for Adam's. He was one of the few people left to call her Marian—to remember her as "one of the handsome Blaisdell girls."

Adam Clow was that rare thing—a handsome old man, having lived a good life so long that he was very full of the beauty of the spirit. His dark eyes were still softly luminous and his thin, delicately cut, finely wrinkled face rather dreamy and remote. But his smile was vivid and youthful and his mouth showed strength and tenderness and humour.

He came once every year to hear the fir-trees whispering on the hills of home. Here where all his race and all his friends, save Marian Blaisdell, had vanished—here was still "home." Here still on purple evenings and starlit midnights and white dawns the little waves murmured and sighed on the harbour shore. And of all those who had once listened to them with him was left only Marian Blaisdell—handsome Marian, who had a certain queen's loveliness about her still. With her he could talk about charming vanished households and the laughing girls of long ago and old summers so sweet they could not wholly die. He shuddered when he thought of a recent evening spent with a former schoolmate who prided herself on keeping up with the times and talked to him the whole time about eugenics and chromosomes and the growing menace of the feebleminded. Dr. Adam Clow thanked his stars for a vine-hung veranda and a woman who had grown old gracefully.

"Oh, well, I haven't got to wheel-chairs and gruel yet," said Grandmother complacently.

They talked of the old days and the new days, and watched the moon rising over the old fields they knew. And Dr. Clow told her all the jokes he could think of. He was the only person in the world who dared tell jokes to Grandmother. And finally Grandmother—proud, reserved Grandmother—found herself telling him all about Marigold—who was asleep in her little room with tears still gemming her lashes. She had not taken any int'rest in Dr. Clow. He was Grandmother's meat and, like Grandmother, must long since have forgotten the way to fairyland.

Grandmother *had* to tell somebody. Adam's coming seemed providential. She had always found it easy to tell things to him—always, until now. To her amazement, she found it incredibly hard to tell Adam Clow that she had locked The Magic Door.

"She doesn't seem to *want* to get better," she concluded helplessly.

"'A wounded spirit who can bear'?" quoted Adam Clow softly.

"I don't understand," said Grandmother in a hurt tone. "I—I think I've been very kind to Marigold."

"And *I* think," said Adam Clow rather sternly, "that she is dying of a broken heart."

Grandmother began to say "Bosh," and stopped. One didn't say bosh to doctors of psychology.

"You don't really mean to say you think she has got so ill because she can't see that Sylvia of hers any more? Or imagines she can't?"

Dr. Clow put his slender finger-tips together.

"I think I might talk a great deal of wise jargon about a neurosis caused by a suppressed desire for her playmate," he said. "But I won't. I simply advise you to give her the key of The Magic Door."

"But—Adam!" Grandmother could not give in so easily. "Is it *right* to encourage her in those pretenses—those falsehoods—"

"They are not falsehoods. They are truths to her. She sees things invisible to us. She is a queen in the lovely Kingdom of Make-Believe. She is not trying to deceive anybody. She has the wonderful gift of creation in an unusual degree. It is such a pity that she will lose it as she grows older—that she will have to forego its wonder and live, like us, in the light of common day. Has this never occurred to you, Marian?"

No, it hadn't. But—Grandmother gave a little sigh—of surrender. Dr. Clow stood up.

"I must be going. We have sat up terribly late for old folks."

"I'm sorry you have to walk to Harmony," said Grandmother. "Our horse is too lame to drive just now—and Horace is away—so his car—"

"I don't like a car after dark. In a car you can never feel the charm of the soft enfolding night. I want to walk. It keeps me limber. Well, it's good-bye for another year. I must go back to-morrow and begin work. And if I have to slip off this 'robe of flesh' before next summer I'll save up my jokes to tell you in eternity. After all, there's nothing quite so satisfying as an old friendship, is there, Marian? As for Marigold—the earth has grown very old for us, Marian. Let us be thankful it is still young and full of magic for Marigold."

4

The next morning after breakfast Grandmother silently laid the key of the orchard door by Marigold's blue bowl. Marigold lifted incredulous eyes.

"Oh, Grandmother! May I—may I?"

"Yes," said Grandmother curtly. In spite of Adam's fine phrases she did not relish defeat by this puss of a Marigold. And there was Lucifer cocking an insolent yellow eye at her, as if he were hugely amused over the whole affair.

Marigold stood still for a moment, transfigured. Her face was as blithe as the day. It was as if a little shower of joy had rained down upon her out of the sky. She flew through the orchard room—through The Magic Door—through the blue-eye grass of the orchard as if there were some Atalanta wizardry in her feet. Through the Green Gate. For another moment she stood, almost afraid. Suppose Sylvia—Then she shut her eyes and said her Rhyme.

5

Grandmother stood in The Magic Door at twilight. There was a pale moon-glow behind the cloud of spruce. There was a dance of great plumy boughs in the western wind. And there was a sound not heard in the orchard for a long time—the sound of Marigold's laughter as she waved goodnight to Sylvia over the Green Gate.

CHAPTER VIII

"It"

1

Mother was home—pink-cheeked and rested and well—and Marigold was going to Blue Water Beach to stay from Friday evening to Sunday night. In other words, a week-end, though that expression had not yet penetrated to Cloud of Spruce. And Marigold was delighted for several good reasons. The best reason was that she would see Nancy—fascinating Nancy of the brown eyes and russet hair; and not only see her but play with her—play with Nancy's beautiful set of dishes kept in the little square box-cupboard in the wall, with the glass door, and not only play with her but sleep with her two whole nights in her fascinating little room, where there was a dressing-table with a lovely frill of sheer white muslin over a pink lining, and a turquoise blue jug and basin with fluted edges, and peacocks on the wallpaper. They would talk delicious little secrets which nobody in the world but their small selves knew. Aunt Stasia's house was near a railroad, and it was such thrilly fun to watch the lighted trains go by in the night, like great dragons breathing smoke and fire.

Then there was to be a party on Saturday afternoon at Lily Johnson's, just across the road from Aunt Stasia's, to which Marigold was invited, and she had the loveliest new dress for it.

Moreover, Blue Water Beach was in that realm of magic "over the bay," where at sunset there were dim old shores of faded gold and dusk. Who knew but that some time she might actually get down to Blue Water Point and see what was beyond it—the Hidden Land, which she had longed all her life to see? She had never dared to ask any one what was beyond Blue Water Point for fear she should be told that there were only the same red coves and headlands and blue silk water that there were on this side of it. Surely there must be something more than that if one could only reach that far purple misty outpost of the "fairylands forlorn" Aunt Marigold talked about. As long as Marigold didn't *know* there wasn't, she could still dream that dear dream.

In the third place, she wanted to wipe out the memory of that old disgrace three years ago, when she had behaved so terribly at Uncle Paul's. Uncle Paul always ragged her about it every time he saw her, and Aunt Flora had never really forgiven her. To be sure, they had to admit that if Marigold had been the good and proper child she should have been, Martin Richard's house would have burned down and Frank Lesley and Hilda Wright would probably never have married each other. Still, Marigold knew she had behaved badly and she burned for a chance to redeem herself.

Standing on the veranda of Cloud of Spruce, Marigold could see three houses in a row over the bay. Three little white dots only six miles away as the crow flew, but nearly fifteen when you had to drive around the Head of the Bay. Though there was a delightful possibility that Uncle Klon just back from the Coast would have his new motor-boat in time to run her over Friday evening.

The middle dot was Aunt Stasia's house—an int'resting house—an unexpected kind of house; like one of those houses in dreams where you are forever discovering new, fascinating rooms; a house where there was red flannel in the glass lamps; a house with a delightful, uncared-for garden where gnarled old apple-trees bent over plots of old-fashioned flowers—thickets of sweet clover, white and fragrant, beds of mint and southernwood, honeysuckles and blush roses; and where there was an old mossy path running up to the ivy-grown front door. Oh, Blue Water

115

Beach was a charming spot, and Marigold couldn't eat or sleep properly for a week because of looking forward to her week-end there.

Of course, this world being as it is, there were one or two small flies in her ointment. Aunt Stasia herself, now. Marigold always felt a little frightened of Aunt Stasia—who wasn't really an aunt but only a cousin. Aunt Stasia of the tragic, wrinkled face, where nothing was left of her traditional beauty but her large dark eyes. Aunt Stasia who always wore black and a widow's veil and never, never smiled. Marigold supposed you couldn't smile if, just a few minutes after you had been married, your husband had been killed by a flash of lightning. But Marigold sometimes wondered, supposing such a thing happened to *her,* if she wouldn't *have* to smile now and then—after years and years had passed, of course. There were so many things in the world to smile at.

Then, too, Aunt Stasia was—fussy. In spite of her romantic and tragic airs, Aunt Stasia was *very* fussy. A crumb on the carpet unfitted her for the day. A fly on the ceiling sent her to bed with a headache. If you got a spot on the tablecloth, Aunt Stasia looked at you as if you had broken all the Ten at once. Marigold knew she would have to be exceedingly proper and perfect at Blue Water Beach if she did not want to smirch the honour of Cloud of Spruce. She liked gentle, kitteny Cousin Teresa better. Cousin Teresa was Aunt Stasia's sister, but she was never called Aunt. There was nothing auntish about her. When Aunt Stasia wasn't around Cousin Teresa could be just like a little girl herself. But then Aunt Stasia mostly was around.

Also, Beulah. Beulah and Nancy were sisters, Aunt Stasia's nieces—real nieces. The children of her dead sister. But whereas Marigold loved Nancy next to Sylvia, she did not like Beulah at all. Not at all. Not the least little bit. Beulah, she thought in her secret soul, was a mean, spiteful little cat. It was Beulah who had once deliberately pushed her into a bush of stick-tights; Beulah who had told her that Mother was disappointed because she wasn't a boy. Marigold had never dared ask Mother about it for fear it was the truth, but it rankled bitterly along with her hatred of Clementine.

2

Marigold was sent from Cloud of Spruce spick and span, with her new dress and her best nightgown in her bag. She arrived at Blue Water Beach spick and span, just in time for supper, to which they at once sat down. Aunt Stasia had welcomed her kindly, though with the usual remote, haunting sound of tears in her voice. Cousin Teresa had kissed and purred; Nancy had given her an ecstatic hug; even Beulah had shaken hands in her superior way and proffered a peck on the cheek.

Marigold was hungry and the supper looked simply gorgeous. There were raspberries in generous blue saucers, and when Aunt Stasia had given her enough cream Cousin Teresa gave her a little more. Nancy was smiling happily and significantly at her across the table, as if to say, "Just wait till we get to bed. I've *heaps* to tell you."

Altogether, in spite of Beulah and Aunt Stasia and the terrible spotlessness of everything, Marigold was rapturously happy. Too happy. The gods didn't like it.

Then—it happened.

Marigold was sitting just where a burst of evening sunshine shone straight down on her shining pale gold hair, with its milk-white parting. Suddenly Aunt Stasia bent forward and looked with awful intentness at Marigold's head. An expression of profound horror came into her eyes. She gasped and looked again. Then looked at Teresa, bent forward and whispered agitatedly in her ear.

"*Im*-possible," said Cousin Teresa.

"See for yourself," said Aunt Stasia.

Cousin Teresa rose and came around the table to the petrified Marigold, who was just realising that something perfectly awful must have happened, but couldn't imagine what. She was so agitated that she slopped her tea over in the saucer. *That* was a terrible break.

"Oh, dear me," wailed Cousin Teresa. *"What* can we do. What *can* we do?"

Cousin Teresa did something. Marigold felt a light touch on her head. Cousin Teresa dashed out of the room and came back a moment later looking ready to faint.

"Do you suppose—there are any more?" demanded Aunt Stasia hollowly.

"I don't *see* any more," said Cousin Teresa.

Beulah was snickering. Nancy was wirelessing sympathy.

"What is the matter with me?" cried Marigold.

No attention was paid to her.

"Is there—a *comb*—in the house?" asked Cousin Teresa in a low, shamed voice.

Aunt Stasia shook her head forcibly. "No—never was. There has never been any need of one here, thank heaven."

Marigold was hopelessly bewildered. No comb at Blue Water Beach? Why, there was an abundance of them—one in every bedroom and one in the kitchen.

"I've a comb of my own in my bag," she said with spirit.

Aunt Stasia looked at her.

"A comb? Do you mean to say that they sent you here— *knowing*—"

"It isn't that kind of a comb," whispered Cousin Teresa. "Oh, Stasia, what can we do?"

"Do. Well, we must keep her away from Nancy and Beulah at all events. Take her up to the spare room, Teresa, until we have consulted over the matter. Run along with Teresa, child—at once. And mind you don't go near the bed. Sit on the hassock by the window. If you haven't finished your supper, take a piece of cake and a cooky with you."

Marigold did not want cake or cooky. She wanted to know what was the matter with her. She dared not ask Aunt Stasia but she indignantly demanded of Cousin Teresa on the stairs what she had done to be put away like this with such scorn and contumely. Marigold didn't use those words but she felt them.

"Hush," said Cousin Teresa nervously, as if the walls around had ears. "The less said about IT the better. Of course, I don't suppose it is your fault. But it's simply terrible."

3

Marigold found herself alone in the spare room. Humiliated—frightened—and a little angry. For all the Lesleys had a bit of temper, and this was no way to treat a visitor. What a hateful grin she had seen on Beulah's face as Cousin Teresa walked her out of the room! She went to the dim mirror and scrutinised her countenance carefully and as much of her sleek head as she could see. Nothing was wrong apparently. Yet that look of horror in Aunt Stasia's eyes!

She must have some terrible disease. Yes, that must be it. Leprosy was an awful thing. Suppose she had leprosy—or smallpox. Or that dreadful thing Uncle Klon flippantly called T. B.? *What* was it she had heard "ran" in the Lesleys. Agatha Lesley had died of it. Something about the heart. But *this* had to do with the head evidently. She wondered if and how soon it would prove fatal. She thought pathetically that she was very young to die. Oh, she must get home right away if she had anything dreadful. Charming Blue Water Beach was now simply a place to get out of as soon as possible. Poor Mother, how terribly she would feel—

Marigold was suddenly aware that Aunt Stasia and Cousin Teresa were talking together in the parlour below the spare room. There was a little grating in the floor under the window, where a small "heat hole" penetrated the parlour ceiling. Marigold had been trained not to eavesdrop. But there were, she felt, exceptions to every rule. She *must* find out what was the matter with her head. Deliberately she lay down on the rag carpet and laid her ear to the grating. She found she could hear tolerably well, save at such times as Aunt Stasia dropped her voice in a fresh access of horror, leaving tantalising gaps which might hold who knew what of ghastly revelation.

"We can't let her go to the party," said Aunt Stasia. "What if any one were to see—what *we* saw. I don't believe such a thing has ever happened to a Lesley before."

"Oh, yes—once—to Charlotte Lesley when she went to school."

Now, Charlotte Lesley was dead. Marigold shuddered. Of course, Charlotte had died of IT.

"And Dan," continued Cousin Teresa. "Remember Dan?"

"A boy is different. And besides, you know how Dan turned out," said Aunt Stasia.

How had Dan turned out? Marigold felt as if she would give anything to know.

"Such a disgrace," Cousin Teresa was wailing when Marigold could hear again. "Her hair will have to be shingled to the bone. I suppose we *could* get a—comb."

"I will not be seen buying a comb," said Aunt Stasia decidedly.

"And where is she to sleep?" moaned Cousin Teresa. "We can't take her home to-night. In the spare room?"

"No—no. She can't sleep *there.* I'd never feel sure of the bed again. We must put her in Annabel's room."

"But Annabel died there," objected Cousin Teresa.

"Marigold doesn't know that," said Aunt Stasia.

Oh, but Marigold did—now. Not that it mattered to her how many people had died in Annabel's room. But she would not be able to sleep with Nancy. This was a far more bitter disappointment than not going to the party.

"There was only *one,*" Cousin Teresa was saying hopefully, when their voices became audible again.

"There are sure to be more of them," said Aunt Stasia darkly.

Them! Marigold had a flash of awful illumination.

Germs, of course. Those mysterious, terrible things she had heard Aunt Marigold speak of. She was—what was it? Oh, yes—a germ-carrier. Germs that perhaps she would never be able to get rid of. She must be an outcast all her life! Horror fell over her small face like a frost.

Aunt Stasia and Cousin Teresa were going out of the parlour. Marigold got up and crept pathetically to the window, feeling as if it were years since she had left home that afternoon, so happy and light-hearted, never dreaming of IT. Away out beyond the harbour, a little lonely ship was drifting over the edge of the world. The lonely red road wound past Blue Water Beach in the twilight. A lonely black wind was blowing. Marigold always felt that winds had colour—and this one was certainly black. Everything was black. No party—no night of soul-satisfying exchange of thought with Nancy. Nothing but—germs.

4

Marigold slept—or did not sleep—in Annabel's room, where there was a man-hole in the ceiling with a black, spooky look. But she never thought of being frightened. What were spooks and devils and things generally compared to the horror of IT. The rain began to pour down—the fir-boughs tapped against the windows. The blankets, which Cousin Teresa had thoughtfully put on because the June night was cold, simply reeked of mothballs. If she were only in her own bed at home between fragrant sheets. Marigold thought the night would never end.

In the morning she had her breakfast at a little table by herself in the corner of the kitchen. Once Nancy slipped in and snuggled down beside her. "I don't care if you have got—them—I love you just the same," said Nancy loyally.

"Nancy Walker! you come right out of there," said Beulah's sharp voice from the door. "Aunt Stasia said you weren't to go near her."

Nancy went out, crying.

"Oh, I'm so sorry for you," said Beulah, before she turned

away.

The malice of Beulah's smile was hard to bear and the pity of Beulah bit deep. Marigold went dismally back to Annabel's room—where the bed had already been stripped to the bones. She could see Cousin Teresa busy over tubs in the wash-house. Nancy was carrying a great sheaf of mauve and gold irises across the road to Johnson's, to help decorate for the party.

Away over the harbour was a soft blur that was Cloud of Spruce—dear Cloud of Spruce—dear home. If she were only there! But Aunt Stasia had told her they could not take her home until after the party. A fog was creeping up to Blue Water Beach. It crept on and on—it blotted out the harbour—it blotted out the distant shore of Cloud of Spruce—it blotted out the world. She was alone in the universe with her terrible, mysterious shame. Poor Marigold's Lesley spirit failed her at last. She broke down and cried.

Aunt Teresa drove her home that evening. Again she was coming home from a visit in disgrace. And when they reached Cloud of Spruce, Mother was away. Thinking Marigold would not be home till Sunday evening, she had gone to South Harmony for a visit. Marigold felt she simply could not bear it.

Cousin Teresa whispered mysteriously to Grandmother.

"Impossible," cried Grandmother peevishly.

"We found one," said Cousin Teresa positively.

One what? Oh, if Marigold only knew *what!*

"Only one." Grandmother's tone implied that Stasia had made a great deal of fuss over a trifle. Grandmother herself would have made enough fuss about IT if *she* had discovered it. But when Stasia made the fuss that was a cat of a different stripe.

"Have you—a comb?" whispered Cousin Teresa.

Grandmother nodded haughtily. She took Marigold upstairs to her room and gave her head a merciless combing with an odd little kind of comb such as Marigold had never seen before. Then she brought her down again.

"No results," she said crisply. "I believe Stasia simply imagined it."

"I saw IT myself," said Cousin Teresa, a trifle shrewishly. She drove away a little offended. Marigold sat down disconsolately on the veranda steps. She dared not ask Grandmother anything. Grandmother was annoyed and when Grandmother was annoyed she was very aloof. Moreover, she had contrived to make Marigold feel that she was in some terrible disgrace—that she had done something no Lesley ever should do. And yet what she had done or how she was responsible, Marigold hadn't the slightest idea. Oh, if Mother were only home!

Then Aunt Marigold came—almost as good as Mother— almost as gentle and tender and understanding. She had been talking with Grandmother.

"So you've been and gone and got into a scrape, Marigold," she said, laughing. "Never mind, precious. There seems to have been only one."

"One what?" demanded Marigold passionately. She simply could not stand this hideous suspense and ignorance any longer. "Aunt Marigold—please—please do tell me what is the matter with my head?"

Aunt Marigold stared.

"Marigold, you dear funny thing, do you mean you don't know?"

Marigold nodded, her eyes like wet pansies.

"And I've just *got* to know," she said desperately.

Aunt Marigold explained.

"It's apt to happen to any child who goes to a public school," she concluded comfortingly.

"Pshaw, is *that* all?" said Marigold. "I guess I got IT when I changed hats with that new girl day before yesterday."

She was so happy she could have cried for joy. Had there then ever been such a starry sky? Such a dear misty, new moon? Such dancing northern lights over the harbour? Down the road Lazarre's dog and Phidime's dog were talking about their feelings at the top of their voices. And Sylvia up in the cloud of spruce.

It was too late to go to her to-night, but she would be there in the morning. Marigold blew an airy kiss to the hill. No germs. No leprosy. Aunt Stasia had made all this fuss about so small a matter. Marigold thought bitterly of the party, the unworn dress, the lost two nights with dear Nancy.

"Aunt Stasia is—" began Aunt Marigold. Then she suddenly snapped her lips together. After all, there was such a thing as clan loyalty, especially in the hearing of the rising generation.

"An old fool," said Marigold, sweetly and distinctly.

CHAPTER IX

A Lesley Christmas

1

It was a Lesley tradition to celebrate Christmas by a royal reunion, and this year it was the turn of Cloud of Spruce. This was the first time it had happened in Marigold's memory, and she was full of delighted anticipation. At heart a thorough clansman, she loved, without knowing she loved, all the old clan customs and beliefs and follies and wisdoms as immutable as law of Mede and Persian. They were all part of that int'resting world where she lived and moved and had her being—a world which could never be dull for Marigold, who possessed the talismanic power of flinging something glamorous over the most commonplace fact of life. As Aunt Marigold said, Marigold saw the soul of things as well as the things themselves.

There were weeks of preparation in which Marigold revelled. Grandmother and Mother and Salome worked like slaves, cleaning Cloud of Spruce from attic to cellar. The last week was given over to cooking. Such things as were concocted in that house! Such weighings and measurings and mixings! Mother thought they were really being too lavish, but for once Grandmother counted no cost.

"I have seen many things come into fashion and go out of fashion but a good meal abides," she said oracularly.

Marigold thrilled with bliss because she was permitted to help. It was such fun to beat egg-whites until you could hold the bowl upside down, and dig the kinkly meats out of the walnuts. Grandmother made a big panful of Devonshire clotted cream. Mother made the mince pies that would be taken in with a sprig of holly stuck in them—piping hot, for lukewarm mince pies were an abomination at Cloud of Spruce. And there was a pound cake that required thirty-two eggs—an extravagance known at Cloud of Spruce only when there was a "reunion." Salome baked a whole box of what she called "hop-and-go-fetch-its"— dear, humpy little cakes with raisins in them and icing over the tops and pink candies over that. Marigold knew what the hop-and-go-fetch-its were for. Just for "pieces" for herself and all the children who came.

Besides, Marigold had her recitation to learn. It was one of the Christmas reunion customs to have a "programme" of speeches and songs and recitations in the parlour after dinner, while the hostesses were cleaning up and washing the dishes. Aunt Marigold had found a cute little recitation for Marigold, and Mother had trained her in the appropriate gestures and inflections. It was to be her first performance of the kind, and Marigold was very anxious to do well. She was not in the least afraid that she wouldn't. She knew her "piece" so perfectly that she could have recited it standing on her head, and every gesture came pat to the word, ending with the graceful little "curtsey" Mother was at such pains to teach her. Beulah would be there and Marigold was sure that curtsey would finish *her* completely.

2

Finally the great day of the feast came. Outside it was a grey squally day, filling the little empty nests in the maple-trees full of snow and surrounding the sad black harbour with meadows of white. But inside there was gaiety and Christmas magic in the very air. The bannisters were garlanded with greenery, the windows hung with crimson rings. The big sideboard was a delectable mountain of good things. The cream was whipped for the banana cake; the kitchen range was singing a lyric of beech and maple; and Salome was purring with importance. The spare room bed really looked too beautiful to be slept in. Grandmother's new pillow slips with crocheted lace six inches deep were on the pillows and Mother had sewed little flat bags of lavender inside them. The Christmas-tree in the hall was covered with lovely red and gold and blue and silver bubbles, such as fairies must have blown. Every one was dressed up—Mother in her brown velvet with little amber earrings against her white neck, Grandmother in her best black silk with a wonderful crêpy purple shawl which was kept in perfumed tissue paper in the lower drawer of the spare room bureau all the year round, save only for big clan affairs like this. Even Lucifer had a new scarlet silk neck-bow, which he considered mere vanity and vexation of spirit.

So far Christmas-Day had been flawless for Marigold. She had got lovely presents from everybody; even Lazarre had given her a near-silver mouse with a blue velvet pin-cushion erupting from its back. Marigold secretly thought it rather awful. It looked as if the mouse wasn't—healthy. But she wouldn't have hurt Lazarre's feelings for the world by letting him suspect this. Again Marigold was disposed to thank goodness people did not know what you thought.

3

It was such fun to watch the arrivals from the window in Salome's room, where she had her shelf of potted plants. The ivies and petunias fell down in a green screen behind which Marigold could peep without being seen—or being caught at it by Grandmother, who thought "peeking" at visitors extremely bad manners. Bad manners it might be, but it was too int'resting to give up. The folks getting out of the cars and buggies and cutters—for all three were in use today—would have been amazed by the things Marigold, whom they still thought of as a mere baby, knew about them.

There was Uncle Peter's Pete, who had poured whiskey into his aunt's dandelion wine and set her drunk. How solemn and stupid he looked, not at all like a boy who would do such a trick. But you could never tell. And Aunt Katherine, who—so Uncle Klon had said—was a witch and turned herself into a grey cat at night. Marigold no longer believed that but she liked to play with the idea. Aunt Katherine certainly looked like a grey cat in her grey coat trimmed with grey fur; but her rosy smiling face was not properly witch-like. Only Uncle Klon said they were the worst kind of witches—the kind that didn't look like witches.

Uncle Mark and Uncle Jerry were coming up the walk together. At some former Christmas feast they had quarrelled and Uncle Mark had pulled Uncle Jerry's nose. It was years before they spoke. But they seemed on good terms now. Even Old Aunt Kitty, who was really only a distant third cousin, was coming with Uncle Jarvis and Aunt Marcia. Aunt Kitty, whose bonnet had fallen off one day when she was sitting in the front pew of the old Harmony church gallery, peering over the railing to see who was sitting below. Aunt Kitty had nearly pitched after the bonnet herself in her frantic effort to grab it and had only been saved by old Mr. Peasely catching hold of her skirt. It had been a gay, wild bonnet of ostrich plumes and flowers, and its descent had made something of a sensation, especially since, by some impish trick of chance, it had landed squarely on Elder Beamish's bald head as neatly as if it had been fitted on. The Beamishes and the Kittys— Marigold couldn't remember Aunt Kitty's family name—had never been good friends and this incident didn't help matters any. Aunt Kitty looked decorous enough now as she hobbled up the walk leaning on her cane, but she had been a wild old girl at one time, Uncle Klon said.

Aunty Clo was coming, too—who really was an aunt of sorts, though Marigold never could get her placed. She did not like Aunty Clo and neither did Uncle Klon, who vowed she was certainly very much too ugly to live. "She is really lovable under her skin," Aunt Marigold had said, fresh from a reading of Kipling. "Then for heaven's sake, tell her to take her skin off," Uncle Klon had retorted.

Uncle Archibald's Martin and his wife Jenny. They were a by-word for their terrible quarrels, but Aunt Marigold declared they loved each other between times enough to make up for it. Martin had left his car at the gate and she saw him stop Jenny and kiss her under the Scotch pine. Before dinner was over they were calling each other awful names across the table and scandalising the whole clan. But as Marigold listened to the amazing epithets she thought of that long kiss under the pine and wondered if a kiss like that wasn't worth a lot of hard names.

Aunt Sybilla, who "went in for spiritualism." Marigold didn't know what spiritualism was but had a vague idea that it had to do with liquor. Still, Aunt Sybilla didn't look like *that*.

Uncle Charlie, whose laughter boomed over the whole garden, and Garnet Lesley, who would come to a bad end—so every one said. It was int'resting to speculate concerning that bad end. George Lesley, who was going to be married to Mary Patterson. Marigold liked George. "I wish he would wait till I grow up," she thought. "I believe he would like me better than Mary, because there is no fun in her. There is a good deal in me when my conscience doesn't bother me."

Gloomy Uncle Jarvis, with his fierce black beard, who never read any book but the Bible and was always "talking religion" to every one within five minutes of meeting them. Aunt Honora—who *must* have had her face screwed up one time when the wind changed and who had taken a vow never to marry—"quite unnecessarily," Uncle Klon said. Uncle Obadiah, whose great ears stuck out like flaps. Uncle Dan, who had a glass eye and thought nobody knew of it. And last of all Uncle Milton and Aunt Charlotte and Aunt Nora. Thirty years before Uncle Milton had jilted Aunt Nora and when he married Aunt Charlotte, Aunt

Nora had decked herself out in widow's weeds and gone to the wedding! And now here they were coming up the walk together, chatting amiably about the weather and their rheumatism. It was very int'resting, looking down on them like this when they couldn't see her, but Marigold paid for her fun when the time came to go in to the parlour and speak to everybody. It was a dreadful ordeal and she shrank back against Mother.

"You must learn to go into a room without thinking every one is staring at you," said Grandmother.

"But they *do* stare," shuddered Marigold. "They're all looking at me to see how much I've grown since the last time or who I look like now. And Aunt Josephine will say I'm not as tall for my age as Gwennie. You know she will."

"It won't kill you if she does," said Grandmother.

"You must act like a lady," whispered Mother.

"Don't be a coward," said Old Grandmother from a faraway moonlit orchard.

It was Old Grandmother who did the trick. Marigold went through the ordeal of handshaking with her head up and her cheeks so crimson that even Aunt Josephine thought her complexion much better. The "big" dinner was in the orchard room, and any one looking at the table would have known that the good old days when nobody bothered about balanced rations had not yet wholly passed at Cloud of Spruce. But Marigold and all the other small fry had theirs in the dining-room.

Marigold rejoiced over this. She never really enjoyed a meal in the orchard room, because she was so busy hating Clementine. They were catered to by Salome, who saw that they all had plenty of dressing and a piece of banana cake besides pudding. Even Uncle Peter's Pete, who had been known to say he wished a fellow could eat two Christmas dinners at once, was satisfied. So everything was beautiful until dinner was over and the "programme" under way in the parlour. And then Marigold crashed down to defeat and not even Old Grandmother's shade could help her.

She got up to say her recitation—and not one word could

she remember of it. She stood there before thousands—more or less—of faces, and could not even recall the title. It was all Uncle Peter's Pete's fault, so Marigold always vowed. Just before her name was called he had whispered into the back of her neck, "You haven't washed behind your ears." Marigold knew that territory *had* been washed—Salome had seen to that—but it rattled her nevertheless. And now she stood dazed, frantic, coming out with goose-flesh all over her body. If Mother had been there just to say the first line—Marigold knew she could go on if she could just remember the first line. But Mother was out helping with the dishes. And there was Pete grinning and Beulah gleefully contemptuous and Nancy squirming in sympathy.

Marigold shut her eyes in a desperate effort to forget every one and straightway saw the most astounding things. Aunt Emma's big cameo brooch with Uncle Ned's hair in it expanded to gigantic size, and Aunt Emma fastened to it—Uncle Jerry with a long nose pulled out like the elephant's child—Uncle Peter's Pete's aunt dancing drunkenly after dandelion wine—Aunt Katherine, a grey cat riding on a broomstick—Aunt Kitty falling headlong after her bonnet—Aunty Clo with her skin off—Uncle Obadiah, just a pair of enormous ears with a tiny manikin between them—Uncle Dan with just one huge eye winking at her all the time—

Dizzy Marigold opened her eyes to come back to reality from that fantastic world into which she had been plunged. But still she could not get that first line.

"Come, come, have you got a bone in your throat?" said Uncle Paul.

"Cat's got her tongue," giggled Uncle Peter's Pete.

"Bit off more than you can chew, eh," said Uncle Charlie, good-naturedly.

Beulah giggled. Flesh and blood could bear no more. Marigold rushed from the room—flew upstairs—tore through Mother's room—slammed shut her door and hurled herself on her bed in an agony of shame and humiliation.

She huddled there all the rest of the afternoon. Mother and Grandmother and Salome were too busy to think about her. Nancy searched but could not find her. Marigold wept in her pillows and wondered what they were saying about her. I don't know if it would have comforted her any had she known they were not thinking about her at all. What was a tragedy to her was only a passing incident to them.

In the rose and purple twilight they went away. Marigold lay and listened to the cars snorting and the sleighbells jingling and then to a tired little lonely motherless wind sobbing itself to sleep in the vines—a wind that had made a fool of itself in the great family of Winds and daren't lift its voice above a whisper.

To Marigold came some one who had never lost the knack of looking at the world through a child's eyes.

"Oh, Aunty Marigold, I've dis-dis-graced myself and—all—the Lesleys," sobbed Marigold.

"Oh, no, darling. There's no disgrace in a little stage fright. We all have it. The first time *I* tried to recite in public my tongue clove to the roof of my mouth and I snivelled—yes, snivelled, and my father had to come up and carry me down from the platform. You got away on your own legs at least."

Marigold could not stop crying all at once, but she sat up and blew her nose.

"Oh, Aunty Marigold—really?"

"Yes, really. Father said to me, 'I am disappointed in you,' and *I* said, 'I wouldn't care for that if I wasn't disappointed in myself.'"

"That's how I feel, too," whispered Marigold. "And then Beulah—"

"Never mind the Beulahs. You'll find heaps of them in life. The only thing to do is ignore them. Beulah would make an excellent mouse-trap, but if she tried for a hundred years she couldn't look as sweet and pretty as you did, standing up there with your puzzled blue eyes. And when you screwed them shut—"

"Oh, I saw such funny things, Aunt Marigold," cried Marigold, bursting into a peal of laughter. Aunt Marigold's little bit of artful flattery was a pick-me-up. It was true poor Beulah was very plain. Oh, how nice to be with some one who just understood and loved. Nothing seemed so disgraceful any more. A truce to vain regrets. She'd show them another time. And here was Lucifer and Salome with a plate of hop-and-go-fetch-its.

"I saved 'em for you," said Salome. "Uncle Peter's Pete was bound to have them but *I* Peted him. He'll not try to sneak into *my* pantry again in a hurry."

"I suppose I can take off this absurd ribbon now," said Lucifer, his very whiskers vibrating with indignation. "A dog doesn't mind making an ass of himself, but a cat has his feelings."

CHAPTER X

The Bobbing of Marigold

1

"Sylvia has bobbed her hair," said Marigold rebelliously.

Grandmother sniffed, as Grandmother was apt to sniff at the mention of Sylvia—though since the day of Dr. Clows visit she had never referred to her, and the key of The Magic Door was always in the lock. But she only said,

"Well, *you're* not going to have yours bobbed, so you can make up your small mind to that. In after years you will thank me for it."

Marigold didn't look or feel very thankful just then. *Everybody* had bobbed hair. Nancy and Beulah—who laughed at her long "tails"—and all the girls in school and even Mrs. Donkin's scared-looking little "home girl" across the road. But she, Marigold Lesley of Cloud of Spruce, had to be hopelessly old-fashioned because Grandmother so decreed. Mother would have been willing for the bob, though she might cry in secret about it. Mother had always been so proud of Marigold's silken fleece. But Grandmother! Marigold knew it was hopeless.

"I don't know if we should do it," said Grandmother—not alluding to bobbed hair. "She has never been left alone before. Suppose something should happen."

"Nothing ever happens here," said Marigold pessimistically and untruthfully. Things happened right along—int'resting things and beautiful things. But this was Marigold's blue day.

She could not go with Grandmother and Mother and Salome to Great-Aunt Jean's golden wedding because Aunt Jean's grandchildren had measles. Marigold did so want to see a golden wedding.

"You can get what you like for supper," said Grandmother. "But remember you are not to touch the chocolate cake. That is for the missionary tea to-morrow. Nor cut any of my Killarney roses. I want them to decorate my table."

"Have a good time, honey-child," whispered Mother. "Why not ask Sylvia down to tea with you? There are doughnuts in the cellar crock and plenty of hop-and-go-fetch-its."

But Marigold did not brighten to this. For the first time she felt a vague discontent with Sylvia, her fairy-playmate of three dream-years.

"I *almost* wish I had a real little girl to play with," she said, as she stood at the gate, watching Grandmother and Mother and Salome drive off up the road—all packed tightly in the buggy. Poor Mother, as Marigold knew, had to sit on the narrow edge of nothing.

2

Perhaps this *was* a Magic Day. Perhaps the dark mind of the Witch of Endor, sitting on the gate post, brewed up some kind of spell. Who knows? At all events, when Marigold turned to look down the other road—the road that ran along the harbour shore to the big Summer Hotel by the dunes—there was the wished-for little girl standing by her very elbow and grinning at her.

Marigold stared in amazement. She had never seen the girl before or any one just like her. The stranger was about her own age—possibly a year older. With ivory outlines, a wide red mouth, long narrow green eyes and little dark eyebrows like wings. Bareheaded, with blue-black hair. Beautifully bobbed, as Marigold instantly perceived with a sigh. She wore an odd, smart green dress with touches of scarlet embroidery and she had wonderful slim white hands—very beautiful and very white. Marigold glanced involuntarily at her own sunburned little paws—and felt ashamed. But—the stranger had *bare knees*. Marigold had never seen this fashion before and she was as much horrified as Grandmother herself could have been.

Who could this girl be? She had appeared so suddenly, so uncannily. She looked different in every way from the Harmony little girls.

"Who are you?" she asked abruptly, before she realised that such a question was probably bad manners.

The stranger grinned.

"I'm me," she said.

Marigold turned haughtily away. A Lesley of Cloud of Spruce was not going to be made fun of by any little nobody from nowhere.

But the girl in green whirled about on tip-toes till she was in front of Marigold once more.

"I'm Princess Varvara," she said. "I'm staying at the hotel down there with Aunt Clara. My uncle is the Duke of Cavendish and Governor-General of Canada. He is visiting the Island and to-day they all went down to visit Cavendish, because it was called after my uncle's great-great-grandfather. All except Aunt Clara and me. She had a headache and they wouldn't take me because there are measles in Cavendish. I was so mad I ran away. I wanted to give Aunt Clara the scare of her life. She's mild and gentle as a kitten but, oh, such a darned tyrant. I can't call my soul my own. So when she went to bed with her headache I just slipped off when Olga was waiting on her. I'm going to do as I like for one day, anyhow. I'm fed up with being looked after. What's the matter?"

"You are telling me a lot of fibs," said Marigold. "You are not a princess. There are no princesses in Prince Edward Island. And you wouldn't be dressed like that if you were a princess."

Varvara laughed. There was some trick about her laugh. It

made you want to laugh too. Marigold had hard work to keep from laughing. But she wouldn't laugh. You couldn't laugh when anybody was trying to deceive you with such yarns.

"She must be one of the Americans down at the hotel," thought Marigold. "And she thinks it fun to fool a silly little down-easter like me if she can. But she *can't!* Imagine a princess having bare knees! Just like Lazarre's kids."

"How do you think a princess should be dressed?" demanded Varvara. "In a crown and a velvet robe. You're silly. I *am* a Princess. My father was a Russian Prince and he was killed in The Terror. Mother is English. A sister of the Duke's. We live in England now, but I came out to Canada with Aunt Clara to visit Uncle."

"I'm not a bad hand at making up things myself," said Marigold. She had an impulse to tell this girl all about Sylvia.

Varvara shrugged her shoulders.

"All right. You needn't believe me if you don't want to. All I want is somebody to play with. You'll do nicely. What is your name?"

"Marigold Lesley."

"How old are you?"

"Ten. How old are *you?*" Marigold was determined that the questions should not be all on one side.

"Oh, I'm just the right age. Come, ask me in. I want to see where you live. Will your mother let us play together?"

"Mother and Grandmother have gone to Aunt Jean's golden wedding," explained Marigold. "And Salome was invited, too, because her mother was a friend of Aunt Jean's. So I'm all alone."

The stranger suddenly threw her arms about Marigold and kissed her rapturously on both cheeks.

"How splendid. Let's have a good time. Let's be as bad as we like. Do you know I love you. You are so pretty. Prettier than I am—and I'm the prettiest princess of my age in Europe."

Marigold was shocked. Little girls shouldn't say things like that. Even if you thought them—sometimes, when you had your blue dress on—you shouldn't say them. But Varvara was talking on.

"That sleek, parted gold hair makes you look like a saint in a stained glass window. But why don't you have it bobbed?"

"Grandmother won't let me."

"Cut it off in spite of her."

"You don't know Grandmother," said Marigold.

She couldn't decide whether she really liked this laughing, tantalising creature or not. But she was int'resting—oh, yes, she was int'resting. Something had happened with a vengeance. Would she tell her about Sylvia? And take her up the hill? No, not yet—somehow, not yet. There was the nice little playhouse in the currant-bushes first.

"What a darling spot," cried Varvara. "But how do you play here all by yourself?"

"I pretend I am the Lady Gloriana Fitzgerald, and sit in the parlour and tell my servant what to do."

"Oh, let me be the servant. I think it must be such fun. Now, you tell me what to do. Shall I sweep the floor?"

Marigold had no trouble telling Varvara what to do. She would show this young Yankee, who thought her soft enough to believe any old yarn, just what it was to be Marigold Lesley of Cloud of Spruce.

3

They had a very good time for a while. When they got tired of it they went to see the pigs—Varvara thought them "very droll animals"—and then they went picking raspberries in the bush behind the pig-house. Varvara kept telling wonderful stories. Certainly, thought Marigold, she was a crackerjack at making up. But they suddenly found all their clothes filled with stick-tights, which was decidedly unpleasant.

"What would you think if I said 'damn'?" demanded Varvara

explosively.

Marigold didn't say what she would think, but her face said it for her.

"Well, I won't," said Varvara. "I'll just say 'lamb' in the same tone and that will relieve my feelings just the same. What berries are those? Eat some and if they don't kill you I'll take some, too. You know there is a kind of berry—if you eat them you can see fairies and talk to them. I've been looking for them all my life."

"Well, these aren't fairy-berries. They are poisonous," said Marigold. "I *did* eat some once and they made me *awful sick*. The minister prayed for me in church," she concluded importantly.

"When *I* was sick the Archbishop of Canterbury prayed for me," said Varvara.

Marigold wished she had made her minister the moderator of the General Assembly at least.

"Let's go and sit on that seat in the orchard and pick these things out of our clothes," suggested Varvara. "And play 'I see' while we do it. The game is which will see the most wonderful things. *I* see a china cat with diamond whiskers walking over the lawn."

"*I* see a bear with wings," said Marigold, who felt she could see things quite as marvellous as any girl from the States trying to pass herself off as a princess.

"*I* see five angels sitting in that apple-tree."

"*I* see three little grey monkeys on a twisted bough with four moons rising behind them."

Varvara drew her black brows together in a scowl. She didn't like being outseen.

"*I* see the devil squatting over there in your garden, with his tail curled up over his back."

Marigold was annoyed. She felt that *she* couldn't see anything more amazing than that.

"You don't!" she cried. "That—that person never comes into *our* garden."

Varvara laughed scornfully.

"It'd be a more interesting place if he did. Do you know"—confidentially—"I pray for the devil every night."

"Pray for him! *For* him!"

"Yes. I'm so sorry for him. Because he wasn't always a devil you know. If he *had* been I suppose he wouldn't mind it so much. There must be spells when he feels awfully homesick, wishing he could be an angel again. Well, we've got all the stick-tights out. What will we do now?"

Again Marigold thought of introducing her to Sylvia. And again for some occult reason she postponed it.

"Let's go and fire potato-balls. Its great fun."

"I don't know how to fire potato-balls. What are they?"

"I'll show you—little tiny things like small green apples. You stick one on the point of a long switch—and whirl it—so—and the potato ball flies through the air for miles. I hit Lazarre in the face with one last night. My, but he was mad."

"Who is Lazarre?"

"Our French hired boy."

"How many servants have you got?"

"Just Lazarre. Salome isn't really a servant. She is related to us."

"We had fifty before The Terror," said Varvara. "And eight gardeners. Our grounds were a dream. I can just barely remember them. Uncle's are wonderful, too. But I like your little garden, and that house of currant-bushes. Isn't it fun to sit and eat currants off your own walls? Well, where are your potato-balls?"

"Over there in Mr. Donkin's field. We must go up the orchard and along by the fence and—"

"Why not cut straight across?" asked Varvara, waving her hand at Mr. Donkin's creamy green oats.

"There's no path there," said Marigold.

"We'll make a path," said Varvara—and made it. Right through the oats. Marigold followed her, though she knew she shouldn't, praying that Mr. Donkin wouldn't see them.

Varvara thought firing potato-balls the best sport ever. In her excitement she fell half-a-dozen times over potato-plants and got her dress in a fearful state in the wet clay a morning shower had left. And the potato-ball juice stained her face and hands till she looked more like a beggar-maid than a princess.

"I never was real dirty in my life before. It's nice," she said complacently.

4

Varvara insisted on helping Marigold to get supper, though Marigold would have preferred being alone. Company did not help to get supper at Cloud of Spruce. But Varvara was out to do as she liked and she did it. She helped set the table, remarking,

"That cup is just like one Aunt Clara used to have. Her husband bit a piece out of it one day when he was in a tantrum."

Marigold knew by this alone that Varvara was no princess. Princess's uncles could never do things like *that*. Why, Phidime had done that once—bit a piece right out of his wife's much prized cut-glass tumbler. The only one she had. A lady she had worked for had given it to her.

Varvara even went to the spare room with Marigold to get the fruit-cake. Marigold decided that for company she must cut some fruit-cake. Grandmother always did. And it was kept in a box under the spare room bed—the sleek, smooth terrible spare room bed where so many people had died. The fruit-cake had always been kept there, ever since Grandmother's children were small and the spare room the only place they dared not go to look for it.

"Oh!" squealed Varvara. "Is that a feather bed? A *real* feather bed?"

"Yes."

Varvara took one wild leap and landed squarely in the middle of it, bounding up and down in ecstasy right on Grandmother's famous spread of filet crochet.

"I've always wanted to see what a feather bed was like. I didn't think there were any left in the world."

Marigold was horrified. That sacred spare room bed! *What* would Grandmother say.

"Every dead person in our family except Old Grandmother has died in that bed," she said.

Varvara turned pale and hastily slid off the bed.

"Why didn't you tell me that before I jumped on it, you little whelp?" she cried excitedly.

"I'm not a little whelp," said Marigold.

"Of course you're not." There was another wild hug and kiss. Marigold emerged from it somewhat discomposed. The Lesleys were not so emotional.

But when Varvara saw the chocolate cake in the pantry, she must have *that* for supper. She must.

"We can't," said Marigold. "Grandmother said I wasn't to touch it."

Varvara stamped her feet.

"I don't care what your grandmother said. I *will* have it. I'm keen on chocolate cake. And they never let me have more than two tiny pieces. Just put that cake right on the table. At once."

"We are not going to have that cake," said Marigold. There was no one by to see it, but at that instant she looked like a pocket-edition of Grandmother. "There is the fruitcake and the date loaf and the hop-and-go-fetch-its."

"I don't want your hop-and-go-what-do-you-call-'ems. Once and for all, are we going to have this cake?"

"Once and for all we're *not*."

Varvara clenched her hands.

"If I were my grandmother I'd order you to be knouted to death—"

"If I were *my* grandmother I'd turn you over my knees and spank you," said Marigold intrepidly.

Varvara at once grew calm—deadly, stonily calm.

"If you don't let me have that chocolate cake for my supper

I'll go out and climb what you call the apple-barn roof and jump down."

"You can't scare me with that," said Marigold scornfully.

Varvara turned without another word and marched out. Marigold followed her a little uneasily. Of course she was only bluffing. She wouldn't do *that*. Why, it would kill her. Even this wild creature couldn't do a thing like that.

Varvara was running nimbly up the ladder. In another second she was on the flat top of the gambrel roof.

"*Now*, will you let me have the chocolate cake?" she cried.

"No," said Marigold resolutely.

Varvara jumped. Marigold screamed. She shut her eyes in anguish and opened them expecting to see Varvara dead and broken on the stones of the path below. What she saw was Varvara hanging, shrieking on the pine-tree by the apple-barn. Her dress had billowed out and caught on the stub of a lopped branch.

Marigold ran to her frantically.

"Oh, you can have the chocolate cake—you can have *anything*."

"How am I to get down?" moaned Varvara, whose temper and determination had evaporated between heaven and earth.

"I'll bring up the step-ladder. I think you can reach it," gasped Marigold.

Varvara managed to escape by the grace of the step-ladder, though she tore her dress woefully in the process.

"I always do just what I say I'll do," she remarked coolly.

"Just look at your dress," shivered Marigold.

"I am more important than my dress," said Varvara loftily.

Marigold was trembling in every limb as she went back to the pantry. Suppose Varvara really had fallen on those stones. Grandmother had said those girls from the States would do *anything*. Marigold believed it.

"Just look how beautifully I've decorated the table," said Varvara proudly.

Marigold looked. Grandmother's Killarney roses were

drooping artistically in the big green basket. Oh, yes, artistically. Varvara had the knack.

"Grandmother told me I wasn't to pick any of those roses," wailed Marigold.

"Well, you didn't, did you, you darling donkey? Tell her *I* did it."

5

The real quarrel did not come until after supper. They had had quite a jolly supper. Varvara was so funny and interesting and said such dreadful things about the picture of Queen Victoria on the dining-room wall.

"Doesn't she look like somebody's old cook with a lace curtain on her head?"

It was really a terrible chromo, originally sent out as a "supplement" with a Montreal paper and framed in hundreds of houses all over the loyal Island. It represented the good queen with a broad blue ribbon across her breast and a crown on her head filled with diamonds, the least of which was as big as a walnut. From the crown descended the aforesaid lace curtain around the face and bust of the queen, and what wasn't lace curtain was diamonds—on ears and throat and breast and hand and arm. Marigold had always had much the same opinion as Varvara about it and had once expressed it. Only once. Grandmother had looked at her as if she had committed *lese-majeste* and said,

"*That is Queen Victoria,*" as if Marigold hadn't known it.

But Marigold wasn't going to have girls from the States coming in and making fun of the royal family.

"I don't think you have any business to talk like that of *our* queen," she said haughtily.

"Silly—she was Mother's aunt," retorted Varvara. "Mother remembers her well. She wasn't a bit handsome, but I'm sure she never looked like *that*. If that's where you get your ideas of a princess's dress from I don't wonder you don't think I'm one. Marigold, this chocolate cake is simply topping."

Varvara ate about half of the chocolate cake and paid it a compliment with every piece. Well, reflected Marigold complacently, certainly Cloud of Spruce cookery was good enough for anybody even if she had been the princess she pretended to be. Varvara certainly was—nice. One couldn't help liking her. Marigold decided that after the dishes were washed she would take Varvara through The Magic Door and the Green Gate and introduce her to Sylvia.

But when she went out to the garden after washing the dishes she found Varvara tormenting her toad—her own pet toad who lived under the yellow rose-bush and knew her. Marigold was certain he knew her. And here was this abominable girl poking him with a sharp stick that must hurt him terribly.

"You stop that!" she cried.

"I won't—it's fun," retorted Varvara. "I'm going to kill it—poke it to death."

Marigold darted forward and wrenched the stick out of Varvara's hand. She broke it in three pieces and confronted her self-invited guest in a true Lesleyan anger.

"You shall not hurt my toad," she said superbly. "I don't care what you threaten—not one bit. You can jump off the apple-barn or down the well or go and throw yourself into the harbour. But you shan't kill my toad, Miss *Princess!*"

The derision that Marigold contrived to put into that "princess" is untransferable to paper. Varvara suddenly was in a most terrible temper. She was almost like an animal in her rage. She bared her teeth and dilated her eyes. Her very hair seemed to bristle.

"Pig! Louse! Flea!" she snarled. "Moon-calf! Beast!" Oh, the venom she contrived to put into her epithets. "You'd make God laugh! Cry-baby! Snivelling thing!"

Marigold *was* crying, but it was with rage. Russian princesses," real or pretended, had no monopoly of temper.

"You have the face of a monkey," Marigold cried.

"I'll—pull—your—ears—out—by—the—roots," said Varvara, with a horrible kind of deliberate devilishness.

She hurled herself against Marigold. She pulled Marigold's hair and she slapped Marigold's face. Marigold had never been so manhandled in her life. She, Marigold Lesley. She struck out blindly and found Varvara's nose. She gave it a fierce, sudden tweak. Varvara emitted a malignant yowl and tore herself loose.

"You—you—do you think you can use me like this—*me?*"

"Haven't I done it?" said Marigold triumphantly.

Varvara looked around. On a garden seat lay Grandmother's shears. With a yell like a demon she pounced on them. Before Marigold could run or stir there was a sudden fierce click—another—and Marigold's two pale gold braids were dangling limply in Varvara's beautiful hand.

"Oh!" shrieked Marigold, clapping her hands to her shorn head.

Suddenly Varvara laughed. Her brief insanity had passed. She dropped the shears and the golden tresses and flung her arms around Marigold.

"Let's kiss and make up. Mustn't let a little thing like this spoil a whole day. Say you forgive me, darlingest."

"Darlingest" said it dazedly. She didn't want to—but she did. This wild girl of laughter and jest had a hundred faults and the one great virtue of charm. She would always be forgiven anything.

But Marigold, in spite of her shorn tresses, was almost glad to see Grandmother and Mother driving into the yard.

"Why? What?" began Grandmother, staring at Marigold's head.

"I did it," interposed the ragged, flushed, juice-stained Varvara resolutely. "You are not to blame her for it. It was all my doings. I did it because I was furious, but I'm glad. You'll have to let her have it trimmed decently now. And *I* ate the chocolate cake and picked the roses and jumped on the feather bed. She is not to be scolded at all for it. Remember that."

Grandmother made an involuntary step forward. The Princess Varvara had the narrowest escape of her royal life.

"Who are you?" demanded Grandmother.

Varvara told her as she had told Marigold. With this difference. She was believed. Grandmother knew all about the Vice-Regal visit to Prince Edward Island, and she had seen Varvara's picture in the Charlottetown *Patriot*.

Grandmother set her lips together. One couldn't, of course, scold a grand-niece of Queen Victoria and the daughter of a Russian Prince. One couldn't. But, oh, if one only could!

An automobile stopped at the gate. A young man and an elderly lady got out of it and came up the walk. A very fine, tall, stately lady, with diamonds winking on her fingers. Her hair snow-white, her face long, her nose long. She could never have been beautiful but she was not under any necessity of being beautiful.

"There's Aunt Clara and Lord Percy," whispered Varvara to Marigold. "I can see she's mad all over—and there's so much of her to get mad. Won't I get a roasting!"

Marigold stiffened in horror. A dreadful conviction came over her that Varvara really was the princess she had claimed to be.

And she had pulled her nose!

The wonderful, great lady walked past Varvara without even looking at her—without looking at anything, indeed. Yet one felt she saw everything and took in the whole situation even to Varvara's muddy dangling rags and dirty face.

"I am sorry," she said to Grandmother, "that my naughty little runaway niece should have given you so much trouble."

"She has not been any trouble to us," said Grandmother graciously, as one queen to another. "I am very sorry I was not at home this afternoon"—combining truth with courtesy to a remarkable degree.

The great lady turned to Varvara.

"Come, my dear," she said softly and sweetly.

Varvara disregarded her for a moment. She sprang past her

and embraced Marigold tempestuously.

"If you were sugar I'd eat you up. Promise me you'll always love me—even if you never see me again. Promise—as long as grass grows and water runs. Promise."

"I will—oh, I will," gasped Marigold sincerely. It was very odd, but in spite of everything she felt that she did and would love Varvara devotedly.

"I've had such a *satisfying* time to-day," said Varvara. "They can't take *that* from me. I really didn't mean to kill your old toad. And you've got your hair bobbed. You can thank me and God for that."

She danced off to the gate, ignoring Lady Clara but throwing an airy kiss to Grandmother. "Laugh, Marigold, laugh," she called imperiously from the car. "I like to leave people laughing."

Marigold managed the ghost of a laugh, after which Varvara deliberately turned a complete double somersault before everybody and hopped into the back seat. Lord Percy smiled at Mother. Mother was a very pretty woman.

"An incorrigible little demon," he said.

6

"I think," said Grandmother quite quietly when she had heard the whole tale, "that princesses are rather too strenuous playmates for you. Perhaps, after all, your imaginary Sylvia is really a better companion."

Marigold thought so too. She ran happily through the dreamy peace of the orchard to meet the twilight that was creeping out of the spruce-grove. Back to Sylvia, her comrade of star-shine and moon-mist, who did not pull hair and slap—or provoke pulling and slapping—Sylvia, who was waiting for her in the shadows beyond the Green Gate. She was very well satisfied with Sylvia again. It was just as Grandmother had said. Princesses were too—too—what was it? Too *it*, anyhow.

She was glad she hadn't told her about Sylvia. She was glad she hadn't shown her the dear fat grey kittens in the apple-barn. Who knew but Varvara would have held them up by their tails? And though she felt sure she could never forget Princess Varvara—the tang of her—the magic of her mirth and storms—there was a queer, bitter little regret far down in her soul.

She had been used to pretend "Suppose a Princess dropped in to tea." And it *had* happened—and she hadn't known it. Besides Varvara wasn't a bit like a Princess. The way she had gobbled things down at supper. Marigold was the poorer for a lost illusion.

Meanwhile down in Cloud of Spruce Mother was putting away Marigold's golden braids and crying over them. Grandmother was girding an apron on with a stern countenance, to make another chocolate cake, late as it was. Salome was counting the hop-and-go-fetch-its and wondering how two children could ever have eaten so many in one afternoon. Marigold's appetite was never very extensive.

"I'll bet that princess will have stomach-ache to-night if she never had it before," she thought vindictively. And Lucifer and the Witch of Endor were talking over the general cussedness of things under the milk bench.

"Take it from me," Lucifer was saying, "princesses aren't what they used to be in the good old days."

CHAPTER XI

A Counsel of Perfection

1

There was really only one creature in the world whom Marigold hated—apart from Clementine, who couldn't be said to be in the world. And that creature was Gwendolen Vincent Lesley—in the family Bible and on the lips of Aunt Josephine. Everywhere else she was Gwennie, the daughter of "Uncle" Luther Lesley, who lived away down east at Rush Hill. She was a second cousin of Marigold's and Marigold had never seen her. Nevertheless she hated her, in her up-rising and her down-sitting, by night and by day, Sundays as well as week-days. And the cause of this hatred was Aunt Josephine.

Aunt Josephine, who was really a second cousin, was a tall severe lady with a pronounced chin and stabbing black eyes which Marigold always felt must see to her very bones—X-ray eyes, Uncle Klon called them. She lived in Charlottetown, when she was home—which wasn't often. Aunt Josephine was an old maid; not a bachelor girl or a single woman but a genuine dyed-in-the-wool old maid. Lazarre added that she "lived on" her relations; by which cannibalish statement he meant that Aunt Josephine was fonder of visiting round than of staying home. She was especially fond of Cloud of Spruce and came as often as she decently could, and every time she came she praised Gwendolen Vincent Lesley to the skies. But she never praised Marigold.

The very first time she had ever seen Marigold she had said, looking at her scrutinisingly,

"Well, you have your father's nose beyond any doubt."

Marigold had never known that her father's nose had been his worst point, but she knew Aunt Josephine was not being complimentary.

"Gwendolen Lesley has such a beautiful little nose," continued Aunt Josphine, who had just come from a visit to Luther's. "Purely Grecian. But *then* everything about *her* is beautiful. I have never in all my life seen such a lovely child. And her disposition is as charming as her face. She is very clever, too, and led her class of twenty in school last term. She showed me the picture of an angel in her favourite book of Bible stories and said, 'That is my model, Aunty.'"

Who wouldn't hate Gwendolen after that? And that was only the beginning. All through that visit and every succeeding visit Aunt Josephine prated about the inexhaustible perfections of Gwendolen Vincent, in season and out of season.

Gwendolen, it appeared, was so conscientious that she wrote down every day all the time she had spent in idleness and prayed over it. She had never, it seemed, given any one a moment's worry since she was born. She had taken the honour diploma for Sabbath-school attendance—Aunt Josephine never said "Sunday"—every year since she had begun going.

"She is *such* a spiritual child," said Aunt Josephine.

"Would she jump if you stuck a pin in her?" asked Marigold.

Grandmother frowned and Mother looked shocked—with a glint of unlawful, unLesleyan amusement behind the shock—and Aunt Josephine looked coldly at her.

"Gwendolen is *never* pert," she rebuked.

It also transpired that Gwendolen always repeated hymns to herself before going to sleep. Marigold, who spent *her* pre-sleep hours in an orgy of wonderful imagery adventures, felt miserably how far short she fell of Gwendolen Vincent. And Gwendolen always ate just what was put before her and *never* ate too much.

"I never saw a child so free from greediness," said Aunt

Josephine.

Marigold wondered uneasily if Aunt Josephine had noticed her taking that third tart.

And with all this Gwendolen, it appeared, was "sensible." Sensible! Marigold knew what that meant. Somebody who would use roses to make soup of if she could.

Gwendolen had never had her hair bobbed.

"And she has such wonderful, luxuriant, thick, long, shining, glossy curls," said Aunt Josephine, who would have added some more adjectives to the curls if she could have thought of them.

Grandmother, who did not approve of bobbed hair, looked scornfully at Marigold's sleek, cropped head. Marigold, who had never before known a pang of jealousy in regard to a living creature, was rent with its anguish now. Oh, how she hated this paragon of a Gwendolen Vincent Lesley—this angelic and spiritual being, who took honour diplomas and led her class but who yet—Marigold clutched avidly at the recollection of the note Gwennie had written her at Christmas—didn't appear to know that "sapphire" shouldn't be spelled "saffire."

Gwendolen Vincent was "tidy." She was brave—"not afraid of thunderstorms," said Aunt Josephine when Marigold cowered in Mother's lap during a terrible one. She always did *exactly* what she was told—"See that, Marigold," said Grandmother. She never slammed doors—Marigold had just slammed one. She was a wonderful cook for her age. She was never late for meals—"See that, Marigold," said Mother. She never mislaid anything. She always cleaned her teeth after *every* meal. She never used slang. She never interrupted. She never made grammatical errors. She had perfect teeth—Marigold's eye-teeth were just a wee bit too prominent. She was never tomboyish—Marigold had been swinging on a gate. She never was too curious about anything— Marigold had been asking questions. She always was early to bed and early to rise because she knew it was the way and the only way to be healthy and wealthy and wise.

"I don't believe *that*," said Marigold rudely. "Phidime gets up at five o'clock every morning of his life and he's the poorest man in Harmony."

And then it appeared that Gwendolen never answered back.

Once and once only did Marigold, for a fleeting moment, think she might like Gwendolen in spite of her goodness. It was when Aunt Josephine told how Gwendolen had once got up in the middle of the night and gone downstairs *in the dark* to let in a poor, cold, miserable pussy-cat crying on the doorstep. But the next minute Aunt Josephine was describing how careful Gwendolen was to keep her nails clean—looking at Marigold's as she talked.

"Gwendolen has such lovely white half-moons at the base of her nails."

Now, Marigold had no half-moons.

"In short"—though it never really was in short with Aunt Josephine—"Gwendolen is a perfect little lady."

Somehow that phrase got under Marigold's skin as nothing else had done.

"I'm fed up with this," she reflected furiously. It was the first time she had ever dared to use this new expression even in thought. Grandmother and Mother merely got rather tired of things. But rather tired was too mild to express her feelings towards the perfect little lady. And under it all that persistent stabbing ache of jealousy. Marigold would have liked as well as any one else to have a clan reputation of being a perfect lady.

And now Gwendolen was coming to Cloud of Spruce for a visit. Luther had written Grandmother that he wanted his little girl to visit Harmony and get acquainted with all her relatives. Especially did he want her to know Cloud of Spruce, where he had had such jolly times when a boy. Grandmother screwed up her lips a bit over the reference to "jolly times"—she remembered some of them—but she wrote back a very cordial invitation.

Aunt Josephine, who was just completing a visit, said she hoped, if Gwendolen came up for the mooted visit, Marigold would learn from her how a really nice little girl should behave. If

Marigold had not been there Grandmother would have bristled up and said that Marigold was a pretty well-behaved child on the whole and her friends reasonably satisfied with her. She would probably have added that Luther Lesley had been a devil of a fellow when he was young and Annie Vincent was the biggest tomboy on the Island before she was married. And that it was curious, to say the least of it, that the pair of them should have produced so saintly an offspring.

But Marigold *was* there, so Grandmother had to look at her sternly and say, "I hope so too."

Marigold did not know that when she had betaken her wounded spirit to the gay ranks of rosy hollyhocks beside the grey-green apple-barn for solace, Grandmother remarked to Mother,

"Thank mercy *that* is over. We won't have another infliction of the old fool for at least three months."

"Aunt Josephine 'likes cats in their place,'" said Lucifer. "*I* know the breed."

2

And then Gwendolen Vincent Lesley came. Marigold got up early the day she was expected, in order to have everything in perfect readiness for the task of entertaining a thorough lady. She was going to be as proper and angelic and spiritual as Gwendolen if it killed her. It was hard to have Mother say pleadingly, "Now, *please* see if you can behave nicely when Gwennie is here," as if she never behaved nicely when Gwennie wasn't there. For a moment Marigold felt an unholy desire that the very first thing she might do would be to scoop up a handful of mud and throw it at the visitor. But that passed. No, she was going to be good—not commonly good, not ordinarily good, but fearfully, extraordinarily, angelically good.

They met. Gwendolen stiffly put out a slender immaculate

154

hand. Marigold glanced apprehensively at her own nails—thank goodness they were clean, even if they had no half-moons. And oh, Gwendolen *was* just as beautiful—and just as ladylike—and just as faultless as Aunt Josephine had painted her. Not one comforting, consoling defect anywhere.

There were the famous nut-brown curls falling around her delicate, spiritual face—there were the large, mild, dewy blue eyes and the exquisitely arched brows—there were the pearly teeth and the straight Grecian nose, the rosebud mouth, the shell-pink ears that lay back so nicely against her head, the cherubic expression, the sweet voice—very sweet. Marigold wondered if it was jealousy that made her think it was a little *too* sweet.

Marigold could have forgiven Gwendolen her beauty but she couldn't forgive her her hopeless perfection of conduct and manners. They had a ghastly week of it. They didn't, as Uncle Klon would have expressed it, click worth a cent in spite of the determined spirituality of both. And oh, how good they both were. Grandmother began to think there might be something in a good example after all.

And they bored each other nearly to death.

Marigold felt forlornly that they *might* have had such a good time if Gwendolen wasn't so horribly proper and if she hadn't to live up to her. Swinging in the apple-barn—housekeeping among the currant-bushes—rollicking in the old grey hay-barn full of cats—prowling about the spruce wood—wading in the brook—gathering mussels down by the shore—making nonsense rhymes—talking sleepy little secrets after they went to bed. But there were no secrets to talk over—nice girls didn't have secrets. And of course Gwendolen was occupied—presumably—repeating hymns.

Once there was a terrible thunderstorm. Marigold was determined she would not show how frightened she was. Gwendolen remarked calmly that the lightning kept her from going to sleep and covered her head with the bedclothes. Marigold wouldn't do that—Gwendolen might think *she* was doing it because she was terrified. Mother came to the door and said, "Darling, are you frightened?"

"No, not a bit," answered Marigold gallantly, hoping that the bed-clothes would keep Gwendolen from noticing how her voice was shaking.

"Aren't thunderstorms jolly?" asked Gwendolen in the morning.

"Aren't they?" answered Marigold most enthusiastically.

It was Gwendolen's beautiful table-manners that were hardest to emulate. This had always been one of Marigold's weak points. She was always in such a hurry to get through and be at something. But now she liked to linger at the table as long as possible. There would be all the less time to spend in Gwendolen's dull company, cudgelling her brains for some amusement that would be proper and spiritual. Gwendolen ate slowly, used her knife and fork with the strictest propriety, apparently enjoyed crusts, said "Excuse me" whenever indicated, and asked, "May I have the butter if you please, Aunt Lorraine?" where Marigold would have polished it off in two words, "Butter, mums?" And oh, but she would have loved Gwendolen if the latter had ever spilled one drop of gravy on the tablecloth!

One night they went to church with Grandmother to hear a missionary speak. Marigold hadn't wanted to go especially, but Gwendolen was so eager for it that Grandmother took them along, though she did not approve of small girls going out to night meetings. Marigold enjoyed the walk to the church—enjoyed it so much that she had an uneasy feeling that it wasn't spiritual to enjoy things to such an extent. But the white young clouds sailing over the moonlit sky were so dear—the shadows of the spruces on the road so fascinating—the sheep so pearly-white in the silver fields—the whole dear, fragrant summer night so friendly and lovesome. But when she said timidly to Gwendolen,

"Isn't the world lovely after dark?" Gwendolen only said starchily,

"I don't worry so much about the heathen in summer when it's warm, but oh, what *do* they do in cold weather?"

Marigold had never worried about the heathen at all, though she faithfully put a tenth of her little allowance every month in a mite-box for them. Again she felt bitterly her inferiority to Gwendolen Vincent and loved her none the better for it.

But it was that night she prayed,

"Please make me pretty good but not quite as good as Gwen, because she never seems to have any fun."

"Those two children get on beautifully," said Grandmother. "They've never had the slightest quarrel. I really never expected that the visit would go off half so well."

Mother agreed—it was better to agree with Grandmother—but she had a queer conviction that the children weren't getting on at all. Though she couldn't have given the slightest reason for it.

3

Came a morning when Grandmother and Mother had to go into Harmony village. Grandmother was getting a new black satin made and Mother had a date with the dentist. They would be away most of the forenoon and Salome had been summoned away by the illness of a relative, but Gwendolen was so good and Marigold so much improved that they did not feel any special anxiety over leaving them alone. But just before they drove away Grandmother said to them,

"Now mind you, don't either of you stick your head between the bars of the gate."

Nobody to this day knows why Grandmother said that. Marigold believes it was simply predestination. Nobody ever *had* stuck her head between the bars of the gate and it had been there for ten years. A substantial gate of slender criss-cross iron bars. No flimsy wire gates for Cloud of Spruce. It had never occurred to Marigold to stick her head between the bars of the gate. Nor

157

did it occur to her now.

But as soon as Grandmother and Mother had disappeared from sight down the road Gwendolen the model, who had been strangely silent all the morning, said deliberately,

"I *am* going to stick my head through the bars of the gate."

Marigold couldn't believe her ears. After what Grandmother had said! The good, so-obedient Gwendolen!

"I'm not going to be bossed by an old woman any longer."

She marched down the steps and down the walk, followed by the suddenly alarmed Marigold.

"Oh, don't—don't, please, Gwennie," she begged. "I'm sure it isn't safe—the squares are so small. What if you couldn't get it out again?"

For answer, Gwendolen stuck her head through one of the oblong spaces between the bars. Pushed her head through to be exact—and it was a tight squeeze.

"There!" she said triumphantly, her mop of curls falling forward over her face and confirming a wild suspicion Marigold had felt at the breakfast-table—that Gwendolen had not washed behind her ears that morning.

"Oh, take it out—please, Gwennie," begged Marigold.

"I'll take it out when I please, Miss Prunes-and-prisms. I'm so sick of being good that I'm going to be just as bad as I want to be after this. I don't care how shocked you will be. You just watch the next thing I do."

Marigold's world seemed to spin around her. Before it grew steady again she heard Gwendolen give a frantic little yowl.

"Oh, I can't get my head out," she cried. "I can't—get—my—head—out."

Nor could she. The thick mop of curls falling forward made just the difference of getting in and getting out. Pull—writhe—twist—squirm as she might, she could not free herself. Marigold, in a panic, climbed over the gate and tried to push the head back—with no results save yelps of anguish from Gwendolen, who, if she were hurt as badly as she sounded, was very badly hurt indeed.

Gwendolen was certainly very uncomfortable. The unnatural position made her back and legs ache frightfully. She declared that the blood was running into her head and she would die. Marigold, shaking in the grip of this new terror, murmured faintly,

"Will it—do—any good—to pray?"

"Pray—pray. If you went for the blacksmith it would do more good than all the prayers in the world, you sickening, pious little cat!" said the spiritual Gwendolen.

The blacksmith! Phidime Gautier. Marigold went cold all over. She was in mortal dread of Phidime, who was a dead shot with tobacco-juice and not the least particular about his targets. She had never really believed the legend about the baby, but the impression of it was still in possession of her feelings. Phidime was very gruff and quick-tempered and never "stood for any kids" hanging round his shop. Marigold felt that she could never have the courage to go to Phidime.

"Oh, don't you think if I took you round the waist and pulled hard I could pull you out?" she gasped.

"Yes, and pull my head clean off," snapped Gwendolen. She gave another agonised squirm but to no effect, except that she nearly scraped one of her ears off. Suddenly she began shrieking like a maniac. "I can't stand this another minute—I can't," she gasped between shrieks. "Oh—I'm dying—I'm dying."

Marigold dared hesitate no longer. She tore off down the road like a mad thing. As she went the wild howls of Gwendolen Vincent could be heard faintly and more faintly. Was Gwennie dead? Or just yelled out?

"Hey, left a pie in the oven?" shouted Uncle Jed Clark as she spun by him.

Marigold answered not. To reach the blacksmith shop, to gasp out her tale, took all the breath she had.

"For de love of all de saints," said Phidime. He killed a nail on the floor with a squirt of tobacco-juice and hunted out a file very deliberately. Phidime had never seen any reason why he should hurry. And Gwennie might be dead!

Eventually the file was found, and he started up the road like the grim black ogre of fairy-tales. Gwendolen was not dead. She was still shrieking.

"Here now, stop dat yelling," said Phidime unsympathetically.

It took some time to file the bar and Phidime was not overly gentle. But at last it was done and Gwendolen Vincent was free, considerably rumpled and dishevelled, with a head that felt as if it were three sizes larger than ordinarily.

"Don't you go for do dat fool t'ing any more again," said Phidime warningly.

Gwendolen looked up at him and said spitefully,

"Old devil-face!"

Marigold nearly dropped in her tracks. Ladylike? Spiritual? Not to speak of commonly grateful?

"You keep dat sassy tongue of yours in your haid," said Phidime blackly as he turned away. Gwendolen stuck her tongue out at him.

Marigold was feeling a bit shrewish after her terror. She looked at Gwendolen and uttered the four most unpopular words in the world.

"I told you so," said Marigold.

"Oh, shut your head!"

This was indecent. "Shut your mouth" was an old friend—Marigold had often heard the boys at school using it—but "shut you head" was an interloper.

"I don't care if you *are* shocked, Miss Prim," said Gwendolen. "I'm through with trying to be as good as you. Nobody could be. I don't care *what* Aunt Josephine says."

"Aunt—Jo-seph-ine!"

"Yes, Aunt Jo-seph-ine! She does nothing all the time she is at Rush Hill but sing your praises."

"Mine!" gasped Marigold.

"Yes. She just held you up as a perfect model—always telling me how good you were! I knew I'd hate you—and I didn't want to come here for a visit—I like to go somewhere where something's happening all the time—but Father made me. And I made up my mind I'd be just as ladylike as you. Such a week!"

"Aunt Josephine told me *you* were a model—a perfect lady. *I*'ve been trying to be as good as you," gasped Marigold.

They looked at each other for a moment—and understood. Gwendolen began to laugh.

"I just couldn't stand it a day longer. That's why I stuck my head in the gate."

"Aunt Josephine told me you said hymns before you went to sleep—and took an angel for your model—and—"

"I was just stuffing Aunt Josephine. My, but it was easy to pull her leg."

Which was wicked of course. But in proportion to the wickedness did Marigold's sudden and new-born affection for Gwendolen Vincent increase.

"She made me so mad praising you. I wanted to show her you weren't the only saint in the world."

"Did you really want to hear that missionary?" asked Marigold.

"I sure did. Wanted to hear if he'd tell any cannibal yarns so's we could make a game of them when I went back to Rush Hill," said Gwennie promptly.

Which was wickeder still. But oh, how Marigold loved Gwennie.

"We've wasted a week," she said mournfully.

"Never mind. We'll make up for it this week," said Gwendolen Vincent ominously.

Grandmother can't understand it to this day. She never forgot that second week.

"One of your deep ones, that," Salome always said afterwards, whenever any one mentioned the name of Gwendolen Vincent.

"You can't always tell a saint by the cut of his jib," remarked Lucifer, who had never felt that his tail was safe in spite of Gwendolen's saintliness.

CHAPTER XII

Marigold Entertains

1

"No more fat for me. I've nearly died eating fat this week," was Gwendolen's declaration of independence that night at supper. Grandmother, who hadn't noticed the gate yet—Phidime had wired it up rather cleverly—wondered what had happened to her.

"You should eat the fat *with* the lean," she said severely.

Gwennie stuck out her tongue at Grandmother. It gave Marigold a shock to realise that anybody could do that and live. Grandmother actually said nothing. What was there to say? But she reflected that Annie Vincent's child possibly ran truer to form than they had supposed after all. Grandmother would never have admitted it, but she was almost as tired of Gwennie's perfection as Marigold was. So she pretended not to see the grimace.

Grandmother had to pretend blindness a good many times in the days that followed, rather than outrage hospitality and incur Annie Vincent's eternal wrath by spanking her offspring or sending her home with a flea in her ear. The famed serenity of Cloud of Spruce was smashed to smithereens. A day without a thrill was a lost day for Gwennie.

Marigold enjoyed it—with reservations. Gwennie cared nothing for story-books or kittens and knew nothing whatever about the dryads that lived in the beech clump or the wind spirits that came up the harbour on stormy nights. Marigold would never have dreamed of telling her about Sylvia or taking her along the secret paths of her enchanted groves. But still Gwennie was a good little scout. There was always something doing when she was about, and she *was* funny. She was always "taking off" some one. She could imitate anyone to perfection. It was very amusing—though you always had a little uneasy feeling that the minute your back was turned she might be imitating *you*. Grandmother really was very cross the day Gwennie spilled soup over Mrs. Dr. Emsley's silk dress at the dinner-table because she was "taking off" the old doctor's way of eating soup and sending poor Marigold into convulsions of unholy mirth.

Of course fun was all right. But Gwennie laughed at so many things Marigold had been taught to hold sacred, and giggled when she should be reverent. It was awful to go to church with her. She said such funny things about everybody and it was so wicked to laugh in church, even silently. Yet laugh Marigold sometimes had to till the pew shook and Grandmother glared at her.

But Marigold would not allow Gwennie to baptise the kittens. Gwen thought it would be "such fun" and had the bowl of water and everything ready. She was to be the minister and Marigold was to hold the kittens.

But Marigold had put her foot down firmly. No kittens were going to be baptised and that was that.

"Grandmother wouldn't allow it," said Marigold.

"I don't care a hang for Grandmother," said Gwennie.

"*I* do."

"You're just afraid of her," said Gwennie contemptuously. "Do have some spunk."

"I've lots of spunk," retorted Marigold. "And it isn't because I'm afraid of her that I won't have the kittens baptised. It just isn't right."

"Do you know," said Gwennie, "what I do at home when Father or Mother won't let me do things. I just sit down and yell at the top of my voice till they give in."

163

"You couldn't yell Grandmother out," said Marigold proudly.

Gwennie sulked all the evening and Marigold felt badly because she really liked Gwennie very much. But there were some things that simply were not done and baptising kittens was one of them. Gwennie announced in the morning that she would forgive Marigold.

"I don't want to be forgiven. I haven't done anything wrong," retorted Marigold. "I *won't* be forgiven."

"I *will* forgive you. You can't prevent me," said Gwennie virtuously. "And now let's arrange for something different to happen to-day. I'm tired of everything we've been doing. Look here, was there ever a day in your life you did *everything* you wanted to?"

Marigold reflected. "No."

"Well, let's do everything we want to to-day. Every single thing."

"Everything *you* want or everything *I* want?" queried Marigold significantly.

"Everything *I* want," declared Gwennie. "I'm the visitor, so you *ought* to let me do as I want. Now, come on, don't be a 'fraid-cat. I won't ask you to baptise kittens. We'll leave the holy things out since you're so squeamish. I'll tell you what I *am* going to do. I'm dying to taste some of that blueberry wine. I asked your grandmother yesterday for some but she said it wasn't good for little girls. That's all in my eye. I'm just going to get a bottle out right now and open it. We'll take a glass apiece and put the bottle back. Nobody'll ever know."

Marigold knew quite well this wasn't right. But it was a different kind of wrongness from the kitten-project. And she knew that Gwennie would do it whether it was right or not; and Marigold had a secret hankering to see what blueberry wine was like. They would never give her any of it, which she thought very mean. Grandmother's blueberry wine was famous, and when evening callers came they were always treated to blueberry wine with their cake.

Grandmother and Mother and Salome were all far up in the orchard picking the August apples. It was a good chance and, as Gwennie said, likely nobody would miss the two glassfuls if they put the bottle away back on the pantry shelf in the dark corner.

The dining-room was cool and shadowy. It had been newly papered in the spring, and Mother had just put up the new cream net curtains that waved softly in the August breezes. Grandmother's beautiful bluebird centrepiece, which Aunt Dorothy had sent her all the way from Vancouver, was on the table under the bowl of purple delphiniums. Hanging over a chair was Salome's freshly laundered blue and white print dress.

Marigold lingered to whisper something to the delphiniums, while Gwennie popped into the pantry and came out with a bottle.

"The cork is wired down," she said. "I'll have to run out to the apple-barn and get the pliers. You wait here and if you hear any one coming pop the bottle back into the pantry."

Nobody came and Marigold watched the bottle with its beautiful purplish-red glow. At last she was going to know what blueberry wine was like. It was really rather jolly to have some one round who dared fly in Grandmother's face.

Gwennie saw nobody but Lazarre on her trip to the apple-barn. Lazarre, whose opinion of Gwennie's ancestry was sulphurous, knew something was in the wind.

"Dat kid she always look special lak de angel w'en she plannin' some devil-work," he muttered. But he said nothing. If three women couldn't look after her it was none of his business.

"I've brought a corkscrew, too," said Gwennie, twisting the wire deftly around with the pliers.

As it happened, there was no need of the corkscrew. None whatever.

Gwennie and Marigold hardly knew what had happened. There had been a noise like a gun-shot—and they were standing in the middle of the dining-room looking wildly at each other. There was not much blueberry wine left in that bottle. The rest of it was on the ceiling—on the walls—on the new curtains—on Salome's dress—on the blue bird centrepiece—on Gwennie's face—on Marigold's pretty pink linen dress! Gwennie had learned something she had never known before about blueberry wine. And if thrills were what she was after, she had had enough in one moment to last several weeks.

For an instant she stood in dismay. Then she seized Marigold's hand. "Come quick," she hissed, "get that dress off—get something on—hurry."

Marigold let herself be whisked upstairs. What dreadful thing had happened? Blueberry stains never came out, she had heard Salome say. But Gwennie gave her no time to think. The stained dress was dragged off and thrown into the closet—Marigold's old tan one was thrown over her head—Gwennie wiped the blueberry wine off her face with one of Mother's towels. There were some spots on her dress, too, but that did not matter.

"Come," she said imperiously, snatching Marigold's hand.

"Where are we going?" gasped Marigold as they tore down the road.

"*Anywhere.* We've got to vamoose until they get over that dining-room. They'd kill us if they saw us when they see *it*. We'll stay away till evening. Their fit will be over by then and maybe we'll get off with whole hides. But I'd like to be a fly on the ceiling when Grandmother sees that room."

"We can't stay away all day. We've nothing to eat," groaned Marigold.

"We'll eat berries and roots—and things," said Gwennie. "We'll be Gipsies and live in the woods. Come to think of it, it will be fun."

"Will you take a drive," said a voice above them.

It was Mr. Abel Derusha, the Weed Man, on his double-seated wagon, bareheaded as always, with his dog Buttons beside him!

2

The Weed Man was one of the few romantic personages the country around the harbour could boast. He lived somewhere up at the Head but was well known all over the surrounding communities—at least people thought they knew him well, whereas perhaps nobody really knew him at all.

In his youth Abel Derusha had gone to college and studied for the ministry. Then that was given up. There was a heresy hunt and the result was that Abel Derusha came home, lived at the Head with his old-maid sister Tabby and set up his weed-wagon. Soon he was known as the "Weed Man." In summer he drove all over the Island gathering medicinal plants and herbs and selling them and the decoctions he made from them. He made only a pittance by it. But he and Tabby had enough to live on, and Abel Derusha's weed-fad was little more than an excuse to live in the open. Marigold thought him very "int'resting" and often felt that it would be a delightful thing to drive about with him on his red wagon. She always felt the strange charm of his personality though she knew little of his history—just what she had heard Salome say to Mrs. Kemp one day.

"Abel Derusha always took things easy. Never seemed to worry over trials and disappointments as most folks do. Seems to me that as long as he can wander over the country hunting weeds and talking to that old red dog of his as if it was a human being he don't care how the world wags on. Didn't even worry when they put him out of the ministry. Said God was in the woods as well as any church. He favours his mother's people, the Courteloes. Sort of shiftless and dreamy. All born with hang-nails on their heels. The Derushas were all ashamed of him. 'Tisn't the way to get on in the world."

No, good and worthy Salome. It is not the way to get on in your world, but there may be other worlds where getting on is estimated by different standards, and Abel Derusha lived in one of these—a world far beyond the ken of the thrifty Harbour farmers. Marigold knew that world, though she knew it didn't do to live in it *all* the time as Abel did. Though you were very happy there. Abel Derusha was the happiest person she knew.

He had a face so short it positively looked square, a long, rippling, silky red beard and an odd, spiky, truculent moustache that didn't seem to belong to the beard at all. There was no doubt he was ugly, but Marigold had always thought it was a nice kind of ugliness. He had beautiful clear blue eyes that told he had kept the child-heart. The red squirrels would come to him in the woods and he called all the dogs in the country by their first name. When he came to Cloud of Spruce—which he did not always do, being "pernickety" in regard to his ports of call—he sat in his red wagon and talked with Lazarre and Salome and Mother and Grandmother by the hour, if they would linger to talk with him, though he would never enter the house. After he had gone Lazarre would shrug his shoulders and say contemptuously,

"Dat man, he's crack." Whereat Salome would inform Lazarre, by way of standing by her race, that Abel Derusha had forgotten more than he, the said Lazarre, ever knew. He had promised once to take Marigold for a drive with him and Marigold hankered after it, though she knew she would never be let go. And now here she and Gwennie were out to do as they liked for a whole day and here was the Weed Man offering them a drive.

"Sure," said Gwennie promptly. But Marigold, in spite of her secret wishes, hung back.

"Where are you going?"

"Anywhere—anywhere," said Abel easily. "I'm just poking along to-day—just poking along, thinking how I'd have made the world if I *had* made it. And if you two small skeesicks want to come along why just come."

"But they wouldn't know what had happened to us at home," said Marigold doubtfully.

"They'll know what has happened to the dining-room," giggled Gwen. "Come on now, Marigold. Be a sport."

"Marigold's right," said the Weed Man. "Doesn't do to worry

folks who worry. *I* never worry myself. Here's Jim Donkin coming along. I'll ask him to drop over to Cloud of Spruce and tell the folks you've come for a day with me. We'll get our dinners somewhere along the road and we'll go home to my place for supper, and I'll bring you back in the evening. How's that?"

Nobody but the Weed Man would have proposed such a plan. But Abel didn't see any reason if the girls wanted a drive why they shouldn't have it on a day God had made specially for people who wanted to be out. Gwennie had quite made up her mind to go and Marigold couldn't help thinking it would be very int'resting.

So Jim Donkin was asked to take the word to Cloud of Spruce, and Marigold and Gwennie were in the back seat of the red wagon, amid fragrant bundles of Abel's harvest, bowling along the road, quite delighted with themselves. Marigold resolved to forget the catastrophe of the blueberry wine. It had been Gwen's doings, anyway. They wouldn't kill Gwen because she was a visitor and meanwhile here was a whole golden day, with the very air seeming alive, flung into their laps as a gift. Perhaps Marigold had a spice of Uncle Klon's wanderlust in her. At any rate the prospect of driving about with the Weed Man filled her with secret delight. She had always known she would like the Weed Man.

"What road are you going to take?" demanded Gwen.

"Whatever road pleases me," said the Weed Man, looking disdainfully at a car that passed. "Look at that critter insulting the daylight. I've no use at all for them. Nor your aeroplanes. If God had meant us to fly He'd have given us wings."

"Did God mean you to drive this poor old horse when He gave you legs?" said Gwen pertly.

"Yes, when He gave him four legs to my two," was the retort. Abel was so well pleased with himself that he chuckled for a mile. Then he turned into a red side road, narrow and woodsy, with daisies blowing by the longer fences, little pole-gates under the spruces, stone dykes overgrown with things he loved to rifle, looping brooks and grassy fields girdled by woods. It was all very dear and remote and lovely and the Weed Man told them tales of every kink and turn, talking sometimes like the educated man he really was and sometimes lapsing into the vernacular of his childhood.

There was one lovely, gruesome tale of a hollow where a murdered woman's body had been found; and at a certain corner of the road a "go-preacher" had been stoned.

"What did they stone him for?" asked Gwen.

"For preaching the truth—or what he believed the truth, anyhow. They always do that if you preach the truth—stone you or crucify you."

"You meant to be a preacher once yourself, didn't you?" Gwen was possessed of a questioning devil.

"The preaching was Tabby's idea. I never wanted to myself—not enough to tell lies for it anyhow. See that house in the hollow. There was a man lived there who used to say his prayers every morning and then get up and kick his wife."

"Why did he kick her?"

"Ah, that's the point, now. Nobody ever knew. Mebbe 'twas just his way of saying 'amen.'"

"He wouldn't have kicked *me* twice," said Gwen.

"I believe you." The Weed Man grinned at her over his shoulder. "Here's the old Malloy place. Used to be a leprechaun living there—the Malloys brought him out from Ireland among their bits of furniture, 'twas said. Guess 'twas true. Never heard of any native leprechauns in Prince Edward Island."

"What is a leprechaun?" asked Marigold who had a thrill at the name.

"A liddle dwarf fairy dressed in red with a peaky cap. If you could see him and keep on seeing him he'd lead you to a pot of buried gold. Jimmy Malloy saw him once but he tuk his eyes off him for a second and the liddle fellow vanished. Howsomever, Jimmy could always wiggle his ears after that. He got that much out of it."

"What good did wiggling his ears do him?"

"Very few can do it. *I* can. Look."

"Oh, will you show me how to do that?" cried Gwennie.

"'Tisn't an accomplishment—it's a gift," said the Weed Man solemnly. "Tom Squirely lives over there. Always bragging he doesn't owe a cent. Good reason why. Nobody would lend him one."

"I heard Lazarre say the same thing about you," said Gwen impudently. "If you live in glass houses you shouldn't throw stones."

"Why not now? Somebody'll be sure to throw a stone at your house whether or no, so you might as well have your fun, too. C. C. Vessey lives on that hill. Not a bad feller—not so mean as his dad. When old Vessey's wife died she was buried with a little gold brooch unbeknown to him. When he found it out he went one night to the graveyard and opened up the grave and casket to get that brooch. Here, wait you a minute. I've got to run in and see Captain Simons for a second. He wanted me to bring him a south-west wind to-day. I have to tell him I couldn't bring it to-day but I'll send him one to-morrow."

"Do you suppose he really sells the winds?" whispered Marigold.

"No," scornfully. "I see through your Weed Man. His head isn't screwed on very tight. But he's good fun and his stories are great. I don't believe that leprechaun yarn though."

"Don't you now?" said the Weed Man, returning creepily from behind, though they had never seen him leave the house, and looking at Gwennie compassionately. "What a lot you're going to miss if you don't believe things. Now, I just drive round believing everything and such fun as I have."

"Lazarre says you're lazy," commented Gwen.

"No, no, not lazy. Just contented. I'm the biggest toad in my own puddle, so it don't worry me none if there's bigger toads in other puddles. I'm king of myself. Now look-a-here. Suppose we call and see old Granny Phin. I haven't seen her for a long while. And maybe she'll let Lily give us a bite of dinner."

Gwen and Marigold surveyed rather dubiously the little house before which the Weed Man was stopping. It was a tumbledown little place with too many brown paper windowpanes. The gate hung by one hinge, the yard was overgrown with Scotch thistle and tansy, and even at a distance the old woman who sat on the crazy veranda did not seem attractive.

"I don't like the look of the place much," whispered Gwen. "Hope we don't catch the itch."

"What is that?"

"Marigold, don't you know *anything?*"

Marigold thought gloatingly of certain things she *did* know—lovely things—things Gwennie never would or could know. But she only said,

"I don't know what *that* is."

"Then pray heaven you never *do* know," said Gwen importantly. "*I* know. Caught it from a kid going to school who lived in just such a place as this. Ugh! Lard and sulphur till you could die."

"Come on, now, and don't you be whispering to each other," said the Weed Man. "Granny Phin won't like that. You don't want to get on the rough side of *her* tongue. She's eighty-seven years old, but she's every inch alive."

3

Physically, Granny Phin was hardly every inch alive, for she could not walk alone, having, as she told her visitors later, "paralattics of the hips." But, mentally, her strength had not abated. She was of striking appearance, with snow-white hair in elf-locks around her dead-white face and flashing greenish-blue eyes. She still possessed all her teeth, but they were discoloured and fang-like and when she drew back her lips in a smile she was certainly a rather wolf-like old dame. She wore a frilled widow's cap tied tightly under her chin, a red calico blouse, and a voluminous skirt of red-and-black checked homespun, and was evidently addicted to bare feet. She liked to sit on the veranda, where she could scream maledictions and shake her long black stick at any persons or objects that incurred her dislike or displeasure. Marigold had heard of Granny Phin, but she had never expected to see her. Curiosity mingled with her trepidation as she followed the Weed Man up the path. What a difference there was in old women, she thought, comparing Old Grandmother and Grandmother to this crone.

"Well, this *is* a treat," said Granny Phin.

"It's a warm day, Mistress Phin," said the Weed Man.

"Ye'll be in a warmer place ere long, no doubt," retorted Granny, "and I'll sit in my high seat in heaven and laugh at yez. Hev ye forgot the last time ye was here that dog o' yourn bit me?"

"Yes, and the poor liddle brute has been ill almost ever since," said the Weed Man rather sternly. "He's only just got well. Don't let me see you letting him bite you again."

"The devil himself can't get the better of yer tongue," chuckled Granny admiringly. "Well, come up, come up. Lucky for you I'm in a good humour to-day. I've had such fun watching old Doc Ramsay's funeral go past. Ten years ago to-day he told me I'd only a year to live. Interduce yer family, please."

"Miss Marigold Lesley of Cloud of Spruce—Miss Gwennie Lesley of Rush Hill."

"Cloud o' Spruce folk, eh? I worked at Cloud o' Spruce in my young days. The old lady was a bigotty one. Yer Aunt Adela was there that summer. She looked like an angel, but they do be saying she p'isened her man."

"She isn't our Aunt Adela. She's only a third cousin," said Gwen. "And she didn't poison her husband."

"Well, well, take it easy. Half the husbands in the world ought to be p'isened, anyhow. I had four so I ought to know something of the breed. Sit down all of yez on the floor of the veranda and let yer feet hang down, till dinner's ready. That's what ye've come for, I reckon. Lily—Lily."

In response to Granny's yells a tall, thin, slatternly woman with a sullen face showed herself for a moment in the doorway.

"Company for dinner, Lily—quality folks from Cloud o' Spruce. Put on a tablecloth and bring out the frog pie. And mind ye brew some skeewiddle tea. And send T. B. out to talk to the girls."

"Lily's peeved to-day," grinned Granny as Lily disappeared without a word. "I boxed her ears this morning 'cause she left the soap in the water."

"And her past sixty. Come, come," protested the Weed Man.

"I believe ye. Ye'd think she could have larned sense in sixty years," said Granny, choosing to misunderstand him. "But some folks never larn sense. Yerself now—ye was a young fool once and now ye're an old one. Sad that. T. B., come here and entertain the young ladies."

T. B. came rather sulkily and squatted down by Gwennie. He was a shock-headed urchin with his grandmother's wicked green eyes. Marigold took little notice of him. She was absorbed in awful visions of frog pie. And *what* was skeewiddle tea? It sounded worse than frog pie because she hadn't the least idea what it was. But Gwennie, who had a flair for all kinds of boys, was soon quite at home, bandying slang with Timothy Benjamin Phin—T. B. for short. T. B. soon learned that there were "no flies on her," even if she were one of those "bigotty Lesleys," and also no great need to be overfussy as to what he said. When a plain "damn" slipped out Gwen only giggled.

"Oh, T. B., aren't you afraid you'll go to the bad place if you say such words?"

"Nix on that," contemptuously. "*I* don't believe there's any heaven or hell. When you die there's an end of you."

"Wouldn't you like to go on living?"

"Nope. There's no fun in it," said the youthful misanthrope. "And heaven's a dull place from all the accounts I've heard."

"You've never been there or you wouldn't call it dull," said Marigold suddenly.

"Have *you* been there?"

Marigold thought of the Hidden Land and the spruce hill and Sylvia.

"Yes," she said.

T. B. looked at her. This Marigold-girl was not as pretty as the Gwen one and there wasn't as much "go" in her; but there was something that made T. B. rather cautious, so instead of saying what he would have said to Gwen, he merely remarked politely,

"You're lying."

"Mind yer manners," Granny suddenly shot at T. B. from her conversation with the Weed Man. "Don't ye let me catch ye calling ladies liars."

"Oh, give your face a rest," retorted T. B.

"No shrimp sauce if ye please," said Granny.

T. B. shrugged his shoulders and turned to Gwen.

"She was picking on Aunt Lily all day 'cause Aunt Lily left the soap in the wash-pan. She used to smack her, but *I* stopped that. I wasn't going to have Granny abuse Aunt Lily."

"How did you stop her?" queried Gwen.

"The last time she smacked Aunt Lily I went up to her and bit her," said T. B. coolly.

"You ought to bite her oftener, if that will stop her," giggled Gwen.

"There ain't nothing else worth standing up to her for," grinned T. B. "Granny's tough biting. No, I let her alone and she lets me alone—mostly. She gave me a jaw last week when I got drunk."

"Apple-sauce. You never," scoffed Gwen.

T. B. *had*—as a sort of experiment, it appeared.

"Jest wanted to see what it was like. And it was awful disappointing. I jest went to sleep. Could do that without getting drunk. No fear of my getting jagged again. No kick in it. Nothing *is* ever like what you expect it to be in this world. It's a dull old hole."

"'Tisn't," interjected Granny again. "It's an int'resting world. Vi'lent int'resting."

Marigold felt there was one thing she had in common with Granny at least. In a sense Marigold was enjoying herself. All this was a glimpse into a kind of life she had never known existed, but it was int'resting—"vi'lent int'resting," as Granny said.

Granny and the Weed Man appeared to be enjoying themselves, too, in spite of an occasional passage-at-arms.

"Going to the Baptist church, are yez?" snarled Granny. "Well, if ye do yer dog'll go to heaven afore ye do. Catch *me* going to a Baptist church. I'm a Episcopalian—always was and always will be, world without end, amen."

"I don't believe you ever saw the inside of an Episcopalian church in your life," taunted the Weed Man.

"Yah, I'd tweak yer nose for that if I could reach it," retorted Granny. "Go to yer Baptist church—go to yer Baptist church. Ye son of a monkey-faced rabbit. And I'll sit here and imagine yez all being fried."

She suddenly turned to Marigold.

"If this Weed Man was as rich as he's poor he'd be riding over the heads of all of us. I tell you the real pride of this man is ridic'lous."

"Dinner's ready," Aunt Lily called sulkily from inside.

"Come and help me in," said Granny, reaching briskly for her black stick. "All that keeps me alive is the little bit I eat."

Before the Weed Man could go gallantly to her assistance a shining new car, filled with gaily dressed people, suddenly swung in at the gate and stopped in front of the veranda. The driver bent from the car to make some request, but Granny, crouched like an old tigress, did not allow him to utter a word. She caught up the nearest missile—which happened to be a plate filled with gravy and bacon scraps—from the bench beside her and hurled it at him. It missed his face by a hair's breadth and landed squarely, gravy and all, in a fashionable lady's silken lap. Granny Phin followed this up by a series of fearsome yells and maledictions of which the mildest were, "May all yer pittaties be rotten" and "May ye always be looking for something and never finding it" and—finally, "May ye all have the seven-year itch. I'll pray for it, that I will."

The half-dazed driver backed his car out of the gate and broke all speed-limits down the road. Gwen was squealing with delight, the Weed Man was grinning and Marigold was trying hard to feel shocked.

Granny was in high good humour.

"My, but that did me good. I kin hold up my end of a row yit. Ye could tell by the look of that fellow his grandfather hanged himself in the horse-stable. Come to dinner, all of yez. If we'd known ye were comin' we'd a killed the old rooster. It's time he was used anyway. But there's always frog pie, hey? Now for the frog pie."

To Marigold's relief and Gwen's disappointment there was no frog pie. Indeed, there wasn't much of anything but fried ham and potatoes with some blueberry jam—which suggested rather dismal recollections to Marigold. The dinner was a dull affair, for Aunt Lily was still sulky, Granny was busy gobbling and the Weed Man was silent. It was one of his peculiarities that he seldom talked inside any house.

"Can't think or talk right with walls round me—never could," he had told Salome once.

After dinner the Weed Man paid for their meal with a bottle of liniment for Granny's "paralattics," and Granny bade them a friendly good-bye.

"It's sorry I am that ye're goin' instead o' comin'," she said graciously.

She pulled Marigold so close to her that Marigold had a horrible idea that Granny Phin was going to kiss her. If *that* happened Marigold knew she would never be the same girl again. But Granny only whispered,

"She's a bit purtier than you, but I like *you* best—ye look like a bit o' spring."

Which was a nicer compliment than one would have expected old Granny Phin to pay.

4

Their afternoon drive led along the winding shore of a little river running into the Head of the Bay. Far down was the blue, beckoning harbour and beyond it the sunny dunes and the misty gulf. The Weed Man shook his whip at it mournfully.

"One poetry has vanished from the gulf forever," he said, more to himself than to the girls. "When I was a boy that gulf there would be dotted with white sails on a day like this. Now there's nothing but gasoline boats and they're not on speaking terms with romance at all. Romance is vanishing—romance is vanishing out of our world."

He shook his head gloomily. But Marigold, looking on the world with the eyes of youth, saw romance everywhere. As for Gwennie she was not concerned with romance or the lack of it but only with her stomach.

"Gee, I'm hungry," she said. "I didn't get half enough at the Phins's. Where'll we have supper?"

"Down at my place," said the Weed Man. "We're going there now. Tabby'll have a bite for us. After supper I'll take you home—if the weather keeps good-humoured. Those weather-gaws aren't out for nothing. It'll rain cats and dogs to-morrow."

Marigold wondered what weather-gaws were—and then forgot in thinking how interesting it would be if it really rained cats and dogs. Little silk-eared kittens everywhere by the basketful—loads of darling pudgy puppies.

The Weed Man's "place" was at the end of a wood road far down by the red harbour shore. He did not like to have his fellow-mortals too close to him. The little white-washed house seemed to be cuddled down among shrubs and blossoms. There were trees everywhere—the Weed Man would never have any cut down—and four blinking, topaz-eyed kittens in a row on the window-sill, all looking as if they had been cut out of black velvet by the same pattern.

"Cloud o' Spruce breed," said the Weed Man as he lifted

the girls down, "Your Old Grandmother gave me the great-grandmother of them. You are very welcome to my poor house, young ladies. Here, Tabby, we've company for supper. Bring along a glass o' water apiece."

"Goodness, aren't we going to have anything for supper but a glass of water?" whispered Gwen.

But Marigold was taken up with Tabby Derusha, about whom she had heard her elders talking. She was not, so Salome said, "all there." She was reported to go Abel one better in the matter of heresy, for she didn't believe in God at all. She laughed a great deal and seldom went from home.

Tabby was very stout and wore a dress of bright red-and-white striped material. Her face was round and blank but her red hair was abundant and beautiful, and she had her brother's kind, childlike blue eyes. She laughed pleasantly at the girls as she brought them the water.

"Down with it—every drop," ordered the Weed Man. "Every one who comes into my house has to drink a full glass of water first thing. People never drink half enough water. If they did they wouldn't have to pay as many doctors' bills. Drink, I say."

Marigold was not in the least thirsty and she found the second half of the generous tumbler hard to "down." Gwennie drank half of hers.

"Finish," said the Weed Man sternly.

"There, then," said Gwennie, and threw the rest of her water in the Weed Man's face.

"Oh, Gwennie!" cried Marigold reproachfully. Miss Tabby laughed. The Weed Man stood quite still, looking comical enough with the water dripping from his whiskers.

"That'll save me washing my face," he said—and it was all he did say.

"How *does* Gwennie do such things and get away with it?" wondered Marigold. "Is it because she's so pretty?"

She was ashamed of Gwennie's manners. Perhaps Gwen was a little ashamed of herself—if shame were possible to her—for she behaved beautifully at the table—making only one break, when she asked Tabby curiously if it were true she didn't believe in God.

"As long as I can laugh at things I can get along without God," said Tabby mysteriously. "When I can't laugh I'll have to believe in Him."

They had a good supper with plenty of Tabby's applecake and cinnamon-buns and raisin-bread and the Weed Man's stories in between. But when he came in after supper and said the rain was very near and they must wait till morning to go home, it was not so very pleasant.

"Oh, we *must* go home," cried Marigold. "Please, please take us home, Mr. Derusha."

"I can't drive you home and then drive back fourteen miles in a rainstorm. I am content with my allotted portion but I am poor—I can't afford a buggy. And my umbrella's full of holes. You're all right here. Your folks know where you are and won't worry. They know we're clean. Your Grandmother was rained in here one night herself seven years ago. You go right to bed and sleep, and morning'll be here 'fore you know it."

5

"I know I won't sleep a wink in this horrid place," said Gwen snappily, looking scornfully around the tiny bedroom and seeing only the bare uneven floor with its round, braided rug, the cheap little bureau with its cracked mirror, the chipped pitcher and bowl, the stained and cracked ceiling, the old-fashioned knitted lace that trimmed the pillow slips. Marigold saw these things, too, but she saw something else—the view of the harbour through the little window, splendid in the savage sunset of approaching storm. Marigold was tired and rather inclined to think that doing everything you wanted wasn't such fun after all; but under the spell of an outlook like that, the sense of romance and adventure persisted. Why couldn't Gwen make the best of things? She had been grumbling ever since supper. She wasn't such a sport after all.

"If the wind changes, your face will always look like that."

"Oh, don't try to be smart," snapped Gwen. "Old Abel should have taken us home. He promised to. I'm scared to death to sleep in the same house with Tabby Derusha. Any one can see she's cracked. She might come in and smother us with a pillow."

Marigold was a little frightened of Tabby herself—now that it was dark. But all she said was,

"I do hope Salome won't forget to give the cats their strippings."

"I do hope there aren't any bed-bugs in this bed," said Gwen, looking at it with disfavour. "It looks like it."

"Oh, no, I'm sure there isn't. Everything is so clean," said Marigold. "Let's just say our prayer and get into bed."

"I wonder you aren't afraid to say your prayers after that lie you told T. B. to-day about having been in Heaven," said Gwen—who was tired and out of sorts and determined to wreak it on somebody.

"It wasn't a lie—it wasn't—oh, you don't understand," cried Marigold. "It was Sylvia—"

She stopped short. She had never told Gwennie about Sylvia. Gwen had somehow got an inkling that Marigold had some secret connected with the spruce wood and teased her to tell it at intervals. She pounced on Marigold's inadvertent sentence.

"Sylvia! You've some secret about Sylvia, whoever she is. You're mean and dirty not to tell me. Friends always tell each other secrets."

"Not some kinds of secrets. I'm *not* going to tell you about Sylvia, and you needn't coax. I guess I have a right to my own secrets."

Gwen threw one of her boots at the wall.

"All right then. Keep it to yourself. Do you think I want to know your horrid secrets? I *do* know one of them, anyhow. You're jealous of Clementine Lawrence."

Marigold coloured hotly. How on earth had Gwennie found that out? She had never mentioned Clementine to her.

"Oh-h-h!" Gwennie chuckled maliciously. She had to torment somebody as an outlet to her nerves, and Marigold was the only one handy. "You didn't think I knew that. You can't hide things from *me*. Gee, how sour you looked when I praised her picture! Fancy being jealous of a dead woman you never saw! It is the funniest thing I ever heard of."

Marigold writhed. The worst of it was it was *true*. She seemed to hate Clementine more bitterly every day of her life. She wished she could stop it. It was a torture when she thought of it. And it was torture to think that Gwennie had stumbled on it.

"Of course," went on Gwen, "the first Mrs. Leander was ever so much handsomer than your mother. Of course your father would love her best. Ma says widowers just marry the second time for a housekeeper. I could just stand and look at Clementine's picture for hours. When I grow up I'm going to have mine taken just like that, looking at a lily, with my hair done the same way. I'm never going to have *my* hair bobbed. It's *common*."

"The Princess Varvara had *hers* bobbed," retorted Marigold.

"Russian princesses don't count."

"She is a grand-niece of Queen Victoria."

"So *she* said. You needn't put on any airs with me, Marigold Lesley, because you had a princess visiting you. I'm a—a—Democrat."

"You're not. It's only in the States there are Democrats."

"Well, it's something that doesn't take stock in kings and queens, anyway. I forget the right word. And as for politics, do you know I'm going to be a Tory after this. Sir John Carter is ever so much better looking than our Liberal man."

"You *can't* be a To—Conservative," cried Marigold, outraged at this topsy-turvy idea. "Why—why—you were *born* a Grit."

"You'll see if I can't. Well—" Gwen had got her clothes off and wriggled into one of the rather skimpy little cotton nightgowns Tabby had unearthed from somewhere for them, "now for prayers. I'm awful tired of saying the same old prayer. I'm going to invent a new one of my own."

"Do you think it's—safe?" asked Marigold dubiously. When you were a stranger in a strange land wouldn't it be best to stick to the tried and tested in prayers as well as politics.

"Why not? But I know what I'll do. I'm going to say *your* prayer—the one your Aunt Marigold made up for you."

"You shan't," cried Marigold. "That's my very own special prayer."

"Selfish pig," said Gwennie.

Marigold said no more. Perhaps it *was* selfish. And anyway Gwennie would say it if she wanted to. She knew her Gwennie. But she also knew her own dear prayer would be spoiled for her forever if that imp from Rush Hill said it.

Gwennie knelt down with one eye on Marigold. And at the last moment she relented. Gwen wasn't such a bad sort after all. But having said that she was going to invent a new prayer it was up to her to invent one. She wouldn't back down altogether, but Gwen suddenly discovered that it was not such an easy thing to invent a prayer.

"Dear God," she said slowly, "please—please—oh, please never let me have moles like Tabby Derusha's. And never mind about the daily bread—I'm sure to have lots of that—but please give me lots of pudding and cake and jam. And please bless all the folks who deserve it."

"There, that's done," she announced, hopping into bed.

"I'm sure God will think that a funny prayer," said Marigold.

"Well, don't you suppose He wants a little amusement sometimes?" demanded Gwennie. "Anyway, it's my own prayer. It isn't one somebody else made up for me. Gee, Marigold, what if there should be a nest of mice in this bed? There's a chaff tick."

What gruesome things Gwennie did think of. They had blown out their lamp and it was very dark. They were fourteen miles from home. The raindrops began to thud against the little windows. *Was* Tabby Derusha "cracked."

"Abel sent in some apples for you."

Gwennie, to use her own expression, let out a yelp. Tabby was standing by their bed. How could she have got there without their hearing her? Certainly it was eerie. And when she had gone out again they did not dare eat the apples for fear there were worms in them.

"What's that snuffing at the door?" whispered Gwen. "Do you s'pose it's old Abel Derusha turned into a wolf?"

"It's only Buttons," scoffed Marigold. But she was glad when a sudden snore proclaimed that Gwen had fallen asleep. Before she went to sleep herself Tabby Derusha came in again—silently as a shadow, with a little candle this time. She bent over the bed. Marigold, cold with sudden terror, kept her eyes shut and held her breath. Were they going to be killed? Smothered with pillows?

"Dear little children," said Tabby Derusha, lifting one of Gwen's lovely curls gently. "Hair soft as silk—sweet little faces—pretty little dears."

There was a touch soft as a rose-leaf on Marigold's cheek. Tabby gloated over them for a few minutes longer. Then she was gone, as noiselessly as she had come. But Marigold was no longer afraid. She felt as safe and as much at home as if she were in her own blue room at Cloud of Spruce. After all, it had been an int'resting day. And Gwen was all right. She hadn't stolen her prayer. Marigold said it over again under her breath—the beautiful little prayer she loved because it *was* so beautiful and because Aunt Marigold had made it up for her—and went to sleep.

6

"I didn't sleep a wink the whole night," vowed Gwen.

"Never mind, here's a new morning—such a lovely new morning," said Marigold.

The rain was over. The southwest wind the Weed Man had promised Captain Simons was blowing. The clouds were racing before it. Down on the beach the water was purring in little blue ripples. The sky in the east was all rosy silver. The grass was green and wet on the high red cliffs. Over the harbour hung a milky mist. Then the rising sun rent it apart and made a rainbow of it. A vessel came sailing through it over a glistening path. Never, thought Marigold, had the world seemed so lovely.

"What are you doing?" said Gwen, struggling impatiently into her clothes, much annoyed because Buttons had got in after all and slept on her dress.

"I—I think—I'm praying," said Marigold dreamily.

7

Uncle Klon came for them in his car before breakfast was over.

"Are they very mad at Cloud of Spruce?" asked Gwennie. Rather soberly for her. She did not like Uncle Klon. He was always too many for her.

"There's a special Providence for children and idiots," said Uncle Klon gently. "Jim Donkin forgot to give the message till late last night and they were so relieved to find out where you had gone, that the dining-room rather sank into the background. You'd better not look again on blueberry wine when it is purple, Miss Gwen."

"It's a good thing we're too big to be spanked," whispered Gwen, when she saw Grandmother's face.

"I believe you," said Lucifer.

CHAPTER XIII

A Ghost Is Laid

1

That affair of the blueberry wine was certainly a bad business. There was some secret talk at Cloud of Spruce of sending Gwennie home after it. But nothing came of it, and Gwennie never even knew it had been mooted. It would never do to offend Luther and Annie, Grandmother concluded, though for her part she couldn't understand Josephine. But the real reason was that they all liked Gwennie in spite of—or maybe because of—her deviltries. "An amusing compound of mischief and precocity," said Uncle Klon, who liked to be amused.

"A darn leetle minx," said Lazarre, but he ran his legs off for her. "A child of Beelzebub," said Salome, but kept the old stone cooky-jar full of hop-and-go-fetch-its for Gwennie. Gwennie might be saintly or devilish as the humour took her, but she was not a bit stuck-up about her looks and she had Annie Vincent's kind, ungrudging heart and Luther Lesley's utter inability to hold any spite. As for Marigold, she and Gwennie had some terrible spats, but they had so much fun between that the fights didn't greatly matter. Though Gwennie had a poisonous little tongue when she got mad and said some things that rankled—especially about Clementine.

Clementine's picture had been left on the orchard room wall when most of Old Grandmother's faded brides had been packed away in the oblivion of the garret. There she hung in

186

the green gloom, with her ivory-white face, her sleek braided flow of hair, her pale beautiful hands and her long-lashed eyes forever entreating the lily. Marigold felt she would not have hated Clementine so much if she had looked squarely and a little arrogantly at you like the other brides—if you could have met her eyes and defied them.

But that averted, indifferent gaze, as if you didn't matter at all—as if what you felt or thought didn't matter at all. Oh, for the others Clementine Lesley might be dead, but for Marigold she was torturingly alive and she knew Father had only married Mother for a housekeeper. All his love belonged to that disdainful Lady of the Lily. And Gwennie, suspecting this secret wound in Marigold's soul, turned the barb in it occasionally by singing the praises of Clementine's picture.

The only faint comfort Marigold had was a hope that if Clementine had lived to be old she might have become enormously fat like her mother up at Harmony village. A good many Lawrences lived in or about Harmony and none of them, it was whispered, cared very much for Lorraine, though they were always painfully polite to her. Marigold knew this, as she knew so many things older folk never dreamed of her knowing, and always felt whenever old Mrs. Lawrence's eye rested on her that she had no right to exist. If she could only have believed thoroughly that Clementine would have looked like her mother when she grew old she would not have been jealous of her.

For old Mrs. Lawrence was a funny old dame, and one is never jealous of funny people.

Mrs. Lawrence was very proud of her resemblance to Queen Victoria and dressed up to it. She had three chins, a bosom like a sheep and a harmless, if irritating, habit of shedding hairpins wherever she went. Her favourite adjective was "Christian," and she had a very decided dislike to being reminded that she was either fat or old. She constantly wore a brooch with Clementine's hair in it and when she talked of her daughter—as she did very often—she snuffled. In spite of this, Mrs. Lawrence had many good qualities and was a decent old soul enough, as Uncle Klon said.

But Marigold saw only her defects and foibles because that was all she wanted to see in Clementine's mother; and it rejoiced her when Uncle Klon poked fun at Mrs. Lawrence's pet peculiarity of saving all her children's boots. It was said she had a roomful of them—every boot or shoe that her family of four had ever worn from their first little slipper up. Which did nobody any harm and need not have given Marigold such fierce pleasure. But when was jealousy ever reasonable?

2

Uncle Peter's son Royal had married and brought his bride home to Harmony. She was said to be unusually pretty, and even Aunt Josephine had said she was the most exquisite bride she had ever seen. There had been the usual clan jollifications in her honour, and now Uncle Klon and Aunt Marigold were giving a party for her—a "fancy dress" dance where all the young fry were to be masked. It sounded very int'resting to Marigold and very provocative to Gwennie as they listened to Mother and Grandmother talking it over at the supper-table. Both wished intensely that they could see that party. But both knew that they must go right to bed as soon as Mother and Grandmother had gone.

"And be good little girls," said Grandmother warningly.

"There's no fun in being a good little girl," said Gwennie, with a pout at Grandmother. "I don't see why we can't go to that party, too."

"You were not invited," said Mother.

"You are not old enough to go to parties," said Grandmother.

"Your day is coming," comforted Salome.

Uncle Klon came out from Harmony for them in his car— already dressed in his fancy costume—a great, flowered-velvet coat that had belonged to some Great-great across the sea, a real sword, and a powdered wig. With lace ruffles at wrist and breast. Mother and Grandmother were not wearing fancy dress, but Grandmother was very splendid in velvet and Mother very pretty in brown brocade and pearls. And Marigold felt delightfully that it was just like a bit out of a story, and she wished she could go up the hill and tell Sylvia about it. She had never even seen Sylvia since Gwennie came, and there were times when she was consumed with longing for her. But she never went up the hill. Gwennie simply must not find out about Sylvia.

"Run on in, kidlets, and go to bed now," said Uncle Klon, grinning rather maliciously, because he knew perfectly well how they hated it.

"Don't call me '*kidlet*,'" flashed Gwen.

After the car had purred off in the twilight, she sat down on the veranda steps and would not say a word. Such a visitation of silence was rare with Gwennie, but Marigold rather welcomed it. She was glad to sit and dream in the lovely twilight, while Lucifer skulked like a black demon among the flower-beds.

It was not the Lucifer of Old Grandmother's days. That Lucifer had gone where good cats go. But there had been another Lucifer to step into his four shoes, looking so exactly like him that in a few weeks it seemed just the same old Lucifer. There had been a procession of Lucifers and Witches for generations at Cloud of Spruce, all looking so much alike that Phidime and Lazarre thought they were one and the same and concluded they were the Old Lady's devils.

Salome, after milking, came along.

"I'm going to bed," she said. "I've got a headache. And it's time you went, too. There's lemonade and cookies for you in the pantry."

"Lemonade and cookies," said Gwennie scornfully, after Salome had gone in, leaving a couple of minxes at large in Cloud of Spruce. "Lemonade and cookies! And they are having all kinds of ices and salads and cakes at the party."

"There's no use thinking about that," said Marigold with a sigh. "It's 9 o'clock. We might as well go to bed."

"Bed! *I'm* going to the party."

Marigold stared.

"The party? But you can't."

"Maybe I can't. But I will. I've been thinking it all out. We'll just go. It's only a mile in—we can easily walk it. We must be dressed up ourselves so that if any one sees us they'll think we belong to the party. There's heaps of things in those chests in the garret and I'll make masks. We won't go in the house—just peep in at the windows and see all the dresses and the fun."

So far had evil communications corrupted good manners that Marigold felt no qualms of conscience at all. It would certainly be int'resting. And she was quite wild to see that "exquisite bride" and all the wonderful costumes. Uncle Peter's Pete, she had heard, was going as a devil. The only thing that gave her to think was whether they could really get away with it.

"What if Grandmother catches us?" she said.

"A fig for your grandmother. She won't—and if she does, what then? She can't kill us. Have some gizzard."

Marigold had lots of "gizzard" and in ten minutes they were in the garret tiptoeing cautiously lest Salome hear them in the retreat of her kitchen chamber. The garret was rather a spooky place by candlelight, and Marigold had never been there after dark before.

Great bunches of dried herbs hung from the nails in the rafters, together with bundles of goose-wings, hanks of yarns and various discarded coats. Grandmother's big loom, where she still wove homespun blankets, was before the window. An old, old piano was in one corner and there was some legend of a ghostly lady who played on it by times. And there was a chest under the eaves filled with silken dresses in which gay girls had danced years ago. Marigold had never seen the contents of that chest, but Gwennie seemed to know all about them. She must have been rummaging, Marigold thought. Gwennie *had*—one rainy day when nobody knew where she was—and she knew what was in the big chest, but she did not know—and neither did Marigold—that the little gown of misty green crêpe with tiny daisies sprinkled over it and a satin girdle with a rhinestone buckle in it, which was lying in a box on the top of the contents of the chest, had been a dress of Clementine's. Marigold knew that Clementine had been buried in her wedding-dress and that old Mrs. Lawrence had taken away the rest of her pretty gowns. But this one had been overlooked; perhaps Mrs. Lawrence did not know it still existed. The first Mrs. Leander had her own reasons for keeping it and it had remained in the box in which she had placed it all those years.

"Here's the very thing for you," said Gwen. "*I'm* going as a fortune-teller, with this scarlet cloak and hood and the pack of cards. They're all here together—somebody must have worn them once to a fancy ball."

Marigold fingered the emerald satin of the girdle lovingly. She adored satin.

"But I can't wear this," she objected. "It's miles too big for me."

"Put it on," ordered Gwen. "I can fix it for you. I'm a crackerjack at that. Ma says I'm a born dressmaker. Let's go down to our room. Salome'll hear us creaking about up here."

Marigold put on the daisy dress, with its pretty, short sleeves of lace and its round low neck. Oh, it *was* pretty even if it were old-fashioned and wrinkled. Marigold was tall for her ten years and Clementine had been small and slight; still the dress was too long—and loose. But resourceful Gwennie, with a paper of safety-pins, worked marvels. The skirt was looped up at intervals all around and the pins hidden under clusters of daisies Gwen got off an old hat and which matched the daisies in the dress admirably.

"Now get your good slippers and pink silk stockings," commanded Gwen, sprinkling her own cloak and the green dress lavishly with Mother's violet water. "I've got to make our masks."

Which she proceeded to do, slashing ruthlessly into Old Grandmother's widow "fall" of stiff black crêpe. Then she put on her own red stockings and fixed up a "wand" for herself out of an old umbrella handle with a silvery Christmas-tree ball at the end and a Japanese snake of scarlet paper wreathed around the handle. Nobody could deny that Gwen was past mistress in her own particular brand of magic, and Marigold was lost in admiration of her cleverness. A few minutes later two black-faced figures, one in green and one in red, slipped silently out of Cloud of Spruce and fled along the dark Harmony road, while Salome slept the sleep of the just in the kitchen chamber and Lucifer told the Witch of Endor that he'd be condemned if he ever let that young demon from Rush Hill walk him about the yard on his hind legs again.

3

Marigold, who was never frightened in the dark if she had any one with her, enjoyed the walk to the village. It was a fairy night, with eerie pixie voices in the bracken. Why were the clouds racing across the moonlit sky in such a hurry? To what mysterious sky-tryst were they hastening? An occasional rabbit frisked across the moonlit road. Marigold was half sorry when they reached the village.

Luckily Uncle Klon's house was in the outskirts, so they had no need of traversing the streets. They slipped up the side lane, squirmed through a gap in the privet hedge, boldly walked across the lawn and found themselves at the window of the big room where the dancing was going on. It was open and the blind was up, and they had a full view of the inside.

Marigold caught her breath with delight. Oh, it was fairyland. It was like a little glimpse into another world. For the second time in her life Marigold thought it might be really quite nice to be grown up. She remembered the first time. Long ago, when she had been only six, curled up on the ottoman in the spare room, watching an eighteen-year-old cousin dressing for a dance. When would she be like that? Not for twelve years. She groaned aloud.

"What's the matter, Sugar-pie? Sick?"

"No. It's only—it takes so long to grow up," sighed Marigold.

"Not so long as you think," remarked Grandmother, passing through the hall.

And now again, for a moment, Marigold felt that it really look too long to grow up.

The room was rosily lighted by a gay enormous Chinese lantern hung from the ceiling. The floor was filled with dancers in the most wonderful dresses. There was gaiety in the very air. Lovely low laughter was everywhere, drifting out over the lawn in front and the flower-garden behind. Aunt Marigold's dog was howling heart-brokenly to the music in his kennel. Such flowers—such lights—such music—such dresses. Most of the younger guests were masked but few of the older ones were, and Marigold liked best to watch them because she knew them. There was Aunt Anne, in grey lace over amber silk—Marigold had never seen Aunt Anne so magnificent before! Cousin Jen, with a diamond wreath in her hair, and Cousin Barbara, who always had runs in her stockings, and Cousin Madge, who was the best dancer in the Lesley clan. Her very slippers would have danced by themselves the night through. Aunt Emma, who still wore her hair pompadour and old Uncle Percy, whose wife had her hair bobbed three months before he ever noticed it. Old Uncle Nathaniel, with his great shock of grey hair reaching to his shoulders and looking, so Uncle Klon was wont to say, like a lion that had eaten a Christian who disagreed with him. And, sitting maskless by Aunt Marigold in the palm corner, a creature so lovely, in her gown of pale pink chiffon embroidered with silver, with her hair folded about her head like a golden hood, that Marigold felt at once that this was the "exquisite bride." *Exquisite* was the word. Marigold could hardly drag her eyes from her. It had been worth it all, just to see her.

Mother was dancing—actually dancing—and Grandmother was sitting by the wall, looking as if she didn't think much of fox-trots and tangos. Beside her, a stately old dowager in mauve satin, with hair arranged a la Victoria, and a cameo brooch with Clementine's hair in it. The sight of Mrs. Lawrence spoiled things for Marigold. She was quite ready to turn away when Gwen said,

"We've seen all we can see here. Let's take a sneak around to the dining-room and have a look at the supper."

But the dining-room blinds were down and they could see nothing.

"We'll go right in and see it," said Gwen.

"Oh, do you think its safe?"

"Of course, it's safe. Look at all the rigs here. We'll never be noticed. I'm going to see all that's to be seen, you bet."

In they went. As Gwen said, nobody noticed them. The supper-table proved such a dream that they hung over it breathlessly. Never in her life had Marigold seen such *pretty* eats—such dainty cakes and cakelets, such wonderful striped sandwiches, such beautiful dishes. Cloud of Spruce could put up a solid banquet, but this alluring daintiness was something new. Gwen perceived sourly that there was no chance of "swiping" anything—there were too many waitresses around, so, after they had looked their fill, she pulled Marigold grumpily away.

"Let's take a peep at the other room again and get out."

Hitherto all had gone well. They were reckless with success. Boldly they crossed the hall and boldly they stood in the doorway of the dancing-room. The floor was not so crowded now. The August night was warm and many of the dancers had gone out to the moonlit lawn. More of the old folks were sitting around the room. Mrs. Lawrence was more Queen-Victorian than ever as she languidly plied a huge ostrich fan of the vintage of the nineties. Old Uncle Percy was down at the end of the hall telephoning, and shouting at the top of his voice as usual. Marigold thought of the clan story about him and snickered.

"What is that racket?" a caller in Uncle Percy's office had once asked.

"Oh, that's only old Mr. Lesley talking to his wife down in Montague," the junior partner had replied.

"Well, why doesn't he phone her instead of yelling across the Island like that?" said the caller.

Gwen turned to see why Marigold was shaking with laughter. Then the end of the world came. Gwen stepped on a small ball that somehow happened to be lying under the fringe of the portière, shot wildly into the room and fell with a curdling scream. As she felt herself shooting she grabbed Marigold—who did not fall but went staggering across the room on the slippery floor and there sat neatly down at the very feet of old Mrs. Lawrence, who had just begun to tell Grandmother how many times she had had the flu.

The next moment Mrs. Lawrence was all but in hysterics, and the room was full. Marigold had scrambled to her feet and was standing there dazedly, but Gwen was still sprawled on the floor. It was Uncle Klon who picked her up and stripped the mask from her face.

"I knew it was you." He stood her beside Marigold, from whose face some one else had removed the mask.

"Oh, Marigold," cried Mother in horror. But old Mrs. Lawrence was still the centre of attraction. Until she could be revived and calmed nobody had any time to spare for Gwen and Marigold.

"Clementine's dress—Clementine's dress," Mrs. Lawrence was shrieking and sobbing. "The dress—she wore—when she came—in to tell me she had just—promised to marry—Leander Lesley. I didn't think—you'd let—your daughter—insult me so—Lorraine."

"Oh, I had nothing to do with it—truly I hadn't," almost sobbed Mother.

"My heart broke—when Clementine died—and now to have it brought up like this—*here*—" people made out between Mrs. Lawrences yoops. "Oh—I shouldn't—have come. I had a presentiment—one of my dark—forebodings came to me."

"Calm yourself, Mrs. Lawrence—here, try a sip of water," said Aunt Marigold.

"Calm—myself! It's—enough—to kill me. We all—die—sudden—unexpected—death—Oh, Lorraine—Lorraine—you took her place—but your daughter—might have left—her dress—her sacred—little—dress—alone."

"Oh, I didn't know," cried Marigold. She wanted to cry—but cry she would not before all those people. Had not Old Grandmother once said that a Lesley should never cry before the world? Yet it was plain to be seen she had involved Mother in some terrible disgrace. All the sense of mystery and romance had fled. She felt that she and Gwennie were only naughty, silly children who had been ignominiously found out.

Mrs. Lawrence yooped more wildly than ever.

"You'd better have her carried upstairs," said Aunt Marigold. "She really has a weak heart—I'm afraid—"

"Oh, Clementine—Clementine," wailed Mrs. Lawrence. "To think—of the dress—you wore—being *here*. That—dreadful—child—Lorraine—how could you—"

Gwen, who had hitherto been rather dazed and sobered by the suddenness of the catastrophe, now wrenched her shoulder from Uncle Klon's restraining hand and sprang forward.

"Shut your face, you old screech-owl," she said furiously. "You've been told Aunt Lorraine had nothing to do with it. Neither had Marigold. It was *me* found that mouldy old dress and made Marigold put it on. Now, get that through your dippy old head and stop making a fuss over nothing. Oh, glare—glare! You'd like to boil me in oil and pick my bones, but I don't care *that* that for you, you fat old *cow*."

And Gwen snapped her fingers under outraged Queen Victoria's very nose.

Mrs. Lawrence, finding some one else could make more noise than she could, ceased yooping. She got on her feet, scattering a shower of hairpins on the floor, with the noted Carberry temper sticking out of every kink and curve of her abundant figure, and assisted by Aunt Marigold and Uncle Percy, moved slowly to the stairs.

"One must—make allowances—of course," she sobbed, for the things—children will do. I am—glad—it wasn't your fault—Lorraine. I didn't—think—I had—deserved that—of you."

"Dear Mrs. Lawrence, don't be angry," implored Lorraine.

"Angry—oh, no. I'm not angry—I'm only—heart-broken. If God—"

"You might as well leave God out of it," said Gwen.

"Gwen, keep quiet," said Uncle Klon furiously.

Whereupon Gwen threw back her head and yelled loud and long.

Everybody was now in the room or the hall, or crowding up to the windows outside. Marigold felt as if everyone in the world were staring at her.

"Could you run us home, Horace?" said Grandmother wearily. "I'm tired—and this has about finished me. Do you want to stay for supper, Lorraine?"

"No—oh, no," said Lorraine, struggling to keep back her tears.

In the back seat of the car Marigold cried for sorrow and Gwen howled for vexation of spirit. But Uncle Klon laughed so uproariously that Grandmother said nervously:

"Horace, *do* pay attention to your steering. I don't see how you can laugh. It's been simply a terrible affair. If it had been any one but old Mrs. Lawrence!"

"Good for her," said Uncle Klon. "I don't believe any one ever told her the truth about herself before. It was priceless."

Gwen stopped sniffling and pricked up her ears. After all, there *was* something nice about Uncle Klon.

"But it *must* have been a shock to see Clementine's dress suddenly come before her like that," said Grandmother. What was the matter with Grandmother's voice? Grandmother couldn't be laughing—she *couldn't*. But was she trying *not* to laugh? "You know, Horace, she really worshipped Clementine—"

"Clementine was a good little scout," said Uncle Klon. "I always liked her. It was to her credit that she wasn't spoiled by such a silly old mother."

"She was a pretty thing," said Grandmother. "I remember her in that dress. People raved about her skin and her hands."

"Clem certainly had pretty hands. It was a pity she had such huge feet," said Uncle Klon.

"She couldn't help her big feet," rebuked Grandmother.

"Of course not. But they were certainly—generous," laughed Uncle Klon. "No wonder the old lady kept all her boots. Too much good leather to waste. Clem had only one quarrel in her life that she never made up. The quarrel with Emmy Carberry. Emmy was going to marry a man neither the Carberrys nor the Lawrences approved of. 'I wouldn't be in your shoes for the world, Emmy,' said Clem solemnly."

"'Don't worry, Clem darling,' said Emmy, sticking out a foot in her little Number Two's beside poor Clem's brogans. 'You could never get into them.' Of course, Clem never forgave her."

Just then in a twinkle something happened to poor, crushed, weeping Marigold in the back seat. The spirit of jealousy departed from her forever—at least as far as Clementine was concerned. *Clementine had big feet.* And Mother had feet that even Uncle Klon thought perfection. Oh—Marigold smiled through her tears in the darkness—oh, she could afford to pity Clementine.

"Give me a good reason why I shouldn't take the hide off you," said Uncle Klon as he lifted Gwen from the car.

"I made you laugh," said Gwen saucily.

"You shameless young hussy," said Uncle Klon.

Grandmother said nothing. Of what use was it saying anything to Gwen? Of what use was it trying to drown fish? And she was going home the next evening. Besides, in her secret soul, Grandmother was not sorry that Caroline Lawrence had got her "come uppance" at last.

"Well, this is the end of Wednesday. Now for Thursday. But they might have given us a bite to eat," grumbled Gwen as she rolled into bed. "I wish I'd swiped that little plate of striped sandwiches. But did you ever see anything so funny as that old dragon yowling? Didn't I shut her up! I hope the devil flies away with her before morning. After all I'm glad I'm going home to-morrow night, Marigold. I like you better than I ever dreamed I'd do after Aunt Jo's sickening praises. But your grandmother gets my goat."

"Aren't you going to say your prayers?" reminded Marigold.

"No use waking God up at this hour of the night," said Gwen drowsily.

She was sleeping like a lamb before Marigold had finished her prayers. Marigold was very very thankful and told God so. Not exactly that Clementine had big feet, of course, but that the horrible feeling of hatred and jealousy had gone completely out of her little heart. It was *so* comfortable.

Mother gave Marigold a little scolding in the morning.

"Mrs. Lawrence might have died of heart-failure. Think how you would have felt. As it is, we heard this morning that she cried all night—cried *violently*," Mother added, fearing that Marigold was not just alive to the awfulness of what she had done.

"Never you worry," said Salome. "It served old Madam right. Her and her old boots. Thinking she's like Queen Victoria. But all the same, I'm thankful that limb of Satan is going home to-night. I should really like to have a few minutes' peace. I feel as if I'd been run through a meat-chopper these three weeks. Heaven help the clan when *she* grows up."

"Amen," said Lucifer with an emphatic whisk of his tail.

Gwennie went home that evening.

"Now maybe we can call our souls our own again," said Salome. And yet she did not say it very briskly. Nor did she snub Lazarre when he remarked mournfully,

"By gosh, you t'ink somebody was die in de house."

The lost serenity of Cloud of Spruce had returned to it, only slightly rippled next day by the arrival of an inky postcard from Gwen, addressed to Grandmother.

"I forgot to tell you that I dropped one of your best silver spoons through a crack in the apple-barn floor day before yesterday. I think you can get it easily if you crawl under the barn."

Marigold missed her badly for two days and in a lesser degree for the third. But after all, it was very nice to be alone with Sylvia again. Laughter and frolics were good things, but one didn't want to laugh and frolic *all* the time. She was like one tasting the beauty of quiet after days of boisterous, stimulating wind. The velvet faces of the pansies were waiting for her in the twilight and her own intimate, beloved trees welcomed her once more to their fraternity. When she shut the little Green Gate behind her she went into a different world—where one could be happy and have beautiful hours without being noisy all the time. She turned and looked down on the old vine-hung house and the harbour beyond. There was no sound in the great quiet world but the song of the wind. And there were soft, dewy shadows in every green meadow-nook of Mr. Donkin's farm.

"If I could have picked my place to be born, I'd have picked Cloud of Spruce," she whispered, holding out her arms as if she wanted to put them around the house—this beautiful old place that so many hands had made and so many hearts had loved.

And Clementine's ghost was forever laid. The next time she went to the graveyard she stole over and put a little flower on Clementine's grave—poor pretty Clementine. She no longer felt that she wanted to push her away from Father's side. And she knew now that Father hadn't married Mother just for a housekeeper. For she had told Mother the whole story, and Mother had laughed a little and cried a little.

"*I* was never jealous of Clementine. They were children. He did love her very dearly. But to me he gave the love of his manhood. I *know*."

So Marigold had no further grudge against Clementine's picture. She could look at it calmly and agree that it was very beautiful. But once she gave herself the satisfaction of remarking to it,

"It's a good thing your feet don't show."

CHAPTER XIV

Bitterness of Soul

1

"Here's a new morning," said Marigold blithe as the day. Somehow she was unusually happy that autumn-tinted morning as she went to school. She always felt as if she had wings on a day like this. She loved October—loved it well in its first crimson pomp, when frosted leaves hung like a flame and the asters along the road were like pale purple songs; and even better in its later quiet of brown autumnal fields and the shadowy interfoldings of the hills over the bay; with its evenings full of the nice smell of burning leaves in Lazarre's bonfires and all its apples to be picked and stored in the apple-barn, until such time as it grew too cold and they must be put away in barrels in the cellar.

A group of girls tittered a little as Marigold passed them on the playground. She did not mind very much. Marigold was, in truth, rather a lonely creature in school. She had never "made up" with any of the girls particularly, and with the new seats that held only one there was not the olden chance for intimacies. Not one of them went her way home. She did not quarrel with them and she played games with them at noon-hour and recess, but in some mysterious way she was not of them and they faintly resented it. "Stuck-up," they called her; though Marigold was not in the least stuck-up.

The sense of cleavage deepened as she grew older, instead of disappearing. Sometimes Marigold felt wistfully that it would be nice to have a real chum, of the kind you read about in books—not a fitful visitor like Varvara or Gwennie, bringing a wild whirl of colour into your life and then vanishing as completely as if they had never existed. But she could not find her in Harmony school. And being of a nature that could not compromise with second best when best was denied Marigold made no lesser friendships. There was always Sylvia—though Sylvia was not *quite* as real as she had once seemed. The old magic still worked but it was not quite so magical now.

This morning Marigold felt something new in the school atmosphere. It was not her imagination that the girls whispered and looked at her—with much of curiosity and a little malice. Marigold felt it all through the forenoon and at recess, but no one said anything in particular to her until noon-hour. Then, as her class sat in a circle among the fern-smothered spruce-stumps on the banks of the brook below the schoolhouse the barrage opened.

"How do you like Mr. Thompson, Marigold?" asked Em Stanton with a giggle.

Marigold wondered why upon earth Mr. Thompson's name was dragged into it. He was the new minister who had come to Harmony in the spring. Marigold was not as yet vitally interested in new ministers. It had been a rather exciting time for the older folks. It would be hard to fill old Mr. Henry's place—Mr. Henry who had filled the pulpit of Harmony church for thirty years and was "a saint if ever there was one."

"He used to make me weep six times every Sunday," sighed Miss Amelia Martin. "I hoped my time would come before his. I've always felt he would be such a lovely man to bury you."

"Oh, Lord," Aunt Kitty Standish had prayed at the first Aid meeting after his retirement, "Oh, Lord, send us as good a minister as Mr. Henry—but, oh, Lord, you can't do it."

Nobody thought Mr. Thompson as good but he seemed the best of the candidates.

"He's a good preacher," said Salome, "but its a pity he's a

widower. He'll marry in the congregation and that'll spoil him."
Adding, however, by way of a comforting after-thought, "But I'm
glad they've picked him. I like a comfortable-looking minister."

Mr. Thompson had one daughter about Marigold's age—
round and rosy little Jane Thompson, who went, however, to
the village school, the church and manse being there, so that
Marigold saw little of her save in Sunday school, where they were
in the same class. Jane always knew her golden text and memory-
verses and cathechism-questions perfectly well—one would
expect a minister's daughter to do that. But it didn't make her any
the more int'resting, Marigold thought. As for Mr. Thompson,
she liked him when she thought about him at all—which was,
to tell the truth, only when he called at Cloud of Spruce. She
liked the jolly, unministerial twinkle in his eye especially. Now,
why should Em Stanton be so suddenly interested in her feelings
towards Mr. Thompson? A disagreeable little sensation came
over Marigold—as if a faint chill wind had blown over the secret
places of her soul.

"I like Mr. Thompson very well," she said stiffly.

Em gave another irritating snigger and exchanged glances
with the other girls.

"That is a good thing," she said significantly.

They expected Marigold to ask why it was a good thing, but
she would not. She bit a dainty little crescent out of a hop-and-
go-fetch-it and chewed it remotely.

"How will you like him for a stepfather?" said Velma Church
slyly.

That particular hop-and-go-fetch-it was never eaten. Marigold
laid it down in her box and stared at Velma.

"Didn't you *know*?"

"Know what?" said Marigold through pale lips.

"That your mother is going to marry him?"

Marigold wondered what had happened to her—or to the
world. Had somebody slapped her in the face? Had the sun been
blotted out of the sky?

"I don't—believe it—" she said helplessly.

"Everybody says so," said Em triumphantly. "We thought you knew, of course. It's funny your mother hasn't told you. Why, he spends half his time at Cloud of Spruce."

This was, of course, an exaggeration. But Marigold suddenly remembered with horror that Mr. Thompson had made a great many calls lately. Of course Grandmother had had a slight attack of bronchitis; but a dreadful conviction assailed her that Mr. Henry had never called so often, even when Salome had pneumonia. She stared miserably at Em.

"They're to be married before spring, *I* heard," said Fanny Collins. "Your mother was in Summerside the other day helping him pick paper for the manse. Aunt Lindy saw them."

"My, won't *your* nose be out of joint," said Sally McLean.

"You'll have to be Marigold Thompson after the wedding," said Lula Nelson.

"They'll send you to a boarding-school, true's you live," said Dot Church.

None of these jabs produced any sign of life in Marigold. She sat as one stunned. Oh, if she could only be alone—far, far away from these hateful girls—to face this!

"Ma says your mother isn't a bit suitable for a minister's wife," said Velma.

"Too dressy and extravagant," added Em.

"Aunt Beth says his first wife was the finest woman that ever lived," said Pet Dixon.

"It's a wonder your mother would marry a bluenose," said Janet Irving.

"I guess she has a hard enough time with the old lady," said Pet.

"Ma says Mrs. Leander has perked up amazing this fall," said Lula.

The school-bell rang and the ring of malicious faces melted away. Marigold followed them slowly into the school. Her feet were like lead and her spirit that had "flown on feathers" in the morning was heavier still. The world had all at once got so very dark. Oh, *could* it be true? It couldn't—Marigold had another awful recollection.

"Mrs. Lesley's engaged," Salome had said gently one day the preceding week, as she had shut the door in the face of a too-persistent insurance-man.

Oh, yes, it must be true.

"Salome," said Marigold that evening, "do you think God ever does things out of spite?"

"Just listen to her," said Salome. "You mustn't ask such wicked questions. That's as bad as anything Gwen Lesley could say."

"I'm sorry," said Marigold with more persistence, "but *does* He?"

"Of course not," said Salome. "It's the Old Gentleman that's spiteful. What's the matter with you? You don't look just right. Have you got a cold?"

Marigold felt that a cold had got her. She was cold and sick to the core of her soul. Everything had been torn out of her little life at once. And not a word could she say to Mother about it.

2

Marigold had thought she was done forever with jealousy when she discovered the truth about Clementine's feet. And now she was in the grip of a jealousy tenfold worse. *That* had been merely a ghostly vexation of the soul. *This* was a burning torment of the heart. Perhaps Marigold was never more bitterly unhappy in all her life than she was during the two months following that day by the brook. Everything fed her suspicion and jealousy. She was filled with hate. She could not enjoy anything because she was hating Mr. Thompson so much. She even hated poor, innocent little Jane Thompson. Would Jane call Mother "mother"? If she did!

November came in, with its dark, dull twilights that made

Marigold feel grown up and old—with its mournful winds rustling the dead leaves on its cold, desolate, moonless nights— with its wintry song of old grey fields and the sorrowful grey ghosts of the goldenrod in the fence corners. And Mr. Thompson's motor-lights burning cheerfully at the gate in so many of its chill evenings. Marigold felt that it was going to be November forever. "To-morrow" had once been a word of magic to her. Now "to-morrow" would only be more cruel than to-day.

But it was a torturing satisfaction to hate Mr. Thompson. She felt sure she had always hated him. Lucifer certainly had—and cats *knew*. You couldn't hoodwink Lucifer. Nothing about him pleased Marigold any more. She remembered what Lazarre had once said about another Frenchman who had done something that reflected on his race.

"But you surely don't want to see him hanged," protested Salome.

"No—no—oh, no, course we not lak to see heem hang," acknowledged Lazarre, "but we lak to see heem *destroyed*."

That exactly expressed Marigold's feelings towards Mr. Thompson. She would not want to see him hanged but she would cheerfully have had him "destroyed." It was a certain ephemeral satisfaction to name the big dead Scotch thistle behind the apple-barn "Rev. Mr. Thompson" and cut it down and burn it. She looked at him drinking his tea and wished there were poison in the cup. Not enough to kill him—oh, no, just enough to make him awfully sick and disgusted with the idea of marrying any one. Once, when he grew angry over what some one in the church had done and pounded the table, Marigold had said under her breath to Mother, "See what a husband you'll have!"

She wished she could refuse to go to church but she could not do that, so she sat there scowling blackly at him. When he came to the house she was the very incarnation of disdain. And he never noticed it! To be disdainful and not have it noticed was unendurable. Half the time he couldn't even remember her name and called her Daffodil. Once he grew fatherly and tried to stroke her hair. "I'm not a cat," said Marigold rudely, jerking away. She had to beg his pardon for that. Cloud of Spruce couldn't imagine why Marigold had taken such a scunner to the minister.

"He preaches such lovely sermons," said Salome reproachfully. "He can draw tears to my eyes."

"So can onions," said Marigold savagely.

And yet when Em Stanton told her that Stanton *père* said Mr. Thompson was a shallow-pated creature Marigold flashed pale lightning at her. This would never do. If Mother were really going to marry him he must be defended.

"Oh, all right," said Em, walking off. "I didn't know you liked him. I didn't suppose any one could like a bluenose."

"He isn't a bluenose," said Marigold, who hadn't the slightest idea what a bluenose was.

"He *is*. Your Uncle Klon told me so himself the day he picked me up on the road. We met the minister in his car and your Uncle Klon said, 'Trust a bluenose to bust the speed-limit every time.' And *I* said, 'Is Mr. Thompson a bluenose?' and he said, 'The very bluest of them.' So there now!"

"But what is a bluenose?" demanded Marigold wildly. She *must* know the worst.

"Well, I'm not sure but I *think* it is a dope-fiend," said Em cautiously. "I asked Vera Church and she said she thought that's what it was. It's a terrible thing. They see hidjus faces wherever they look. There's nothing too bad for them to do. And they're that sly. Nobody would ever suspect them at first until they get so they can't hide it. Then they have to be put away."

Put away! What did "put away" mean? But Marigold would ask no more questions of Em. Every question answered seemed to make a bad matter worse. But if Mr. Thompson ever had to be "put away" she wished it might happen before he married Mother.

Things constantly happened that tortured her. Mr. Thompson came more and more often to Cloud of Spruce. He took Mother to Summerside to pick more wallpaper; he came one evening and said to Mother,

"I want to consult you about Jane's adenoids."

Mother took him into the orchard room and closed the door. Marigold haunted the hall outside like an uneasy little ghost. What was going on behind that closed door? *She* had a sore throat, but was Mother troubled over *that*? Not at all. She was wrapped up in Jane's adenoids—whatever they were.

When nothing happened to torture her she tortured herself. Would she have to leave dear Cloud of Spruce when Mother married Mr. Thompson? Or perhaps Mother would leave her all alone there with Grandmother, as Millie Graham's mother had done. And there would be no one to meet her any more when she came from school; or stand at the door in the twilight calling her in to shelter out of the dark; or sit by her bed and talk to her before she went to sleep. Though now her bedtime talks with Mother were not what they had been. Always some veil of strangerhood hung between them.

Lorraine feared her child was growing away from her— growing into the hard Blaisdell reserve perhaps. She could not ask Marigold what had changed her—that would be to admit change. When Aunt Anne wanted Mother to let Marigold go to her for a visit and Mother consented, Marigold refused almost tearfully—though she had once wanted so much to go. Suppose Mother would get married while she was away? Suppose that was why she wanted her to go to Aunt Anne's? And they wouldn't even have the same name! How terrible it would be to hear people say, "Oh, that is Marigold Lesley—Mrs. *Thompson's* daughter, you know."

They might even call her Marigold Thompson!

Marigold felt she could not bear it. Why, she wouldn't be wanted anywhere. Oh, couldn't something—or somebody— prevent it?

"I wonder if it would do any good to pray about it," she thought wearily and concluded it wouldn't. It would be of no use to pray against a minister, of course. Gwen had said she jumped up and down and screamed until she got her own way. But Marigold could not quite see herself doing that. Just suppose she did. Why the brides in the garret would come rushing down—Clementine would at last look up from her lily—Old Grandmother would jump out of her frame in the orchard room. But still Mother would marry Mr. Thompson. Mother who was looking so pretty and blooming this fall. Before she knew this ghastly thing Marigold had been so pleased when people said, "How well Lorraine is looking." Now it was an insult.

As Christmas grew near, Cloud of Spruce was fairly haunted by Marigold's sad little face. "How thin you're getting, darling," said Mother anxiously.

"Jane Thompson's fat enough," said Marigold pettishly.

Mother smiled. She thought Marigold was a little jealous of the rose-faced Jane. Probably some Josephinian person had been praising Jane too much. Mother thought she understood—and Marigold thought *she* understood. And still the gulf of misunderstanding between them widened and deepened.

Would this be the last Christmas she would ever spend with Mother? The day before Christmas they went to the graveyard as usual. Marigold crushed the holly wreath down on Fathers grave with savage intensity. *She* hadn't forgotten him, if Mother had.

"And I'll never call *him* 'Father,'" she sobbed. "Not if they kill me."

3

The Christmas reunion was at Aunt Marcia's that year, and Grandmother could not go because her bronchitis was worse and Mother would not leave her. Marigold was glad. She was in no mood for Christmas reunions.

In the afternoon Salome got Lazarre to hitch up the buggy and drove herself over to the village to see some old friends. She took Marigold with her and Marigold prowled about the streets while Salome gossiped. It was a very mild, still day. The wind had fallen asleep in the spruce woods behind South Harmony and great beautiful flakes were floating softly down. Some impulse she could not resist drew her to the manse. Would Mother soon be living I here? Such an ugly square house, with not even a tree about it. And no real garden. Only a little kitchen-plot off to one side. With an old pig rooting in it.

Marigold perceived that the pig was in Mr. Thompson's parsnip-bed. Well, what of it? *She* wasn't going to tell Mr. Thompson. He could look after his own parsnips. She turned and walked deliberately to the main street. Then she turned as deliberately back. If Mother were living in that manse in the spring she must have parsnips. Mother was so fond of parsnips.

Marigold went firmly up the walk and up the steps and to the door. There she stood for a few minutes, apparently turned to stone. The door was open. And the door of a room off the hall was open. An unfurnished room, still littered with the mess paperhangers make but with beautiful walls blossoming in velvety flowers. And Mr. Thompson was standing in this room with Third Cousin Ellice Lesley from Summerside. Marigold knew "Aunt" Ellice very well. A comfortable woman who never counted calories and always wore her hair in smooth glossy ripples just like the wave marks on the sand. Aunt Ellice was not handsome, but as old Mr. McAllister said, she was "a useful wumman—a verra useful wumman." She was also a well-off woman and she wore just now a very smart hat and a rich plush coat with a big red rose pinned to the collar.

And Mr. Thompson was kissing her!

Marigold turned and stole noiselessly away—but not before she had heard Mr. Thompson say,

"Sweetums," and Aunt Ellice say "Honey-boy!"

The pig was still rooting in the parsnips. Let him root—while the minister kissed women he had no business to kiss—women with complexions like tallow candles and ankles like sausages and eyes so shallow that they looked as if they were pasted on their faces. And called them "Sweetums!"

Marigold was so full of indignation for her mother's sake that she would not wait for Salome. She tore homeward through the white flakes to Cloud of Spruce, and found Mother keeping some tryst with the past before a jolly open fire in the orchard room.

"Mother," cried Marigold in breathless fury, "Mr. Thompson's kissing Aunt Ellice—in the manse—*kissing* her."

"Well, why shouldn't he kiss her?" asked Mother amusedly.

"Don't you—*care?*"

"Care? Why should I care? He is going to marry Aunt Ellice in two weeks' time."

Marigold stared. All her life seemed to have been drained out of her body and concentrated in her eyes.

"I—thought—that—*you* were going to marry him, Mother."

"Me! Why, Marigold, whatever put such a silly idea into your head, darling?"

Marigold continued to stare. Great tears slowly formed in her eyes and rolled down her cheeks.

"Marigold—Marigold!" Mother folded her arms about her and drew her to her knee. "Why are you so disappointed because I'm not going to marry Mr. Thompson?"

Disappointed!

"I'm so happy—so happy, Mother," sobbed Marigold. "I was so afraid you *were.*"

"And that's why you've been so funny to him. Marigold, why didn't you ask me—"

"I couldn't bear to. I was so afraid you'd say it was true."

Lorraine Lesley cuddled her baby closer. She understood and did not laugh at the torture the little soul had endured.

"Darling, no one who had loved your father could ever love any one else. I've *had* love—and now I have its memory—and *you.* That is enough for me."

"Mother," whispered Marigold, "were you—disappointed because—I wasn't a boy?"

"Never. Not for one minute. I wanted you to be a girl. And so did your father. There hadn't been a little girl at Cloud of Spruce for so long, he said."

Marigold sat very still with her face against her mother's. She knew this was one of the moments that last forever.

4

Mr. Thompson was such a nice man. Such a nice, jolly, friendly man. She hoped that pig hadn't eaten *all* his parsnips. She was dreadfully sorry for him because he wasn't going to get Mother, but Aunt Ellice would do very well. She was so useful. A ministers wife should be useful. And Jane was a darling. How jolly it was not to hate anybody any more. Life and she were good friends again.

It had stopped snowing. A big round silvery moon was floating up over a snowy hill. The little hollow in Mr. Donkin's field that would be a pool, blue-flagged, in summer, was a round white dimple, as if some giantess had pressed her finger down. The orchard was full of fine, faint blue shadows on the snow. It was a lovely world and life was beautiful. The paper that day had said a king's son had been born in Europe and a millionaire's son in Montreal. A far more interesting event which the paper had not chronicled, was that the Witch of Endor had three lovely kittens in the apple-barn. And to-morrow she would go up the hill and tryst again with Sylvia.

CHAPTER XV

One Clear Call

1

I am afraid that if Marigold could have defined her state of mind when her mother told her she must go to the missionary meeting in the church that evening, she would have said she was bored with the prospect. For a little girl who had three fourth cousins in the foreign-mission field it must be confessed that Marigold was shamefully indifferent to missionary work in general.

She had planned to spend the evening with Sylvia and she didn't want to exchange Sylvia's alluring company for a dull, stupid, poky, old missionary meeting. The adjectives are Marigold's, not mine, and if you blame her for them, please remember that very few lasses of eleven, outside of memoirs, have any very clear ideas of the heathen in their blindness. For Marigold, foreign missions were something that grown-ups and ministers naturally took to but which were far removed from her sphere of thought and action. So she didn't see why she should be dragged out to hear a foreign missionary speak. She had heard one the night she went with Gwennie—a queer, sun-burned spectacled man, tremendously in earnest but dreadfully dull. And Marigold considered she had had enough of it. But Grandmother could not go out after night because of her rheumatism and Salome had a sore foot; and Mother, for some strange reason, was set on going. It seemed that the speaker of the evening was a lady and an old

214

schoolmate of hers. She wanted Marigold for company. Marigold would have done anything and gone anywhere for Mother— even to a missionary meeting. So she trotted resignedly along the pleasant, star-lit road with Mother and thought mainly about the new dress of apricot georgette that Mother, in spite of Grandmother's pursed lips, had promised her for Willa Rogers's birthday-party.

Marigold got her first shock when the missionary rose to speak. Could that wonderful creature be a missionary? Marigold had never seen any one so entrancingly beautiful in her life. What strange, deep, dark, appealing eyes! What cheek of creamy pallor despite India's suns! What a crown of burnished, red-gold hair! What exquisite out-reaching hands that seemed to draw you magnetically whither they would! What a haunting voice, full of pathos and unnameable charm! And what a lovely, lovely white dress with a pale, seraphic-blue girdle hanging to the hem of it!

Dr. Violet Meriwether had not been speaking for ten minutes before Marigold was longing through all her soul to be a foreign missionary, with the uttermost ends of the earth for her inheritance. The only thing that surprised her was that there was no visible halo around Dr. Violet's head.

Oh, what a thrilling address! Marigold had a moment of amazed wonder at herself for ever supposing foreign missions were poky before she was swept out on that flood-tide of eloquence to a realm she had never known existed—a realm in which self-sacrifice and child-widows and India's coral strand were all blended together into something indescribably fascinating and appealing. Nay, more than appealing—demanding. Before Dr. Violet was half through her address Marigold Lesley, entranced in the old Lesley pew, was dedicating her life to foreign missions.

It was a sudden conversion but a very thorough one. Already Marigold felt that she was cut off forever from her old life—her old companions—her old dreams. *She* was not the silly, wicked little girl who had come unwillingly to the missionary meeting an hour ago, thinking of apricot dresses and fairy playmates on the hill. Not she. Consecrated. Set apart. All the rest of her life to follow that shining, upward path of service Dr. Violet Meriwether pointed out. Some day she, too, might be Dr. Marigold Lesley. Think of it. She had sometimes wondered whom she would like to resemble when she grew up. Mother? But Mother was "put upon." Everybody bossed her. But she had no longer any doubt. She wanted to be exactly like Dr. Violet Meriwether.

She hated Em Church for giggling behind her. She looked with scornful contempt at Elder MacLeod's four grown-up daughters. Why weren't *they* in the foreign-mission field? She almost died of shame when she sneezed rapidly three times in succession just when Dr. Violet was making her most impassioned appeal to the young girls. Was there not *one* in this church to-night who would answer, "Here Am I" to the "one-clear call"? And Marigold, who longed to spring to her feet and say it, could only sneeze until the great moment was passed and Dr. Meriwether had sat down.

Mr. Thompson followed with a few words. He lacked entirely the fascination of Dr. Meriwether, but one of his sentences struck burningly across Marigold's thrilled soul. A foreign missionary, he said, must be calm, serene, patient, tactful, self-reliant, resourceful and deeply religious. Marigold remembered every one of his adjectives. It was something of a large order but Marigold in her uplift had no doubt she could fill it eventually. And she would begin at once to prepare herself for her life-work. At once. She went down the aisle as if she trod on air. Oh, how wicked and foolish she had been before this wonderful night! But now her face was—what had been Dr. Meriwether's phase—"set towards the heights"—distant, shining heights of service and sacrifice. Marigold shivered in ecstasy.

Tommy Blair was going down the opposite aisle. Marigold had hated Tommy Blair bitterly ever since the day he had written across the front page of her reader in his sprawling, inky hand,

"This book is one thing, my fist is another. If you steal the one, you'll feel the other."

But she must forgive him—a missionary must forgive everybody. She smiled at him so radiantly across the church that Tommy Blair went out and told his cronies that Marigold Lesley was "gone" on him.

2

Marigold could not tell her mother of her great resolve. It would make poor Mother feel so badly. If Father had been alive, it would be different. But she was all Mother had. That was where part of the self-sacrifice lay. As for telling Grandmother, Marigold never dreamed of it. But she plunged at once with all her might into the preparation for her life-work. Grandmother and Mother knew there was something in the wind, though they couldn't imagine what. I do not know if they considered Marigold calm, serene, patient, tactful, etc., but I do know they thought her very funny.

"Whatever it is I suppose it will run its course," said Grandmother resignedly, out of her experience. But Mother was secretly a little bit worried. Something must be the matter when Marigold said she would rather not have a new apricot dress— her old one was quite good enough. And she didn't even want to go to Willa's party—only Grandmother insisted because the Rogerses would be offended. Marigold went under protest and condescended to the other little girls, pitying them for the dull, commonplace lives before them. Pitying Algie Rogers too. Every one knew his mother had vowed he should be a minister when he wanted furiously to be a carpenter. How different from her high, self-elected lot.

"My, but ain't Marigold Lesley getting stuck-up," Willa Rogers said.

Marigold laid aside the tiny diamond ring Aunt Marigold had given her on her last birthday. Consecrated people should not, she felt, wear diamond rings. Uncle Klon offered to get her one of the new striped silk parasols she had craved, but Marigold thanked him firmly and serenely and would he please give her a concordance instead. Uncle Klon chuckled and gave it to her. He did not know what particular magic Marigold was making now, but he knew she was getting a tremendous lot of satisfaction out of it.

She was. It was positive rapture to refuse the new ribbon hat-streamers for which her soul had once longed and wear her old hat to Cousin Nellie's wedding. Once Marigold had been interested in weddings. Who knew—when one grew up—? But that was past. She must never ever think of being married. Marigold was nothing if not thorough. Naught but counsels of perfection for her. She washed dishes and beat eggs and weeded her garden rapt as a saint.

She gave up reading everything except missionary literature. She pored over the missionary books from the Sunday-school library—especially one fascinating little fat brown volume, the biography of a missionary who had "prepared" herself from the age of six. Marigold felt she had lost many precious years. But she would do her best to catch up. She rose at five o'clock—once—to read the Bible and pray. *That* would sound well in a memoir. The said missionary had arisen at five o'clock every morning of her life from her sixth birthday. But said missionary did not have a Grandmother. That made all the difference.

The only thing that really hurt very badly was giving up Sylvia. At first Marigold felt that she could not—could not—do this. But she must. Sacrifice was not really sacrifice unless it hurt you. Dr. Violet had said so. She explained it all tearfully to Sylvia. Was it only fancy or did a mocking elfin-rill of laughter follow her down the orchard from the cloud of spruce? It almost seemed as if Sylvia didn't think she meant it.

Marigold tried to fill up the resulting gap in her life by imagining herself being carried about on the backs of elephants and rescuing child-widows from burning, at the risk of her life. To be sure, Dr. Violet had not said anything about riding on elephants—she had even mentioned a prosaic motor-car—and Mr. Thompson said widows were no longer burned. But no doubt something just as dreadful was done to them. Marigold stifled her longing for Sylvia in rescuing them by the dozen. Oh, I fancy Uncle Klon was right.

Marigold had some moments of agonised wonder if she would ever be able to pray in public. She tried to make a small beginning by saying "Amen" under her breath whenever Mr. Thompson said anything in his prayers that appealed to her. And it was very hard to decide where she would go as a missionary. She shuddered for days between Japanese earthquakes and Indian snakes. Until she got a book about the lepers in India. The lepers carried the day. *They* must be attended to, snakes or no snakes. She would be a missionary to the lepers. And meanwhile Grandmother was horribly cross because Marigold had forgotten to water the geraniums. She couldn't explain to Grandmother that she had forgotten because she was bringing an Indian village through a famine. But she was calm and serene under Grandmother's disapproval. Very.

3

For two or three weeks this was all very well and satisfying. Then Marigold yearned for what Alexander the Great would have called more worlds to conquer and Dr. Violet Meriwether might have termed a wider field of service. The heroine of the memoirs was always visiting some one who was sick or in trouble and working wonders of consolation. Marigold felt she should do the same. But whom to visit? There was nobody sick or in trouble—that Marigold knew of—near Cloud of Spruce just then. Unless it might be Mrs. Delagarde. The thought of her came to Marigold like an inspiration. Mrs. Delagarde of the black robes and the sad, sad face. Who never went anywhere but wandered about in her big garden all day long in South Harmony.

Marigold had heard some one say that Mrs. Delagarde was a "little off." She did not know what that meant exactly but she felt sure any one with that sorrowful face was in need of comforting. She would go to see her and—and—what? Read the Bible to her as the Lady of the Memoirs had done? Marigold could not see herself doing that. But she would just go to see her—and perhaps the way would be opened up. In the Memoirs a way was always opened up. Marigold slipped up to her room before she went, and said a little special prayer. A very earnest, sincere little prayer, in spite of the fact that it was couched largely in the language of the Memoirs. Then she stole away through the fragrant evening.

Marigold had a moment of panic when she found herself really inside Mrs. Delagarde's gate facing a grim house that looked black against the sunset. But a missionary must be self-reliant. A missionary must not give way to panic. With a gallant smile Marigold marched down the aisle of daffodils to where Mrs. Delagarde was standing among the pale gold of lemon lilies in the shadows, with an amber sky and dark hills behind her, staring unseeingly before her with her large, strange agate-grey eyes.

Mrs. Delagarde surprised Marigold. Her whole sad face lighted up with a wonderful radiance of joy. She stepped forward and held out her hands. Marigold was to be haunted for weeks by those long pale hands held out in supplication.

"Delight—Delight—you have come back to me—" she said.

Marigold let Mrs. Delagarde take her hands—put her arms round her—press her lips to her forehead. She suddenly felt very queer—and frightened. There was something about Mrs. Delagarde—and she was being drawn into the house. What was Mrs. Delagarde saying—in that quick, strange, passionate voice of hers, that wasn't like any voice Marigold knew?

"I've often seen you walking before me—with your face turned away. You'd never wait for me. But now you have come back, Delight. So you must have forgiven me. Have you forgiven me, Delight?"

"Oh—yes—yes." Marigold would have said "yes" to any question. She did not know what she was saying. She was no brave missionary—no ambitious candidate for Memoirs—she was only a very badly frightened little girl—shut up in a strange house with a strange—a very strange woman.

Again that wonderful flash of joy crossed Mrs. Delagarde's face.

"Come up to your room, Delight. It is all ready for you. I have kept it all ready. I knew you would come back to me sometime—when I had been punished enough. So I have kept it ready for you."

Marigold was being drawn up the stairs by that insistent arm—across the hall—into a room. A large, shadowy room with four great windows. And in the midst a huge white bed with something lying on it. Marigold felt a prickling in the roots of her hair—Was it—was it—?

"There is your big doll, Delight," said Mrs. Delagarde, laughing a little wildly. "I've kept it for you, you see. Take it up and play with it. I want to see you play, Delight. It's so long since I have seen you play. And your dresses are all in the closet for you. See."

She opened the closet-door and Marigold saw them—rows of dainty dresses hanging there, awfully like Bluebeard's wives in a picture-book she had.

Marigold found her voice—a shaky, panicky voice.

"Please may I go home now?" she gasped. "I—I think Mother will be wanting me. It's—getting late."

A look of alarm crossed Mrs. Delagarde's pale face—followed by a look of cunning.

"But you *are* home, Delight. You are my child—though you have left me so long. Oh, it was cruel to leave me so long. But I will not scold you—I will never scold you again. Now you have come back. You must never leave me again. Never. I am going to find your father and tell him you have come back. I have never spoken to him since you went away—but I will speak now. Oh, Delight, Delight!"

Marigold eluded the outstretched arms.

"Please, please let me go," she entreated desperately. "I'm not your little Delight—really I'm not—my name is Marigold Lesley. Please, dear Mrs. Delagarde, let me go home."

"You are still angry with me," said Mrs. Delagarde sorrowfully. "That is why you talk so. Of course you are Delight. Don't you think I know your golden hair? But you are angry with me because I whipped you that day before you went away. I will never do that again, Delight. You need not be afraid of me, darling. Tell me again that you forgive me, sweetest—tell me again that you forgive me."

"Oh, I do—I do." If only Mrs. Delagarde would let her out! But Mrs. Delagarde knelt down by her entreatingly.

"Oh, we will be so happy now that you have come back, Delight. Kiss me—kiss me. You have turned your face away from me so long, my golden-haired Delight."

Her voice was so appealing that Marigold, in spite of her terror, could not refuse. She bent forward and kissed Mrs. Delagarde—then found herself seized in a wild embrace and smothered with hungry kisses.

Marigold tore herself from the encircling arms and darted towards the door. But Mrs. Delagarde caught her as she reached it—pushed her aside with a strange little laugh and slipped out. Marigold heard the key turn in the lock. She was a prisoner in the house of a crazy woman. She knew now. *That* was what people meant when they called Mrs. Delagarde "a little off."

What could she do? Nothing. Nobody knew where she was. Alone in this horrible, big, darkening room with the shrouded windows. With those dreadful dresses of dead Delight hanging in the closet. With that terrible doll lying on the bed like a dead thing. With a huge, black bearskin muff on a little stand by the bed. What wild tale had Lazarre once told her about those big, old-fashioned bearskin muffs? That they were really witches and went out on moonlit nights and danced in the snow. There was a moon to-night—already its faint radiance was stealing into the room—suppose the muff began to dance around the room before her!

Marigold stifled the scream that rose to her lips. It might bring Mrs. Delagarde back. Nothing would be so dreadful as that—not even a bewitched bearskin muff. She was afraid even to move—but she managed to tiptoe to window after window. They were all nailed down—every one of them. Anyway, all of them opened on a steep bare wall. No chance of escape there. And through one she saw the home-light at Cloud of Spruce. Had they missed her? Were they searching for her? But they would never think of coming here.

She sat down in an old cretonne-covered wing-chair by the window—as far as possible from the bed and the muff! She sat there through the whole of the chilly, incredible, everlasting night. Nobody came. At first there was only a dreadful stillness. There did not seem to be a sound in the whole earth. The wind rose and the moonlight went out and the windows rattled unceasingly. And she was sure the muff moved. And the dresses in the closet surely stirred. Twice she heard footsteps in the hall.

Morning came—a cloudy morning with a blood-red sunrise sky. The windows all looked out on green widespread fields. There was no way in which she could attract attention. No way of escape. She would die here of starvation, and Mother would never know what had become of her. Again and again she heard footsteps passing along the hall—again and again she held her breath with fear lest they pause at the door. She suffered with thirst as the day wore on but she felt no hunger. A queer, numb resignation was stealing over her. Perhaps she would die very soon—but that no longer seemed terrible. The only terrible thing was that Mrs. Delagarde might come back.

Evening again—moonlight again—wind again—a snarling, quarrelsome wind that worried a vine at the window and sent a queer shadow flying across the room to the bearksin muff. It seemed to move—it *was* moving—Marigold suddenly went to pieces. She shrieked madly—she flew across the room—she tugged frantically at the locked door. It opened so suddenly that she nearly fell over backward. She did not pause to reflect that it could never have been locked at all, in spite of the turned key—she was past thinking or reflecting. She fled across the hall—down the stairs—out—out into freedom. She never stopped running till she stumbled into the hall at Cloud of Spruce—a hall full of wild, excited people, amid which she caught one glimpse of Mother's white anguished face before—for the first time in her life—she fainted.

"Good God," said Uncle Klon. "Here she is."

4

It was next day and Marigold was in bed with Mother sitting by her bedside and Grandmother coming in and out trying to look disapproving but too relieved and thankful to make a success of it. The whole story had been told—and much more. Marigold knew all about Mrs. Delagarde now—poor Mrs. Delagarde, who had lost her only little child a year ago, and had not been right in her mind ever since. Who had sat for hours by her little girl's side entreating her to speak to her once more—just one word. Who could not forget for a moment that she had whipped Delight the day before her sudden illness. Who had never forgiven her husband because he had been away when Delight took ill and there was no one to go for the doctor through the storm.

"The poor unhappy lady is greatly to be pitied," Mother said. "But, oh, darling, what a terrible time you have had."

"Some of the rest of us have had a terrible time, too," said Grandmother grimly. "Mrs. Donkin was sure she saw you at dusk in an automobile with two strange-looking men. And Toff LeClerc's boat is missing and we thought you had floated out into the channel in it. The whole country has been combed for you, miss."

"I'm afraid I'm not fit to be a missionary, Mother," sobbed

Marigold when Grandmother had gone out. "I wasn't brave—or resourceful—or serene—or anything."

Mother cuddled her—compassionate, tender, understanding.

"It's a very fine, splendid thing to be a missionary, dear, and if, when you grow up, you feel called to that particular form of service nobody will try to hinder you. But the best way to prepare for it is just to learn all you can and get a good education and live as happily and pleasantly as a small girl can, meanwhile. Dr. Violet Meriwether was the jolliest little tomboy in the world when we were girls together—a perfect mischief and madcap."

Aunt Marigold made her namesake stay in bed for a week. On the day Marigold was allowed to get up Mother came in smiling.

"After all, your missionary effort seems to have done some good, Marigold. Mrs. Delagarde's doctor says she is very much better. She has ceased to talk about Delight and she has forgiven her husband. Dr. Ryan says she is quite rational in many ways and he thinks if she is taken away for a complete change of scene and association she will recover completely. He says she told him she was 'forgiven' and this conviction seems to have cured some sick spot in her soul."

"Humph," said Grandmother—rather gently, however.

"Isn't it funny she never came back to the room?" said Marigold.

"She probably forgot all about you the minute you were out of her sight."

"I was so afraid she would. I thought I heard her outside all the time. That was why I never dared go near the door. And it wasn't locked at all—though I *know* I heard the key turn."

"I suppose it didn't turn all the way. Keys sometimes stick like that."

"Wasn't it silly to think I was locked in when I might have got out right away? I guess I've been silly right through. But—"

Marigold sighed. After having been consecrated and set apart for three weeks it was somewhat flat and savourless to come back to ordinary, memoirless life.

But visions of a new apricot dress were again flickering alluringly before her eyes. And Sylvia was on the hill—a forgiving Sylvia, who made no difference at all because of her brief defection.

CHAPTER XVI

One of Us

1

"I'm going travelling to-morrow. It makes me feel very important," Marigold told Sylvia one evening.

Hitherto Marigold had not done a great deal of visiting. Grandmother disapproved of it and Mother seldom dared to disagree with Grandmother. Besides Marigold herself had no great hankering to visit—by which she meant going away from home by herself to stay overnight. Only twice had she done it before—to Uncle Paul's and to Aunt Stasia's, and neither "visit" had been much of a success. Marigold still tingled with shame and resentment whenever she thought of "IT." She vowed she would never go to Aunt Stasia's again.

But, of course, it was different at Aunt Anne's. Marigold loved Aunt Anne best of all her aunts. So when Aunt Anne came one day to Cloud of Spruce and said:

"I want to borrow Marigold for awhile," Marigold was very glad that Grandmother raised no objections.

Grandmother thought it was time the child was seeing something of the world. She had her head stuffed too full of nonsense, like that Sylvia business. Despite Dr. Adam Clow—who came no more to Cloud of Spruce, having fared forth on an adventurous journey beyond our bourne of time and space—Grandmother thought it was hanging on too long. What might be tolerated at eight was inexcusable at eleven. Anne and

Charles were sensible people—though Anne was too indulgent. Grandmother expected Marigold to come home with her digestion ruined for life.

But Marigold went to Aunt Anne's with no cloud over her golden anticipations. Aunt Anne was a twinkly-eyed lady who was always saying, "I must go and see if there is anything nice in the pantry." You couldn't help adoring an aunty like that. It may be that Grandmother's fears were not altogether unfounded.

But she had to content herself with exacting a promise from Anne that Marigold must eat porridge every morning—real oatmeal porridge. If that were done, Grandmother felt that the rest of the day might be trusted to take care of itself.

So Marigold went to Broad Acres and loved it at first sight. An old grey homestead right down by the sea—the real, wonderful sea, not merely the calm, land-locked harbour. Built on a little point of land running out into a pond, with a steep fir-clad hill behind it and slender silver birch-trees all over it. With an old thorn-hedge the slips of which had been brought out from the Old Country—that mysterious land across the ocean where the Lesley clan had its roots. Enclosing a garden even more wonderful and fascinating than the garden at home—for a garden by the sea has in it something no inland garden can ever have. An old stone dyke between the house and the hill, with gorgeous hollyhocks flaunting over it. And a dear little six-sided room in "the tower," where you could lie at night and watch the stars twinkling through the fir-boughs. All this, with an uncle who knew a joke when he saw it and an aunty who let you alone so beautifully made Broad Acres just the spot for a vacation-visit.

And at first—Mats. Mats lived on the next farm and had been christened Martha. But she had lived that down. She was a fat, jolly little soul with round grey eyes, notorious freckles, luxuriant unbobbed sugar-brown curls, a face meant for laughter, and a generous mother who made enchanting pies. For a week she and Marigold had "no end of fun" together and got into no more mischief than two normal small girls should with no grandmothers around. And the soul of Marigold was knit into the soul of Mats and all was harmony and joy—until Paula came. Came and took immediate possession of the centre of the stage, as is the way of the Paulas.

2

It happened at Sunday-school. All the Lesleys were Presbyterians—of course—but the Presbyterian church over-the-bay was three miles away, so Marigold was sent to Sunday-school in the little white Baptist church on the other side of the pond, with the spruce-trees crowding all around it. Marigold loved it. She thought it seemed like a nice, friendly little church. She wore her pretty new green dress, with its little embroidered collar, and her smart little white hat with its green bow. *And* kid gloves—new kid gloves—*real* kid gloves. Mats, who knew no jealousy, was puffed up with pride over having for a chum a girl who wore real kid gloves. All the other little girls in Sunday-school cast envious glances at her and Marigold.

All but one. That one was sitting by herself on a bench, reading her Bible. And when Marigold and Mats sat down beside her that one got up and moved away—not contemptuously or proudly, but as some consecrated soul might remove itself automatically and unconsciously from the contamination of worldly contact.

"Well, I never," said Mats. "Aren't we good enough to sit beside you, Paula Pengelly?"

Paula turned and looked at them—or rather at Marigold. Mats she seemed entirely to ignore. Marigold looked back at her, spellbound from the start. She saw a girl, perhaps a year older than herself, slight as a reed, with large, glowing hazel eyes in a small, pale-brown face. A braid of long, straight, silky, dark-brown hair fell over each shoulder. Her cheek-bones were high and her lips thin and red. She was hatless and shabbily dressed and the Bible she clasped dramatically against her breast in her very long, very slender hands seemed to have been a Bible a great many years. She was not pretty but there was Something in her face. "Int'resting" was hardly a strong enough word and Marigold had not yet picked up "fascinating." She could not help looking at this Paula. There was—something—in her eyes that made you suddenly feel she saw things invisible to others—things you wanted ardently to see, too. A look that made Marigold think of a picture over Aunt Marigold's desk—the look of a white saint in ecstasy.

"No," said Paula, in an intense, dramatic way that made Marigold shiver deliciously, "you are *not*. You are not Christians. You are children of wrath."

"We ain't," cried Mats indignantly. But Marigold felt that they might be. Somehow one believed what Paula said. And she did not want to be a child of wrath. She wanted to be like Paula. She fairly ached with her desire for it.

"We're just as good as you," continued Mats.

"Goodness isn't enough, wretched child," answered Paula. "Hold your peace."

"What does she mean?" whispered Mats as Paula turned away. Whispered it rather fearfully. *Was* she a wretched child? She had never thought so, but Paul Pengelly *made* you believe things.

"She means hold your yap," said another girl passing. "Paulas 'got religion,' didn't you know?—like her father." Whatever it was that Paula had, Marigold felt she wanted it too. All through Sunday-school she yearned for it as she watched Paula's saintly little profile under that prim, straight hair. Grandmother and Mother were Christians, of course. But they never made her feel as Paula had done. At one time Marigold had believed Gwennie was very saintly. But Gwennie's supposed goodness only aggravated her. *This* was different. Marigold stayed for church that day because Mats was a Baptist, and Paula sat opposite them in a side seat. All through the waiting time before service Paula read her Bible. When the service began she fixed her eyes unwinkingly on the top of one of the little oriel windows. Oh, thought Marigold passionately, to be saintly and wonderful like that! She felt religious and sorrowful herself. It was a beautiful feeling. She had never felt anything quite like it before, not even when listening to Dr. Violet Meriwether. Once Paula looked from the window and right at her—with those compelling, mystical eyes. They said "Come" and Marigold felt that she must go—to the world's end and further.

When church was out Paula came straight up to Marigold.

"Do you want to come with me on the way of the cross?" she asked solemnly and dramatically. Paula had the knack of making every scene in which she took part dramatic—which was probably a large part of her fascination. And she had a little way of saying things, as if she could have said so much more and didn't. One yearned to discover the mystery of what she didn't say.

"If you do, meet me under the lone pine-tree at the head of the pond to-morrow."

"Can Mats come too?" asked Marigold loyally.

Paula flung Mats a condescending glance.

"Do *you* want to go to Heaven?"

"Y-e-es—but not for a long time yet," stammered Mats uncomfortably.

"You see." Paula looked eloquently at Marigold. "She's not One of Us. I knew *you* were the moment I saw you."

"I am," cried Mats, who couldn't bear to be left out of anything. "And of course I want to go to heaven."

"Then you must be a saint." Paula was inexorable. "Only saints go to heaven."

"But—do you have any fun?" wailed Mats.

"*Fun!* We are saving our souls. Would you," demanded Paula hollowly, "rather have fun and go to—to—a place too dreadful to speak of?"

"No—no." Mats was quite subdued and willing—temporarily—to do and surrender everything.

"To-morrow then—at nine o'clock—under the lone pine," said

Paula.

The very tone of her voice as she uttered "lone pine" gave you a thrilling sense of mystery and consecration. Marigold and Mats went home, the former expectant and excited, the latter very dubious.

"Paula's always got some bee in her bonnet," she grumbled. "Last summer she read a book called *Rob Roy,* and she made all us girls call ourselves a clan and have a chieftain and wear thistles and tartans. Of course *she* was chieftain. But there was some fun in that. I don't believe this religious game will be as good."

"But it's not a game," Marigold was shocked.

"Maybe not. But you don't know Paula Pengelly."

Marigold felt she did—better than Mats—better than anybody. She longed for Monday and the lone pine.

"Old Pengelly's her father," said Mats. "He used to be a minister long ago—but he did something dreadful and they put him out. I think he used to get drunk. He's—" Mats tapped her forehead with a significant gesture, as she had seen her elders do. "He preaches a lot yet, though in barns and places like that. I'm scared to death of him but lots of people say he's a real good man and very badly used. They live in that little house on the other side of the pond. Paula's aunt keeps house for them. Her mother is long since dead. Some people say she has Indian blood in her. She's never decently dressed—all cobbled together with safety pins, Ma says. Are you really going to the head of the pond tomorrow?"

"Of course."

"Well," Mats sighed, "I s'pose I'll have to go too. But I guess our good times are over."

3

Monday and the lone pine came though Marigold thought they never would. She told Aunt Anne and Uncle Charlie at the breakfast-table where she was going, and Uncle Charlie looked questioningly at Aunt Anne. As Marigold went out, he asked,

"What is that young devil in petticoats up to now?"

Marigold thought he was referring to her and wondered what on earth she had done to be called a young devil. Her conduct had really been very blameless. But she forgot all such minor problems when they reached the lone pine. Paula was awaiting them there—still rapt, still ecstatic. She had not, so she informed them, slept a wink all night.

"I couldn't—thinking of all the people in the world who are going to be—*lost*."

Marigold immediately felt it was dreadful of her to have slept so soundly. She and Mats sat down, as commanded, on the grass. Paula gave a harangue, mainly compounded of scraps of her father's theology. But Marigold did not know that, and she thought Paula more wonderful than ever. Mats merely felt uncomfortable. Paula hadn't even told them to sit in the shade. All very fine if you had the Lesley pink-and-white or the Pengelly brown. But when you hadn't! Right here in the boiling sun! It must be admitted, I am afraid, that Mats just then was much more concerned with her freckles than with her soul.

"And now," concluded Paula with tragic earnestness, "both of you ask yourselves this question, 'Am I a child of God or of the devil?'"

Mats thought it was horrid to be confronted with such a problem.

"Of course I'm not a child of the devil," she said indignantly.

But Marigold was all at sea. Under the spell of Paula's eloquence she did not know what her ancestry ought to be.

"What'll—we do—about it—if we are?" she asked unsteadily.

"Repent. Repent of your sins."

"Oh, I haven't any sins to repent of," said Mats, relieved.

"You can never go to heaven if you haven't committed sins, because you can't repent of them and be forgiven," said Paula inexorably.

This new kind of theology dumbfounded Mats. While she was wrestling with it, Paula's mesmeric eyes were on Marigold.

"What would—you call sins?" Marigold asked timidly.

"Have you ever read stories that weren't true?" demanded Paula.

"Ye-es—and—" Marigold was seized with the torturing delight of confession, "and—made them up—too."

"Do you mean to say you've *lied?*"

"Oh, no. Not lies. Not lies. I mean—"

"They must be lies if they weren't true."

"Well—perhaps. And I've thought of—things—when Uncle Charlie was having family prayers."

"What things?" said Paula relentlessly.

"I—I thought of a door in a picture on the wall—I thought of opening it—and going in—seeing what was inside—what people lived there—"

Paula waved her hand. After all what did it matter if Marigold did think of queer things while Charlie Marshall was praying? What did *his* prayers matter? Paula was after things that mattered.

"Have you ever eaten meat?"

"Why—yes—is that—"

"Its wicked—very wicked. To sacrifice life to your appetites. Oh, shame!"

Shame, indeed!

Marigold writhed with it. It was intolerable to have Paula looking at her in such scorn. Paula saw the shame and promptly assuaged it.

"Never mind. You didn't know. I've et meat—too—till last spring. I had an awful rash. I knew it was a judgment because I'd done something wrong. I knew it was eating meat—Father said so. He said the finger of God had touched me. So I vowed I'd never eat any more. Oh, how my conscience vexed me. It was awful how I suffered."

There was real anguish in Paula's voice. She stood, a flaming, fascinating figure under the old pine—a young priestess, inspired, devoted. Marigold felt she would follow her to the stake.

"What are we going to do about it?" said that detestable practical Mats.

"We are going to form a society for saving our souls and the world," said Paula. "I've thought it all out. We'll call ourselves the Lighted Lamps. Don't you think that's a splendid name? I'll be head of it and you must do just as I tell you. We will live such beautiful lives that everybody will admire us and want to join us. We will be just as good every day as we are on Sunday"—here Mats emitted a "marvellous grisly groan"—"but we will be very exclusive. No one can come in who is not ready to be a martyr."

"But what are we to *do*?" said Mats with a sigh. She must go where Marigold went, but her chubby personality had no heritage of martyrdom.

Paula allowed herself to sit down.

"First, we must *never* eat anything more than is absolutely necessary. No meat—no pudding—no cake—"

"Oh, I have to eat *some*," cried Marigold sorrowfully. "Aunty would think I was sick or something and send me home."

"Well, then, there must be no second helpings," said Paula inexorably. They pledged themselves—Marigold thinking guiltily of the delicious little strawberry shortcakes Aunt Anne had said she was going to make for dinner.

"We must never read or tell anything that isn't strictly true. Never *pretend* anything"—Marigold gave a gasp but recovered herself gallantly—"never wear any jewelry—and *never* play silly games."

"Can't we play at all?" implored Mats.

"Play. In a world where we must prepare for eternity? *You* can play if you like but *I* shall not."

"What will we do if we can't play?" asked Marigold humbly.

"Work. The world is full of work waiting to be done."

"I always help Aunt Anne every way I can. But when I get through what can I do?"

"Meditate. But we'll find lots to do when we get going. Now,

Mats, if you're coming in on this, come with all your soul. You *must* sacrifice. You have to be miserable or you can't be good. You mustn't forget for *one* moment that you're a sinner. You can't be both religious and happy in this world of sin and woe. We must live up to our name. And every time our light goes out we must do penance."

"How?" Mats again.

"Oh, lots of ways. *I* put some burrs next my skin yesterday because I only *wanted* a second helping at dinner. And kneel on peas. And *fast*. I fast often—and do you know, girls, when I fast I hear *voices* calling me by name." Paula's face took on a strange, unearthly radiance that completed Marigold's subjugation. "And I know it is angels calling me to my life's work—singling me out—setting me apart."

Mats had a hazy idea that it was going to be pretty hard to live up to Paula. But she meant to get to the bottom of things. "You've told us what we mustn't do. Now tell us what we must do."

"We must visit sick people—"

"I hate sick people," muttered Mats rebelliously, while Marigold thought with a shudder of her experience with Mrs. Delagarde. Paula, she felt, would not have been a bit frightened of Mrs. Delagarde.

"And read the Bible every day and say our prayers night and morning—"

"I don't see any use in saying prayers in the morning. I ain't scared in daytime," protested Mats.

Paula tried to ignore her and addressed herself to Marigold—who, as she felt instinctively, was a devotee of promise. You could never make anything of Mats—always chattering like a silly little parrot—but this new girl was after her own heart.

"We must hand out tracts—Father has stacks of them—and ask people if they're Christians—you can ask your father's hired man, Mats."

"He'd leave if I did and Father'd kill me," said Mats uncomfortably.

"Well, we're organised," said Paula. "Repeat after me, 'Lighted lamps we are and lighted lamps we will be as long as grass grows and water runs.'"

"Ow," whimpered Mats. But she repeated the vow glibly, comforted by recollections of other vows with the same implication of eternity which had proved to be of time when Paula grew tired of them.

"And now," concluded Paula, "I'll lead in prayer"—which she did, so beautifully and fervently, with her pale hands clasped and her eyes fixed on the sky, that Marigold's soul was uplifted and even Mats was impressed.

"There may be some fun in this after all," she reflected. "But I wish Paula would repent in winter. That's the best time for repenting."

4

As the days went on, Mats grimly concluded that there wasn't much fun in it. She was with them but not of them. As she had foreseen, it was very hard to live up to Paula. At least, for her, Marigold didn't seem to find it hard. Marigold, who went about with stars in her eyes, so unnaturally good that Aunt Anne was worried. Good on the outside, at least. Marigold knew she was full of sin inside because Paula told her so. Marigold was by now wholly in the power of this pale brown girl and thought her the most wonderful saintly creature that ever lived. She grieved constantly because she fell so far short of her. Paula fasted so much—as that wan, rapt face and those purple-ringed eyes testified eloquently. Marigold couldn't fast because of unsympathetic relatives. She could only refuse second helpings and "pieces" and writhe in bitterness when she heard Paula say loftily,

"*I* haven't touched a morsel of food since yesterday morning."

Neither could she hand out little time-yellowed tracts at

church as Paula did every Sunday and as Mats flatly refused to do at all.

"You can amuse yourselves by being miserable if you want to," said Uncle Charlie, "but I'm not going to have you making a nuisance of yourself as Paula Pengelly does."

Paula a nuisance! That self-sacrificing little saint who was positively happy in wearing a shabby, faded dress to church and who knew whole chapters of the Bible by heart. Not the int'resting ones, either, but the—the—dull ones like those in Numbers and Leviticus. Who wouldn't play games—not even jackstones, though she was crazy about them—because it was wrong. Who cried all night about her sins, when she, Marigold, could only squeeze out a few tears and then fall ignominiously asleep. Who never laughed—there was no place in religion for laughter, not even with an Uncle Charlie forever saying things that nearly made you die. Who *never* did anything she liked to do because if you liked a thing it was a sure sign it was wrong. Marigold was furious with Uncle Charlie.

"It's lovely here at Aunt Anne's," she sighed. "But it's so hard to be religious. I suppose it's easier at Paula's. Her father doesn't hinder her."

Marigold knew Paula's father by this time. She had been to have tea with Paula and stay all night with her—a great privilege which Aunt Anne did not properly appreciate.

Paula lived in a little grey house on the other side of the pond. A tired little house that looked as if it were on the point of lying down. Inside, the blinds were very crooked and the furniture very dusty. There was nothing for supper but nuts, apples, brown bread and some stale, sweet crackers. But that did not matter, for Marigold could not have eaten anyhow, she was in such awe of Mr. Pengelly—a tall old man with long grey hair, a wonderful grey beard, a great hawk nose and eyes that shone in his lined face like a cat's in the dark. He never spoke a word to her or any one. Paula told her it was because he had one of vows of silence on.

"Sometimes he never says a word for a whole week," said Paula proudly. "He is such a good man. Once Aunt Em made a pudding for dinner Christmas—a *little* pudding—and Father grabbed it from the pot and hurled it out of doors. But even *he* isn't as good as Great-Uncle Josiah was. *He* let his nails grow till they were as long as birds' claws, just to please God."

Marigold couldn't help wondering what particular pleasure Uncle Josiah's nails would give God, but she crushed back the thought rigidly as a sin.

They slept in a stuffy little hall-bedroom that had shabby, faded pink curtains and a broken pane, and was lighted by a lamp that seemed never to have been cleaned.

The head of the funny little old wooden bedstead was just against the rattling window.

"The snow drifts in on my pillow in winter," said Paula, the fires of martyrdom burning in her eyes as she knelt on peas to say her prayers.

The rain beat against the panes. Marigold half wished she were back in the tower room at Broad Acres. This was not one of the nights Paula lay awake to worry over her sins. She slept like a log. She *snored*. Marigold did the lying-awake.

Breakfast. No salt in the porridge. Paula had burned the toast. The tablecloth was dirty. And Marigold had a chipped cup. Then she drank avidly. This was certainly a good chance to do something for penance. Penance for certain thoughts she had been thinking. But not about Paula. Paula, in spite of the snores, still shone amid all her shabby surroundings like a star far above the soil and mist of earth—a star for worship and reverence. Marigold worshipped and reverenced. She was strangely happy in all her renunciations and denials. She would give up anything rather than face Paula's scornful smile. It was all the reward she wanted when Paula said graciously, as a priestess might stoop to approve the acolyte,

"I knew, as soon as I saw you, that you were One of Us."

Aunt Anne and Uncle Charlie couldn't understand it.

"That Pengelly imp seems to have a power to bewitch the other girls," grumbled Uncle Charlie. "Marigold is absolutely infatuated with her and her kididoes. But there's one thing—if this keeps on after she goes home, old Madam Lesley will make short work of it."

5

Marigold spent a considerable part of her time doing penance in various small ways for various small misdemeanours. It was not always easy to find a penance to do—something Aunt Anne would let you do. No fasting or kneeling on peas for Aunt Anne. And even when Marigold and Paula between them—Mats bluntly declined to have anything to do with penances—hit on a workable penance, Marigold was apt to discover that she rather liked it—it was int'resting—and Paula had said,

"Just as soon as you like doing a thing it isn't penance of course."

But one "penance" was an experience that always stood out clearly in Marigold's memory. At its first conception it looked like a real penance. She had fallen from grace terribly—she and Mats, if Mats could ever have been considered in a state of grace by Paula's standards. She had been invited to supper at Mats's; and she couldn't resist that supper.

Mats's mother was a notable cook and she had four different kinds of cake. And, alas, every one was a kind of which Marigold was particularly fond. Banana cake with whipped cream—strawberry shortcake—date layer-cake—jelly-roll cake. Marigold took a piece of each and *two* pieces of the shortcake. She *knew* she was doing wrong—from Mother's point of view as well as Paula's; but with Mats gobbling industriously by her side and Mats's mother saying reproachfully,

"You haven't eaten *anything*, child,"

What was one to do?

And after supper she and Mats had got a big fashion-book and picked out the dresses they'd have when they grew up; and filled their cup of iniquity to overflowing by "boxing" the bed of the hired man in the kitchen loft. At that, he probably slept better than Marigold, who was sick all night and had horrible dreams. Which might have been thought a sufficient penance. But Paula had a different opinion.

Marigold's conscience gave her no rest until she had confessed everything to Paula.

"You are a Pharisee," said Paula sorrowfully.

"Oh, I'm *not*," wailed Marigold. "It was just—"

Then she stopped. No, she was *not* going to say,

"Mats and her mother just *made* me eat."

That wasn't altogether true. She had been very willing to eat and she must bear her own iniquities. But had she lost caste forever in Paula's eyes? Would she no longer be considered One of Us?

"You've been very wicked," said Paula. "Your lamp has almost gone out and you must do a specially hard penance to atone."

Marigold sighed with relief. So she was not to be cast off. Of course she would do a penance. But what penance—at once severe enough and practicable. Paula thought of it.

"You're afraid of being alone in the dark. Sleep out all night on the roof of the veranda. *That* will be a real penance."

It certainly would. How real, Marigold knew too well. It was true that she was afraid of being alone in the dark. She was never afraid in the dark if any one was with her, but to be alone in it was terrible. She was becoming very ashamed of this terror. Grandmother said severely that a girl of eleven should not be such a baby and Marigold was sure that Old Grandmother would have scorned her for a coward. But so far she had not been able to conquer her dread of it. And the thought of spending the night *alone* on the veranda roof appalled her. Nevertheless she agreed to do it.

It was easy enough from one point of view. There was a door

in her little tower-room opening on the veranda roof and there was a little iron bedstead on it. All Marigold had to do was to slip out of bed as soon as everybody was asleep and drag her bedclothes and mattress out.

She did it—in a cold perspiration—and crept into bed trembling from head to foot.

"I *won't* be scared of you," she gasped gallantly to the night.

But she was. She felt all the primitive, unreasoning fear known to the childhood of the race. The awe of the dark and the shadowy—the shrinking from some unseen menace lurking in the gloom. The night seemed creeping down through the spruce wood behind the house like a living—but not human—thing to pounce on her. Darkness all about her—around—above—below. And in that darkness—what?

She wanted to cover up her head but she would not. That would be shirking part of the penance. She lay there and looked up at the sky—that terrible ocean of stars which Uncle Klon had told her were suns, millions of millions of millions of miles away. There did not seem to be a sound in the whole earth. It was waiting—waiting—for *what?* Suppose every one in the world was dead! Suppose she was the only person left alive in that terrible silence!

Then—she could not have told whether it was hours or minutes later—something changed. All at once. She was no longer frightened. She sat up and looked about her. On a world of velvet and shadow and stars. The boughs of the spruces tossed in a sudden wind against the sky. The gulf waters were silver under the rising moon. The trees were whispering in the garden like old friends. The fern scents of a warm summer night drifted down from the hill.

"Why—I like the dark," Marigold whispered to herself. "It's nice—and kind—and friendly. I never thought it could be so beautiful."

She stretched out her arms to it. It seemed a Presence, hovering, loving, enfolding. She lay down again in its shadow and surrendered herself utterly to its charm, letting her thoughts run out into it far beyond the Milky Way. She did not want to sleep—but after a time she slept. And wakened in the pale, windless morning just as a new dawn came creeping across Broad Acres. The dreamy dunes along the shore were lilac and blue and gold. Above her were high and lovely clouds just touched by sunrise. Below in the garden the dews were silver in the hearts of unblown roses. Uncle Charlie's sheep in the brook pasture looked amazingly white and pearly and plump in the misty morning light. The world had a look Marigold had never seen it wear before—an expectant, untouched look as if it were a morning in Eden. She sighed with delight. A mystic happiness possessed her.

Paula was over soon after breakfast to find out if Marigold really had stuck it out on the veranda all night.

"You look too happy about it," she said reproachfully.

"It *was* a penance for a little while at first and then I enjoyed it," said Marigold honestly.

"You enjoy too many things," said Paula despairingly. "A penance isn't a penance if you *enjoy* it."

"I can't help liking things and I'm glad I do," said Marigold in a sudden accession of common sense. "It makes life so much more int'resting."

6

Marigold was going to the post-office to mail a letter for Aunt Anne. It was a lovely afternoon. Never had the world seemed so beautiful, in spite of the hundreds of millions of sinful people living in it. When she passed Mats's gate, Mats was playing by herself at jackstones under the big apple-tree. Mats had backslidden sadly of late and had returned to her wallowing in jackstones—thereby proving conclusively that she was not One of Us. She beckoned a gay invitation to Marigold, but Marigold shook her head and walked righteously on.

A little further down there was a sharp turn in the red road and Miss Lula Jacobs's little white house was in the angle. And Miss Lula's famous delphiniums were holding up their gleaming blue torches by the white paling. Marigold stopped for a moment to admire them. She would have gone in, for she and Miss Lula were very good friends, but she knew Miss Lula was not home, being in fact at Broad Acres with Aunt Anne at that very moment.

Marigold could see the pantry-window through the delphinium-stalks. And she saw something else. A dark-brown head popped out of the window, looked around, then disappeared. The next moment Paula Pengelly slipped nimbly over the sill to the ground and marched off through the spruce-bush behind Miss Lula's house. And Paula held in her hands a cake—a whole cake—which she was devouring in rapid mouthfuls.

Marigold stood as if turned to stone, in that terrible moment of disillusion. That was the cake Miss Lula had made for the Ladies' Aid social on the morrow—a very special cake with nut and raisin filling and caramel icing. She had heard Miss Lula telling Aunt Anne all about it just before she came away.

And Paula had stolen it!

Paula the Lighted Lamp—Paula the consecrated, Paula the rigid devotee of fasts and self-immolation, Paula the hearer of unearthly voices. Paula had stolen it and was gobbling it up all by herself.

Marigold went on to the post-office, torn between the anguish of disillusionment and the anger of the disillusioned. Nothing was quite the same—never could be again, she thought gloomily. The sun was not so bright, the sky so blue, the flowers so flowery. The west wind, purring in the grass, and the mad merry dance of the aspen-leaves hurt her.

An ideal had been shattered. She had believed so in Paula. She had believed in her vigils and her denials. Marigold thought bitterly of all those untaken second helpings.

Mats was not in when Marigold returned, but Marigold went

home to Broad Acres and played jackstones by herself. And let herself go in a mad orgy of pretending, after all these weeks when, swallowed up in a passion of sacrifice, she had not even allowed herself to think of her world of fancy. Also she remembered with considerable satisfaction that Aunt Anne was making an apple-cake for supper.

Paula found her there and looked at her reproachfully—with purple-ringed eyes which, Marigold reflected scornfully, certainly did not come from fasting this time. Indigestion more likely.

"Is this how you, the possessor of an immortal soul, are wasting your precious time?" she asked rebukingly.

"Never mind my soul," cried Marigold stormily. "Just you think of poor Miss Lula's cake."

Paula bounced up, her pale face for once crimson.

"What do you mean?" she cried.

"I saw you," said Marigold.

"Do you want your nose pulled?" shrieked Paula.

"Try it," said Marigold superbly.

Suddenly Paula collapsed on the grey stone and burst into tears.

"You needn't make—such a fuss—over a trifle," she sobbed.

"Trifle. You *stole* it."

"I—I was so hungry for a piece of cake. I *never* get any—Father won't let Aunt Em make any. Nothing but porridge and nuts for breakfast and dinner and supper, day in and day out. And that cake looked so scrumptious. You'd have taken it yourself. Miss Lula has heaps of them. She *loves* making cake."

Marigold looked at Paula, all the anger and contempt gone out of her eyes. Little sinning, human Paula, like herself. Marigold no longer worshipped her but she suddenly loved her.

"Never mind," she said softly. "I—guess I understand. But—I can't be a Lighted Lamp any longer, Paula."

Paula wiped away her tears briskly.

"Don't know's I care. I was getting awfully tired of being so religious, anyhow."

"I—I think we didn't go the right way about being religious," said Marigold timidly. "Aunt Marigold says religion is just loving God and people and things."

"Maybe," said Paula—going down on her knees—but not to pray. "Anyhow I got all the cake I wanted for *once*. Let's have a game of jacks before Mats shows up. She always spoils everything with her jabber. She isn't really One of Us."

CHAPTER XVII

Not by Bread Alone

1

Salome had gone to Charlottetown for the day—rather unwillingly, for she had had a horrible dream of fourteen people coming to supper and nothing in the house for them to eat but cold boiled potatoes.

"And there's more truth than poetry in *that,* ma'am," she said, "for there isn't a thing baked except the raisin-bread. I assure you I don't dream dreams like that for nothing. And there's the Witch of Endor polishing her face out by the apple-barn."

It was an inflexible Cloud of Spruce tradition that there must always be cake in the pantry—fresh, flawless cake—lest unexpected company come to tea. No company had ever found Cloud of Spruce cakeless. Grandmother and Mother would both have died of horror on the spot if such a thing had happened. Kingdoms of Europe might rise and fall—famines might ravage India and revolutions sweep China—Liberals and Conservatives, Republicans and Democrats might crash down to defeat, but so long as cake-box and cooky-jar were filled there was balm in Gilead.

Yet this unthinkable thing had actually occurred. The evening before three car-loads of visitors had come out from Summerside and found cake in the pantry—but left none. No wonder Salome was upset.

"*I* have made cake before now," said Grandmother rather

sarcastically. Every once in so long Salome had to be snubbed. "And so has Mrs. Leander."

When Grandmother called Lorraine Mrs. Leander before Salome, Salome knew she was snubbed.

"I am well aware," she said with meek stateliness, "that I am not the only cook at Cloud of Spruce. I merely thought, ma'am, that seeing it was my duty to keep the pantry well filled, I ought not to neglect it for the sake of my own pleasure. *I* am not like my sister-in-law Rose John, ma'am. *She* hasn't any sense of shame. When unexpected company comes to tea she just runs out and borrows a cake from a neighbour. Whatever John saw in *her* enough to marry her I have never been able to imagine."

"Go and enjoy your holiday, Salome," said Lorraine kindly, knowing that if Salome once fairly embarked on the delinquencies of Rose John there was no telling when she would stop. "You deserve it. Grandmother and I will soon fill up the pantry."

Alas! Mother had got only as far as getting out her mixing-bowl when Uncle Jack's Jim arrived. ". . . bloody with spurring, fiery red with haste,"—or the modern equivalent for it. Great-Uncle William Lesley was dying at the Head of the Bay, or thought he was. And he wanted to see Grandmother and Leander's wife. They must lose no time if they were to get there before he died.

It was a tragedy.

"I have never," said Grandmother in a tone of anguish as she tied on her bonnet, "gone away from home and left absolutely *no* cake in the house."

"Surely no one will come to-day," moaned Mother, equally wretched. Really, it was a most inconvenient time for Great-Uncle to die.

"Don't forget to feed the cats," Grandmother told Marigold. "And mind you don't go wandering in Mr. Donkin's hill pasture. He's turned his ox in there."

"That's not his ox," said Marigold. "That's his old red bull."

Grandmother would have died before she would have said the word "bull" aloud. She drove away with Uncle Jack's Jim, sadly wondering what the young people of this generation were coming to. Apart from that she did not worry over leaving Marigold alone. Marigold was eleven now and tall for her age. One year she had been measured by the rose-bush—the next by the blue-bells. This year she was as tall as the phlox.

She liked being alone very well once in a while. It was quite important being in charge of Cloud of Spruce. She swept the kitchen, and got dinner for herself and Lazarre; she fed the cats and washed the dishes and wrote a letter to Paula.

Then the end of the world came. A car stopped at the gate; seven people descended therefrom and marched in past the platoons of hollyhocks with the air of people coming to stay. Marigold, staring aghast through the window, recognised them. She had met them all two weeks ago at a clan-funeral, where Grandmother had proffered them all a warm invitation to Cloud of Spruce. Second-Cousin Marcus Carter, his wife and son and daughter from Los Angeles; Second-Cousin Olivia Peake from Vancouver; *and* Third-Cousin Dr. Palmer of Knox College, Toronto, with *his* wife.

And there was no cake at Cloud of Spruce!

Marigold accepted the situation. In that moment she had decided what she would do.

As graciously as Mother herself could have done, she welcomed the guests at the door.

"Aunt Marian and Lorraine away? Then I don't suppose we'll stay," exclaimed Cousin Marcella Carter, who had a long thin face, a long thin nose, and a long thin mouth.

"You must stay for supper of course," said Marigold resolutely.

"Have you got anything good for us to eat?" asked Cousin Marcus with a chuckle. He had a square face with a spiky moustache and bristly white eyebrows. Marigold thought she did not like him and was glad she did not have to call him "uncle."

"I know the Cloud of Spruce pantry is always well supplied," said Mrs. Dr. Palmer, smiling. In her smooth grey silk dress she looked, Marigold decided, just like a nice sleek grey cat.

"Well, give us something that will stick to our ribs," said Cousin Marcus. "We've had dinner at a place—I won't say where—but there was heaps of style and precious little comfort."

"Marcus," said Cousin Marcella rebukingly.

"Fact. And now, Marigold, I'll give you a quarter for a kiss."

Cousin Marcus was quite genial. A joke was his idea of being kind and friendly. But Marigold did not know this and she resented it. Lifting her head as she had seen Varvara do, she said freezingly,

"I don't sell my kisses."

The visitors laughed. Jack Carter said,

"She's saving her kisses for *me*, Dad."

There was another laugh. Marigold shot a furious glance at Jack. She did not like boys—any boys. And she at once hated Jack. He was about thirteen with a fat moon-face, straight whitish hair parted in the middle, staring china-blue eyes and spectacles. Under ordinary circumstances Marigold could and would have annihilated him with ease and pleasure. She had not sparred with Tommy Blair four years without learning how to handle the sex. But a Cloud of Spruce hostess must not show discourtesy to any guest.

"She's got a nice mouth for kissing, anyhow," said Cousin Marcus more genially than ever.

2

Marigold left her guests in the orchard room and flew to the pantry. She was breathless with excitement, but she knew exactly what was to be done. There was plenty of cold boiled chicken and ham left over from the previous day; the Cloud of Spruce jam-pots were full as always. Cream galore for whipping. But hot biscuits—there *must* be hot biscuits—and cake!

If Marigold had been asked if she could cook she might have answered like canny Great-Uncle Malcolm when asked if he could play the violin. "He couldna' say. He had never tried."

Marigold had never tried. She could boil potatoes—and fry eggs—but further than that her culinary accomplishments as yet did not go. But she was going to try now. She had the Cloud of Spruce cook-book and she had helped Salome and Mother scores of times, looking forward with delight to the time when she would be allowed to do it off her own bat.

She clasped floury hands over the cake-bowl.

"Oh, dear God, I think I can manage the biscuits but You *must* help me with the cake."

Then she proceeded to mix, measure and beat. To make matters worse, Jack appeared. Jack was not happy unless he was teasing somebody. He proceeded to tease Marigold, not having any idea that it was a dangerous pastime, even when protected by Cloud of Spruce custom.

"I'm a terrible fellow," he declared. "I throw dead cats into wells. S'pose I throw *yours?*"

"I'll get Lazarre to call the new pig after you," said Marigold scornfully, and cracked an egg with violence.

Jack stared. What kind of girl was this?

"I'm just over the measles," he said. "Black measles. Ever had measles?"

"No."

"Mumps?"

"No."

"I've had mumps and whooping cough and scarlet fever and chicken pox and pneumonia. I'm a wow to have things. You ever had any of them?"

"No."

"Did you ever have *anything?*" Jack was plainly contemptuous.

"Yes," said Marigold, suddenly recalling some of Aunt Marigold's diagnoses. "I've had urticaria."

Jack stared again—but more respectfully.

"Golly. Is it bad?"

"Incurable," said Marigold mendaciously. "You never get over it."

Jack edged away.

"Is it catching?"

"*You* couldn't catch it." There was that in Marigold's tone Jack didn't like. Did this puling girl think she had something he couldn't have?

"Look here," he said furiously, "you give yourself airs that don't belong to you. And your nose is crooked. See!"

Marigold crimsoned to the tip of the offending nose. But tradition held. She spared Jack's life.

"But if I ever meet you away from Cloud of Spruce I'll ask you who put your ears on for you," she thought as she measured the baking-powder.

"What are you thinking of?" queried Jack, resenting her silence.

"I'm imagining how you'll look in your coffin," answered Marigold deliberately.

This gave Jack to think. Was it safe to be alone with a girl who could imagine such things? But to leave her, was to confess defeat.

"In five minutes by that clock I'm going to kiss you," he said with a fiendish grin.

Marigold shuddered and shut her eyes.

"If you do I'll tell everybody at supper what a sweet-looking baby you were."

That got under Jack's skin. He wished he was well out of the pantry and the presence of this exasperating creature. He shifted to a new point of attack.

"My, but I'm sorry for the man you're going to marry."

Marigold cast tradition to the winds.

"Oh, never mind," she said. "Your wife will be able to sympathise with him."

"Don't waste your breath now," drawled Jack.

"It's *my* breath."

"Think you're smart, don't you?"

"I don't think it, I know it," retorted Marigold, beating her cake-batter terrifically.

"After all, you're only a female," said Jack insolently.

"I heard you pinned a dishcloth to a minister's coat once," said Marigold.

But the minute she said it she knew she had made a mistake. He was proud of it.

"What are you two young divvils up to?" demanded Cousin Marcus, peering in at the door. "Oh, fond of the boys I see, Marigold. Come alone, Jack. Lazarre is going to show us the apple-orchard."

Jack, as relieved to be rid of Marigold as she was to be rid of him, vanished. Marigold breathed a sigh of thanksgiving. Oh, would her cake be all right? That wretched boy had bothered her so. *Had* she put in the baking-powder?

The cake was a gorgeous success. Marigold was a Lesley, and besides there was Providence—or Luck. It was a delicious feathery concoction with whipped cream and golden orange crescents on it—*the* special company-cake of Cloud of Spruce. And Marigold had just as good fortune with her biscuits. Then she set the table with the hemstitched cloth and Grandmother's best Coalport. Every domestic rite of Cloud of Spruce was properly performed. The ham was sliced in thin pink slices, the chicken platter was parsley-fringed, the white cake-basket with the china roses round it was brought out, the water in the tumblers was ice-cold.

3

Marigold sat behind the tea-cups facing the ordeal before her, a gallant and smiling hostess. She could feel her pulses beating to her fingertips. If only her hands would not tremble! She steadied her legs by twisting them around the rungs of the chair. Cousin Marcus did what in him lay to rattle her by conjuring her not to fill the cups so full of tea that there wasn't room for cream— as mean Aunt Harriet always did—and Dr. Palmer helped the chicken so lavishly that she broke out into a cold perspiration lest there shouldn't be enough to go round. Mrs. Dr. Palmer took cream and no sugar and Dr. Palmer took sugar and no cream and Cousin Marcella took neither and Cousin Marcus took both. Cousin Olivia took cambric tea. It was very difficult to remember everything, but she thoroughly enjoyed asking Jack how he took his. It seemed to put him in his place for once. Eventually everybody got something to drink and the chicken *did* go round.

Jack kept quiet for awhile, being fully occupied with gorging. But just as it had dawned on Marigold that the supper was almost over and had gone very well, Jack said,

"Say, Marigold, *you can cook.* If you'll promise to have my slippers warm for me every night when I come home, I'll come back and marry you when I grow up."

"I wouldn't marry you—"

"Oh, come, come now, my duck," said Jack, with an irritating snigger, "wait till you're asked."

"So you were courting in the pantry," chuckled Cousin Marcus.

Jack grinned like a Chessy cat.

"Marigold has such a nice little way of cuddling in your arms, Dad."

He hadn't really meant to say it, but it suddenly struck him as a very clever thing to say.

Marigold positively came out in goose-flesh.

"I haven't—I mean—*you* couldn't know it if I had."

"You're beginning young," said Cousin Marcus solemnly, pretending to shake his head over the doings of modern youth.

Marigold had a stroke of diabolical inspiration.

"*Johnsy* is telling his dreams," she said coolly.

That "Johnsy" was what Jack would have called "a mean wallop." He dared not open his mouth again at the table and did not recover his impudence until they were leaving.

"Isn't that a lovely moon?" said Marigold softly, more to herself than to any one, as she stood by the car.

"You should see the moons we have in Los Angeles," he boasted.

"What do you really think of him?" said Uncle Marcus in a pig's whisper, giving Marigold a poke in the ribs.

Marigold remembered that Salome had once said that Rose John had once said that if there was one thing more than another that lent spice to life, it was tormenting the men.

"I think Johnsy isn't really half as big a fool as he looks," she said condescendingly.

Cousin Marcus roared with laughter. "You've said a mouthful!" he exclaimed. Jack was crimson with rage. The car rolled away and Marigold stood by the gate, victress.

"I don't know how it is some girls like boys," she said.

4

When Grandmother and Mother came home—slightly annoyed, though they did not know it, that Great-Uncle William Lesley had been so inconsiderate as not to have died after all the bother but had rallied surprisingly—they had already heard the news, having met Cousin Marcus's car on the road.

"Marigold, *did you make the cake?* Cousin Marcella said she wanted the recipe of our cake."

"Yes," said Marigold.

Grandmother sighed with relief.

"Thank goodness. When I heard there was cake I thought you must have borrowed it from Mrs. Donkin—like Rose John. You didn't forget to put the pickles on."

"No. I put pickles and chow both."

"And you didn't—you're sure you didn't—slop any tea over in the saucers."

"I'm sure."

Mother hugged Marigold in the blue room upstairs.

"Darling, you're a brick! Grandmother and I felt *dreadful* until we found out there was cake."

CHAPTER XVIII

Red Ink or—?

1

Marigold thought the world a charming place at all times but especially in September, when the hills were blue and the great wheat-fields along the harbour-shore warm gold and the glens of autumn full of shimmering leaves. Marigold always felt that there was something in the fall that *belonged* to her and her alone if she could only find it, and this secret quest made of September and October months of magic.

To be sure there was generally school in September. But not this September for Marigold. She had not been quite herself through the August heat, so Mother and Grandmother and Aunt Marigold, who remembered that she was an M.D. in her own right when Uncle Klon let her remember it, advised that she be kept out of school for some weeks longer.

Then Aunt Irene Winthrop wrote to Mother and asked her to let Marigold visit her and Uncle Maurice. Aunt Irene was Mother's sister, and the Winthrops and the Lesleys were none too fond of each other. Grandmother rather grimly said she thought Marigold would be just as well at home.

"We let her visit Aunt Anne last year," said Mother. "I suppose Irene thinks it is her turn now."

Mother was too timid—or too good a diplomat—to say that she thought Marigold should visit her mother's people as well as her father's. But Grandmother understood it that way and offered no further objection. So Marigold went to Uncle Maurice and Aunt Irene at Owl's Hill. A name that fascinated Marigold. Any name with a hill in it was beautiful and Owl's Hill was magical.

Uncle Maurice and Aunt Irene were secretly a little afraid that Marigold might be lonesome and homesick. But Marigold never thought of such a thing. She liked Owl's Hill tremendously. Such a romantic spot on a high sloping hill with a little tree-smothered village snuggling at its foot and above it woods where at night sounded laughter that was merry but not human, while other hills lay beyond like green wave after wave. Uncle Maurice's face was so red and beaming that Marigold felt he made fine weather out of the gloomiest day. And Aunt Irene was like Mother. Only she laughed more, not being a widow. And having no Grandmother living with her.

There was a long letter to be written every night to Mother, in which Marigold told her everything that happened during the day. She always went down the lane to put it in the mail-box herself every morning. And there was Amy Josephs, of the chubby, agreeable brown face, next door, to play with. Amy was the daughter of Uncle Maurice's brother, so a cousin of sorts if you like. Amy made a fairly satisfactorily playmate who really seemed to have a dim conception of what Marigold meant when she talked of the laughter of bluebells and daisies, and they had good fun together.

Amy's two village chums came up the hill to play with them. Marigold liked them fairly well also. Not one of the three was anything like as good a playmate as Sylvia but Marigold carefully concealed this thought because she was beginning to feel that it was a bit queer that she should like an imaginary playmate better than real ones. But there it was.

One of Amy's chums was a very fat little girl with a most romantic name—June Page. A fair girl with hair so flaxen that beside it Marigold's shone like spun gold. Caroline Chrysler was a missionary's daughter. Sent home from India. Caroline, apart from her insistence on the fact that she was going to be a missionary, too—had been "consecrated to it in her cradle"—was quite a nice girl. It wasn't her fault that she was dark and sallow—perhaps not her fault that she wouldn't be called Carrie. Too frivolous for a consecrated. Marigold, who had once believed herself consecrated, too, could not be too hard on Caroline's poses. So they all got on very well, each having her own private opinion of the others, and every new dawn that broke across the autumn upland, ushered in a day full of interest and delight.

Even Sundays. Marigold loved going down to church Sunday evenings with Aunt Irene and Amy. They always went down across the fields to the road. Aunt Irene always carried a little lantern because, though it was only crisp steel-blue twilight when they left, it was dark long before they reached the church. The lantern cast such fascinating shivery, giant shadows. They went along the edge of the sheep-pasture. Marigold loved the cool grass under her feet and the soft eerie sighs in the trees, the sweet wild odours of the wandering winds and the elfin laugh of the hidden brook down under the balsam-boughs. There was a smell of aftermath clover in the air and the Milky Way was overhead. All around were misty stars over the harvest-fields. One really felt too happy for Sunday.

Aunt Irene never talked much and Amy and Marigold talked in whispers.

"I wonder if Hip Price will be in church to-night," said Amy.

"Who is Hip Price?" asked Marigold.

"He's the minister's son. His real name is Howard Ingraham Price, but he never gets anything but Hip—from his initials. He's awfully clever. I never," vowed Amy, speaking out of her tremendous experience of eleven and a half years, "met any one who knew so much. And he's so brave. He saved a little girl from drowning once, at the risk of his life."

"When?"

"Oh, before he came here. They only moved to this church last spring. He says he can lick his weight in wildcats. And he took the diploma for learning the whole Shorter Catechism by heart."

Marigold felt rather bored with this prodigy.

"What does he look like?"

"He's handsome. His eyes are just like an archangel's," said Amy fervently.

"How do you know? Did you ever see an archangel's eyes?" demanded Marigold relentlessly.

2

The choir was singing *Joy to the World,* and Marigold was thinking of "Tidal, king of nations," in the chapter the minister had just read. That phrase always fascinated her whenever she heard it. There was something so mysterious about it. Tidal, king of nations, was so much grander than just Tidal, king of one little country. Splendid. Triumphal. An entrancing figure of royalty ruling over hundreds of subject peoples. And just then Marigold saw Hip and thought no more forever of Tidal, king of nations.

He was sitting right across from her in the corner seat, staring at her. He continued to stare at her. Marigold felt that glance on her inescapably. She tried to look away—she fought against looking back—but in the end *her* eyes always returned to the corner seat to find *his* eyes still intent on her. Eyes can say so much in a second. Marigold felt very queer.

And, oh, he *was* handsome. Just like the slim princeling of fairy-tales. Brown curls shining in the lamplight. Cheeks rose-red under golden-tan. Dark-blue, romantic eyes. She felt that she would die of shame and humiliation when an old lady behind her suddenly held a peppermint out to her over the back of the seat. Marigold had to take it—and could not help looking at Hip as she did it. She could not—would not—did not eat it, but she felt as if Hip must see it all the time, moist and sticky in her warm, unwilling hand, and despise her for a baby who had to be kept good in church with peppermints. Marigold, to her dying day, never quite forgave Aunt Lucy Bates, who thought she had done a kind act to Lorraine Winthrop's little girl.

Marigold found her legs were trembling when she got up for the last hymn. Her face was burning under Hip's seemingly mesmerised eyes. She was sure every living soul in the church must notice him.

One at least had. Marigold met Caroline on the porch, going out, and it seemed to her that Caroline was a bit cool.

"Did you see Hip Price?" asked Caroline.

"Hip Price?" Marigold was not without the feminine knack of protective coloration. "Who is he?"

"That boy in the corner seat. I saw him staring at you. He always stares like that at a new girl."

"Sly thing," thought Marigold—not meaning Hip.

Amy did not go back with them. She was staying all night with June. So Marigold walked home alone with Aunt Irene. Not altogether alone.

On the other side of the road, until they reached the pasture gate, stalked a slender figure with a smart cap worn a bit rakishly on the back of its head. The figure whistled *The Long, Long Trail*. Marigold knew that it was Hip Price and she also knew that the manse was away on the other side of the church. It is terrific what damsels of eleven do know sometimes. But she was—almost— glad when they left the road and started up over the fields.

As they walked along Marigold was not thinking of the charm of starlit evening or the wind in the trees or the pixy lantern-shadows. I shall not tell you what she was thinking of. I will only state that next day she scorched a panful of cookies she had been left to watch because she was thinking of the same thing. Aunt Irene was annoyed. A Cloud of Spruce Lesley was supposed never to be careless. But Marigold with shining eyes and a dreamy smile lingering on her lips, did not worry about the cookies at all.

3

During the following three weeks life was a thing of rainbows for our Marigold. She had a delightful secret—a secret that nobody knew. Even when she wrote "everything" to Mother she did not tell her about Hip Price. Though she put an extra row of kisses in to make up for it.

The morning after that memorable Sunday evening, when Marigold went down to the end of the lane to mail Mother's letter, she found a letter in the box addressed to herself. Marigold trembled again—a delicious trembling. She sat down among the goldenrod under a friendly little spruce-tree and read it. It was a very wonderful epistle. Ask Marigold. To be told she was beautiful! Once in awhile she had heard a hint that she was pretty. But beautiful! And what did it matter that he spelled "angel" angle? Angel really was a very tricky word. *Anybody* might spell it wrong. Besides, doesn't everybody know that it doesn't make a mite of difference how a love-letter is spelled? He signed himself "fondestly yours" with lots of flourishes and curlicues. And there was a little x for a P. S.

Marigold's cheeks were so rosy when she went back to the house that Aunt Irene thought the child was picking up wonderfully. Marigold slept that night with Hip's letter under her pillow. And found another in the mailbox the next morning! In which he asked her if she were going to June Page's party Thursday evening and would she wear the blue dress she had worn to church? Would she? She had been wondering which of her two "good" dresses became her most and had been dangerously near selecting the green. And he wrote, "When the moon rises to-night think of me and I'll think of you." Marigold hunted out the time of moonrise in the almanac. Really, the moons of Owl's Hill were wonderful. Cloud of Spruce never had such moons. And would any other boy she knew ever think of saying a thing like that? Not in a thousand years.

Hip cornered her off at the party and asked her why she hadn't answered his letters. Marigold didn't think she could without Aunt Irene knowing.

"But you don't mind my writing them?" asked Hip softly—tenderly. Looking at her as if his very life depended on her answer. Marigold, dyed in blushes, confessed she didn't. Whereupon Hip surveyed the room with the air of a conqueror. When called upon to recite he gave "Casabianca" in ringing tones, standing all beautiful and brave as the immortal hero. A horrible thought suddenly arose in Marigold's mind. Did he *know* he was all beautiful and brave. She strangled and buried the hateful intruder instantly.

Hip was certainly captivating. He said such smart up-to-date things like "attaboy" and "apple-sauce" and "I'll tell the world!"—looking at Marigold to see if she admired his smartness. And he walked home with her—not exactly from the house. He joined her on the road, having dashed across lots. And at the gate of Owl's Hill lane he took her hand and kissed it. Marigold had read of young knights doing that but that it should happen to *her!*

It was thrilling to hear of all the deeds of high emprise Hip had done. That he had once saved a little girl from being burned to death—Amy must have got it twisted—that he often climbed to the very top of telegraph-poles—that he had once stopped a team of runaway horses by his own unaided prowess—that he would, on occasion, really relish a fight with blood-maddened tigers. As for sea-serpents, take Hip's word for it, they ate out of his hand.

"I don't believe he's done all the wonderful things he's always talking about," Amy said scornfully once.

Marigold knew what *that* meant. Just sheer jealousy. And of course it was also jealousy that led Caroline to say that Hip had bitten his sister when he was four years old and left open old Mr. Simon's gate on purpose so that the pigs could get into the garden. Marigold did not believe a word of it.

She had such a funny feeling when other people pronounced his name. It was thrilling to go to church and listen to Mr. Price preaching. *His* father. Marigold hated old Tom Ainsworth for sleeping in church. And there was one almost painfully rapturous day when she and Amy were invited to the manse to tea. To eat a meal at the same table with Hip was something in the nature of a rite, with the big maple rustling outside the window on which, Hip told her, he had cut their intertwined initials. How bitterly she resented it when his mother told him to keep his elbow off the table and not talk with his mouth full!

And every morning that romantic journey to the mailbox to find a letter—a delightful letter. There were times when Marigold felt, though she would not admit it even to herself, that she really liked Hip's letters much better than Hip himself.

In one he told her she was his Little Queen. And he had written that especial sentence in red ink—or—was it?—could it be—Marigold had heard of such things. She pitied every other girl, especially the consecrated Caroline, and thought of Hip every time the moon rose or didn't rise.

"You are so different from everybody else," Hip told her. Clever Hip.

4

The course of true love even at eleven never runs smooth. There came a dreadful day when she and Hip almost quarrelled. Marigold had been told a certain shameful little secret by Netta Caroll about Em Dawes. Em Dawes was living with an aunt down in the village because her father and mother were divorced, true's you live. Netta had heard it over in Halifax and cross your heart you were never to tell a word of it. Marigold promised solemnly she would never tell. And then Hip, with his uncanny nose for secrets, discovered that Marigold had one and coaxed her to tell him.

Marigold wanted to tell him—yearned to tell him—felt her heart must really break if she didn't tell him. But there was her solemn promise. Lesleys did not break their solemn promises. It was a custom of their caste. Hip grew angry when he found her so unexpectedly unmalleable, and when anger gave him nothing—except perhaps the look in Marigold's face—he became sad and reproachful. She didn't like him a bit, of course, when she wouldn't tell him what she and Netta had been whispering about that time.

"If you don't tell me," said Hip earnestly, "I'll go and drown myself. When you see me lying dead you'll wish you'd told me."

Hip rather overreached himself there, because Marigold didn't believe at all that there was the slightest fear of his drowning himself. She stuck gallantly to her determination not to tell, despite his pleadings. And then the next afternoon, when it became known that Hip Price had disappeared and could not be found anywhere, though everybody in the community was madly searching for him, Marigold thought she must die. *Had* Hip actually drowned himself because he thought she did not like him? *Had* he? The dread was intolerable. How terrible to live all your life remembering that some one had drowned himself because of you! Who could support such a prospect?

"I heard a dog howling under my window last night," sobbed Amy. "Mother says that's a sure sign of death."

"That was only old Lazy Murphy's dog. Surely you don't think *he* knows anything," protested Marigold. She was resentful of Amy's crying. What right had Amy to cry about Hip? She, Marigold, could not cry. Her dread went too deep for tears.

"His mother believes he's kidnapped," said Amy, hunting for a dry spot in her handkerchief. "She's just been going from one fainting fit to another all day. But some say he was seen going down the river in that leaky old boat of Shanty George's. Certain death, Shanty George says it was. Oh, I won't sleep a wink to-night."

Then came Caroline and June, and Caroline and June were also in tears—which did not improve the looks of either of them. Or their tempers, evidently. Caroline was shrewish.

"I don't see what *you're* crying about, June Page. He wasn't *your* minister's son. You're a Baptist."

"I guess I've as good a right to cry as you," retorted June. "Hip was my friend—my special friend. He thought more of me than of any girl in Owl's Hill. He's told me so *dozens* of times. He told me I was different from anybody he'd ever met. Cry! I will cry. Just you try to stop me."

An unbecoming red flush had risen in Caroline's pale face.

"Did Hip Price really tell you that?" she asked in a queer voice. Marigold, in the background, stood as if turned to the proverbial stone. Amy had put her handkerchief in her pocket.

"Yes, he did. And wrote it. I've had a letter from him every day for weeks."

"So have I," said Caroline.

June in her turn stopped crying and glared at Caroline.

"You haven't."

"I have. I can show them to you. And he told *me* I was different from any one he ever knew and that he couldn't help being crazy about me."

"He wrote me that, too," said June.

They looked at each other. No more tears were shed for Hip— nor would be if he were lying forty fathoms deep.

"Did he ever kiss your hand?" demanded Caroline.

June giggled—a giggle that seemed to make everything ugly. "More than that," she said significantly.

Marigold involuntarily brushed something from her hand. The power of thought had returned to her. She was very thankful now that she hadn't been able to cry. There were no stains on her face. Calmly, proudly as any Lesley of them all, she drained her cup of wormwood and gall.

June began to cry again—in self-pity this time. The Pages, Marigold reflected disdainfully, had no pride.

"He called me his Little Queen," she sobbed, "and said I had a crown of golden hair."

To call June Page's hair golden when it was just tow-coloured!

And fancy a Little Queen with a nose like a dab of putty! Oh, it was to laugh.

Caroline did not cry. But she looked very limp. She had been also Little-Queened. "And he said my eyes were so sweet and provoking."

To think of those round pale eyes of Caroline's being called sweet and provoking! Oh, of course Hip had left old Simon's gate open and bit his sister—bit her frequently. Not a doubt of it.

"He's just been a regular mean two-faced deceitful little sneak," said June violently, "and I hope he *is* drowned, I do."

"I didn't think a minister's son would do that," said Caroline mournfully. There was something especially terrible about a minister's son doing a thing like that. Whom could one trust if not a minister's son?

"I believe they are the worst sometimes," said June. "Well, you can have him."

"I don't want him!" said Caroline superbly, remembering at last that she was consecrated.

They went away on that note. Amy looked guiltily at Marigold.

"I—I wasn't going to tell *them*," she said, "but I got letters from Hip, too. Lovely letters. I *can't* believe he didn't mean them. Of course he was just fooling *them* but—"

"He was fooling everybody," said Marigold shortly. "And we needn't worry over his being drowned. He'll turn up safe and sound. I'm going home to write to Mother."

Marigold did write to Mother—not telling her *quite* everything, however. But first she burned a packet of schoolboy love-letters. She felt as if she had been mixed up in something very grimy. And she suddenly felt a great longing to be sitting on the old wharf below Cloud of Spruce, watching the boats coming in and feeling the clear, fresh sea-breeze from the dunes blowing in her face. Oh, how she hated and despised Hip Price.

But what was it Old Grandmother had said once?—That it was the hardest thing in the world to be just.

"I guess I was as much to blame as Hip," admitted Marigold

candidly.

All that saved her self-respect was the fact that she had not told him The Secret.

5

Hip turned up safe and sound next day. He had gone for a day's ride with Lazy Murphy's son-the-pedlar and Lazy Murphy's horse had taken sick eighteen miles away, in a place where there was no telephone. So Owl's Hill folks gave up searching and Mrs. Price recovered from her fainting fits and Hip came straight up to Owl's Hill to see Marigold. It was rather unfortunate that Hip should have selected that day for appearing out in kilts. He had thin legs.

"Come on for a walk down to the pasture-spring," he whispered.

"No, thank you, Howard."

Hip had never heard that an enchantment is at an end as soon as the enchanter is called by name. But he knew there was something wrong with Marigold, standing there, the very incarnation of disdain.

"What's the matter? You don't look as if you were glad to see me back. And I was thinking of you every minute I was away."

"And about June and Caroline, too?" asked Marigold sweetly, as one who knew her Hip at last.

For the first time since she had known him Hip lost face.

"So they've blabbed," he said. "Why, I was just seeing how much they'd believe. It was different with you—honest—You've got *them* skinned a mile."

"I think you'd better go home," said Marigold sarcastically. "Your mother may be anxious about you. She might even take a fainting-fit. Good-bye."

Marigold went away stiffly, regally, without a backward glance. Hip had not drowned himself in despair over her lack of confidence, but he was for her not only dead but, as the French would say, very dead.

"He was never very int'resting, anyhow—not even as much as Johnsy," she thought, suddenly clear-sighted.

It seemed years since she had left home. At the end of that long red road were Mother and Sylvia and Cloud of Spruce. She felt clean once more.

"I guess it was only red ink after all," she said.

CHAPTER XIX

How It Came to Pass

1

When Marigold had gone to visit Aunt Anne and then Aunt Irene, something was started. Grandmother gloomily said,

"They'll all be wanting her now," and her prediction was speedily fulfilled. Aunt Marcia wanted her share of Marigold, too.

"If Anne and Irene Winthrop could have her I think I should too. She's never spent a night in my house—my favourite brother's child," she said reproachfully.

So Grandmother with a look of I-told-you-so and Mother with a look of How-can-I-do-without-Marigold again consented rather unwillingly.

"Jarvis is so—odd," said Grandmother to Mother.

Grandmother had very little use for Jarvis Pringle, even if he were her son-in-law. Nobody in the clan had much use for him. He was known to have got up once in the middle of the night to dot an "i" in a letter he had written that evening. As Uncle Klon said, that was carrying things rather too far.

Marigold did not know, as the grown-ups of the clan knew, that he had lived all his life with the shadow of madness hanging over him. She didn't know what Uncle Klon meant when he said Jarvis took the universe too seriously. But she did know she had never seen Uncle Jarvis smile. And when Uncle Jarvis once asked her if she loved God and she had said "yes," she had the oddest feeling that she was really telling a lie, because her God was certainly not the God Uncle Jarvis was inquiring about. And she did know that she didn't like Uncle Jarvis. She loved him, of course—you have to love your relations—but she didn't like him—not one little bit. She always made her small self scarce when he came to visit Cloud of Spruce. She did not know he had the face of a fanatic; but she knew he had a high, narrow, knobby forehead, deep-set, intolerant eyes, austere, merciless mouth, and a probing nose, which he had a horrible habit of pulling. Also a fierce, immense, black beard which he would never even trim because that would have been un-Scriptural and contrary to the will of God.

Uncle Jarvis knew all about the will of God—or thought he did. Nobody could go to heaven who did not believe exactly as he did. He argued, or rather dogmatised, with every one. Marigold was so small a fish that she generally slipped through the meshes of his theological nets and he paid scant attention to her. But she wondered sometimes if Uncle Jarvis would really be contented in heaven. With nobody to frown at. And a dreadful God who hated to see you the least bit happy.

Nevertheless she was pleased at the prospect of another visit. Uncle Jarvis and Aunt Marcia also lived "over the bay," which of course had a magic sound in Marigold's ears. And she loved Aunt Marcia, who had calm, sea-blue eyes and one only doctrine— that "everybody needs a bit of spoiling now and then." Her pies praised her in the gates and she was renowned for a lovely cake called "Upside-down cake," the secret of which nobody else in the clan possessed. Marigold knew she would have a good time with Aunt Marcia. And Uncle Jarvis couldn't be 'round all the time. Grain must be cut and chores done no matter how dreadful the goings-on might be in your household during your absence.

So she went to Yarrow Lane farm, where she found a low-eaved old house under dark spruces and a garden that looked as if God smiled occasionally at least. Aunt Marcia's garden, of course. The only thing in the gardening line Uncle Jarvis concerned himself with was the row of little round, trimmed spruces along the fence of the front yard. Uncle Jarvis really enjoyed pruning them every spring, snipping off all rebellious tips as he would have liked to snip off the holder of every doctrine he didn't agree with.

Marigold had a room with a bed so big she felt lost in it and a small, square window looking out on the silver-tipped waves of the bay. She had the dearest little bowl to eat her porridge out of—it made even porridge taste good. And the Upside-down cake was all fond fancy had painted it.

Uncle Jarvis did not bother her much, though she was always secretly terrified at his gloomy prayers.

"Why," Marigold wondered, "must one groan so when one talks to God?" Her own little prayers were cheerful affairs. But perhaps they oughtn't to be.

The only unpleasant day was Sunday. Uncle Jarvis was almost as bad as the man in another of graceless Uncle Klon's stories— who hung his cat because she caught a mouse on Sunday. When he heard Marigold laugh the first Sunday she was at Yarrow Lane he told her sternly that she must never laugh on Sunday in his house.

"Whatever may be done at godless Cloud of Spruce," his manner seemed to say though his tongue didn't.

2

Marigold was not long at Yarrow Lane before she picked up a chum. By the end of a week she and Bernice Willis had known each other all their lives. Aunt Marcia had rather expected Marigold to chum with Babe Kennedy on the next farm, who lived much nearer than Bernice. And Babe was very ready to be chummed with. But chumship, like kissing, goes by favour. Marigold simply did not like Babe—a pretty little doll, with hair of pale, shining, silky-red; pale green eyes, an inquisitive expression and an irritating little snigger that set Marigold's nerves on edge. She would have none of her. Bernice was the choice of her heart—the first real friend she had ever had—the first real rival to Sylvia. Bernice lived half a mile away, with an odd old aunt in "the house behind the young spruce wood." The very description intrigued Marigold. The *young* spruce wood— so delightful. What charming things must foregather in a *young* spruce wood. Bernice was ugly but clever. She had uncut mouse-coloured hair and big, friendly grey eyes in a thin, freckled face—a face that seemed meant for laughter, although it was generally a little sad. Her father and mother were both dead and Bernice did not seem to have any relatives in the world except the aforesaid odd old aunt. Lots of the girls in Ladore—even magical, over-the-bay places have to have post-office names—didn't like her.

But it happened that she and Marigold talked the same language—liked the same things. They could both have supped on a saucer of moonshine and felt no hunger—for a time, anyhow. They both understood the stories the wind told. They both liked silk-soft kittens and the little fir woods that ran venturesomely down to the shore and the dancing harbour ripples like songs. A bluebird singing on the point of a picket in the Yarrow Lane thrilled them and an imaginary trip to the moon was all in the evening's work. And they made every day a gay adventure for themselves.

"You'll find out she isn't as good as you think her," Babe told Marigold with sinister significance.

But that, Marigold believed, was only Babe's jealousy.

3

Then one night Marigold and Bernice had the supreme bliss of sleeping together. And not only of sleeping together but sleeping in the granary-loft—the little white granary across the small, hollow field carpeted with sheets of green moss and full of birch-trees. Such a romantic thing.

Aunt Marcia had told Marigold to ask Bernice to stay all night with her. And soon after Bernice's arrival two loaded automobiles came out from Charlottetown. The guests must be put up somehow for the night. The little house was taxed to its limit. Marigold's room must be commandeered in the emergency. But what was the matter with sleeping in the neat little granary-loft this warm September night? Aunt Marcia would make them up a comfortable bed. If they wouldn't be afraid!

Afraid! Bernice and Marigold hooted at the idea. They were all for it at once. So after they had prowled about till nearly ten—Bernice had gone to bed at eight every night of her life and Marigold was supposed to go—they went through the moonlit birches with their nighties under their arms and a huge piece of apple-pie in their paws. Aunt Marcia actually let people eat pie at night. Perhaps that accounted for some of Uncle Jarvis's religious gloom. They took a drink from the truly delightful stoned-up spring behind the granary, which Uncle Jarvis called the barn-well, and then mounted the outside granary stairs to the loft. Its bare boards were beautifully white-washed, and Aunt Marcia had made up a bed on the floor and covered it with a charming white quilt that had red "rising suns" all over it. And she had set a lighted candle on a barrel for them, feeling that it would never do to give them a kerosene lamp in the granary.

They bolted the door—more romance—and blew out the candle to have the fun of undressing by moonlight.

It was when they were ready for bed that Marigold made her shocking discovery.

"Now, let's say our prayers and snuggle down for a good jaw," she said. "We can talk just as long as we like to-night and nobody to pound on the wall and tell us to stop."

Bernice turned from the loft window whence she had been gazing rapturously on the glimpse of moonlit bay over the birches.

"I never say any prayers," she announced calmly.

Marigold gasped.

"Why, Bernice Willis, that is wicked. Aren't you afraid God will punish you?"

"There isn't any God," said Bernice, "and I won't pray to any one I don't believe in."

Marigold stared at her. This thing had been *said*—and yet the granary still stood and Bernice still stood, a slim, white sceptic in the moonlight.

"But—but—Bernice, there *must* be a God."

"How do you know?"

"Mother told me," said Marigold, gasping at the first argument that presented itself to her dumbfounded mind.

"She told you there was a Santa Claus, too, didn't she?" asked Bernice relentlessly. "Mind you, I'd like to believe in God. But I can't."

"Why not?" wondered Marigold helplessly.

"Because—because I haven't *anybody*. Nobody but Aunt Harriet—and she's only a half-aunt and she doesn't like me a bit. Father and mother are dead—and she won't even talk to me about them. I had a kitten and it died and she won't let me have another. As for this praying-business, I used to pray. Once when I was so small I can just remember it Aunt Harriet sent me down to the store on an errand. The wind was awful cold. And I knelt right down on the road behind a little spruce-bush and asked God to make the wind warmer before I came out of the store. He *didn't*—it was colder than ever and right in my face. And when my kitten took sick I asked God to make it well. But it died. And then I knew there was no God. Because if there had been He wouldn't have let my kitten die when it was the only thing I had to love. So I never prayed any more. Of course I have to kneel down when Aunt Harriet has family prayers. But I just kneel and make faces at God."

"You just said you didn't believe in Him," cried Marigold.

"Well—" Bernice was not going to be posed, "I just make faces at the idea of Him."

So this, Marigold reflected bitterly, was what Babe Kennedy

had meant.

"Besides, look at me," continued Bernice rebelliously. "See how ugly I am. Look at the size of my mouth. Why did God make me ugly? Babe Kennedy says I've got a face like a monkey's."

"You haven't. And think how clever you are," cried Marigold.

"I want to be pretty," said Bernice stubbornly. "Then people might like me. But I don't believe in God and I'm not going to pretend I do."

Marigold got up with a long sigh of adjustment and flung her arms about Bernice.

"Never mind. *I* love you. I love you whether you believe in God or not. I only wish you did. It's—it's so much nicer."

"I won't have *you* long," said Bernice, determinedly pessimistic. "Something'll happen to take you away, too."

"Nothing can happen," Marigold challenged fate. "Oh, of course I'll have to go home when my visit's ended—but we'll write—and I'll get Mother to ask you to Cloud of Spruce. We'll be friends forever."

Bernice shook her head.

"No. Something will happen. You'll see. This is too good to last."

A new fear assailed Marigold.

"Bernice, if you don't believe in God how can you expect to go to heaven?"

"I don't. And I don't want to," Bernice answered defiantly. "Aunt Harriet read about heaven in the Bible. All shut in with walls and gates. I'd hate that."

"But wouldn't it be better than—than—"

"Hell? No. You wouldn't have to pretend you liked hell if you didn't. But I don't believe in either place."

"Bernice, don't you believe in the Bible *at all*?"

"Not one word of it. It's all about God and there isn't any God. It's just a—just a fairy-tale."

Somehow, this seemed more terrible to Marigold than not believing in God. God was far-away and invisible but the Bible was right in your hand, so to speak. She sighed again as she knelt to say her own prayers. It seemed a very lonely performance—with that little sceptic of a Bernice standing rigidly by the window, disbelieving. But Marigold prayed for her very softly. "Please, dear God, make Bernice believe in You. Oh, *please,* make Bernice believe in You."

4

At dinner-time next day Marigold made the mistake of her life. Aunt Marcia asked what she was worrying about. And Marigold confessed that she was—not exactly worrying about Bernice but so sorry for her.

"Because, you see, she doesn't believe in God. And it must be terrible not to believe in God."

"What's that?" Uncle Jarvis shot at her suddenly. "What's that about Bernice Willis not believing in God?"

"She says she doesn't," said Marigold mournfully.

"Poor child," said Aunt Marcia.

"Poor child? Wicked child!" thundered Uncle Jarvis. "If she doesn't believe in God you'll not play with her again, Marigold."

"Oh, Jarvis," protested Aunt Marcia.

"I've said it." Uncle Jarvis stabbed a potato with a fork as if he were spearing an infidel. "Woe to them that are at ease in Zion. We keep the Ten Commandments in *this* house."

"Oh, Jarvis, remember the poor child has no one to teach her really. That queer old—"

"Marcia, be silent. She has had plenty of opportunity in a Christian land to learn that there is a God. Doesn't she go to Sunday-school and church? And Harriet Caine is an earnest Christian woman. There is no doubt that Bernice has been taught the truth. But she is plainly not of the elect and she is too wicked for you to play with. Why, I refused to shake hands with Dr. Clarke because he said he believed there were two Isaiahs. Do you think I'll tolerate infidelity?"

Aunt Marcia knew he was inexorable and Marigold felt he was. She began to cry, though she knew tears would have no influence on Uncle Jarvis.

"Oh, Uncle Jarvis—if Bernice—if Bernice comes to believe there is a God can't I play with her then?"

"Yes, but not till them." Uncle Jarvis gave his nose a frantic tweak and left the table, his black beard fairly bristling with indignation. Uncle Jarvis had one of his headaches that day and so was more than usually theological. Aunt Marcia wanted him to take an aspirin to relieve it but he would not. It was flying in the face of God to take aspirin. If He sent you pain it was for you to endure it.

Aunt Marcia tried to comfort Marigold but could not hold out much hope that Uncle Jarvis would change his mind.

"Oh, if I'd only held my tongue," moaned Marigold.

"It would have been wiser," agreed Aunt Marcia sadly. Thirty years of living with Jarvis Pringle had taught her that.

Marigold never forgot Bernice's sad little face when she told her Uncle Jarvis wouldn't let them play together any longer.

"Didn't I tell you? I knew something would happen," she said, her lips quivering.

"Oh, Bernice, couldn't you—couldn't you—*pretend* you believe in Him?" Marigold's voice faltered. She *knew*, deep in her soul, that this wasn't right—that a friendship so purchased must be poisoned at the core. Bernice knew it, too.

"I can't, Marigold. Not even for you. It wouldn't be any use."

"Oh, Bernice, if you come to find out—sometime—that you do believe in Him after all, you'll tell me, won't you? And then we can be friends again. Promise."

Bernice promised.

"But I won't. Isn't this very thing that's happened a proof? If there was a God He'd know it would make me feel more than ever there wasn't."

The week that followed was a very lonely one for Marigold. She missed Bernice dreadfully—and that hateful Babe was always poking round, triumphing.

"Didn't I tell you. *I* knew ages ago Bernice didn't believe there was a God. I'll bet He'll punish her right smart some of these days."

"She doesn't pronounce sepulchre 'see-pulker,' anyhow," retorted Marigold, thinking of the verse Babe had read in Sunday-school the day before.

Babe reddened.

"I don't believe Miss Jackson knows how to pronounce it herself. You make me *sick,* Marigold Lesley. You're just mad because you've found out your precious Bernice isn't the piece of perfection you thought her."

"I'm not mad," said Marigold calmly. "I'm only sorry for you. It must be so terrible to be *you.*"

Marigold prayed desperately every night for Bernice's conversion—prayed without a bit of faith that her prayer would be answered. She even tried to consult the minister about the matter, the night he came to Yarow Lane for supper.

"Tut, tut, everybody believes in God," he said when Marigold timidly put a supposititious case.

So *that* wasn't much help. Marigold thought wildly of refusing to eat unless Uncle Jarvis let her play with Bernice. But something told her that wouldn't move Uncle Jarvis a hair's breadth. He would only tell Aunt Marcia to send her home.

And, oh, the raspberries were thick on the hill—and there was a basketful of adorable kittens in the old tumbledown barn— Uncle Jarvis was always so busy with theology that he hadn't time to patch up his barns. And it was a shame, so it was, that Bernice must miss all this just because she couldn't believe in God.

5

"I've found out something about Bernice Willis. I've found out something about Bernice Willis," chanted Babe Kennedy triumphantly, rocking on her heels and toes in the door of the granary-loft, grinning like a Cheshire cat.

Marigold looked scornfully over her shoulder from the corner where she was arranging her cupboard of broken dishes.

"What have you found out?"

"I'm not going to tell *you*," crowed Babe. "I'm going to tell Bernice, though. I gave her a hint of it this afternoon at the store but I wasn't going to tell her then—I just gave her something to think of. I'm going right down to her aunt's to tell her as soon as I've taken Mrs. Carter's eggs to her. Oh, it's awful—the awfullest thing you ever heard of. You'll find it out pretty soon. Everybody will. Well, bye-bye. I've got to be off. It's coming up a storm, I guess."

Marigold made one swift bound across the granary, caught Babe by the arm, pulled her with scant regard for her eggs into the loft, slammed and bolted the door and stood with her back to it.

"Now, you just tell me what you mean and no more nonsense about it."

Marigold was not a Lesley for nothing. Babe surrendered. She snapped her thin-lipped, cruel little mouth shut, then opened it.

"Very well then. Bernice Willis's father isn't dead. Never was dead. He's in the penitentiary at Dorchester, for stealing money."

"I—don't believe it."

"It's true—cross my heart. I overheard Mrs. Dr. Keyes from Charlottetown telling Ma all about it. He was in a bank—and he—em—embezzled the money. So he was sent to the pen for twelve years and his wife died of a broken heart—though Mrs. Keyes said it was her extravagance drove him to stealing. And Bernice's Aunt Harriet took her. She was just a baby—and brought her up to think her father was dead, too."

Marigold wanted to disbelieve it. But it was too hopelessly, horribly, evidently true.

"My, ain't I glad I've never played with Bernice!" gloated Babe. "The daughter of a jail-bird. Just think of her face when I tell her!"

"Oh, Babe—" Marigold stooped to plead with Babe Kennedy piteously, "oh, you're not going to tell her. Please—please don't tell her."

"I will so tell her. It'll bring that pride of hers down. Carrying her head as high as if she came of honest people."

"If you were changed into a toad this minute you'd only look like what you are," cried Marigold passionately.

Babe laughed condescendingly.

"Of course you're sore—after thinking nobody was good enough for you to play with but Bernice. Oh, my, Miss Lesley. You can pull in your horns now, I guess. I'm going to tell Bernice right off. She'd have to know it, anyhow, soon—her father'll soon be out of jail. I'm going to have the fun of telling her first. Think of her face. Now, you just open that door and let me out."

Marigold did as she was ordered. The spirit was clean gone out of her.

This was dreadful—dreadful. No hope now that Bernice would ever believe in God. Marigold felt she could hardly blame her. "Think of her face—" Marigold did think of it—that dear, freckled, sensitive, homely little face—when Babe told her the terrible truth. And of course Babe would tell. Babe did so love to tell ugly things. Hadn't she told Kitty Houseman she was going to die? Hadn't she told the teacher Sally Ford had stolen Jane McKenzie's pencil in school?

"If I could get there and tell Bernice first," said Marigold. "If she *has* to hear it she could stand it better from me. I could go by the Lower road—Mrs. Carter lives on the Upper road and I could get there before Babe. But it's dark—and going to rain—"

Marigold shuddered. She didn't mind being out after dark on a road she knew. But a road she didn't know was different.

She ran down the granary stairs and across the birch field to the Lower road. She *must* get to Bernice first. But, oh, how weird and lonely that Lower road was in the sudden swoops of wind and the sudden gushes of wan moonlight between the clouds. Melancholy dogs were howling to each other across the dark farms. The wind whistled dolefully in the fence corners. *Something*—with red eyes—glared out at her from under a bush. And the trees!

By daylight Marigold was a little sister to all the trees in the world. But trees took on such extraordinary shapes in the dark. A huge lion prowled through John Burnham's field. An enormous, diabolical rooster strutted on the fence. A queer elfish old man leered at her over a gate. A very devil squatted at the turn of the road. The whole walk was full of terrors. Marigold was in a cold reek of perspiration when she reached the house behind the young spruce wood and stumbled into the little kitchen, where Bernice was—fortunately—alone.

"Bernice," gasped Marigold, "Babe's coming to tell you something—something dreadful. I—tried to stop her but I couldn't."

Bernice looked at Marigold with fear in her sad grey eyes.

"I knew she meant something this afternoon. She asked me where my father was buried. I said in Charlottetown. 'Go and see if his grave is there,' she said. What is it? Tell me. I'd rather hear it from you than her."

"Oh, I can't, Bernice—I can't," cried Marigold in agony. "I thought I could—but I can't."

"You *must*," said Bernice.

In the end Marigold told her—haltingly—tearfully. Then buried her face in her hands.

"Oh, I'm so happy," said Bernice.

Marigold pulled her away. Bernice was radiant. Eyes like stars. "Happy?"

"Yes—oh, don't you see. I've got *somebody* after all. It was so dreadful to think I didn't belong to anybody. And Father'll *need* me so much when he comes out next year. There'll be so much I can do for him. Oh, Marigold—I *do* believe in God now—I'm sorry I ever said I didn't. Of course there's a God. I love Him—and I love everybody in the world. I don't mind a bit how poor and ugly I am now that I have a father to love."

In Marigold's utter confusion of thought only one idea stood out clearly.

"Oh, Bernice—if you do—believe in God—Uncle Jarvis will let us play together again."

"Well, I do declare." Babe Kennedy stood in the doorway. A vicious, disappointed Babe. "So *that* was why you didn't want me to tell—so's you could tell yourself."

"Exactly."

Marigold put her arm around Bernice and faced Babe defiantly. "And I *have* told it first. So you can just go home, Miss Meow. Nobody wants you here."

CHAPTER XX

The Punishment of Billy

1

"I have the evil eye," said Billy ominously. "People are scared of me."

"If you are going to talk nonsense we can't be friends," said Marigold coldly. "If you're sensible we can have some fun."

Billy—nobody but Aunt Min ever called him William— looked at this sprite-like Marigold and decided to be sensible. When Aunt Min had told him that Marigold Lesley was coming to Windyside for a week Billy had two reactions.

Firstly, he was mad. He didn't want a girl poking and snooping round. Secondly, he was rather pleased. It would be good fun to tease her and teach her her place. Now came a third. Marigold, sleek of hair, blue of eye, light of foot, found favour in his eyes. As sign and seal that evening, sitting on the granary steps, he told her all his troubles. Marigold listened and sympathised with one side of her mind, and with the other carried on her own small thought-processes. As is the way of womenkind of all ages, whether men knew it or not.

Marigold could not quite understand why Billy detested staying at Aunt Min's so bitterly. For herself she rather liked it. Billy thought Aunt Min too strict to live, but in Marigold's eyes her regimen compared very favourably with Grandmother's. Though Marigold called her Aunt Min, according to the custom of the caste, she was really only a cousin of the Cloud of Spruce

Lesleys. But she was a genuine aunt of Billy's, that is to say, she had once been married to a half-brother of his father's. So Marigold and Billy might call themselves cousins of a sort.

This was Marigold's first visit to Aunt Min, and was to be the final one of the autumn. Next week she must go to school again.

Marigold liked Windyside. She liked the big airy house with its rooms full of quaint old furniture. There were so many beautiful things to look at, especially the scores of strange and exquisite Indian shells, brought home by Aunt Min's sailor-husband, and the case of stuffed parrots in the hall, with the model of a full-rigged ship atop of it.

To be sure, Aunt Min was very strict about her diet—which was why Grandmother had been so willing to let her come—and her table was something of the leanest. Aunt Min's temper was a bit uncertain also. She could say sharp things on occasion and had been known to slam doors. But there were compensations. For one thing, Aunt Min always asked her casually how she took her tea. For another, cats. Dozens of adorable animals basking on the window-sills, sunning themselves in the garden walks, and prowling about the barn. A batch of kittens was all in the days work at Windyside. For once in her life Marigold felt that she had all the cats she wanted.

Now, all the use Billy had for a cat was a target.

Marigold thought Billy very funny to look at. He had a round moon face of pink and white, large china-blue eyes, a shock of fine straight yellow hair and a mouth so wide he seemed to be perpetually grinning. But she rather liked him. He was the first boy she had ever liked.

Hip? No, she had never *liked* Hip. This was entirely different.

She listened sympathetically to his tale of woe. She thought Billy had a case.

Billy, it seemed, had not wanted to come to Aunt Min's at all. His mother was dead and he and his father lived together at a boarding-house, where life was tolerable because of Dad. But Dad had to go to South America on a prolonged business-trip and hence Billy's sojourn with Aunt Min.

"Rotten, I call it," he growled. "I wanted to go to Aunt Nora's. She's a real aunt—Mamma's own sister. Not a half-aunt like Aunt Min. I tell you Aunt Nora's great. Always cuts a pie in six pieces. Aunt Min, 'jever notice, always cuts it in eight. A feller can do as he likes at Aunt Nora's. You haven't gotter sit up on your hind-legs and act real pretty *all* the time there. *She* ain't one of your fussy old things."

"Aunt Min is pretty particular," agreed Marigold, thinking how lovely that little blue glimpse of the harbour was at the end of the orchard aisle.

"Particular! Say, I've gotter wash my face *every* day, and brush my teeth more times 'n you could shake a stick at. And live on health foods. Say, you ought to taste Aunt Nora's raspberry buns."

"They sound good," agreed Marigold, who herself felt certain hankerings after Salome's pantry.

"Just think how splendid it would 'a' been there. I wouldn't have to be respectable for one minute—only on Sundays and then I could 'a' stood it for a change. I could go barefoot—and slide down the pighouse roof—and eat everything that come handy. Hot dogs. There's a hot-dog stand just outside Aunt Nora's gate."

Billy groaned. It was agonising to think of the delights one might enjoy at Aunt Nora's and contrast them with the bitter reality at Aunt Min's.

"Why wouldn't your father let you go to Aunt Nora's?" asked Marigold.

"Search *me*. I think he had some fool notion Aunt Min would be offended. I was to Aunt Nora's last summer and Aunt Min thought it was her turn. Mind you, it isn't because she likes me. She's got some fool idea of doing her duty by Dad. And mind you, she thinks Aunt Nora's is an awful place because Aunt Nora is poor. She thinks I wouldn't be 'happy' there. Happy!"

Billy groaned again.

"I *never* had such a good time as I had at Aunt Nora's. Say, I had to hunt her turkeys up every evening. Roam everywhere I liked and no questions asked so long's I turned up at bedtime with the turks. Here if I go outer the gate it's, 'William, *where* have you been?' and 'William, did you scrape your boots?' Why, the cats here have to wipe their feet afore they go in."

"Now, Billy, *that's* exaggerating," said Marigold rebukingly.

"Well, 'tain't exaggerating to say I don't dast throw a single stone here," said Billy defiantly. "It's aggravating, that's what it is. Millions of cats and not a chance to throw a stone at one of 'em. I *did* throw one first day I was here—gave her old yellow Tom the thrill of his life—and she jawed at me for a week and made me read a chapter of the Bible every day. I'd rather she'd taken it out of my hide. She thinks out so many different ways of punishing me and I never know what to expect. And then—'ja hear her?—telling Mrs. Kent what I looked like when I was a baby? She's always at it. Catch Aunt Nora telling on a feller like that. Or kissing me goodnight. Aunt Min always does. Thinks it's her 'duty,' I s'pose."

Billy thrust his hands in his pockets and scowled at the universe. But he was feeling better. Remained only one grievance to be discussed. The worst of all.

"I could worry along if it wasn't for Sundays," he said. "I hate Sunday here—hate it worse'n p'isen."

"Why?"

"'Cause I have to write a snopsis."

"What's a snopsis?"

"Why, you go to church and when you come home you gotter write out all you can remember of the sermon. And if you can't remember enough—oh, boy! She says *her* children always done it. She'll make *you* do it, too, next Sunday, I'll bet."

Marigold reflected a bit. She didn't think she would mind. It might be int'resting—a kind of game in fact. For *one* Sunday. But poor Bill had to do it every Sunday.

"Well, never mind," she said soothingly. "Sunday's a long way off yet. Let's see how much fun we can have before that."

Decidedly, thought Billy, here was a girl.

2

Sunday might be far off—but Sunday came. After a week during which Billy forgot to hanker for Aunt Nora's. That was all very well. But Marigold was going home Tuesday. Billy would have been torn in pieces by wild horses before he would have confessed how he hated the thought.

But here was Sunday afternoon—and church. To which Billy and Marigold must go alone because Aunt Min had been summoned to Charlottetown to see an old friend who was passing through and could be seen on no other day.

"I'm sorry I can't go to church," she said, "because young Mr. Harvey Nelson is preaching for a call and I'd like to hear him. But it can't be helped. I've left your suppers in the pantry for you. Now be good children. Marigold, you'll see that Billy behaves properly, won't you? Don't forget to pay close attention to the sermon. You must both write out a synopsis of it this evening, and I want to see a better result than last Sunday, Billy."

"A-ha," gloated Billy as Aunt Min went out. "I told you you'd have to do it, too."

Marigold did not resent his gloating. He was really behaving very well, considering she had been told to look after his behaviour. That was too awful of Aunt Min. Why *couldn't* people understand certain perfectly plain, self-evident things?

"Oh, my, ain't we Sundayfied!" chanted Davy Dixon on the fence, as they went down the lane. Davy was freckled and snubnosed, bareheaded and barefooted. With no more clothes on than decency required. But he did look so jolly and care-free. All the Dixons did. But they were a family Aunt Min detested. She never let Billy and Marigold play with them, though they lived only a cat's walk away through the bush behind Aunt Min's.

"Comin' to the picnic?" asked Davy.

"What picnic?"

"Oh, just the Dixon family picnic," grinned Davy. "This is Mom's and Pop's wedding-day. Twelve years married 'n' ain't sorry for it yit. We're going to take our new car 'n' go to the sand-hills. Got a basket of eats 'd make your eyes stick out. Yum-yum. 'N' mom said to ask youse to come along, too, 'cause she knew your Aunt Min was going away 'n' youse'd be lonesome."

Marigold found herself wishing they could go. At home she liked going to church, but she was sure she wouldn't like going to Windyside church. She didn't like the look of it; a big, bare, wind-beaten, drab-tinted church with a spire as long and sharp as a needle; somehow it was not a friendly church. And she knew nobody there. A drive in a motor-car to the sand-hills sounded very alluring. But of course it was unthinkable.

What was Billy saying?

"I'll go if you'll lend me that book at your place—*The Flying Roll.*"

"Bill-*ee*," said Marigold.

"Oh, all right," said Dave. "It belongs to old Aunt Janey but she won't care."

"I'll go," said Billy decidedly. "Coming, Marigold?"

"Oh, please, remember what day this is," implored Marigold, with a wild wish in the back of her mind that she could go. "And what will Aunt Min say?"

"Aunt Min isn't going to know a thing about it. I've got a plan. Aw, come on. We'll have a rip-roaring time."

"Billy, you don't mean it."

"You bet I do. You can go to church if you want to and stick all the afternoon to varnishy seats."

"Gotter make up your mind quick," said Dave. "Lizzie's waiting."

Marigold reflected rapidly. She *couldn't* go alone to a strange church. And it would be so lonesome to stay home. The sand-dunes—the waves—the wind on the sea—

"I'll—go," she said helplessly.

"I knew you'd some gizzard in you. Atta girl," gloated Bill. "Let's scoot back and take off our proud rags. Jes' a minute, Dave."

A few minutes later they were running along the path through a scented field of hay on a short cut to the Dixons. Ordinarily Marigold felt she had wings on a day like this. Now she suddenly felt leaden-footed. But Billy must not suspect it. He would despise her if he found out she really did not care for all this lawlessness.

The Dixons' new car proved to be a very second-hand snub-nosed little Ford, into which they all piled and rattled and bounced down a narrow deep-rutted lane to the sand-dunes. Marigold sat on the knee of Mrs. Dixon, a big, pink, overblown lady who used what even Billy knew to be bad grammar, in a cheerful, excruciating voice. Marigold thought the bones would be shaken out of her before they got to the dunes.

It should have been a wonderful afternoon. Polly Dixon was a pretty, gentle little girl and Marigold liked her. They slid down the sand-hills and made shore pies and dug wells in the sand. They gathered clam-shells and went bathing in a little sand-cove up the shore where the water was like soft, warm, liquid turquoise. They played games with the boys. They laughed and ran and scampered. And under it all Marigold knew perfectly well that she was not having a good time. She was only trying to make herself think she was.

Even the lunch—to which she looked forward a little ashamedly after a week of Aunt Min's diet—was a disappointment. There was plenty of it—but Mrs. Dixon was not a good cook. Marigold ate stale sandwiches, and cookies that reeked of soda, and a piece of mushy lemon-pie. She always believed that she also ate two crickets that had got tangled up in the meringue of the pie. But Billy thought that feed was extra-x. "I wish to goodness I could eat some more but I can't," he sighed, bolting the last morsel of a gorgeous piece of cake whose iced surface was decorated with violent red-and-yellow candies.

3

"Wasn't it jolly?" said Billy, drawing a long unregretful breath as they walked home together through the hayfield.

"Won't it be jolly when Aunt Min asks you to write a synopsis and you can't?" demanded Marigold rather wearily and sarcastically.

Billy grinned.

"I'll just write it. This *Flying Roll* book is full of sermons. I read some dandy ones in it one day down at Dixons' before you came. We'll just write a snopsis of one of them, and Aunt Min will never know the difference."

"*We* won't," cried Marigold. "You can do as you like, but I won't cheat like that."

"Then you'll go and give the whole thing away," said Billy pale with wrath and fear.

"No-o-o, I won't. I'll just tell Aunt Min I couldn't write a synopsis."

"She'll send you to bed 'thout any supper."

"I don't care," said Marigold pathetically, putting her hand on her stomach. "That lemon-pie was awful."

Billy betook himself to a little room Aunt Min called her library. His opinion was that writing a "snopsis" with the printed sermon before you was a snap. When Aunt Min came home he was ready for her. Marigold said, with a very good imitation of Grandmother Lesley's manner, that she could not write a synopsis.

Aunt Min looked at her for a moment but said nothing. She took Billy's copious sheets with a very grim smile—a smile that speedily changed to a frown.

"Surely—surely Harvey Nelson never preached such stuff as this."

"Why, what's the matter with it?" cried Billy.

"Matter. It's heresy—rank heresy. Why, the man must be a Second Adventist. I never read such doctrines. Well, he'll not get any call to Windyside if I can prevent it. I was in favour of him because he's engaged to Dovie Sinclair and she is a distant relation of mine. But this preposterous sermon is too much."

Aunt Min rustled indignantly out of the room, leaving Billy to reflect on the snares and pitfalls of existence.

"What do you suppose was wrong with it?" he whispered miserably.

"I don't know," said Marigold agitatedly, "but I do know that if Mr. Nelson is engaged to Dovie Sinclair he's *got* to get that call. Dovie is my Sunday-school teacher at home and I won't have her disappointed through our fault."

"Don't you dare snitch on me," cried Billy. "Let things alone. Maybe she'll cool down—or find out from some one else he didn't preach it."

Marigold's face was white and tragic.

"She never will. She'll just say he doesn't preach sound doctrine and she won't explain anything about it. You know Aunt Min. She's got to be told and I'm going to tell her. But you needn't come if you're scared."

"I'm scared but I'm coming. You don't suppose I'm going to leave you to do it all alone?" said Billy staunchly. "Besides it was all my doings. I made you go. If Aunt Min has to be told, she's gotter be told that, too."

No wonder folks liked Billy.

4

Half an hour later Billy and Marigold were sitting on the granary steps. The fatal interview was over and it had not been a pleasant one, to state it mildly.

None the pleasanter for Marigold in that Aunt Min forgave her readily because Billy had led her astray. Perhaps Aunt Min did not want to get in wrong with the Cloud of Spruce people. But all the vials of her wrath were uncorked on Billy's devoted head. She told Billy he had disgraced his name and ordered him to go out and stay out until she had decided on his punishment.

If it had not been for Billy, Marigold would have been feeling very happy. It was so delightful to be good friends with herself again. And—if only one knew what was going to be done to Billy—it was such a perfect evening. Those little golden dells among the sunset hills—that path of moonrise glitter on the harbour over which a ship of dreams might come sailing—those gossiping poplars—the green creaminess of that field of buckwheat-blossom in the shade of the wood—those pines behind the well like big green purring pussy-cats—that sweetest imp-faced kitten purring at her from under the milk-bench—but—

"*What* do you suppose she'll do?" she whispered to Billy. The subject had such a gruesome fascination.

"Oh, likely make me wear a girl's apron for a week," groaned Billy. "She made we wear one for two days the time I put the peanut-shells in Elder Johnny's pocket at prayer-meeting. Say—" Billy began to laugh, "that *was* fun. When he pulled out his hanky in the middle of his prayer the shells flew every which way for a Sunday. One struck the minister on the nose."

Marigold *saw* the picture and laughed satisfyingly. Billy reflected gloomily that she was going home Tuesday. If only she were to be around to help him through whatever Aunt Min would visit on him. To be sure, she had got him into the scrape but he bore her no grudge for that. She was a good little scout.

The moon had come up until she seemed to be resting on the very tip of the tall Lombardy on the hills when Aunt Min came across the yard, a rigid figure of outraged majesty. She looked scornfully at Billy and spoke in a sad, gentle way. When Aunt Min banged doors and looked or spoke sourly or sharply no one worried. But when Aunt Min smiled in that curious sweet fashion and spoke in that low, even tone, then beware. It was the calm before the levin-bolt.

"Do you realise that you have behaved very badly?" she asked.

"Yes'm," gulped Billy.

"I have decided—" Aunt Min paused.

Billy was speaking. *What* fiendish punishment had Aunt Min devised? Marigold slipped a little cold hand of backing into his.

"I don't feel equal to the responsibility of looking after you any longer," resumed Aunt Min more gently than ever, "so I have decided to send you to your Aunt Nora's to-morrow."

CHAPTER XXI

Her Chrism of Womanhood

1

A new magic had fallen over Cloud of Spruce. Grandmother solemnly decreed that Marigold might play with Sidney Guest. Grandmother would not, of course, call him Budge as everybody else did. His mother was a Randolph from Charlottetown, so that he was a quite permissible playmate for a Lesley of Harmony. Mr. Guest had bought Mr. Donkin's farm and so Budge lived right next door to Cloud of Spruce.

He was a "nice-mannered" little boy, so Grandmother said. Rather thin and scrawny as to looks, with sandy hair but fine clear grey eyes. The only thing Grandmother was seriously afraid of was that they might poison themselves in some of their prowls and rambles. Not an ill-founded fear at all. For, in spite of all warnings, they ate or tried to eat nearly everything they came across.

Marigold had never had a real playmate in Harmony before, save for Gwen's hectic three weeks. She did not seem to care for any of the girls in Harmony, and though she wrote fat gossipy letters to Gwen and Paula and Bernice she did not see them very often. Perhaps Sylvia spoiled her for other little girls, as Mother sometimes thought rather anxiously. Mother had always defended Sylvia sympathisingly against a Grandmother who did not understand some things. But sometimes lately she wondered if she had been wise in so doing. It would not be a good thing if the wild secret charm of fairy-playmates spoiled Marigold for the necessary and valuable companionship of her kind. Marigold was twelve. Her golden hair was deepening to warm brown and she had at last learned not to pronounce interesting "int'resting." Surely it was time she was outgrowing Sylvia.

So Lorraine Lesley was glad when, just at the beginning of vacation, the Guests bought the Donkin place and Marigold and Budge took a prompt liking to each other. Marigold was amazed to find herself really liking a boy. She had never liked any of the boys in school. She had liked Billy but she had forgotten him. She had detested Cousin Marcus's Jack. As for Hip Price, he had made her hate all boys for a time. But Budge was different from any boy she had ever known.

For weeks Marigold's existence became one of hair-raising excitement. She did things to win Budge's approval that she had never dreamed of doing. They went trouting up the brook and Marigold was such a sport in regard to worms that Budge thought in his heart—but did not say—that she was almost as good as a boy. They waded under the bridge. They climbed to the ventilator on top of the big Guest barn. They played pirate on an old green boat—the *Daisy Dean*—stranded on the harbour shore, with a black flag made out of Salome's old black silk skirt and decorated with a skull and cross-bones. In it they sailed on amazing voyages hunting for gold and glamour and adventure. They had a password and a secret sign. They fixed up a stove of stones and cooked mussels and potatoes over it.

With Budge, Marigold could explore all the pretty play-lands down the harbour where she would never have dared to go alone. They even went as far as that grey misty end of the world known as the harbour's mouth, where the silver-and-lilac sand-dunes stretched in all their wild sweet loveliness of salt-withered grasses and piping sea-winds. Nobody ever knew *that,* or that they had got caught by the tide and had to climb the banks and come home through dripping wet meadows. 'Twas a guilty triumphant secret. And another was the driftwood fire they made on the shore one twilight. They had both been told never to play with fire, but that did not spoil their enjoyment of it one bit. Rather heightened it, I am afraid. This secret forbidden thing had a charm all its own. And some days they fairly lived in the froggy marsh—where a very decent dragon also had his abode and grizzly bears grizzled.

Marigold had a deadly horror of frogs but she never let Budge know it, and she compelled herself to carry a dead snake—on a stick—to win his admiration. She also brought herself to say "Holy cats," but try as she would she could never compass a "darn," which was just as well. Because in his heart Budge did not care for girls who said "darn."

She was never able to learn to whistle on a blade of grass, as he did. But she could do one thing he couldn't do—make the dearest pudding-bags out of the fat live-forever leaves. Budge tried and tried but his thumb pressure was always too heavy, so the balance of respect was kept true. And when Budge sat down on a hot oven door one day, in trousers that needed a patch, Marigold never even asked him how his burns were getting on. By such tact is friendship preserved.

Budge patted Marigold's kitten, Pops, and Marigold loved his dog, Dix. But Sylvia she could not yet share with him. Budge had somehow got the idea that Marigold had some pet mystery connected with the hill of spruce, and sometimes teased her to tell him what it was. But Marigold always refused. Not yet—not yet. She had never, in spite of fleeting temptation, told any of her playmates about Sylvia—not even Bernice. Sylvia was so much her own. Although—Marigold owned it to herself occasionally with a sorrowful sigh—somehow Sylvia wasn't just the same. Not so vivid—so living—so *real*. The change had come about so slowly that Marigold did not yet realise how far her jolly chumship with Budge had replaced that goblin-comradeship of her lonely years. She clung to Sylvia, remembering what Aunt Marigold had said to her one evening as they sat in the orchard.

"Keep your dream, little Marigold, as long as you can. A

dream is an immortal thing. Time cannot kill it or age wither it. You may tire of reality but never of dreams."

"It hurts—to wake up, though," said Marigold timidly. "When I come back through the Green Gate I always feel that it's just terrible to think there really isn't any Sylvia—that she's just something I've dreamed."

"The dreamer's joy is worth the dreamer's pain," said Aunt Marigold, knowing that since Marigold had begun to think of Sylvia as a dream the sad awakening was near.

So, almost every day, some time of it, Marigold slipped through The Magic Door and the Green Gate and summoned Sylvia. Sylvia always came—still. But there was a difference.

Marigold would have told Budge about Sylvia if she could have been sure how he would take her. Marigold knew of a side of his nature which made her think he might understand Sylvia. Rarely, Budge gave her glimpses of this side. When they grew tired of prowling and pirating and sat on the wharf watching the ghostly sails of outgoing ships in the twilight, Budge would recite to her shyly the queer little verses of poetry he sometimes made up. Marigold thought they were wonderful. Budge understood, too, the secret thrill that came when you opened a new book. And he was a crackerjack at yarns. She liked his scarlet boy-stories better than her rose-pink and moon-blue girl-fancies. That one of the wolf-skin rug on the Guest parlour floor coming alive and prowling at night with burning eyes. Marigold couldn't sleep when she went to bed for the delicious horror of it. Was it coming across the road now—snuffing through the garden—padding up the stairs? Marigold screamed aloud and Mother came in and said she'd had a nightmare.

2

And then. The Austins bought the old Burnaby place and moved in. Tad Austin was a boy of Budge's age. And Marigold found herself deserted.

"'Tis an old tale and often told."

Tad Austin's parents, for some inscrutable reason, had seen fit to christen him Romney, but he never got anything but Tad. He was really not a bad-looking boy, with a chubby, agreeable brown face, although Marigold, who naturally could see nothing attractive about him, thought that his round, prominent blue eyes looked absurdly like the fat blue plums on the tree by the apple-barn.

The world was suddenly a cold, lonely, empty place for our poor Marigold. Always hitherto she had taken her troubles to her mother. But she couldn't take this—she couldn't. Not even Mother could understand. Certainly Grandmother couldn't. Grandmother, who, passing Marigold sitting disconsolately on the twilight steps, had remarked humorously,

"'Don't sigh but send. And if he doesn't come let him be hanged.'"

Send, indeed. Marigold would have died the death before she would have made the slightest effort to get Budge back. The cats could have him. She got an enormous satisfaction out of picturing to herself how haughty and implacable she would be if he *did* come back. At least this was how she felt about it at first.

"Perhaps he'll be sorry when I'm dead," thought Marigold darkly. But she would show Budge—show everybody—*she* didn't care. She went and made candy and sang like a lark.

But there was nobody to share the candy with when it was made. She gave Lazarre the most of it to take to his children.

Life was a howling wilderness for Marigold the next few weeks. It seemed to her that Budge and Tad literally flaunted their intimacy and fun in her face—though the shameful truth was that they never thought about her at all. They got up a show and all the boys of Harmony could see it for a cent, but no girls. Oh, it was *mean*!

Budge and Tad went fishing up the brooks. Budge and Tad dug for pirate gold. Budge and Tad had a smuggler's rendezvous in the cave Marigold had discovered on the harbour shore. Budge and Tad had the kitten-hunt in the Guest barn which Marigold and Budge had planned to have in the fulness of time when there should be kittens to hunt.

This was the last straw that broke Marigold's pride. She would so have loved a kitten-hunt with Budge in the great dusky hay-scented old barn.

She must get Budge back. She *must*. Existence was quite impossible without him. But how? What could she do? Marigold knew she must not show her hand too plainly. Instinct told her that. Besides she had a dim old memory of something Old Grandmother had said long, long ago.

"If you run after a man he'll run away. It's instinct. We *have* to run when anything chases us."

Wherefore she, Marigold, would *not* run after Budge. Was there any other way?

"I wonder if it would do any good to pray about it," she thought. Then she decided she couldn't try it anyway.

"I don't want him to come back because God made him come. I want him to come back because he *wants* to."

Like an inspiration came the thought of Sylvia. She would tell him about Sylvia. He had always wanted to know about Sylvia. He might come back then.

It was a fortunate coincidence that Salome asked her to go over to the Guest place on an errand that very afternoon. Budge was sitting on the side door-steps packing fish-worms in a tin can. He grinned at her cheerfully and absently. It had never occurred to Budge that he had treated Marigold shamelessly. She had simply—for the time—ceased to count.

"I have something to tell you," whispered Marigold.

"What is it?" said Budge indifferently.

Marigold sat down beside him and told him all about Sylvia at last. About The Magic Door and the Green Gate and the Land of Butterflies and The Rhyme. She had a curious unpleasant sense of loss and disloyalty as she told it. As if she were losing something that was very precious.

And she had her reward.

"Aw, that sounds awful silly," said Budge.

Marigold went away without another word. She would *never* speak to Budge Guest again. She would *never* have anything to do with *any* boy again. All tarred with the same brush, as Lazarre said. She would go back to Sylvia—darling, neglected Sylvia. Through The Magic Door—up the slope of fern—through the Green Gate. Then The Rhyme.

And no Sylvia!

Marigold stared helplessly around her with a quivering lip. No Sylvia. Sylvia would not come. Would never come again. Marigold felt this as we feel certain things irrevocably. Was it because she had told Budge about her? Or was it because she had suddenly grown too old and wise for fairyland. Were the "ivory gates and golden" of which Mother sometimes sang, closed behind her forever? Marigold flung herself down among the ferns in the bitterest tears she had ever shed—ever would shed, perhaps. Her lovely dream was gone. Who of us is there who has not lost one?

3

It was the next day Budge came back—an indignant Budge, avid to pour out his wrongs to somebody. And that somebody was the disdained and disdainful Marigold, who had vowed afresh the night before that if Budge Guest ever spoke to her again she would treat him with such scorn and contempt that even his thick hide would feel it.

Budge and Tad had fought because their dogs had fought.

"*My* dog won," gulped Budge. "And Tad got mad. He said Dix was only a *mongrel cur.*"

"He's jealous," said Marigold comfortingly. "And he has an awful temper. I heard that long ago from a girl who knew him *well.*"

"*I* dared him to fight *me*, then—and he said he *wouldn't* fight me because I was such a sissy."

"He wouldn't fight you because he knew he'd get licked even worse than his dog did," said Marigold, oh, so scornfully. But the scorn was all for Tad.

"He *wouldn't* fight—but he kept on saying mean things. He said I wore a *nightcap.* Well, I did once, years ago—when I was little but—"

"Everybody wears nightcaps when they're *little*," said Marigold.

"And he said that I was a coward and that I wouldn't walk through the graveyard at night."

"Let's go through it to-night and *show* him," said Marigold eagerly.

"Not to-night," said Budge hastily. "There's a heavy dew. You'd get wet."

Happiness flowed through Marigold like a wave. Budge was thinking of *her* welfare. At least, so she believed.

"He said *his* grandfather had whiskers and mine hadn't. *Should* a grandfather have whiskers?"

"It's ever so much more *aristocratic* not to have them," said Marigold with finality.

"And he said *I* wasn't tattooed and couldn't stand tattooing. He's always been so conceited about that snake his sailor-uncle tattooed on his arm."

"What if he is tattooed?" Marigold wanted to know. She recalled what Grandmother had said about that tattooed snake. "It's a barbaric disfigurement. Didn't *you* say anything to *him?*"

Budge gulped.

"Everything *I* said he said it over again and *laughed.*"

"There's something so insulting about *that*," agreed Marigold.

"And he called me a devilish pup."

"*I* wouldn't mind being called a devilish pup," said Marigold, who thought it sounded quite dashing and romantic.

But there was something yet worse to be told.

"He—said—I was *unladylike.*"

This was a bit of a poser for Marigold. It would never do to imply that Budge *was* ladylike.

"Why didn't you tell him that he's pop-eyed and that he eats like a rhinoceros?" she inquired calmly.

Budge was at the end of his list of grievances. His anger was ebbing and he had a horrible feeling that he was going to—cry. And back of that a delicious feeling that even if he did Marigold would understand and not despise him. What a brick of a girl she was! Worth a million Tad Austins.

As a matter of fact Budge got off without crying but he never forgot that feeling.

"I'm never going to have anything to do with him again," he said darkly. "Say, do you want one of them grey kittens? If you do I'll bring it over to-morrow."

"Oh, do," said Marigold. "The Witch's are all black this summer."

They sat there for an hour eating nut-sweet apples, entirely satisfied with themselves. To Marigold the tiny roses on the bush by the steps seemed like the notes or echoes of the little song that was singing itself in her heart. All that had once made magic made it again. And she asked Budge if he had told Tad about Sylvia.

"Of course not. That's *your* secret," said Budge, grandly. "And he doesn't know about the password and the secret sign either. That's *our* secret."

When Budge went home it was agreed that he should bring the kitten the next afternoon and that they should go on a quest for the Holy Grail up among the spruces.

"I'll *never* forget to-night," said Marigold. Some lost ecstasy had returned to life.

4

But the next morning it seemed as if the night before had never been. When Marigold had sprung eagerly out of her blue-and-white bed, slipped into her clothes and run liltingly down to the front door—what did she see?

Budge and Tad walking amiably down the road with fishing-poles and worm-cans, while two dogs trotted behind in entire amity.

Marigold stood rigid. She made no response when Budge waved his pole gaily at her and shouted hello. Her heart, so full of joy a moment ago, was lead, heavy and cold.

That was a doleful forenoon. Her new dress of peach silk came home but Marigold was not interested in it. A maiden forsaken and grieved in spirit has no vanity.

But just let Budge Guest come to her again for comfort!

Budge came that afternoon but not in search of comfort. He was cheerful and grinful and he brought an adorable clover-scented kitten with a new pattern of stripes. But Marigold was cold and distant. Very.

"What's biting you?" asked Budge.

"Nothing," said Marigold.

"Look here," expostulated Budge, "I came over to go Grailing with you. But if you don't want to go just say so. Tad wants me to go to the harbour mouth."

For a moment, pride and—something else—struggled fiercely together in Marigold's heart. Something else won.

"Of course I want to go Grail-hunting," she said.

They did not find the Grail but they found one of Grandmother's precious pink-lustre cups which had been lost for two years, ever since a certain Lesley Reunion Picnic had been held on the spruce hill. Found it safe and unharmed in a crevice of the stone dyke. And Grandmother was so pleased that she gave them a whole plateful of hop-and-go-fetch-its to eat—which was symbolic. She would not have given them hop-and-go-fetch-its if it had really been the Grail they found.

5

Budge went home. He had a tryst with Tad for the evening. Marigold sat down on the veranda steps. The little streak of yellow sky above the dark hills over the harbour was very lonely. The sound of breakers tumbling on the far away outer shore was very lonely. She was very lonely—in spite of her jolly afternoon with Budge.

Aunt Marigold coming out, noted Marigold's face and sat down beside her. Aunt Marigold, who had never had any children of her own, knew more mothercraft than many women who had. She had not only the seeing eye but the understanding heart as well. In a short time she had the whole story. If she smiled over it Marigold did not see it.

"You must not expect to have Budge wholly to yourself, dear, as you had Sylvia. Our earthly house of love has many mansions and many tenants. Budge will be always coming back to you. He finds something in your companionship Tad can't give him. He'll come for it, never fear. But you must share him with others. We—women—must always share."

Marigold sat awhile longer after Aunt Marigold had gone away. But she was no longer unhappy. A dreamy smile lingered on her lips. The new kitten purred on her lap. The twilight wrapped her round. Robber winds came down out of the cloud of spruce to rifle spices from the flower-beds in the orchard. There was gold of her namesake flowers all along the dusk of the walk. The stars twinkled through the fir-trees and right and left the harbour range-lights shone like great earth stars. Presently a moon rose and there was a sparkling trail over the harbour like a lady's silken dress.

Yes, she must share Budge. The old magic was gone forever— gone with Sylvia and the Hidden Land and all the dear, sweet fading dreams of childhood. But after all there were compensations. For one thing, she could be as big a coward as she wanted to be. No more hunting snakes and chivying frogs. No more pretending to like horrible things that squirmed. She was no longer a boy's rival. She stood on her own ground.

"And I'll always be here for him to come back to," she thought.

THE END

JANE OF LANTERN HILL

First published in 1937

1

Gay street, so Jane always thought, did not live up to its name. It was, she felt certain, the most melancholy street in Toronto . . . though, to be sure, she had not seen a great many of the Toronto streets in her circumscribed comings and goings of eleven years.

Gay Street should be a *gay* street, thought Jane, with gay, friendly houses, set amid flowers, that cried out, "How do you do?" to you as you passed them, with trees that waved hands at you and windows that winked at you in the twilights. Instead of that, Gay Street was dark and dingy, lined with forbidding, old-fashioned brick houses, grimy with age, whose tall, shuttered, blinded windows could never have thought of winking at anybody. The trees that lined Gay Street were so old and huge and stately that it was difficult to think of them as trees at all, any more than those forlorn little things in the green pails by the doors of the filling station on the opposite corner. Grandmother had been furious when the old Adams house on that corner had been torn down and the new white-and-red filling station built in its place. She would never let Frank get petrol there. But at that, Jane thought, it was the only gay place on the street.

Jane lived at 60 Gay. It was a huge, castellated structure of brick, with a pillared entrance porch, high, arched Georgian windows, and towers and turrets wherever a tower or turret could be wedged in. It was surrounded by a high iron fence with wrought-iron gates . . . those gates had been famous in the Toronto of an earlier day . . . that were always closed and locked by Frank at night, thus giving Jane a very nasty feeling that she was a prisoner being locked in.

There was more space around 60 Gay than around most of the houses on the street. It had quite a bit of lawn in front, though the grass never grew well because of the row of old trees just inside the fence . . . and quite a respectable space between the side of the house and Bloor Street; but it was not nearly wide enough to dim the unceasing clatter and clang of Bloor, which was especially noisy and busy where Gay Street joined it. People wondered why old Mrs Robert Kennedy continued to live there when she had oodles of money and could buy one of those lovely new houses in Forest Hill or in the Kingsway. The taxes on a lot as big as 60 Gay must be ruinous and the house was hopelessly out of date. Mrs Kennedy merely smiled contemptuously when things like this were said to her, even by her son, William Anderson, the only one of her first family whom she respected, because he had been successful in business and was rich in his own right. She had never loved him, but he had compelled her to respect him.

Mrs Kennedy was perfectly satisfied with 60 Gay. She had come there as the bride of Robert Kennedy when Gay Street was the last word in streets and 60 Gay, built by Robert's father, one of the finest "mansions" in Toronto. It had never ceased to be so in her eyes. She had lived there for forty-five years and she would live there the rest of her life. Those who did not like it need not stay there. This, with a satirically amused glance at Jane, who had never said she didn't like Gay Street. But grandmother, as Jane had long ago discovered, had an uncanny knack of reading your mind.

Once, when Jane had been sitting in the Cadillac, one dark, dingy morning in a snowy world, waiting for Frank to take her to St Agatha's, as he did every day, she had heard two women, who were standing on the street-corner, talking about it.

"Did you ever see such a dead house?" said the younger. "It looks as if it had been dead for ages."

"That house died thirty years ago, when Robert Kennedy died," said the older woman. "Before that it was a lively place. Nobody in Toronto entertained more. Robert Kennedy liked social life. He was a very handsome, friendly man. People could never understand how he came to marry Mrs James Anderson

. . . a widow with three children. She was Victoria Moore to begin with, you know, old Colonel Moore's daughter . . . a very aristocratic family. But she was pretty as a picture then and was she crazy about him! My dear, she worshipped him. People said she was never willing to let him out of her sight for a moment. And they said she hadn't cared for her first husband at all. Robert Kennedy died when they had been married about fifteen years . . . died just after his first baby was born, I've heard."

"Does she live all alone in that castle?"

"Oh, no. Her two daughters live with her. One of them is a widow or something . . . and there's a granddaughter, I believe. They say old Mrs Kennedy is a terrible tyrant, but the younger daughter . . . the widow . . . is gay enough and goes to everything you see reported in *Saturday Evening*. Very pretty . . . and can she dress! She was the Kennedy one and took after her father. She must hate having all her fine friends coming to Gay Street. It's worse than dead . . . it's decayed. But I can remember when Gay Street was one of the most fashionable residential streets in town. Look at it now."

"Shabby genteel."

"Hardly even that. Why, 58 Gay is a boarding-house. But old Mrs Kennedy keeps 60 up very well, though the paint is beginning to peel off the balconies, you notice."

"Well, I'm glad I don't live on Gay Street," giggled the other, as they ran to catch the car.

"You may well be," thought Jane. Though, if she had been put to it, she could hardly have told you where she would have liked to live if not at 60 Gay. Most of the streets through which she drove to St Agatha's were mean and uninviting, for St Agatha's, that very expensive and exclusive private school to which grandmother sent Jane, now found itself in an unfashionable and outgrown locality also. But St Agatha's didn't mind that . . . St Agatha's would have been St Agatha's, you must understand, in the desert of Sahara.

Uncle William Anderson's house in Forest Hill was very

handsome, with landscaped lawns and rock gardens, but she wouldn't like to live there. One was almost terrified to walk over the lawn lest one do something to Uncle William's cherished velvet. You had to keep to the flat stepping-stones path. And Jane wanted to run. You couldn't run at St Agatha's either, except when you were playing games. And Jane was not very good at games. She always felt awkward in them. At eleven she was as tall as most girls of thirteen. She towered above the girls of her class. They did not like it and made Jane feel that she fitted in nowhere.

As for running at 60 Gay . . . had anybody ever run at 60 Gay? Jane felt as if mother must have . . . mother stepped so lightly and gaily yet that you thought her feet had wings. But once, when Jane had dared to run from the front door to the back door, straight through the long house that was almost half the length of the city block, singing at the top of her voice, grandmother, who she had thought was out, had emerged from the breakfast-room and looked at her with the smile on her dead-white face that Jane hated.

"What," she said in the silky voice that Jane hated still more, "is responsible for this outburst, Victoria?"

"I was running just for the fun of it," explained Jane. It seemed so very simple. But grandmother had just smiled and said, as only grandmother could say things:

"I wouldn't do it again if I were you, Victoria."

Jane never did it again. That was the effect grandmother had on you, though she was so tiny and wrinkled . . . so tiny that lanky, long-legged Jane was almost as tall as she was.

Jane hated to be called Victoria. Yet everybody called her that, except mother, who called her Jane Victoria. Jane knew somehow that grandmother resented that . . . knew that for some reason unknown to her, grandmother hated the name of Jane. Jane liked it . . . always had liked it . . . always thought of herself as Jane. She understood that she had been named Victoria after grandmother, but she did not know where the Jane had come from. There were no Janes in the Kennedys or Andersons. In her eleventh year she had begun to suspect that it might have come from the Stuart side. And Jane was sorry for that, because she did not want to think she owed her favourite name to her father. Jane hated her father in so far as hatred could find place in a little heart that was not made for hating anybody, even grandmother. There were times Jane was afraid she did hate grandmother, which was dreadful, because grandmother was feeding and clothing and educating her. Jane knew she ought to love grandmother, but it seemed a very hard thing to do. Apparently mother found it easy; but, then, grandmother loved mother, which made a difference. Loved her as she loved nobody else in the world. And grandmother did not love Jane. Jane had always known that. And Jane felt, if she did not yet know, that grandmother did not like mother loving her so much.

"You fuss entirely too much about her," grandmother had once said contemptuously, when mother was worried about Jane's sore throat.

"She's all I have," said mother.

And then grandmother's old white face had flushed.

"I am nothing, I suppose," she said.

"Oh, mother, you know I didn't mean *that*," mother had said piteously, fluttering her hands in a way she had which always made Jane think of two little white butterflies. "I meant . . . I meant . . . she's my only child. . . ."

"And you love that child . . . his child . . . better than you love me!"

"Not better . . . only differently," said mother pleadingly.

"Ingrate!" said grandmother. It was only one word, but what venom she could put into a word. Then she had gone out of the room, still with that flush on her face and her pale blue eyes smouldering under her frosty hair.

2

"Mummy," said Jane as well as her swelled tonsils would let her, "why doesn't grandmother want you to love me?"

"Darling, it isn't like that," said mother, bending over Jane, her face like a rose in the light of the rose-shaded lamp.

But Jane knew it was like that. She knew why mother seldom kissed her or petted her in grandmother's presence. It made grandmother angry with a still, cold, terrible anger that seemed to freeze the air about her. Jane was glad mother didn't often do it. She made up for it when they were alone together . . . but then they were so very seldom alone together. Even now they would not have very long together, for mother was going out to a dinner party. Mother went out almost every evening to something or other and almost every afternoon too. Jane always loved to get a glimpse of her before she went out. Mother knew this and generally contrived that Jane should. She always wore such pretty dresses and looked so lovely. Jane was sure she had the most beautiful mother in the whole world. She was beginning to wonder how any one so lovely as mother could have a daughter so plain and awkward as herself.

"You'll never be pretty . . . your mouth is too big," one of the girls at St Agatha's had told her.

Mother's mouth was like a rosebud, small and red, with dimples tucked away at the corners. Her eyes were blue . . . but not an icy blue like grandmother's. There is such a difference in blue eyes. Mother's were just the colour of the sky on a summer morning between the great masses of white clouds. Her hair was a warm, wavy gold and to-night she was wearing it brushed away from her forehead, with little bunches of curls behind her ears and a row of them at the nape of her white neck. She wore a dress of pale yellow taffeta, with a great rose of deeper yellow velvet at one of her beautiful shoulders. Jane thought she looked like a lovely golden princess, with the slender flame of the diamond bracelet on the creamy satin of her arm. Grandmother had given her the bracelet last week for her birthday. Grandmother was always giving mother such lovely things. And she picked out all her clothes for her . . . wonderful dresses and hats and wraps. Jane did not know that people said Mrs Stuart was always rather overdressed, but she had an idea that mother really liked simpler clothes and only pretended to like better the gorgeous things grandmother bought for her for fear of hurting grandmother's feelings.

Jane was very proud of mother's beauty. She thrilled with delight when she heard people whisper, "Isn't she lovely?" She almost forgot her aching throat as she watched mother put on the rich brocaded wrap, just the colour of her eyes, with its big collar of grey fox.

"Oh, but you're sweet, mummy," she said, putting up her hand and touching mother's cheek as mother bent down and kissed her. It was like touching a rose-leaf. And mother's lashes lay on her cheeks like silken fans. Some people, Jane knew, looked better farther off; but the nearer you were to mother, the prettier she was.

"Darling, do you feel very sick? I hate to leave you but . . ."

Mother didn't finish her sentence but Jane knew she meant, "Grandmother wouldn't like it if I didn't go."

"I don't feel very sick at all," said Jane gallantly "Mary will look after me."

But after mother had gone, with a swish of taffeta, Jane felt a horrible lump in her throat that had nothing to do with her tonsils. It would be so easy to cry . . . but Jane would not let herself cry. Years ago, when she had been no more than five, she had heard mother say very proudly, "Jane never cries. She never cried even when she was a tiny baby." From that day Jane had been careful never to let herself cry, even when she was alone in bed at night. Mother had so few things to be proud of in her: she must not let her down on one of those few things.

But it was dreadfully lonely. The wind was howling along the street outside. The tall windows rattled drearily and the big house seemed full of unfriendly noises and whispers. Jane wished Jody could come in and sit with her for a while. But Jane knew it was useless to wish for that. She could never forget the only time Jody had come to 60 Gay.

"Well, anyhow," said Jane, trying to look on the bright side of things in spite of her sore throat and aching head, "I won't have to read the Bible to them to-night."

"Them" were grandmother and Aunt Gertrude. Very seldom mother because mother was nearly always out. But every night before Jane went to bed she had to read a chapter in the Bible to grandmother and Aunt Gertrude. There was nothing in the whole twenty-four hours that Jane hated doing more than that. And she knew quite well that that was just why grandmother made her do it.

They always went into the drawing-room for the reading and Jane invariably shivered as she entered it. That huge, elaborate room, so full of things that you could hardly move about in it without knocking something over, always seemed cold even on the hottest night in summer. And on winter nights it was cold. Aunt Gertrude took the huge family Bible, with its heavy silver clasp, from the marble-topped centre table and laid it on a little table between the windows. Then she and grandmother sat, one at each end of the table, and Jane sat between them at the side, with Great-grandfather Kennedy scowling down at her from the dim old painting in its heavy, tarnished gilt frame, flanked by the dark blue velvet curtains. That woman on the street had said that Grandfather Kennedy was a nice friendly man but his father couldn't have been. Jane always thought candidly that he looked as if he would enjoy biting a nail in two.

"Turn to the fourteenth chapter of Exodus," grandmother would say. The chapter varied every night, of course, but the tone never did. It always rattled Jane so that she generally made a muddle of finding the right place. And grandmother, with the hateful little smile which seemed to say, "So you can't even do this as it should be done," would put out her lean, crapy hand, with its rich old-fashioned rings, and turn to the right place with uncanny precision. Jane would stumble through the chapter, mispronouncing words she knew perfectly well just because she was so nervous. Sometimes grandmother would say, "A little louder if you please, Victoria. I thought when I sent you to St Agatha's they would at least teach you to open your mouth when reading even if they couldn't teach you geography and history." And Jane would raise her voice so suddenly that Aunt Gertrude would jump. But the next evening it might be, "Not quite so loud, Victoria, if you please. We are not deaf." And poor Jane's voice would die away to little more than a whisper.

When she had finished grandmother and Aunt Gertrude would bow their heads and repeat the Lord's Prayer. Jane would try to say it with them, which was a difficult thing because grandmother was generally two words ahead of Aunt Gertrude. Jane always said "Amen" thankfully. The beautiful prayer, haloed with all the loveliness of age-long worship, had become a sort of horror to Jane.

Then Aunt Gertrude would close the Bible and put it back in exactly the same place, to the fraction of a hair, on the centre table. Finally Jane had to kiss her and grandmother good night. Grandmother would always remain sitting in her chair and Jane would stoop and kiss her forehead.

"Good night, grandmother."

"Good night, Victoria."

But Aunt Gertrude would be standing by the centre table and Jane would have to reach up to her, for Aunt Gertrude was tall. Aunt Gertrude would stoop just a little and Jane would kiss her narrow grey face.

"Good night, Aunt Gertrude."

"Good night, Victoria," Aunt Gertrude would say in her thin, cold voice.

And Jane would get herself out of the room, sometimes lucky enough not to knock anything over.

"When I grow up I'll never, never read the Bible or say that prayer," she would whisper to herself as she climbed the long, magnificent staircase which had once been the talk of Toronto.

One night grandmother had smiled and said, "What do you think of the Bible, Victoria?"

"I think it is very dull," said Jane truthfully. The reading had been a chapter full of "knops" and "taches," and Jane had not the least idea what knops or taches were.

"Ah! But do you think your opinion counts for a great deal?" said grandmother, smiling with paper-thin lips.

"Why did you ask me for it then?" said Jane, and had been icily rebuked for impertinence when she had not had the least intention of being impertinent. Was it any wonder she went up the staircase that night fairly loathing 60 Gay? And she did not want to loathe it. She wanted to love it . . . to be friends with it . . . to do things for it. But she could not love it . . . it wouldn't be friendly . . . and there was nothing it wanted done. Aunt Gertrude and Mary Price, the cook, and Frank Davis, the houseman and chauffeur, did everything for it. Aunt Gertrude would not let grandmother keep a housemaid because she preferred to attend to the house herself. Tall, shadowy, reserved Aunt Gertrude, who was so totally unlike mother that Jane found it hard to believe they were even half-sisters, was a martinet for order and system. At 60 Gay everything had to be done in a certain way on a certain day. The house was really frightfully clean. Aunt Gertrude's cold grey eyes could not tolerate a speck of dust anywhere. She was always going about the house putting things in their places and she attended to everything. Even mother never did anything except arrange the flowers for the table when they had company and light the candles for dinner. Jane would have liked the fun of doing that. And Jane would have liked to polish the silver and cook. More than anything else Jane would have liked to cook.

Now and then, when grandmother was out, she hung about the kitchen and watched good-natured Mary Price cook the meals. It all seemed so easy. . . . Jane was sure she could do it perfectly if she were allowed. It must be such fun to cook a meal. The smell of it was almost as good as the eating of it.

But Mary Price never let her. She knew the old lady didn't approve of Miss Victoria talking to the servants.

"Victoria fancies herself as domestic," grandmother had once said at the midday Sunday dinner where, as usual, Uncle William Anderson and Aunt Minnie and Uncle David Coleman and Aunt Sylvia Coleman and their daughter Phyllis were present. Grandmother had such a knack of making you feel ridiculous and silly in company. All the same, Jane wondered what grandmother would say if she knew that Mary Price, being somewhat rushed that day, had let Jane wash and arrange the lettuce for the salad. Jane knew what grandmother would do. She would refuse to touch a leaf of it.

"Well, shouldn't a girl be domestic?" said Uncle William, not because he wanted to take Jane's part but because he never lost an opportunity of announcing his belief that a woman's place was in the home. "Every girl should know how to cook."

"I don't think Victoria wants very much to learn how to cook," said grandmother. "It is just that she likes to hang about kitchens and places like that."

Grandmother's voice implied that Victoria had low tastes and that kitchens were barely respectable. Jane wondered why mother's face flushed so suddenly and why a strange, rebellious look gleamed for a moment in her eyes. But only for a moment.

"How are you getting on at St Agatha's, Victoria?" asked Uncle William. "Going to get your grade?"

Jane did not know whether she was going to get her grade or not. The fear haunted her night and day. She knew her monthly reports had not been very good . . . grandmother had been very angry over them and even mother had asked her piteously if she couldn't do a little better. Jane had done the best she could, but history and geography were so dull and drab. Arithmetic and spelling were easier. Jane was really quite brilliant in arithmetic.

"Victoria can write wonderful compositions, I hear," said grandmother sarcastically. For some reason Jane couldn't fathom at all, her ability to write good compositions had never pleased grandmother.

"Tut, tut," said Uncle William. "Victoria could get her grade easily enough if she wanted to. The thing to do is to study hard. She's getting to be a big girl now and ought to realize that. What is the capital of Canada, Victoria?"

Jane knew perfectly well what the capital of Canada was but Uncle William fired the question at her so unexpectedly and all the guests stopped eating to listen . . . and for the moment she couldn't remember for her life what the name was. She blushed . . . stammered . . . squirmed. If she had looked at mother she would have seen that mother was forming the world silently on her lips but she could not look at any one. She was ready to die of shame and mortification.

"Phyllis," said Uncle William, "tell Victoria what the capital of Canada is."

Phyllis promptly responded: "Ottawa."

"O-t-t-a-w-a," said Uncle William to Jane. Jane felt that they were all, except mother, watching her for something to find fault with and now Aunt Sylvia Coleman put on a pair of nose-glasses attached to a long black ribbon and looked at Jane through them as if wishing to be sure what a girl who didn't know the capital of her country was really like. Jane, under the paralysing influence of that stare, dropped her fork and writhed in anguish when she caught grandmother's eye. Grandmother touched her little silver bell.

"Will you bring Miss Victoria another fork, Davis?" she said in a tone implying that Jane had had several forks already.

Uncle William put the piece of white chicken meat he had just carved off on the side of the platter. Jane had been hoping he would give it to her. She did not often get white meat. When Uncle

William was not there to carve, Mary carved the fowls in the kitchen and Frank passed the platter around. Jane seldom dared to help herself to white meat because she knew grandmother was watching her. On one occasion when she had helped herself to two tiny pieces of breast grandmother had said:

"Don't forget, my dear Victoria, there are other people who might like a breast slice, too."

At present Jane reflected that she was lucky to get a drumstick. Uncle William was quite capable of giving her the neck by way of rebuking her for not knowing the capital of Canada. However, Aunt Sylvia very kindly gave her a double portion of turnip. Jane loathed turnip.

"You don't seem to have much appetite, Victoria," said Aunt Sylvia reproachfully when the mound of turnip had not decreased much.

"Oh, I think Victoria's appetite is all right," said grandmother, as if it were the only thing about her that was all right. Jane always felt that there was far more in what grandmother said than in the words themselves. Jane might then and there have broken her record for never crying, she felt so utterly wretched, had she not looked at mother. And mother was looking so tender and sympathetic and understanding that Jane spunked up at once and simply made no effort to eat any more turnip.

Aunt Sylvia's daughter Phyllis, who did not go to St Agatha's but to Hillwood Hall, a much newer but even more expensive school, could have named not only the capital of Canada but the capital of every province in the Dominion. Jane did not like Phyllis. Sometimes Jane thought drearily that there must be something the matter with her when there were so many people she didn't like. But Phyllis was so condescending . . . and Jane hated to be condescended to.

"Why don't you like Phyllis?" grandmother had asked once, looking at Jane with those eyes that, Jane felt, could see through walls, doors, everything, right into your inmost soul. "She is pretty, lady-like, well behaved and clever . . . everything that you are not," Jane felt sure grandmother wanted to add.

"She patronizes me," said Jane.

"Do you really know the meaning of all the big words you use, my dear Victoria?" said grandmother. "And don't you think that . . . possibly . . . you are a little jealous of Phyllis?"

"No, I don't think so," said Jane firmly. She knew she was not jealous of Phyllis.

"Of course, I must admit she is very different from that Jody of yours," said grandmother. The sneer in her voice brought an angry sparkle into Jane's eyes. She could not bear to hear any one sneer at Jody. And yet what could she do about it?

3

She and Jody had been pals for a year. Jody matched Jane's eleven years of life and was tall for her age, too . . . though not with Jane's sturdy tallness. Jody was thin and weedy and looked as if she had never had enough to eat in her life . . . which was very likely the case, although she lived in a boarding-house—58 Gay, which had once been a fashionable residence and was now just a dingy three-story boarding-house.

One evening in the spring of the preceding year Jane was out in the back yard of 60 Gay, sitting on a rustic bench in an old disused summer-house. Mother and grandmother were both away and Aunt Gertrude was in bed with a bad cold, or else Jane would not have been sitting in the back yard. She had crept out to have a good look at the full moon . . . Jane had her own particular reasons for liking to look at the moon . . . and the white blossoming cherry-tree over in the yard of 58. The cherry-tree, with the moon hanging over it like a great pearl, was so beautiful that Jane felt a queer lump in her throat when she looked at it . . . almost as if she wanted to cry. And then . . . somebody really was crying over in the yard of 58. The stifled, piteous sounds came clearly on the still, crystal air of the spring evening.

Jane got up and walked out of the summer-house and around the garage, past the lonely dog-house that had never had a dog in it . . . at least, in Jane's recollection . . . and so to the fence that had ceased to be iron and become a wooden paling between 60 and 58. There was a gap in it behind the dog-house where a slat had been broken off amid a tangle of creeper and Jane, squeezing through it, found herself in the untidy yard of 58. It was still quite light and Jane could see a girl huddled at the root of the cherry-tree, sobbing bitterly, her face in her hands.

"Can I help you?" said Jane.

Though Jane herself had no inkling of it, those words were the keynote of her character. Any one else would probably have said, "What is the matter?" But Jane always wanted to help: and, though she was too young to realize it, the tragedy of her little existence was that nobody ever wanted her help . . . not even mother, who had everything heart could wish.

The child under the cherry-tree stopped sobbing and got on her feet. She looked at Jane and Jane looked at her and something happened to both of them. Long afterwards Jane said, "I knew we were the same kind of folks." Jane saw a girl of about her own age, with a very white little face under a thick bang of black hair cut straight across her forehead. The hair looked as if it had not been washed for a long time but the eyes underneath it were brown and beautiful, though of quite a different brown from Jane's. Jane's were goldy-brown like a marigold, with laughter lurking in them, but this girl's were very dark and very sad . . . so sad that Jane's heart did something queer inside of her. She knew quite well that it wasn't right that anybody so young should have such sad eyes.

The girl wore a dreadful old blue dress that had certainly never been made for her. It was too long and too elaborate and it was dirty and grease-spotted. It hung on the thin little shoulders like a gaudy rag on a scarecrow. But the dress mattered nothing to Jane. All she was conscious of was those appealing eyes.

"Can I help?" she asked again.

The girl shook her head and the tears welled up in her big eyes. "Look," she pointed.

Jane looked and saw between the cherry-tree and the fence what seemed like a rudely made flower-bed strewn over with roses that were ground into the earth.

"Dick did that," said the girl. "He did it on purpose . . . because it was my garden. Miss Summers had them roses sent her last week . . . twelve great big red ones for her birthday . . . and this morning she said they were done and told me to throw them in the garbage pail. But I couldn't . . . they were still so pretty. I come out here and made that bed and stuck the roses all over it. I knew they wouldn't last long . . . but they looked pretty and I pretended I had a garden of my own . . . and now . . . Dick just come out and stomped all over it . . . and *laughed.*"

She sobbed again. Jane didn't know who Dick was but at that moment she could cheerfully have wrung his neck with her strong, capable little hands. She put her arm about the girl.

"Never mind. Don't cry any more. See, we'll break off a lot of little cherry boughs and stick them all over your bed. They're fresher than the roses . . . and think how lovely they'll look in the moonlight."

"I'm scared to do that," said the girl. "Miss West might be mad."

Again Jane felt a thrill of understanding. So this girl was afraid of people, too.

"Well, we'll just climb up on that big bough that stretches out and sit there and admire it," said Jane. "I suppose that won't make Miss West mad, will it?"

"I guess she won't mind that. Of course she's mad at me anyhow to-night because I stumbled with a tray of tumblers when I was waiting on the supper table and broke three of them. She said if I kept on like that . . . I spilled soup on Miss Thatcher's silk dress last night . . . she'd have to send me away."

"Where would she send you?"

"I don't know. I haven't anywhere to go. But she says I'm not worth my salt and she's only keeping me out of charity."

"What is your name?" asked Jane. They had scrambled up into the cherry-tree as nimbly as pussy cats and its whiteness enclosed and enfolded them, shutting them away into a fragrant world all their own.

"Josephine Turner. But every one calls me Jody."

Jody! Jane liked that.

"Mine's Jane Stuart."

"I thought it was Victoria," said Jody. "Miss West said it was."

"It's Jane," said Jane firmly. "At least, it's Jane Victoria but I am

Jane. And now"—briskly—"let's get acquainted."

Before Jane went back through the gap that night she knew practically all there was to be known about Jody. Jody's father and mother were dead . . . had been dead ever since Jody was a baby. Jody's mother's cousin, who had been the cook at 58, had taken her and was permitted to keep her at 58 if she never let her out of the kitchen. Two years ago Cousin Millie had died and Jody had just "stayed on." She helped the new cook . . . peeling potatoes, washing dishes, sweeping, dusting, running errands, scouring knives . . . and lately had been promoted to waiting on the table. She slept in a little attic cubby-hole which was hot in summer and cold in winter, she wore cast-off things the boarders gave her and went to school every day there was no extra rush. Nobody ever gave her a kind word or took any notice of her . . . except Dick who was Miss West's nephew and pet and who teased and tormented her and called her "charity child." Jody hated Dick. Once when everybody was out she had slipped into the parlour and picked out a little tune on the piano but Dick had told Miss West and Jody had been sternly informed that she must never touch the piano again.

"And I'd love to be able to play," she said wistfully. "That and a garden's the only things I want. I do wish I could have a garden."

Jane wondered again why things were so criss-cross. She did not like playing on the piano but grandmother had insisted on her taking music lessons and she practised faithfully to please mother. And here was poor Jody hankering for music and with no chance at all of getting it.

"Don't you think you could have a bit of a garden?" said Jane. "There's plenty of room here and it's not too shady, like our yard. I'd help you make a bed and I'm sure mother would give us some seeds. . . ."

"It wouldn't be any use," said Jody drearily. "Dick would just stomp on it, too."

"Then I'll tell you," said Jane resolutely, "we'll get a seed catalogue . . . Frank will get me one . . . and have an *imaginary* garden."

"Ain't you the one for thinking of things?" said Jody admiringly. Jane tasted happiness. It was the first time any one had ever admired her.

4

Of course it was no time before grandmother knew about Jody. She made a great many sweetly sarcastic speeches about her but she never actually forbade Jane going over to play with her in the yard of 58. Jane was to be a good many years older before she understood the reason for that . . . understood that grandmother wanted to show any one who might question it that Jane had common tastes and liked low people.

"Darling, is this Jody of yours a nice little girl?" mother had asked doubtfully.

"She is a very nice little girl," said Jane emphatically.

"But she looks so uncared for . . . positively dirty. . . ."

"Her face is always clean and she never forgets to wash behind her ears, mummy. I'm going to show her how to wash her hair. Her hair would be lovely if it was clean . . . it's so fine and black and silky. And may I give her one of my jars of cold cream. . . . I've two, you know . . . for her hands? They're so red and chapped because she has to work so hard and wash so many dishes."

"But her clothes. . . ."

"She can't help her clothes. She just has to wear what's given her and she never has more than two dresses at a time . . . one to wear every day and one to go to Sunday school in. Even the Sunday school one isn't very clean . . . it was Mrs Bellew's Ethel's old pink one and she spilled coffee on it. And she has to work so hard . . . she's a regular little slave, Mary says. I like Jody very much, mummy. She's sweet."

"Well" . . . mother sighed and gave way. Mother always gave way if you were firm enough. Jane had already discovered that. She adored mother but she had unerringly laid her finger on the weak spot in her character. Mother couldn't "stand up to" people.

Jane had heard Mary say that to Frank one time when they didn't think she heard and she knew it was true.

"She'll go with the last one that talks to her," said Mary. "And that's always the old lady."

"Well, the old lady's mighty good to her," said Frank. "She's a gay little piece."

"Gay enough. But is she happy?" said Mary.

"Happy? Of course, mummy is happy," Jane had thought indignantly . . . all the more indignantly because, away back in her mind, there was lurking a queer suspicion that mother, in spite of her dances and dinners and furs and dresses and jewels and friends, wasn't happy. Jane couldn't imagine why she had this idea. Perhaps a look in mother's eyes now and then . . . like something shut up in a cage.

Jane could go over and play in the yard of 58 in the spring and summer evenings after Jody had finished washing stacks of dishes. They made their "imaginary" garden, they fed crumbs to the robins and the black and grey squirrels, they sat up in the cherry-tree and watched the evening star together. And talked! Jane, who could never find anything to say to Phyllis, found plenty to say to Jody.

There was never any question of Jody coming to play in the yard of 60. Once, early in their friendship, Jane had asked Jody to come over. She had found Jody crying under the cherry-tree again and discovered that it was because Miss West had insisted on her putting her old Teddy bear in the garbage pail. It was, Miss West said, utterly worn out. It had been patched until there was no more room for patches and even shoe buttons couldn't be sewn any more into its worn-out eye-sockets. Besides, she was too old to be playing with Teddy bears.

"But I've nothing else," sobbed Jody. "If I had a doll, I wouldn't mind. I've always wanted a doll . . . but now I'll have to sleep alone away up there . . . and it's so lonesome."

"Come over to our house and I'll give you a doll," said Jane.

Jane had never cared much for dolls because they were not

alive. She had a very nice one which Aunt Sylvia had given her the Christmas she was seven but it was so flawless and well dressed that it never needed to have anything done for it and Jane had never loved it. She would have loved better a Teddy bear that needed a new patch every day.

She took Jody, wide-eyed and enraptured, through the splendours of 60 Gay and gave her the doll which had reposed undisturbed for a long time in the lower drawer of the huge black wardrobe in Jane's room. Then she had taken her into mother's room to show her the things on mother's table . . . the silver-backed brushes, the perfume bottles with the cut-glass stoppers that made rainbows, the wonderful rings on the little gold tray. Grandmother found them there.

She stood in the doorway and looked at them. You could feel the silence spreading through the room like a cold, smothering wave.

"What does this mean, Victoria . . . if I am allowed to ask?"

"This is . . . Jody," faltered Jane. "I . . . I brought her over to give her my doll. She hasn't any."

"Indeed? And you have given her the one your Aunt Sylvia gave you?"

Jane at once realized that she had done something quite unpardonable. It had never occurred to her that she was not at liberty to give away her own doll.

"I have not," said grandmother, "forbidden you to play with this . . . this *Jody* in her own lot. What is in the blood is bound to come out sooner or later. But . . . if you don't mind . . . please don't bring your riff-raff here, my dear Victoria."

Her dear Victoria got herself and poor hurt Jody away as best she could, leaving the doll behind them. But grandmother did not get off scot-free for all that. For the first time the worm turned. Jane paused for a moment before she went out of the door and looked straight at grandmother with intent, judging brown eyes.

"You are not fair," she said. Her voice trembled a little but she felt she had to say it, no matter how impertinent grandmother thought her. Then she followed Jody down and out with a strange feeling of satisfaction in her heart.

"I ain't riff-raff," said Jody, her lips quivering. "Of course I'm not like you. . . . Miss West says you're *people* . . . but my folks were respectable. Cousin Millie told me so. She said they always paid their way while they were alive. And I work hard enough for Miss West to pay my way."

"You aren't riff-raff and I love you," said Jane. "You and mother are the only people in the whole world I love."

Even as she said it a queer little pang wrung Jane's heart. It suddenly occurred to her that two people out of all the millions in the world . . . Jane never could remember the exact number of millions but she knew it was enormous . . . were very few to love.

"And I like loving people," thought Jane. "It's nice."

"I don't love anybody but you," said Jody, who forgot her hurt feelings as soon as Jane got her interested in building a castle out of all the old tin cans in the corner of the yard. Miss West hoarded her tin cans for a country cousin who made some mysterious use of them. He had not been in all winter and there were enough cans to build a towering structure. Dick kicked it down next day, of course, but they had had the fun of building it. They never knew that Mr Torrey, one of the 58 boarders who was a budding architect, saw the castle, gleaming in the moonlight, when he was putting his car in the garage and whistled over it.

"That's rather an amazing thing for those two kids to build," he said.

Jane, who should have been asleep, was lying wide awake that very moment, going on with the story of her life in the moon which she could see through her window.

Jane's "moon secret," as she called it, was the one thing she hadn't shared with mother and Jody. She couldn't, somehow. It was her very own. To tell about it would be to destroy it. For three years now Jane had been going on dream voyages to the moon. It was a shimmering world of fancy where she lived very splendidly and sated some deep thirst in her soul at unknown, enchanted springs among its shining silver hills. Before she had found the trick of going to the moon, Jane had longed to get into the looking-glass as Alice did. She used to stand so long before her mirror hoping for the miracle to happen that Aunt Gertrude said Victoria was the vainest child she had ever seen.

"Really?" said grandmother, as if mildly inquiring what Jane could possibly have to be vain about.

Eventually Jane had sadly concluded that she could never get into the looking-glass world, and then one night, when she was lying alone in her big unfriendly room, she saw the moon looking in at her through one of the windows ... the calm, beautiful moon that was never in a hurry; and she began to build for herself an existence in the moon, where she ate fairy food and wandered through fairy fields, full of strange white moon-blossoms, with the companions of her fancy.

But even in the moon Jane's dreams ran true to the ruling passion. Since the moon was all silver it had to be polished every night. Jane and her moon friends had no end of fun polishing up the moon, with an elaborate system of rewards and punishments for extra good polishers and lazy ones. The lazy ones were generally banished to the other side of the moon ... which Jane had read was very dark and very cold. When they were allowed back, chilled to the bone, they were glad to warm themselves up by rubbing as hard as they could. Those were the nights when the moon seemed brighter than usual. Oh, it was fun! Jane was never lonely in bed now except on nights when there was no moon. The clearest sight Jane knew was the thin crescent in the western sky that told her her friend was back. She was supported through many a dreary day by the hope of going on a moon spree at night.

5

Up to the age of ten Jane had believed her father was dead. She could not recall that anybody had ever told her so, but if she had thought about it at all she would have felt quite sure of it. She just did not think about it . . . nobody ever mentioned him. All she knew about him was that his name must have been Andrew Stuart, because mother was Mrs Andrew Stuart. For anything else, he might as well never have existed as far as Jane was concerned. She did not know much about fathers. The only one she was really acquainted with was Phyllis's father, Uncle David Coleman, a handsome, oldish man with pouches under his eyes, who grunted at her occasionally when he came to Sunday dinners. Jane had an idea his grunts were meant to be friendly and she did not dislike him, but there was nothing about him that made her envy Phyllis for having a father. With a mother so sweet and adorable and loving, what did one want of a father?

Then Agnes Ripley came to St Agatha's. Jane liked Agnes well enough at first, though Agnes had stuck her tongue out at Jane rather derisively on the occasion of their first meeting. She was the daughter of somebody who was called "the great Thomas Ripley" . . . he had built "railroads and things" . . . and most of the St Agatha's girls paid court to her and plumed themselves if she noticed them. She was much given to "secrets," and it came to be thought a great honour among the St Agathians if Agnes told you a secret. Therefore Jane was conscious of a decided thrill when one afternoon on the playground Agnes came up to her and said, darkly and mysteriously, "I know a secret."

"I know a secret" is probably the most intriguing phrase in the world. Jane surrendered to its allure.

"Oh, tell me," she implored. She wanted to be admitted to that charmed inner circle of girls who had been told one of Agnes's secrets; and she wanted to know the secret for its own sake. Secrets must always be wonderful, beautiful things.

Agnes wrinkled up her fat little nose and looked important.

"Oh, I'll tell you some other time."

"I don't want to hear it some other time. I want to hear it now," pleaded Jane, her marigold eyes full of eager radiance.

Agnes's little elfish face, framed in its straight brown hair, was alive with mischief. She winked one of her green eyes at Jane.

"All right. Don't blame me if you don't like it when you hear it. Listen."

Jane listened. The towers of St Agatha's listened. The shabby streets beyond listened. It seemed to Jane that the whole world listened. She was one of the chosen . . . Agnes was going to tell her a secret.

"Your father and mother don't live together."

Jane stared at Agnes. What she had said didn't make any sense.

"Of course they don't live together," she said. "My father is dead."

"Oh, no, he isn't," said Agnes. "He's living down in Prince Edward Island. Your mother left him when you were three years old."

Jane felt as if some big cold hand were beginning to squeeze her heart.

"That . . . isn't . . . true," she gasped.

"'Tis, too. I heard Aunt Dora telling mother all about it. She said your mother married him just after he came back from the war, one summer when your grandmother took her down to the Maritimes. Your grandmother didn't want her to. Aunt Dora said everybody knew it wouldn't last long. He was poor. But it was you that made the most trouble. You should never have been born. Neither of them wanted you, Aunt Dora said. They fought like cat and dog after that and at last your mother just up and left him. Aunt Dora said she would likely have divorced him only divorces are awful hard to get in Canada and anyhow all the Kennedys think divorce is a dreadful thing."

The hand was gripping Jane's heart so tightly now that she could hardly breathe.

"I . . . I don't believe it," she said.

"If that's how you're going to talk when I tell you a secret, I'll never tell you another one, Miss Victoria Stuart," said Agnes, reddening with rage.

"I don't want to hear any more," said Jane.

She would never forget what she had heard. It couldn't be true . . . it couldn't. Jane thought the afternoon would never end. St Agatha's was a nightmare. Frank had never driven so slowly home. The snow had never looked so grimy and dirty along the dingy streets. The wind had never been so grey. The moon, floating high in the sky, was all faded and paper-white but Jane didn't care if it was never polished again.

An afternoon tea was in progress at 60 Gay when she arrived there. The big drawing-room, decorated lavishly with pale pink snapdragons and tulips and maidenhair fern, was full of people. Mother, in orchid chiffon, with loose trailing lace sleeves, was laughing and chatting. Grandmother, with blue-white diamonds sparkling in her hair, was sitting on her favourite needle-point chair, looking, so one lady said, "Such an utterly sweet silver-haired thing, just like a Whistler mother." Aunt Gertrude and Aunt Sylvia were pouring tea at a table covered with Venetian lace, where tall pink tapers were burning.

Straight through them all Jane marched to mother. She did not care how many people were there . . . she had one question to ask and it must be answered at once. At once. Jane could not bear her suspense another moment.

"Mummy," she said, "is my father alive?"

A strange, dreadful hush suddenly fell over the room. A light like a sword flashed into grandmother's blue eyes. Aunt Sylvia gasped and Aunt Gertrude turned an unbecoming purple. But mother's face was as if snow had fallen over it.

"Is he?" said Jane.

"Yes," said mother. She said nothing more. Jane asked nothing more. She turned and went out and up the stairs blindly. In her own room she shut the door and lay down very softly on the big white bearskin rug by the bed, her lace buried in the soft fur. Heavy black waves of pain seemed rolling over her.

So it was true. All her life she had thought her father dead while he was living . . . on that far-away dot on the map which she had been told was the province of Prince Edward Island. But he and mother did not like each other and she had not been wanted. Jane found that it was a very curious and unpleasant sensation to feel that your parents hadn't wanted you. She was sure that all the rest of her life she would hear Agnes's voice saying, "You should never have been born." She hated Agnes Ripley . . . she would always hate her. Jane wondered if she would live to be as old as grandmother and how she could bear it if she did.

Mother and grandmother found her there when everybody had gone.

"Victoria, get up."

Jane did not move.

"Victoria, I am accustomed to be obeyed when I speak."

Jane got up. She had not cried . . . hadn't somebody ages ago said that "Jane never cried" . . . but her face was stamped with an expression that might have wrung anybody's heart. Perhaps it touched even grandmother, for she said, quite gently for her:

"I have always told your mother, Victoria, that she ought to tell you the truth. I told her you were sure to hear it from someone sooner or later. Your father is living. Your mother married him against my wish and lived to repent it. I forgave her and welcomed her back gladly when she came to her senses. That is all. And in future when you feel an irresistible urge to make a scene while we are entertaining, will you be good enough to control the impulse until our guests are gone?"

"Why didn't he like me?" asked Jane dully.

When all was said and done, that seemed to be what was hurting most. Her mother might not have wanted her either, to begin with, but Jane knew that mother loved her now.

Mother suddenly gave a little laugh so sad that it nearly broke Jane's heart.

"He was jealous of you, I think," she said.

"He made your mother's life wretched," said grandmother, her voice hardening.

"Oh, I was to blame, too," cried mother chokingly.

Jane, looking from one to the other, saw the swift change that came over grandmother's face.

"You will never mention your father's name in my hearing or in your mother's hearing again," said grandmother. "As far as we are concerned . . . as far as *you* are concerned . . . he is dead."

The prohibition was unnecessary. Jane didn't want to mention her father's name again. He had made mother unhappy, and so Jane hated him and put him out of her thoughts completely. There were just some things that didn't bear thinking of and father was one of them. But the most terrible thing about it all was that there was something now that could not be talked over with mother. Jane felt it between them, indefinable but there. The old perfect confidence was gone. There was a subject that must never be mentioned and it poisoned everything.

She could never bear Agnes Ripley and her cult of "secrets" again and was glad when Agnes left the school, the great Thomas having decided that it was not quite up-to-date enough for his daughter. Agnes wanted to learn tap-dancing.

6

It was a year now since Jane had learned that she had a father . . . a year in which Jane had just scraped through as far as her grade was concerned. . . . Phyllis had taken the prize for general proficiency in her year and did Jane hear of it! . . . had continued to be driven to and from St Agatha's, had tried her best to like Phyllis and had not made any great headway at it, had trysted with Jody in the back yard twilights and had practised her scales as faithfully as if she liked it.

"Such a pity you are not fonder of music," said grandmother. "But of course, how could you be?"

It was not so much what grandmother said as how she said it. She made wounds that rankled and festered. And Jane was fond of music . . . she loved to listen to it. When Mr Ransome, the musical boarder at 58, played on his violin in his room in the evenings, he never dreamed of the two enraptured listeners he had in the back yard cherry-tree. Jane and Jody sat there, their hands clasped, their hearts filled with some nameless ecstasy. When winter came and the bedroom window was shut, Jane felt the loss keenly. The moon was her only escape then and she slipped away to it oftener than ever, in long visitations of silence which grandmother called "sulks."

"She has a very sulky disposition," said grandmother.

"Oh, I don't think so," faltered mother. The only times she ever dared to contradict grandmother were in defence of Jane. "She's just rather . . . sensitive."

"Sensitive!" Grandmother laughed. Grandmother did not often laugh, which Jane thought was just as well. As for Aunt Gertrude, if she had ever laughed or jested it must have been so long ago that nobody remembered it. Mother laughed when people were about . . . little tinkling laughs that Jane could never feel were real. No, there was not much real laughter at 60 Gay, though Jane, with her concealed gift for seeing the funny side of things, could have filled even that big house with laughter. But Jane had known very early that grandmother resented laughter. Even Mary and Frank had to giggle very discreetly in the kitchen.

Jane had shot up appallingly in that year. She was rather more angular and awkward. Her chin was square and cleft.

"It gets more like *his* every day," she once heard grandmother saying bitterly to Aunt Gertrude. Jane winced. In her bitter new wisdom she suspected that "his" was her father's chin and she straightway detested hers. Why couldn't it have been a pretty rounded one like mother's?

The year was very uneventful. Jane would have called it monotonous if she had not as yet been unacquainted with the word. There were only three things in it that made much impression on her . . . the incident of the kitten, the mysterious affair of Kenneth Howard's picture and the unlucky recitation.

Jane had picked the kitten up on the street. One afternoon Frank had been in a great hurry to get somewhere on time for grandmother and mother and he had let Jane walk home from the beginning of Gay Street when he was bringing her from St Agatha's. Jane walked along happily, savouring this rare moment of independence. It was very seldom she was allowed to walk anywhere alone . . . to walk anywhere at all, indeed. And Jane loved walking. She would have liked to walk to and from St Agatha's or, since that really was too far, she would have liked to go by street-car. Jane loved travelling on a streetcar. It was fascinating to look at the people in it and speculate about them. Who was that lady with the lovely shimmering hair? What was the angry old woman muttering to herself about? Did that little boy like having his mother clean his face with her handkerchief in public? Did that jolly looking little girl have trouble getting her grade? Did that man have toothache and did he ever look pleasant when he hadn't it? She would have liked to know all about them and sympathize or rejoice as occasion required. But it was very seldom any resident of 60 Gay had a chance to go on a street-car. There was always Frank with the limousine.

Jane walked slowly to prolong the pleasure. It was a cold day in late autumn. It had been miserly of its light from the beginning, with a dim ghost of sun peering through the dull grey clouds, and now it was getting dark and spitting snow. The lights gleamed out: even the grim windows of Victorian Gay were abloom. Jane did not mind the bitter wind but something else did. Jane heard the most pitiful, despairing little cry and looked down to see the kitten, huddled miserably against an iron fence. She bent and picked it up and held it against her face. The little creature, a handful of tiny bones in its fluffed-out Maltese fur, licked her cheek with an eager tongue. It was cold, starving, forsaken. Jane knew it did not belong to Gay Street. She could not leave it there to perish in the oncoming stormy night.

"Goodness sake, Miss Victoria, wherever did you get that?" exclaimed Mary, when Jane entered the kitchen. "You shouldn't have brought it in. You know your grandmother doesn't like cats. Your Aunt Gertrude got one once but it clawed all the tassels off the furniture and it had to go. Better put that kitten right out, Miss Victoria."

Jane hated to be called "Miss Victoria," but grandmother insisted on the servants addressing her so.

"I *can't* put it out in the cold, Mary. Let me give it some supper and leave it here till after dinner. I'll ask grandmother to let me keep it. Perhaps she will if I promise to keep it out here and in the yard. You wouldn't mind it round, would you, Mary?"

"I'd like it," said Mary. "I've often thought a cat would be great company . . . or a dog. Your mother had a dog once but it got poisoned and she would never have another."

Mary did not tell Jane that she firmly believed the old lady had poisoned the dog. You didn't tell children things like that and anyway she couldn't be dead sure of it. All she was sure of was that old Mrs Kennedy had been bitterly jealous of her daughter's love for the dog.

"How she used to look at it when she didn't know I saw her," thought Mary.

Grandmother and Aunt Gertrude and mother were taking in a couple of teas that day so Jane knew she could count on at least an hour yet. It was a pleasant hour. The kitten was happy and frolicsome, having drunk milk until its little sides tubbed out almost to the bursting point. The kitchen was warm and cosy. Mary let Jane chop the nuts that were to be sprinkled over the cake and cut the pears into slim segments for the salad.

"Oh, Mary, blueberry pie! Why don't we have it oftener? You can make such delicious blueberry pie."

"There's some who can make pies and some who can't," said Mary complacently. "As for having it oftener, you know your grandmother doesn't care much for any kind of pie. She says they're indigestible . . . and my father lived to be ninety and had pie for breakfast every morning of his life! I just make it occasional for your mother."

"After dinner I'll tell grandmother about the kitten and ask her if I may keep it," said Jane.

"I think you'll have your trouble for your pains, you poor child," said Mary as the door closed behind Jane. "Miss Robin ought to stand up for you more than she does . . . but there, she's always been under the thumb of her mother. Any way, I hope the dinner will go well and keep the old dame in good humour. I wisht I hadn't made the blueberry pie after all. It's lucky she won't know Miss Victoria fixed the salad . . . what folks don't know never hurts them."

The dinner did not go well. There was a tension in the air. Grandmother did not talk . . . evidently some occurrence of the afternoon had put her out. Aunt Gertrude never talked at any time. And mother seemed uneasy and never once tried to pass Jane any of the little signals they had . . . the touched lip . . . the lifted eyebrow . . . the crooked finger . . . that all meant "honey darling" or "I love you" or "consider yourself kissed."

Jane, burdened by her secret, was even more awkward than usual, and when she was eating her blueberry pie she dropped a forkful of it on the table.

"This," said grandmother, "might have been excused in a child of five. It is absolutely inexcusable in a girl of your age. Blueberry stain is almost impossible to get out and this is one of my best table-cloths. But of course that is a matter of small importance."

Jane gazed at the table in dismay. How such a little bit of pie could have spread itself over so much territory she could not understand. And of course it had to be at this inauspicious moment that a little purry furry creature escaped the pursuing Mary, skittered across the dining-room and bounded into Jane's lap. Jane's heart descended to her boots.

"Where did that cat come from?" demanded grandmother.

"I mustn't be a coward," thought Jane desperately.

"I found it on the street and brought it in," she said bravely . . . defiantly, grandmother thought. "It was so cold and hungry . . . look how thin it is, grandmother. Please may I keep it? It's such a darling. I won't let it trouble you . . . I'll . . ."

"My dear Victoria, don't be ridiculous. I really supposed you knew we do not keep cats here. Be good enough to put that creature out at once."

"Oh, not out on the street, grandmother, *please*. Listen to the sleet . . . it would die."

"I expect you to obey me without argument, Victoria. You cannot have your own way all the time. Other people's wishes must be considered occasionally. Please oblige me by making no further fuss over a trifle."

"Grandmother," began Jane passionately. But grandmother lifted a little wrinkled, sparkling hand.

"Now, now, don't work yourself into a state, Victoria. Take that thing out at once."

Jane took the kitten to the kitchen.

"Don't worry, Miss Victoria. I'll get Frank to put it in the garage with a rug to lie on. It will be quite comfy. And to-morrow

I'll find a good home for it at my sister's. She's fond of cats."

Jane never cried, so she was not crying when mother slipped rather stealthily into her room for a good-night kiss. She was only tense with rebellion.

"Mummy, I wish we could get away . . . just you and I. I hate this place, mummy, I hate it."

Mother said a strange thing and said it bitterly: "There is no escape for either of us now."

7

Jane could never understand the affair of the picture. After her hurt and anger passed away she was just hopelessly puzzled. Why . . . *why* . . . should the picture of a perfect stranger matter to anybody at 60 Gay . . . and to mother, least of all?

She had come across it one day when she was visiting Phyllis. Every once in so long Jane had to spend an afternoon with Phyllis. This one was no more of a success than the former ones had been. Phyllis was a conscientious hostess. She had shown Jane all her new dolls, her new dresses, her new slippers, her new pearl necklace, her new china pig. Phyllis was collecting china pigs and apparently thought any one "dumb" who was not interested in china pigs. She had patronized and condescended even more than usual. Consequently Jane was stiffer than usual and both of them were in agonies of boredom. It was a relief to all concerned when Jane picked up a *Saturday Evening* and buried herself in it, though she was not in the least interested in the society pages, the photographs of brides and debutantes, the stock market or even in the article, "Peaceful Adjustment of International Difficulties," by Kenneth Howard, which was given a place of honour on the front page. Jane had a vague idea that she ought not to be reading *Saturday Evening*. For some unknown reason grandmother did not approve of it. She would not have a copy of it in her house.

But what Jane did like was the picture of Kenneth Howard on the front page. The moment she looked at it she was conscious of its fascination. She had never seen Kenneth Howard . . . she had no idea who he was or where he lived . . . but she felt as if it were the picture of someone she knew very well and liked very much. She liked everything about it . . . his odd peaked eyebrows . . . the way his thick rather unruly hair sprang back from his forehead .

. . the way his firm mouth tucked in at the corners . . . the slightly stern look in the eyes which yet had such jolly wrinkles at the corners . . . and the square, cleft chin which reminded Jane so strongly of something, she couldn't remember just what. That chin seemed like an old friend. Jane looked at the face and drew a long breath. She knew, right off, that if she had loved her father instead of hating him she would have wanted him to look like Kenneth Howard.

Jane stared at the picture so long that Phyllis became curious.

"What are you looking at, Jane?"

Jane suddenly came to life.

"May I have this picture, Phyllis . . . please?"

"Whose picture? Why . . . that? Do you know him?"

"No. I never heard of him before. But I like the picture."

"I don't." Phyllis looked at it contemptuously. "Why . . . he's old. And he isn't a bit handsome. There's a lovely picture of Norman Tait on the next page, Jane . . . let me show it to you."

Jane was not interested in Norman Tait nor any other screen star. Grandmother did not approve of children going to the movies.

"I'd like this picture if I may have it," she said firmly.

"I guess you can have it," condescended Phyllis. She thought Jane "dumber" than ever. How she did pity such a dumb girl! "I guess nobody here wants *that* picture. I don't like it a bit. He looks as if he was laughing at you behind his eyes."

Which was a bit of surprising insight on the part of Phyllis. That was just how Kenneth Howard did look. Only it was nice laughter. Jane felt she wouldn't mind a bit being laughed at like that. She cut the picture carefully out, carried it home, and hid it under the pile of handkerchiefs in her top bureau drawer. She could hardly have told why she did not want to show it to anybody. Perhaps she did not want any one to ridicule the picture as Phyllis had done. Perhaps it was just because there seemed some strange bond between her and it . . . something too beautiful to be talked about to any one, even mother. Not that there was much chance of talking to mother about anything just now. Never had mother been so brilliant, so gay, so beautifully dressed, so constantly on the go to parties and teas and bridges. Even the goodnight kiss had become a rare thing . . . or Jane thought it had. She did not know that always when her mother came in late, she tiptoed into Jane's room and dropped a kiss on Jane's russet hair . . . lightly so as not to waken her. Sometimes she cried when she went back to her own room but not often, because it might show at breakfast and old Mrs Robert Kennedy did not like people who cried o' nights in her house.

For three weeks the picture and Jane were the best of friends. She took it out and looked at it whenever she could . . . she told it all about Jody and about her tribulations with her homework and about her love for mother. She even told it her moon secret. When she lay lonely in her bed, the thought of it was company. She kissed it good night and took a peep at it the first thing in the morning.

Then Aunt Gertrude found it.

The moment Jane came in from St Agatha's that day she knew something was wrong. The house, which always seemed to be watching her, was watching her more closely than ever, with a mocking, triumphant malice. Great-grandfather Kennedy scowled more darkly than ever at her from the drawing-room wall. And grandmother was sitting bolt-upright in her chair flanked by mother and Aunt Gertrude. Mother was twisting a lovely red rose to pieces in her little white hands but Aunt Gertrude was staring at the picture grandmother was holding.

"*My* picture!" cried Jane aloud.

Grandmother looked at Jane. For once her cold blue eyes were on fire.

"Where did you get this?" she said.

"It's mine," cried Jane. "Who took it out of my drawer? Nobody had any business to do that."

"I don't think I like your manner, Victoria. And we are not discussing a problem in ethics. I asked a question."

Jane looked down at the floor. She had no earthly idea why it seemed such a crime to have Kenneth Howard's picture but she knew she was not going to be allowed to have it any more. And it seemed to Jane that she just could not bear that.

"Will you be kind enough to look at me, Victoria? And to answer my question? You are not tongue-tied, by any chance, I suppose."

Jane looked up with stormy and mutinous eyes.

"I cut it out of a paper . . . out of *Saturday Evening*."

"That rag!" Grandmother's tone consigned *Saturday Evening* to unfathomable depths of contempt. "Where did you see it?"

"At Aunt Sylvia's," retorted Jane, plucking up spirit.

"Why did you cut this out?"

"Because I liked it."

"Do you know who Kenneth Howard is?"

"No."

"'No, grandmother,' if you please. Well, I think it is hardly necessary to keep the picture of a man you don't know in your bureau drawer. Let us have no more of such absurdity."

Grandmother lifted the picture in both hands. Jane sprang forward and caught her arm.

"Oh, grandmother, don't tear it up. You mustn't. I want it terribly."

The moment she said it, she knew she had made a mistake. There had never been much chance of getting the picture back but what little there had been was now gone.

"Have you gone completely mad, Victoria?" said grandmother . . . to whom nobody had ever said, "You mustn't," in her whole life before. "Take your hand off my arm, please. As for this . . ." grandmother tore the picture deliberately into four pieces and threw them on the fire. Jane, who felt as if her heart were being torn with it, was on the point of a rebellious outburst when she happened to glance at mother. Mother was pale as ashes, standing there with the leaves of the rose she had torn to pieces strewing the carpet around her feet. There was such a dreadful look of pain

347

in her eyes that Jane shuddered. The look was gone in a moment but Jane could never forget that it had been there. And she knew she could not ask mother to explain the mystery of the picture. For some reason she could not guess at, Kenneth Howard meant suffering to mother. And somehow that fact stained and spoiled all her beautiful memories of communion with the picture.

"No sulks now. Go to your room and stay there till I send for you," said grandmother, not altogether liking Jane's expression. "And remember that people who belong here do not read *Saturday Evening*."

Jane had to say it. It really said itself.

"I don't belong here," said Jane. Then she went to her room, which was huge and lonely again, with no Kenneth Howard smiling at her from under the handkerchiefs.

And this was another thing she could not talk over with mother. She felt just like one big ache as she stood at her window for a long time. It was a cruel world . . . with the very stars laughing at you . . . twinkling mockingly at you.

"I wonder," said Jane slowly, "if any one was ever happy in this house."

Then she saw the moon . . . the new moon, but not the thin silver crescent the new moon usually was. This was just on the point of sinking into a dark cloud on the horizon and it was large and dull red. If ever a moon needed polishing up this one did. In a moment Jane had slipped away from all her sorrows . . . two hundred and thirty thousand miles away. Luckily grandmother had no power over the moon.

8

Then there was the affair of the recitation.

They were getting up a school programme at St Agatha's to which only the families of the girls were invited. There were to be a short play, some music and a reading or two. Jane had secretly hoped to be given a part in the play, even if it were only one of the many angels who came and went in it, with wings and trailing white robes and home-made haloes. But no such good luck. She suspected that it was because she was rather bony and awkward for an angel.

Then Miss Semple asked her if she would recite.

Jane jumped at the idea. She knew she could recite rather well. Here was a chance to make mother proud of her and show grandmother that all the money she was spending on Jane's education was not being wholly wasted.

Jane picked a poem she had long liked in spite, or perhaps because, of its *habitant* English, "The Little Baby of Mathieu," and plunged enthusiastically into learning it. She practised it in her room . . . she murmured lines of it everywhere until grandmother asked her sharply what she was muttering about all the time. Then Jane shut up like a clam. Nobody must suspect . . . it was to be a "surprise" to them all. A proud and glad surprise for mother. And perhaps even grandmother might feel a little pleased with her if she did well. Jane knew she would meet with no mercy if she didn't do well.

Grandmother took Jane down to a room in Marlborough's big department store . . . a room that had panelled walls, velvety carpets and muted voices . . . a room that Jane didn't like, somehow. She always felt smothered in it. And grandmother got her a new dress for the concert. It was a very pretty dress . . . you had to admit grandmother had a taste in dresses. A dull green silk that brought out the russet glow of Jane's hair and the gold-brown of her eyes. Jane liked herself in it and was more anxious than ever to please grandmother with her recitation.

She was terribly worried the night before the concert. Wasn't she a little hoarse? Suppose it got worse? It did not . . . it was all gone the next day. But when Jane found herself on the concert platform facing an audience for the first time, a nasty little quiver ran down her spine. She had never supposed there would be so many people. For one dreadful moment she thought she was not going to be able to utter a word. Then she seemed to see Kenneth Howard's eyes, crinkling with laughter at her. "Never mind them. Do your stuff for *me,*" he seemed to be saying. Jane got her mouth open.

The St Agatha staff were quite amazed. Who could have supposed that shy, awkward Victoria Stuart could recite any poem so well, let alone a *habitant* one? Jane herself was feeling the delight of a certain oneness with her audience . . . a realization that she had captured them . . . that she was delighting them . . . until she came to the last verse. Then she saw mother and grandmother just in front of her. Mother, in her lovely new blue fox furs, with the little wine hat Jane loved tilted on one side of her head, was looking more frightened than proud, and grandmother . . . Jane had seen that expression too often to mistake it. Grandmother was furious.

The last verse, which should have been the climax, went rather flat. Jane felt like a candle-flame blown out, though the applause was hearty and prolonged, and Miss Semple behind the scenes whispered, "Excellent, Victoria, excellent."

But there were no compliments on the road home. Not a word was said . . . that was the dreadful part of it. Mother seemed too frightened to speak and grandmother preserved a stony silence. But when they got home she said:

"Who put you up to that, Victoria?"

"Put me up to what?" said Jane in honest bewilderment.

"Please don't repeat my questions, Victoria. You know perfectly well what I mean."

"Is it my recitation? No one. Miss Semple asked me to recite, and I picked the recitation myself because I liked it," said Jane. It might even be said she retorted it. She was hurt . . . angry . . . a little "pepped up" because of her success. "I thought it would please you. But you are never pleased with anything I do."

"Don't be cheaply theatrical, please," said grandmother. "And in future if you *have* to recite," very much as she might have said, "if you have to have smallpox" . . . "please choose poems in decent English. I do not care for patois."

Jane didn't know what patois was, but it was all too evident that she had made a mess of things somehow.

"Why was grandmother so angry, mummy?" she asked piteously, when mother came in to kiss her good night, cool, slim and fragrant, in a dress of rose *crêpe* with little wisps of lace over the shoulders. Mother's blue eyes seemed to mist a little.

"Someone she . . . did not like . . . used to be . . . very good at reading *habitant* poetry. Never mind, heart's delight. You did splendidly. I was proud of you."

She bent down and took Jane's face in her hands. Mother had such a dear way of doing that.

So, in spite of everything, Jane went very happily through the gates of sleep. After all, it does not take much to make a child happy.

9

The letter was a bolt from the blue. It came one dull morning in early April . . . but such a bitter, peevish, unlovely April . . . more like March in its disposition than April. It was Saturday, so there would be no St Agatha's and when Jane wakened in her big black walnut bed she wondered just how she would put in the day because mother was going to a bridge and Jody was sick with a cold.

Jane lay a little while, looking through the window, where she could see only dull grey sky and old tree tops having a fight with the wind. She knew that in the yard below the window on the north there was still a lingering bank of dirty grey snow. Jane thought dirty snow must be the dreariest thing in the world. She hated this shabby end of winter. And she hated the bedroom where she had to sleep alone. She wished she and mother could sleep together. They could have such lovely times talking to each other with no one else to hear, after they went to bed or early in the morning. And how lovely it would be when you woke up in the night to hear mother's soft breathing beside you and cuddle to her just a wee bit, carefully, so as not to disturb her.

But grandmother would not let mother sleep with her.

"It is unhealthy for two people to sleep in the same bed," grandmother had said with her chill, unsmiling smile. "Surely in a house of this size everybody can have a room to herself. There are many people in the world who would be grateful for such a privilege."

Jane thought she might have liked the room better if it had been smaller. She always felt lost in it. Nothing in it seemed to be related to her. It always seemed hostile, watchful, vindictive. And yet Jane always felt that if she were allowed to do things for it . . . sweep it, dust it, put flowers in it . . . she would begin to love it, huge as it was. Everything in it was huge . . . a huge black walnut wardrobe like a prison, a huge chest of drawers, a huge walnut bedstead, a huge mirror over the massive black marble mantelpiece . . . except a tiny cradle which was always kept in the alcove by the fireplace . . . a cradle that grandmother had been rocked in. Fancy grandmother a baby! Jane just couldn't.

Jane got out of bed and dressed herself under the stare of several old dead grands and greats hung on the walls. Below on the lawn robins were hopping about. Robins always made Jane laugh . . . they were so saucy, so sleek, so important, strutting over the grounds of 60 Gay just as if it were any common yard. Much they cared for grandmothers!

Jane slipped down the hall to mother's room at the far end. She was not supposed to do this. It was understood at 60 Gay that mother must not be disturbed in the mornings. But mother, for a wonder, had not been out the night before and Jane knew she would be awake. Not only was she awake but Mary was just bringing in her breakfast tray. Jane would have loved to do this for mother but she was never allowed.

Mother was sitting up in bed wearing the daintiest breakfast jacket of tea-rose *crêpe de Chine* edged with cobwebby beige lace. Her cheeks were just the colour of her jacket and her eyes were fresh and dewy. Mother, Jane reflected proudly, looked as lovely when she got up in the mornings as she did before she went to bed.

Mother had chilled melon balls in orange juice instead of cereal, and she shared them with Jane. She offered half of her toast, too, but Jane knew she must save some appetite for her own breakfast and refused it. They had a lovely time, laughing and talking beautiful nonsense, very quietly, so as not to be overheard. Not that either of them ever put this into words; but both knew.

"I wish it could be like this every morning," thought Jane. But she did not say so. She had learned that whenever she said anything like that mother's eyes darkened with pain and she would not hurt mother for the world. She could never forget the time she had heard mother crying in the night.

She had wakened up with toothache and had crept down to mother's room to see if mother had any toothache drops. And, as she opened the door ever so softly, she heard mother crying in a dreadful smothered sort of way. Then grandmother had come along the hall with her candle.

"Victoria, what are you doing here?"

"I have toothache," said Jane.

"Come with me and I will get you some drops," said grandmother coldly.

Jane went . . . but she no longer minded the toothache. Why was mother crying? It couldn't be possible she was unhappy . . . pretty, laughing mother. The next morning at breakfast mother looked as if she had never shed a tear in her life. Sometimes Jane wondered if she had dreamed it.

Jane put the lemon verbena salts into the bath water for mother and got a pair of new stockings, thin as dew gossamers, out of the drawer for her. She loved to do things for mother and there was so little she could do.

She had breakfast alone with grandmother, Aunt Gertrude having had hers already. It is not pleasant to eat a meal alone with a person you do not like. And Mary had forgotten to put salt in the oatmeal.

"Your shoe-lace is untied, Victoria."

That was the only thing grandmother said during the meal. The house was dark. It was a sulky day that now and then brightened up a little and then turned sulkier than ever. The mail came at ten. Jane was not interested in it. There was never anything for her. Sometimes she thought it would be nice and exciting to get a letter from somebody. Mother always got no end of letters . . . invitations and advertisements. This morning Jane carried the mail into the library where grandmother and Aunt Gertrude and mother were sitting. Jane noticed among the letters one addressed to her mother in a black spiky handwriting which Jane was sure she had never seen before. She hadn't the least idea that that letter was going to change her whole life.

Grandmother took the letters from her and looked them over as she always did.

"Did you close the vestibule door, Victoria?"

"Yes."

"Yes what?"

"Yes, grandmother."

"You left it open yesterday. Robin, here is a letter from Mrs

Kirby . . . likely about that bazaar. Remember it is my wish that you have nothing to do with it. I do not approve of Sarah Kirby. Gertrude, here is one for you from Cousin Mary in Winnipeg. If it is about that silver service she avers my mother left her, tell her I consider the matter closed. Robin, here is . . ."

Grandmother stopped abruptly. She had picked up the black-handed letter and was looking at it as if she had picked up a snake. Then she looked at her daughter.

"This is from . . . him," she said.

Mother dropped Mrs Kirby's letter and turned so white that Jane involuntarily sprang towards her but was barred by grandmother's outstretched arm.

"Do you wish me to read it for you, Robin?"

Mother trembled piteously but she said, "No . . . no . . . let me . . ."

Grandmother handed the letter over with an offended air and mother opened it with shaking hands. It did not seem as if her face could turn whiter than it was, but it did as she read it.

"Well?" said grandmother.

"He says," gasped mother, "that I must send Jane Victoria to him for the summer . . . that he has a right to her sometimes. . . ."

"Who says?" cried Jane.

"Do not interrupt, Victoria," said grandmother. "Let me see that letter, Robin."

They waited while grandmother read it. Aunt Gertrude stared unwinkingly ahead of her with her cold grey eyes in her long white face. Mother had dropped her head in her hands. It was only three minutes since Jane had brought the letters in and in those three minutes the world had turned upside down. Jane felt as if a gulf had opened between her and all humankind. She knew now without being told who had written the letter.

"So!" said grandmother. She folded the letter up, put it in its envelope, laid it on her table and carefully wiped her hands with her fine lace handkerchief.

"You won't let her go, of course, Robin."

For the first time in her life Jane felt at one with grandmother. She looked imploringly at mother with a curious feeling of seeing her for the first time . . . not as a loving mother or affectionate daughter but as a woman . . . a woman in the grip of some terrible emotion. Jane's heart was torn by another pang in seeing mother suffer so.

"If I don't," she said, "he may take her from me altogether. He could, you know. He says . . ."

"I have read what he says," said grandmother, "and I still tell you to ignore that letter. He is doing this simply to annoy you. He cares nothing for her . . . he never cared for anything but his scribbling."

"I'm afraid . . ." began mother again.

"We'd better consult William," said Aunt Gertrude suddenly. "This needs a man's advice."

"A man!" snapped grandmother. Then she seemed to pull herself up. "You may be right, Gertrude. I shall lay the matter before William when he comes to supper to-morrow. In the meantime we shall not discuss it. We shall not allow it to disturb us in the least."

Jane felt as if she were in a nightmare the rest of the day. Surely it must be a dream . . . surely her father could not have written her mother that she must spend the summer with him, a thousand miles away in that horrible Prince Edward Island which looked on the map to be a desolate little fragment in the jaws of Gaspé and Cape Breton . . . with a father who didn't love her and whom she didn't love.

She had no chance to say anything about it to mother . . . grandmother saw to that. They all went to Aunt Sylvia's luncheon . . . mother did not look as if she wanted to go anywhere . . . and Jane had lunch alone. She couldn't eat anything.

"Does your head ache, Miss Victoria?" Mary asked sympathetically.

Something was aching terribly but it did not seem to be her head. It ached all the afternoon and evening and far on into the night. It was still aching when Jane woke the next morning with a sickening rush of remembrance. Jane felt that it might help the ache a little if she could only have a talk with mother, but when she tried mother's door it was locked. Jane felt that mother didn't want to talk to her about this and that hurt worse than anything else.

They all went to church . . . an old and big and gloomy church on a downtown street where the Kennedys had always gone. Jane was rather fond of going to church for the not very commendable reason that she had some peace there. She could be silent without someone asking her accusingly what she was thinking of. Grandmother had to let her alone in church. And if you couldn't be loved, the next best thing was to be let alone.

Apart from that Jane did not care for St Barnabas's. The sermon was beyond her. She liked the music and some of the hymns. Occasionally there was a line that gave her a thrill. There was something fascinating about coral strands and icy mountains, tides that moving seemed asleep, islands that lifted their fronded palms in air, reapers that bore harvest treasures home and years like shadows on sunny hills that lie.

But nothing gave Jane any pleasure to-day. She hated the pale sunshine that sifted down between the chilly, grudging clouds. What business had the sun even to try to shine while her fate hung in the balance like this? The sermon seemed endless, the prayers dreary, there was not even a hymn line she liked. But Jane put up a desperate prayer on her own behalf.

"Please, dear God," she whispered, "make Uncle William say I needn't be sent to him."

Jane had to live in suspense as to what Uncle William would say until the Sunday supper was over. She ate little. She sat looking at Uncle William with fear in her eyes, wondering if God really could have much influence over him. They were all there . . . Uncle William and Aunt Minnie, Uncle David and Aunt Sylvia, and Phyllis; and after supper they all went to the library and sat in a stiff circle while Uncle William put on his glasses and read the letter. Jane thought every one must hear the beating of her heart.

Uncle William read the letter . . . turned back and read a certain paragraph twice . . . pursed his lips . . . folded up the letter and fitted it into its envelope . . . took off his glasses . . . put them into their case and laid it down . . . cleared his throat and reflected. Jane felt that she was going to scream.

"I suppose," said Uncle William at last, "that you had better let her go."

There was a good deal more said, though Jane said nothing. Grandmother was very angry.

But Uncle William said, "Andrew Stuart could take her altogether if he had a mind to. And, knowing him for what he is, I think he very likely would if you angered him. I agree with you, mother, that he is only doing this to annoy us, and when he sees that it has not annoyed us and that we are taking it quite calmly he will probably never bother about her again."

Jane went up to her room and stood alone in it. She saw with eyes of despair the great, big, unfriendly place. She saw herself in the big mirror reflected in another dim unfriendly room.

"God," said Jane distinctly and deliberately, "is no good."

10

"I think your father and mother might have got on if it hadn't been for you," said Phyllis.

Jane winced. She hadn't known that Phyllis knew about her father. But it seemed that everybody had known except her. She did not want to talk about him but Phyllis was bent on talking.

"I don't see," said Jane miserably, "why I made so much difference to them."

"Mother says your father was jealous because Aunt Robin loved you so much."

This, thought Jane, was a different yarn from the one Agnes Ripley had told. Agnes had said her mother hadn't wanted her. What was the truth? Perhaps neither Phyllis nor Agnes knew it. Anyhow, Jane liked Phyllis's version better than Agnes's. It was dreadful to think you ought never to have been born . . . that your mother wasn't glad to have you.

"Mother says," went on Phyllis, finding that Jane had nothing to say, "that if you lived in the States Aunt Robin could get a divorce easy as wink, but it's harder in Canada."

"What is a divorce?" asked Jane, remembering that Agnes Ripley had used the same word.

Phyllis laughed condescendingly.

"Victoria, don't you know anything? A divorce is when two people get unmarried."

"Can people get unmarried?" gasped Jane to whom it was an entirely new idea.

"Of course they can, silly. Mother says your mother ought to go to the States and get a divorce but father says it wouldn't be legal in Canada and anyway the Kennedys don't believe in it. Father says grandmother wouldn't allow it either, for fear Aunt

Robin would just go and marry somebody else."

"If . . . if mother got a divorce does that mean that he wouldn't be my father any more?" querried Jane hopefully.

Phyllis looked dubious.

"I shouldn't suppose it would make any difference that way. But whoever she married would be your stepfather."

Jane did not want a stepfather any more than she wanted a father. But she said nothing again and Phyllis was annoyed.

"How do you like the idea of going to P. E. Island, Victoria?"

Jane was not going to expose her soul to the patronizing Phyllis.

"I don't know anything about it," she said shortly.

"*I* do," said Phyllis importantly. "We spent a summer there two years ago. We lived in a big hotel on the north shore. It's quite a pretty place. I daresay you'll like it for a change."

Jane knew she would hate it. She tried to turn the conversation but Phyllis meant to thrash the subject out.

"How do you suppose you'll get along with your father?"

"I don't know."

"He likes clever people, you know, and you're not very clever, are you, Victoria?"

Jane did not like being made feel like a worm. Phyllis always made her feel like that . . . when she didn't make her feel like a shadow. And there was not a bit of use in getting mad with her. Phyllis never got mad. Phyllis, everybody said, was such a sweet child . . . had such a lovely disposition. She just went on condescending. Jane sometimes thought if they could have just one good fight she would like Phyllis better. Jane knew mother was a bit worried because she didn't make more friends among girls of her own age.

"You know," went on Phyllis, "that was one of the things. . . . Aunt Robin thought she couldn't talk clever enough for him."

The worm turned.

"I am not going to talk any more about my mother . . . or him," said Jane distinctly.

Phyllis sulked a little and the afternoon was a failure. Jane was more thankful than usual when Frank came to take her home.

Little was being said at 60 Gay about Jane's going to the Island. How quickly the days flew by! Jane wished she could hold them back. Once, when she had been very small, she had said to mother, "Isn't there any way we can stop time, mummy?"

Jane remembered that mother had sighed and said, "We can never stop time, darling."

And now time just went stonily on . . . tick tock, tick tock . . . sunrise, sunset, ever and ever nearer to the day when she would be torn away from mother. It would be early in June . . . St Agatha's closed earlier than the other schools. Grandmother took Jane to Marlborough's late in May and got some very nice clothes for her . . . much nicer than she had ever had before. Under ordinary circumstances Jane would have loved her blue coat and the smart little blue hat with its tiny scarlet bow . . . and a certain lovely frock of white, eyelet-embroidered in red, with a smart red leather belt. Phyllis had nothing nicer than that. But now she had no interest in them.

"I don't suppose she'll have much use for very fine clothes down there," mother had said.

"She shall go fitted out properly," said grandmother. "He shall not need to buy clothes for her, of that I shall make sure. And Irene Fraser shall have no chance to comment. I suppose he has some kind of a hovel to live in or he would not have sent for her. Did any one ever tell you, Victoria, that it is not proper to butter your whole slice of bread at once? And do you think it would be possible, just for a change, to get through a meal without letting your napkin slip off your knee continually?"

Jane dreaded meal-times more than ever. Her preoccupation made her awkward and grandmother pounced on everything. She wished she need never come to the table, but unluckily one cannot live without eating a little. Jane ate very little. She had no appetite and grew noticeably thinner. She could not put any heart into her studies and she barely made the Senior Third while

Phyllis passed with honours.

"As was to be expected," said grandmother.

Jody tried to comfort her.

"After all, it won't be so long. Only three months, Jane."

Three months of absence from a beloved mother and three months' presence with a detested father seemed like an eternity to Jane.

"You'll write me, Jane? And I'll write you if I can get any postage stamps. I've got ten cents now . . . that Mr Ransome gave me. That will pay for three stamps anyhow."

Then Jane told Jody a heart-breaking thing.

"I'll write you often, Jody. But I can write mother only once a month. And I'm never to mention him."

"Did your mother tell you that?"

"No, oh, no! It was grandmother. As if I'd want to mention him."

"I hunted up P. E. Island on the map," said Jody, her dark velvet-brown eyes full of sympathy. "There's such an awful lot of water round it. Ain't you afraid of falling over the edge?"

"I don't believe I'd mind if I did," said Jane dismally.

11

Jane was to go to the Island with Mr and Mrs Stanley who were going down to visit a married daughter. Somehow Jane lived through the last days. She was determined she would not make any fuss because that would be hard on mother. There were no more good-night confidences and caressings . . . no more little tender loving words spoken at special moments. But Jane, somehow, knew the two reasons for this. Mother could not bear it, for one thing, and, for another, grandmother was resolved not to permit it. But on Jane's last night at 60 Gay mother did slip in when grandmother was occupied by callers below.

"Mother . . . mother!"

"Darling, be brave. After all, it is only three months and the Island is a lovely spot. You may . . . if I'd known . . . once I . . . oh, it doesn't matter now. Nothing matters. Darling, there's one thing I must ask you to promise. You are never to mention me to your father."

"I won't," choked Jane. It was an easy promise. She couldn't imagine herself talking to him about mother.

"He will like you better if . . . if . . . he thinks you don't love me too much," whispered mother. Down went her white lids over her blue eyes. But Jane had seen the look. She felt as if her heart was bursting.

The sky at sunrise was blood-red but it soon darkened into sullen grey. At noon a drizzle set in. "I think the weather is sorry at your going away," said Jody. "Oh, Jane, I'll miss you so. And . . . I don't know if I'll be here when you come back. Miss West says she's going to put me in an orphanage, and I don't want to be put in an orphanage, Jane. Here's the pretty shell Miss Ames brought from the West Indies for me. It's the only pretty thing I have. I want you to have it because if I go to the orphanage I s'pose they'll take it away from me."

The train left for Montreal at eleven that night and Frank took Jane and her mother to the station. She had kissed grandmother and Aunt Gertrude good-bye dutifully.

"If you meet your Aunt Irene Fraser down on the Island remember me to her," said grandmother. There was an odd little tone of exultation in her voice. Jane felt that grandmother had got the better of Aunt Irene in some way, at some time, and wanted it rubbed in. It was as if she had said, "She will remember me." And who was Aunt Irene?

60 Gay seemed to scowl at her as they drove away. She had never liked it and it had never liked her, but she felt drearily as if some gate of life were shut behind her when the door closed. She and mother did not talk as they drove along over the elfish underground city that comes into view under the black street on a rainy night. She was determined she would not cry and she did not. Her eyes were wide with dismay but her voice was cool and quiet as she said good-bye. The last Robin Stuart saw of her was a gallant, indomitable little figure waving to her as Mrs Stanley herded her into the door of the Pullman.

They reached Montreal in the morning and left at noon on the Maritime Express. The time was to come when the very name of Maritime Express was to thrill Jane with ecstasy but now it meant exile. It rained all day. Mrs Stanley pointed out the mountains but Jane was not having any mountains just then. Mrs Stanley thought her very stiff and unresponsive and eventually left her alone . . . for which Jane would have thanked God, fasting, if she had ever heard of the phrase. Mountains! When every turn of the wheels was carrying her farther away from mother!

The next day they went down through New Brunswick, lying in the grey light of a cheerless rain. It was raining when they got to Sackville and transferred to the little branch line that ran down to Cape Tormentine.

"We take the car ferry there across to the Island," Mrs Stanley explained. Mrs Stanley had given up trying to talk to her. She thought Jane quite the dumbest child she had ever encountered. She had not the slightest inkling that Jane's silence was her only bulwark against wild, rebellious tears. And Jane *would not* cry.

It was not actually raining when they reached the Cape. As they went on board the car ferry the sun was hanging, a flat red ball, in a rift of clouds to the west. But it soon darkened down again. There was a grey choppy strait under a grey sky with dirty rags of clouds around the edges. By the time they got on the train again it was pouring harder than ever. Jane had been seasick on the way across and was now terribly tired. So this was Prince Edward Island . . . this rain-drenched land where the trees cringed before the wind and the heavy clouds seemed almost to touch the fields. Jane had no eyes for blossoming orchard or green meadow or soft-bosomed hills with scarfs of dark spruce across their shoulders. They would be in Charlottetown in a couple of hours, so Mrs Stanley said, and her father was to meet her there. Her father, who didn't love her, as mother said, and who lived in a hovel, as grandmother said. She knew nothing else about him. She wished she knew something . . . anything. What did he look like? Would he have pouchy eyes like Uncle David? A thin, sewed-up mouth like Uncle William? Would he wink at the end of every sentence like old Mr Doran when he came to call on grandmother?

She was a thousand miles away from mother and felt as if it were a million. Terrible waves of loneliness went over her. The train was pulling into the station.

"Here we are, Victoria," said Mrs Stanley in a tone of relief.

12

As Jane stepped from the train to the platform a lady pounced on her with a cry of "Is *this* Jane Victoria . . . can this be my *dear* little Jane Victoria?"

Jane did not like to be pounced on . . . and just then she was not feeling like anybody's Jane Victoria.

She drew herself away and took in the lady with one of her straight, deliberate glances. A very pretty lady of perhaps forty-five or fifty, with large, pale blue eyes and smooth ripples of auburn hair around her placid creamy face. Was this Aunt Irene?

"Jane, if you please," she said politely and distinctly.

"For all the world like her grandmother Kennedy, Andrew," Aunt Irene told her brother the next morning.

Aunt Irene laughed . . . an amused little gurgle.

"You dear funny child! Of course it can be Jane. It can be just whatever you like. I am your Aunt Irene. But I suppose you've never heard of me?"

"Yes, I have." Jane kissed Aunt Irene's cheek obediently. "Grandmother told me to remember her to you."

"Oh!" Something a little hard crept into Aunt Irene's sweet voice. "That was very kind of her . . . *very* kind indeed. And now I suppose you're wondering why your father isn't here. He started . . . he lives out at Brookview, you know . . . but that dreadful old car of his broke down half-way. He phoned in to me that he couldn't possibly get in to-night but would be along early in the morning and would I meet you and keep you for the night. Oh, Mrs Stanley, you're not going before I've thanked you for bringing our dear little girl safely down to us. We're so much obliged to you."

"Not at all. It's been a pleasure," said Mrs Stanley, politely and untruthfully. She hurried away, thankful to be relieved of the odd silent child who had looked all the way down as if she were an early Christian martyr on her path to the lions.

Jane felt herself alone in the universe. Aunt Irene did not make a bit of difference. Jane did not like Aunt Irene. And she liked herself still less. What was the matter with her? Couldn't she like anybody? Other girls liked some of their uncles and aunts at least.

She followed Aunt Irene out to the waiting taxi.

"It's a terrible night, lovey . . . but the country needs rain . . . we've been suffering for weeks . . . you must have brought it with you. But we'll soon be home. I'm so glad to have you. I've been telling your father he ought to let you stay with me anyhow. It's really foolish of him to take you out to Brookview. He only boards there, you know . . . two rooms over Jim Meade's store. Of course, he comes to town in the winter. But . . . well, perhaps you don't know, Jane darling, how very determined your father can be when he makes up his mind."

"I don't know anything about him," said Jane desperately.

"I suppose not. I suppose your mother has never talked to you about him?"

"No," Jane answered reluctantly. Somehow, Aunt Irene's question seemed charged with hidden meaning. Jane was to learn that this was characteristic of Aunt Irene's questions. Aunt Irene squeezed Jane's hand, which she had held ever since she had helped her into the taxi, sympathetically.

"You poor child! I know exactly how you feel. And I couldn't feel it was the right thing for your father to send for you. I'm sure I don't know why he did it. I couldn't fathom his motive . . . although your father and I have always been very close to each other . . . very close, lovey. I am ten years older than he is and I've always been more like a mother to him than a sister. Here we are at home, lovey."

Home! The house into which Jane was ushered was cosy and sleek, just like Aunt Irene herself, but Jane felt about as much at home as a sparrow alone on an alien house-top. In the living-room Aunt Irene took off her hat and coat, patted her hair and put her arm around Jane.

"Now let me look you over. I hadn't a chance in the station, and I haven't seen you since you were three years old."

Jane didn't want to be looked over and shrank back a little stiffly. She felt that she was being appraised and in spite of Aunt Irene's kindness of voice and manner she sensed that there was something in the appraisal not wholly friendly.

"You are not at all like your mother. She was the prettiest thing I ever saw. You are like your father, darling. And now we must have a bite of supper."

"Oh, no, please no," cried Jane impulsively. She knew she couldn't swallow a mouthful . . . it was misery to think of trying.

"Just a bite . . . just one little bite," said Aunt Irene persuasively as if coaxing a baby. "There's such a nice chocolate peppermint cake. I really made it for your father. He's just like a boy in some ways, you know . . . such a sweet tooth. And he has always thought my chocolate cakes just about perfection. Your mother did try so hard to learn to make them like mine . . . but . . . well, it's a gift. You have it or you haven't. One really couldn't expect a lovely little doll like her to be a cook . . . or a manager either for that matter and I told your father that often enough. Men don't always understand, do they? They expect everything in a woman. Sit here, Janie."

Perhaps the "Janie" was the last straw. Jane was not going to be "Janied."

"Thank you, Aunt Irene," she said very politely and very resolutely, "but I can't eat anything and it wouldn't be any use at all to try. Please may I go to bed?"

Aunt Irene patted her shoulder.

"Of course, you poor darling. You're all tired out and everything so strange. I know how hard it is for you. I'll take you right upstairs to your room."

The room was very pretty, with hangings of basket-weave rose-patterned cretonne and a silk-covered bed so smooth and sleek that it looked as if it had never been slept in. But Aunt Irene deftly removed the silk spread and turned down the sheets.

"I hope you'll have a good sleep, lovey. You don't know what it means to me to have you sleeping under my roof... Andrew's little girl... my only niece. And I was always so fond of your mother .. . but... well, I don't quite think she ever really liked me. I always felt she didn't, but I never let it make any difference between us. She didn't like to see me and your father talking much together ... I always realized that. She was so much younger than your father... a mere child... it was natural for him to turn to me for advice as he'd always been used to do. He always talked things over with me first. She was a little jealous, I think ... she could hardly help that, being Mrs Robert Kennedy's daughter. Never let yourself be jealous, Janie. It wrecks more lives than anything else. Here's a puff, lovey, if you're chilly in the night. A wet night in P. E. Island is apt to be cool. Good night, lovey."

Jane stood alone in the room and looked about her. The bed lamp had a lamp-shade painted with roses with a bead fringe. For some reason Jane couldn't endure that lamp-shade. It was too smooth and pretty just like Aunt Irene. She went to it and put out the light. Then she went to the window. Beat, beat went the rain on the panes. Splash, splash went the rain on the roof of the veranda. Beyond it Jane could see nothing. Her heart swelled. This black, alien, starless land could never be home to her.

"If I only had mother," she whispered. But, though she felt that something had taken her life and torn it apart, she did not cry.

13

Jane was so tired after the preceding sleepless nights on the train that she went to sleep almost at once. But she wakened while it was still night. The rain had ceased. A bar of shining light lay across her bed. She slipped out from between Aunt Irene's perfumed sheets and went to the window. The world had changed. The sky was cloudless and a few shining, distant stars looked down on the sleeping town. A tree not far away was all silvery bloom. Moonlight was spilling over everything from a full moon that hung like an enormous bubble over what must be a bay or harbour and there was one splendid, sparkling trail across the water. So there was a moon in Prince Edward Island, too. Jane hadn't really believed it before. And polished to the queen's taste. It was like seeing an old friend. That moon was looking down on Toronto as well as Prince Edward Island. Perhaps it was shining on Jody, asleep in her little attic room, or on mother coming home late from some gay affair. Suppose she were looking at it at this very moment! It no longer seemed a thousand miles to Toronto.

The door opened and Aunt Irene came in, in her nightdress.

"Lovey, what is the matter? I heard you moving about and was afraid you were ill."

"I just got up to look at the moon," said Jane.

"You funny childy! Haven't you seen moons before? You gave me a real fright. Now go back to bed like a darling. You want to look bright and fresh for father when he comes, you know."

Jane didn't want to look bright and fresh for anybody. Was she always to be spied upon? She got into bed silently and was tucked in for the second time. But she could not sleep again.

Morning comes at last, be the night ever so long. The day that was to be such a marvellous day for Jane began like any other.

The mackerel clouds . . . only Jane didn't know then they were mackerel clouds . . . in the eastern sky began to take fire. The sun rose without any unusual fuss. Jane was afraid to get up too early for fear of alarming Aunt Irene again but at last she rose and opened the window. Jane did not know she was looking out on the loveliest thing on earth . . . a June morning in Prince Edward Island . . . but she knew it all seemed like a different world from last night. A wave of fragrance broke in her face from the lilac hedge between Aunt Irene's house and the next one. The poplars in a corner of the lawn were shaking in green laughter. An apple-tree stretched out friendly arms. There was a far-away view of daisy-sprinkled fields across the harbour where white gulls were soaring and swooping. The air was moist and sweet after the rain. Aunt Irene's house was on the fringe of the town and a country road ran behind it . . . a road almost blood-red in its glistening wetness. Jane had never imagined a road coloured like that.

"Why . . . why, P. E. Island is a pretty place," thought Jane half grudgingly.

Breakfast was the first ordeal and Jane was no hungrier than she had been the night before.

"I don't think I can eat anything, Aunt Irene."

"But you must, lovey. I'm going to love you but I'm not going to spoil you. I expect you've always had a little too much of your own way. Your father may be along almost any minute now. Sit right down here and eat your cereal."

Jane tried. Aunt Irene had certainly prepared a lovely breakfast for her. Orange juice . . . cereal with thick golden cream . . . dainty triangles of toast . . . a perfectly poached egg . . . apple jelly between amber and crimson. There was no doubt Aunt Irene was a good cook. But Jane had never had a harder time choking down a meal.

"Don't be so excited, lovey," said Aunt Irene with a smile as to some very young child who needed soothing.

Jane did not think she was excited. She had merely a queer, dreadful, empty feeling which nothing, not even the egg, seemed able to fill up. And after breakfast there was an hour when Jane discovered that the hardest work in the world is waiting. But everything comes to an end and when Aunt Irene said, "There's your father now," Jane felt that everything had come to an end.

Her hands were suddenly clammy but her mouth was dry. The ticking of the clock seemed unnaturally loud. There was a step on the path . . . the door opened . . . someone was standing on the threshold. Jane stood up but she could not raise her eyes . . . she could not.

"Here's your baby," said Aunt Irene. "Isn't she a little daughter to be proud of, 'Drew? A bit too tall for her age perhaps, but . . ."

"A russet-haired jade," said a voice.

Only four words . . . but they changed life for Jane. Perhaps it was the voice more than the words . . . a voice that made everything seem like a wonderful secret just you two shared. Jane came to life at last and looked up.

Peaked eyebrows . . . thick reddish-brown hair springing back from his forehead . . . a mouth tucked in at the corners . . . square cleft chin . . . stern hazel eyes with jolly looking wrinkles around them. The face was as familiar to her as her own.

"Kenneth Howard," gasped Jane. She took a quite unconscious step towards him.

The next moment she was lifted in his arms and kissed. She kissed him back. She had no sense of strangerhood. She felt at once the call of that mysterious kinship of soul which has nothing to do with the relationships of flesh and blood. In that one moment Jane forgot that she had ever hated her father. She liked him . . . she liked everything about him from the nice tobaccoey smell of his heather-mixture tweed suit to the firm grip of his arms around her. She wanted to cry but that was out of the question so she laughed instead . . . rather wildly, perhaps, for Aunt Irene said tolerantly, "Poor child, no wonder she is a little hysterical."

Father set Jane down and looked at her. All the sternness of his eyes had crinkled into laughter.

"Are you hysterical, my Jane?" he said gravely.

How she loved to be called "my Jane" like that!

"No, father," she said with equal gravity. She never spoke of him or thought of him as "he" again.

"Leave her with me a month and I'll fatten her up," smiled Aunt Irene.

Jane felt a quake of dismay. Suppose father did leave her. Evidently father had no intention of doing anything of the sort. He pulled her down on the sofa beside him and kept his arm about her. All at once everything was all right.

"I don't believe I want her fattened up. I like her bones." He looked at Jane critically. Jane knew he was looking her over and didn't mind. She only hoped madly that he would like her. Would he be disappointed because she was not pretty? Would he think her mouth too big? "Do you know you have nice little bones, Janekin?"

"She's got her Grandfather Stuart's nose," said Aunt Irene. Aunt Irene evidently approved of Jane's nose but Jane had a disagreeable feeling that she had robbed Grandfather Stuart of his nose. She liked it better when father said:

"I rather fancy the way your eyelashes are put on, Jane. By the way, do you like to be Jane? I've always called you Jane but that may be just pure cussedness. You've a right to whatever name you like. But I want to know which name is the real *you* and which the shadowy little ghost."

"Oh, I'm Jane," cried Jane. And was she glad to be Jane!

"That's settled then. And suppose you call me dad? I'm afraid I'd make a terribly awkward father but I think I could be a tolerable dad. Sorry I couldn't get in last night but my jovial, disreputable old car died right on the road. I managed to restore it to life this morning . . . at least long enough to hop into town like a toad . . . our mode of travelling added to the gaiety of P. E. Island . . . but I'm afraid it's got to go into a garage for a while. After dinner we'll drive across the Island, Jane, and get acquainted."

"We're acquainted now," said Jane simply. It was true. She felt that she had known dad for years. Yes, "dad" was nicer than "father." "Father" had unpleasant associations . . . she had hated father. But it was easy to love dad. Jane opened the most secret chamber of her heart and took him in . . . nay, found him there. For dad was Kenneth Howard and Jane had loved Kenneth Howard for a long, long time.

"This Jane person," dad remarked to the ceiling, "knows her onions."

14

Jane found that waiting for something pleasant was very different from waiting for something unpleasant. Mrs Stanley would not have known her with the laughter and sparkle in her eyes. If the forenoon seemed long it was only because she was in such a hurry to be with dad again . . . and away from Aunt Irene. Aunt Irene was trying to pump her . . . about grandmother and mother and her life at 60 Gay. Jane was not going to be pumped, much to Aunt Irene's disappointment. Questioned she never so cleverly, Jane had a disconcerting "yes" or "no" for every question and still more disconcerting silence for suggestive remarks that were disguised questions.

"So your Grandmother Kennedy is good to you, Janie?"

"Very good," said Jane unflinchingly. Well, grandmother *was* good to her. There were St Agatha's and the music lessons and the pretty clothes, the limousine and the balanced meals as evidence. Aunt Irene had looked carefully at all her clothes.

"She never had any use for your father, you know, Janie. I thought perhaps she might take her spite out on you. It was really she that made all the trouble between him and your mother."

Jane said nothing. She would not talk about that secret bitterness to Aunt Irene. Aunt Irene gave up in disgust.

Dad came back at noon without his car but with a horse and buggy.

"It's going to take all day to fix it. I'm borrowing Jed Carson's rig and he'll take it back when he brings the car and Jane's trunk out to-morrow. Did you ever have a buggy ride, my Jane?"

"You're not going without your dinners," said Aunt Irene.

Jane enjoyed that dinner, having eaten next to nothing ever since she left Toronto. She hoped dad wouldn't think her appetite terrible. For all she knew he was poor . . . that car hadn't looked like wealth . . . and another mouth to fill might be inconvenient. But dad himself was evidently enjoying his dinner . . . especially that chocolate peppermint cake. Jane wished she knew how to make chocolate peppermint cake, but she made up her mind that she would never ask Aunt Irene how to make it.

Aunt Irene made a fuss over dad. She purred over him . . . actually purred. And dad liked her purring and her honey-sweet phrases just as well as he had liked her cake. Jane saw that clearly.

"It isn't really fair to the child to take her out to that Brookview boarding-house of yours," said Aunt Irene.

"Who knows but I'll get a house of my own for the summer?" said dad. "Do you think you could keep house for me, Jane?"

"Yes," said Jane promptly. She *could*. She knew how a house should be kept even if she had never kept one. There are people who are born knowing things.

"Can you cook?" asked Aunt Irene, winking at dad, as if over some delicious joke. Jane was pleased to see that dad did not wink back. And he saved her the ordeal of replying.

"Any descendant of my mother's can cook," he said. "Come, my Jane, put on thy beautiful garments and let's be on our way."

As Jane came downstairs in her hat and coat she could not help hearing Aunt Irene in the dining-room.

"She's got a secretive strain in her, Andrew, that I confess I don't like."

"Knows how to keep her own counsel, eh?" said dad.

"It's more than that, Andrew. She's deep . . . take my word for it, she's deep. Old Lady Kennedy will never be dead while she is alive. But she is a very dear little girl for all that, Andrew . . . we can't expect her to be faultless . . . and if there is anything I can do for her you have only to let me know. Be patient with her, Andrew. You know she's never been taught how to love you."

Jane fairly gritted her teeth. The idea of her having to be taught "how to love" dad! It was . . . why, it was funny! Jane's annoyance with Aunt Irene dissolved in a little chuckle, as low-pitched and impish as an owl's.

"*Do* be careful of poison ivy," Aunt Irene called after them as they drove away. "I'm told there is so much of it in Brookview. *Do* take good care of her, Andrew."

"You've got it wrong end foremost, Irene, like all women. Any one could see with half an eye that Jane is going to take care of *me.*"

A blithe soul was Jane as they drove away. The glow at her heart went with her across the Island. She simply could not believe that only a few hours had elapsed since she had been the most miserable creature in the world. It was jolly to ride in a buggy, just behind a little red mare whose sleek hams Jane would have liked to bend forward and slap. She did not eat up the long red miles as a car would have done, but Jane did not want them eaten up. The road was full of lovely surprises . . . a glimpse of far-off hills that seemed made of opal dust . . . a whiff of wind that had been blowing over a clover field . . . brooks that appeared from nowhere and ran off into green shadowy woods where long branches of spicy fir hung over the laced water . . . great white cloud mountains towering up in the blue sky . . . a hollow of tipsy buttercups . . . a tidal river unbelievably blue. Everywhere she looked there was something to delight her. Everything seemed just on the point of whispering a secret of happiness. And there was something else . . . the sea tang in the air. Jane sniffed it for the first time . . . sniffed again . . . drank it in.

"Feel in my right-hand pocket," said dad.

Jane explored and found a bag of caramels. At 60 Gay she was not allowed to eat candy between meals . . . but 60 Gay was a thousand miles away.

"We're neither of us much for talking, it seems," said dad.

"No, but I think we entertain each other very well," said Jane, as distinctly as she could with her jaws stuck together with caramel.

Dad laughed. He had such a nice understanding laugh.

"I can talk a blue streak when the spirit moves me," he said. "When it doesn't I like people to let me be. You're a girl after my own heart, Jane. I'm glad I was predestined to send for you. Irene argued against it. But I'm a stubborn dud, my Jane, when I take a notion into my noddle. It just occurred to me that I wanted to get acquainted with my daughter."

Dad did not ask about mother. Jane was thankful he did not . . . and yet she knew it was all wrong that he did not. It was all wrong that mother had asked her not to speak of her to him. Oh, there were too many things all wrong but one thing was indisputably and satisfyingly right. She was going to spend a whole summer with dad and they were here together, driving over a road which had a life of its own that seemed to be running through her veins like quicksilver. Jane knew that she had never been in any place or any company that suited her so well.

The most delightful drive must end.

"We'll soon be at Brookview," said dad. "I've been living at Brookview this past year. It is still one of the quiet places of the earth. I've a couple of rooms over Jim Meade's store. Mrs Jim Meade gives me my meals and thinks I'm a harmless lunatic because I write."

"What do you write, dad?" asked Jane, thinking of "Peaceful Adjustment of International Difficulties."

"A little of everything, Jane. Stories . . . poems . . . essays . . . articles on all subjects. I even wrote a novel once. But I couldn't find a publisher. So I went back to my pot-boilers. Behold a mute inglorious Milton in your dad. To you, Jane, I will confide my dearest dream. It is to write an epic on the life of Methuselah. What a subject! Here we are."

"Here" was a corner where two roads crossed and in the corner was a building which was a store at one end and a dwelling place at the other. The store end was open to the road but the house end was fenced off with a paling and a spruce hedge. Jane learned at once and for ever the art of getting out of a buggy and they went through a little white gate, with a black wooden decoy duck on one of its posts, and up a red walk edged with ribbon grass and big quahaug shells.

"Woof, woof," went a friendly little brown and white dog sitting on the steps. A nice gingery smell of hot cookies floated out of the door as an elderly woman came out . . . a trim body wearing a white apron edged with six-inch-deep crochet lace and with the reddest cheeks Jane had ever seen on anybody in her life.

"Mrs Meade, this is Jane," said dad, "and you see now why I shall have to shave every morning after this."

"Dear child," said Mrs Meade and kissed her. Jane liked her kiss better than Aunt Irene's.

Mrs Meade at once gave Jane a slice of bread and butter and strawberry jam to "stay her stomach" till supper. It was wild-strawberry jam and Jane had never tasted wild-strawberry jam in her life before. The supper table was spread in a spotless kitchen where all the big windows were filled with flowering geraniums and begonias with silver-spotted leaves.

"I like kitchens," thought Jane.

Through another door that opened into a garden was a far-away view of green pastures to the south. The table in the centre of the room was covered with a gay red and white checked cloth. There was a fat, squat little bean-pot full of golden-brown beans before Mr Meade who gave Jane a liberal helping, besides a big square of fluffy cornmeal cake. Mr Meade looked very much like a cabbage in spectacles and flying jibs but Jane liked him.

Nobody found fault with Jane for things done or left undone. Nobody made her feel silly and crude and always in the wrong. When she finished her johnny-cake Mr Meade put another slice on her plate without even asking her if she wanted it.

"Eat all you like but pocket nothing," he told her solemnly.

The brown and white dog sat beside her, looking up with hungry hopeful eyes. Nobody took any notice when Jane fed him bits of johnny-cake.

Mr and Mrs Meade did most of the talking. It was all about people Jane had never heard of, but somehow she liked to listen. When Mrs Meade said in a solemn tone that poor George Baldwin was very ill with an ulster in his stomach, Jane's eyes and dad's laughed to each other though their faces remained as solemn as Mrs Meade's. Jane felt warm and pleasant all over. It was jolly to have someone to share a joke with. Fancy laughing with your eyes at any one in 60 Gay! She and mother exchanged glimmers but they never dared laugh.

The east was paling to moonrise when Jane went to bed in Mrs Meade's spare-room. The bureau and the wash-stand were very cheap, the bed an iron one enamelled in white, the floor painted brown. But there was a gorgeous hooked rug of roses and ferns and autumn leaves on it, the prim starched lace curtains were as white as snow, the wallpaper was so pretty . . . silver daisy clusters on a creamy ground with circles of pale blue ribbon round them . . . and there was a huge scarlet geranium with scented velvety leaves on a stand before one of the windows.

There was something friendly about the room. Jane slept like a top and was up and down in the morning when Mrs Meade was lighting the kitchen fire. Mrs Meade gave Jane a big fat doughnut to stay her stomach till breakfast and sent her out into the garden to wait till dad came down. It lay in the silence of the dewy morning. The wind was full of wholesome country smells. The little flower-beds were edged with blue forget-me-nots and in one corner was a big clump of early, dark red peonies. Violets and plots of red and white daisies grew under the parlour windows. In a near field cows were cropping gold-green grass and a dozen little fluffy chicks were running about. A tiny yellow bird was tilting on a spirea spray. The brown and white dog came out and followed Jane about. A funny, two-wheeled cart, such as Jane had never seen before, went by on the road and the driver, a lank youth in overalls, waved to her as to an old friend. Jane promptly waved back with what was left of her doughnut.

How blue and high the sky was! Jane liked the country sky. "P. E. Island is a lovely place," thought Jane, not at all grudgingly. She picked a pink cabbage rose and shook the dew from it all over her face. Fancy washing your face with a rose! And then she remembered how she had prayed that she might not come here.

"I think," said Jane decidedly, "that I should apologize to God."

15

"We must go and buy us a house soon, duck," said dad, jumping right into the middle of the subject as Jane was to find was his habit.

Jane turned it over in her mind.

"Is 'soon' to-day?" she asked.

Dad laughed.

"Might as well be. This happens to be one of the days when I like myself reasonably well. We'll start as soon as Jed brings our car."

Jed did not bring the car till noon so they had dinner before they set out, and Mrs Meade gave Jane a bag of butter cookies to stay their stomachs till supper-time.

"I like Mrs Meade," Jane told dad, a pleasant warmth filling her soul as she realized that here was somebody she did like.

"She's the salt of the earth," agreed dad, "even if she does think the violet ray is a girl."

The violet ray might have been a girl for anything Jane knew to the contrary ... or cared. It was enough to know that dad and she were off in a car that would have given Frank a conniption at sight, bouncing along red roads that were at once friendly and secretive, through woods that were so gay and bridal with wild cherry-trees sprinkled through them and over hills where velvet cloud-shadows rolled until they seemed to vanish in little hollows filled with blue. There were houses on every side in that pleasant land and they were going to buy one. . . . "Let's buy a house, Jane" . . . just like that, as one might have said, "Let's buy a basket." Delightful!

"As soon as I knew you were coming I began inquiring about possible houses. I've heard of several. We'll take a look at them all before we decide. What kind of a house would you like, Jane?"

"What kind of a house can you afford?" said Jane gravely.

Dad chuckled.

"She's got some of the little common sense still left in the world," he told the sky. "We can't pay a fancy price, Jane. I'm not a plutocrat. On the other hand, neither am I on relief. I sold quite a lot of stuff last winter."

"'Peaceful Adjustment of International Difficulties'," murmured Jane.

"What's that?"

Jane told him. She told him how she had liked Kenneth Howard's picture and cut it out. But she did not tell him that grandmother had torn it, nor about the look in mother's eyes.

"*Saturday Evening* is a good customer of mine. But let us return to our muttons. Subject to the fluctuations of the market, what kind of a house would you like, my Jane?"

"Not a big one," said Jane, thinking of the enormous 60 Gay. "A little house . . . with some trees around it . . . young trees."

"White birches?" said dad. "I rather fancy a white birch or two. And a few dark green spruces for contrast. And the house must be green and white to match the trees. I've always wanted a green and white house."

"Couldn't we paint it?" asked Jane.

"We could. Clever of you to think of that, Jane. I might have turned down our predestined house just because it was mud colour. And we must have at least one window where we can see the gulf."

"Will it be near the gulf?"

"It must be. We're going up to the Queen's Shore district. All the houses I've heard about are up there."

"I'd like it to be on a hill," said Jane wistfully.

"Let's sum up . . . a little house, white and green or to be made so . . . with trees, preferably birch and spruce . . . a window looking seaward . . . on a hill. That sounds very possible . . . but there is one other requirement. There must be magic about it, Jane . . .

lashings of magic . . . and magic houses are scarce, even on the Island. Have you any idea at all what I mean, Jane?"

Jane reflected.

"You want to feel that the house is *yours* before you buy it," she said.

"Jane," said dad, "you are too good to be true."

He was looking at her closely as they went up a hill after crossing a river so blue that Jane had exclaimed in rapture over it . . . a river that ran into a bluer harbour. And when they reached the top of the hill, there before them lay something greater and bluer still that Jane knew must be the gulf.

"Oh!" she said. And again, "Oh!"

"This is where the sea begins. Like it, Jane?"

Jane nodded. She could not speak. She had seen Lake Ontario, pale blue and shimmering, but this . . . this? She continued to look at it as if she could never have enough of it.

"I never thought anything could be so blue," she whispered.

"You've seen it before," said dad softly. "You may not know it but it's in your blood. You were born beside it, one sweet, haunted April night . . . you lived by it for three years. Once I took you down and dipped you in it, to the horror of . . . of several people. You were properly baptized before that in the Anglican church in Charlottetown . . . but that was your real baptism. You are the sea's child and you have come home."

"But you didn't like me," said Jane, before she thought.

"Not like you! Who told you that?"

"Grandmother." She had not been forbidden to mention grandmother's name to him.

"The old . . ." dad checked himself. A mask seemed to fall over his face.

"Let us not forget we are house-hunting, Jane," he said coolly.

For a little while Jane felt no interest in house-hunting. She didn't know what to believe or whom to believe. She thought dad liked her now . . . but did he? Perhaps he was just pretending. Then she remembered how he had kissed her.

"He does like me now," she thought. "Perhaps he didn't like me when I was born but I know he does now." And she was happy again.

16

House-hunting, Jane decided, was jolly. Perhaps it was really more the pleasure of the driving and talking and being silent with dad that was jolly, for most of the houses on dad's list were not interesting. The first house they looked at was too big; the second was too small.

"After all, we must have room to swing the cat," said dad.

"Have you a cat?" demanded Jane.

"No. But we can get one if you like. I hear the kitten crop is tops this year. Do you like cats?"

"Yes."

"Then we'll have a bushel of them."

"No," said Jane, "two."

"And a dog. I don't know how you feel about dogs, Jane, but if you're going to have a cat, I must have a dog. I haven't had a dog since . . ."

He stopped short again, and again Jane had the feeling that he had been just on the point of saying something she wanted very much to hear.

The third house looked attractive. It was just at the turn of a wooded road dappled with sunshine through the trees. But on inspection it proved hopeless. The floors were cut and warped and slanted in all directions. The doors didn't hang right. The windows wouldn't open. There was no pantry.

There was too much gingerbread about the fourth house, dad said, and neither of them looked twice at the fifth . . . a dingy, square, unpainted building with a litter of rusty cans, old pails, fruit baskets, rags and rubbish all over its yard.

"The next on my list is the old Jones house," said dad.

It was not so easy to find the old Jones house. The new Jones house fronted the road boldly, but you had to go past it and away down a deep-rutted, neglected lane to find the old one. You could see the gulf from the kitchen window. But it was too big and both dad and Jane felt that the view of the back of the Jones barns and pig-sty was not inspiring. So they bounced up the lane again, feeling a little dashed.

The seventh house seemed to be all a house should be. It was a small bungalow, new and white, with a red roof and dormer windows. The yard was trim though treeless; there were a pantry and a nice cellar and good floors. And it had a wonderful view of the gulf.

Dad looked at Jane.

"Do you sense any magic about this, my Jane?"

"Do *you?*" challenged Jane.

Dad shook his head.

"Absolutely none. And, as magic is indispensable, no can do."

They drove away, leaving the man who owned the house wondering who them two lunatics were. What on earth was magic? He must see the carpenter who had built the house and find out why he hadn't put any in it.

Two more houses were impossible.

"I suppose we're a pair of fools, Jane. We've looked at all the houses I've heard of that are for sale . . . and what's to be done now? Go back and eat our words and buy the bungalow?"

"Let's ask this man who is coming along the road if he knows of any house we haven't seen," said Jane composedly.

"The Jimmy Johns have one, I hear," said the man. "Over at Lantern Hill. The house their Aunt Matilda Jollie lived in. There's some of her furniture in it, too, I hear. You'd likely git it reasonable if you jewed him down a bit. It's two miles to Lantern Hill and you go by Queen's Shore."

The Jimmy Johns and a Lantern Hill and an Aunt Matilda Jollie! Jane's thumbs pricked. Magic was in the offing.

Jane saw the house first . . . at least she saw the upstairs window in its gable end winking at her over the top of a hill. But they had to drive around the hill and up a winding lane between two dikes, with little ferns growing out of the stones and young spruces starting up along them at intervals.

And then, right before them, was the house . . . *their* house!

"Dear, don't let your eyes pop quite out of your head," warned dad.

It squatted right against a little steep hill whose toes were lost in bracken. It was small . . . you could have put half a dozen of it inside 60 Gay. It had a garden, with a stone dike at the lower end of it to keep it from sliding down the hill, a paling and a gate, with two tall white birches leaning over it, and a flat-stone walk up to the only door, which had eight small panes of glass in its upper half. The door was locked but they could see in at the windows. There was a good-sized room on one side of the door, stairs going up right in front of it, and two small rooms on the other side whose windows looked right into the side of the hill where ferns grew as high as your waist, and there were stones lying about covered with velvet green moss.

There was a bandy-legged old cook-stove in the kitchen, a table and some chairs. And a dear little glass-paned cupboard in the corner fastened with a wooden button.

On one side of the house was a clover field and on the other a maple grove, sprinkled with firs and spruces, and separated from the house lot by an old, lichen-covered board fence. There was an apple-tree in the corner of the yard, with pink petals falling softly, and a clump of old spruces outside the garden gate.

"I like the pattern of this place," said Jane.

"Do you suppose it's possible that the view goes with the house?" said dad.

Jane had been so taken up with her house that she had not looked at the view at all. Now she turned her eyes on it and lost her breath over it. Never, never had she seen . . . had she dreamed anything so wonderful.

Lantern Hill was at the apex of a triangle of land which had the gulf for its base and Queen's Harbour for one of its sides.

There were silver and lilac sand-dunes between them and the sea, extending into a bar across the harbour where great, splendid, blue and white waves were racing to the long sun-washed shore. Across the channel a white lighthouse stood up against the sky and on the other side of the harbour were the shadowy crests of purple hills that dreamed with their arms around each other. And over it all the indefinable charm of a Prince Edward Island landscape.

Just below Lantern Hill, skirted by spruce barrens on the harbour side and a pasture field on the other, was a little pond . . . absolutely the bluest thing that Jane had ever seen.

"Now, that is my idea of a pond," said dad.

Jane said nothing at first. She could only look. She had never been there before but it seemed as if she had known it all her life. The song the sea-wind was singing was music native to her ears. She had always wanted to "belong" somewhere and she belonged here. At last she had a feeling of home.

"Well, what about it?" said dad.

Jane was so sure the house was listening that she shook her finger at him.

"Sh . . . sh," she said.

"Let's go down to the shore and talk it over," said dad.

It was about fifteen minutes' walk to the outside shore. They sat down on the bone-white body of an old tree that had drifted from heaven knew where. The snapping salty breeze whipped their faces; the surf creamed along the shore; the wee sand-peeps flitted fearlessly past them. "How clean salt air is!" thought Jane.

"Jane, I have a suspicion that the roof leaks."

"You can put some shingles on it."

"There's a lot of burdocks in the yard."

"We can root them out."

"The house may have once been white . . ."

"It can be white again."

"The paint on the front door is blistered."

"Paint doesn't cost very much, does it?"

"The shutters are broken."

"Let's fix them."

"The plaster is cracked."

"We can paper over it."

"Who knows if there's a pantry, Jane?"

"There are shelves in one of the little rooms on the right. I can use that for a pantry. The other little room would do you for a study. You'd have to have some place to write, wouldn't you?"

"She's got it all planned out," dad told the Altantic. But added, "That big maple wood is a likely place for owls."

"Who's afraid of owls?"

"And what about magic, my Jane?"

Magic! Why, the place was simply jammed with magic. You were falling over magic. Dad knew that. He was only talking for the sake of talking. When they went back Jane sat down on the big red sandstone slab which served as a doorstep, while dad went through the maple wood by a little twisted path the cows had made to see Jimmy John—otherwise Mr J. J. Garland. The Garland house could be seen peeping around the corner of the maples—a snug, butter-coloured farmhouse decently dressed in trees.

Jimmy John came back with dad, a little fat man with twinkling grey eyes. He hadn't been able to find the key but they had seen the ground floor and he told them there were three rooms upstairs with a spool bed in one of them and a closet in each of them.

"And a boot-shelf under the stairs."

They stood on the stone walk and looked at the house.

"What are you going to do with me?" said the house as plainly as ever a house spoke.

"What is your price?" said dad.

"Four hundred with the furniture thrown in for good measure," said Jimmy John, winking at Jane. Jane winked rakishly back. After all, grandmother was a thousand miles away.

"Bang goes saxpence," said dad. He did not try to "jew" Jimmy

John down. That he could buy all this loveliness for four hundred dollars was enough luck.

Dad handed over fifty dollars and said the rest would be paid next day.

"The house is yours," said Jimmy John with an air of making them a present of it. But Jane knew the house had always been theirs.

"The house . . . and the pond . . . and the harbour . . . and the gulf! A good buy," said dad. "And half an acre of land. All my life I've wanted to own a bit of land . . . just enough to stand on and say, 'This is mine.' And now, Jane, it's brillig."

"Four o'clock in the afternoon." Jane knew her *Alice* too well to be caught tripping on that.

Just as they were leaving, a pocket edition of Jimmy John, with a little impudent face came tearing through the maple grove with the key which had turned up in his absence. Jimmy John handed it to Jane with a bow. Jane clutched it tightly all the way back to Brookview. She loved it. Think what it would open for her!

They discovered they were hungry, having forgotten all about dinner, so they fished out Mrs Meade's butter cookies and ate them.

"You'll let me do the cooking, dad?"

"Why, you'll have to. *I* can't."

Jane glowed.

"I wish we could move in to-morrow, dad."

"Why not? I can get some bedding and some food. We can go on from there."

"I just can't bear to have this day go," said Jane. "It doesn't seem as if there could ever be another so happy."

"We've got to-morrow, Jane . . . let me see . . . we've got about ninety-five to-morrows."

"Ninety-five," gloated Jane.

"And we'll do just as we want to inside of decency. We'll be clean but not too clean. We'll be lazy but not too lazy . . . just do enough to keep three jumps ahead of the wolf. And we'll never have in our house that devilish thing known as an intermittent alarm clock."

"But we must have some kind of a clock," said Jane.

"Timothy Salt down at the harbour mouth has an old ship's clock. I'll get him to lend it to us. It only goes when it feels like it, but what matter? Can you darn my socks, Jane?"

"Yes," said Jane, who had never darned a sock in her life.

"Jane, we're sitting on the top of the world. It was a piece of amazing luck, your asking that man, Jane."

"It wasn't luck. I *knew* he'd know," said Jane. "And oh, dad, can we keep the house a secret till we've moved in?"

"Of course," agreed dad. "From every one except Aunt Irene. We'll have to tell her, of course."

Jane said nothing. She had not known till dad spoke that it was really from Aunt Irene she wished to keep it secret.

Jane didn't believe she would sleep that night. How could one go to sleep with so many wonderful things to think of? And some that were very puzzling. How could two people like mother and dad hate each other? It didn't make sense. They were both so lovely in different ways. They must have loved each other once. What had changed them? If she, Jane, only knew the whole truth, perhaps she could do something about it.

But as she drifted off into dreams of spruce-shadowed red roads that all led to dear little houses, her last conscious thought was "I wonder if we can get our milk at the Jimmy Johns'."

17

They "moved in" the next afternoon. Dad and Jane went to town in the forenoon and got a load of canned stuff and some bedding. Jane also got some gingham dresses and aprons. She knew none of the clothes grandmother had bought for her would be of any use at Lantern Hill. And she slipped into a bookstore unbeknown to dad and bought a *Cookery for Beginners*. Mother had given her a dollar when she left and she was not going to take any chances.

They called to see Aunt Irene but Aunt Irene was out, and Jane had her own reasons for being pleased about this but she kept them to herself. After dinner they tied Jane's trunk and suitcase on the running-boards and bounced off to Lantern Hill. Mrs Meade gave them a box of doughnuts, three leaves of bread, a round pat of butter with a pattern of clover-leaves on it, a jar of cream, a raisin pie and three dried codfish.

"Put one in soak to-night and broil it for your breakfast in the morning," she told Jane.

The house was still there. Jane had been half afraid it would be stolen in the night. It seemed so entirely desirable to her that she couldn't imagine any one else not wanting it. She felt so sorry for Aunt Matilda Jollie who had had to die and leave it. It was hard to believe that, even in the golden mansions, Aunt Matilda Jollie wouldn't miss the house on Lantern Hill.

"Let me unlock the door, please, dad." She was trembling with delight as she stepped over the threshold.

"This . . . this is home," said Jane. Home . . . something she had never known before. She was nearer crying then than she had ever been in her life.

They ran over the house like a couple of children. There were three rooms upstairs . . . a quite large one to the north, which Jane decided at once must be father's.

"Wouldn't you like it yourself, blithe spirit? The window looks over the gulf."

"No, I want this dear little one at the back. I want a *little* room, dad. And the other one will do nicely for a guest-room."

"Do we need a guest-room, Jane? Let me remind you that the measure of any one's freedom is what he can do without."

"Oh, but of course we need a guest-room, dad." Jane was quite tickled over the thought. "We'll have company sometimes, won't we?"

"There isn't a bed in it."

"Oh, we'll get one somewhere. Dad, the house is glad to see us . . . glad to be lived in again. The chairs just want someone to sit on them."

"Little sentimentalist!" jeered dad. But there was understanding laughter behind his eyes.

The house was surprisingly clean. Jane was to learn later that as soon as they knew Aunt Matilda Jollie's house was sold, Mrs Jimmy John and Miranda Jimmy John had come over, got in at one of the kitchen windows and given the whole place a Dutch cleaning from top to bottom. Jane was almost sorry the house was clean. She would have liked to clean it. She wanted to do everything for it.

"I am as bad as Aunt Gertrude," she thought. And a little glimmer of understanding of Aunt Gertrude came to her.

There was nothing to do just now but put the mattresses and clothes on the beds, the cans in the kitchen cupboard, and the butter and cream in the cellar. Dad hung Mrs Meade's codfish on the nails behind the kitchen stove.

"We'll have sausages for supper," Jane was saying.

"Janekin," said dad, clutching his hair in dismay, "I forgot to buy a frying-pan."

"Oh, there's an iron frying-pan in the bottom of the cupboard," said Jane serenely. "And a three-legged cooking-pot," she added in triumph.

There was nothing about the house that Jane did not know by this time. Dad had kindled a fire in the stove and fed it with some of Aunt Matilda Jollie's wood, Jane keeping a watchful eye on him as he did it. She had never seen a fire made in a stove before but she meant to know how to do it herself next time. The stove was a bit wobbly on one of its feet but Jane found a piece of flat stone in the yard which fitted nicely under it and everything was shipshape. Dad went over to the Jimmy Johns' to borrow a pail of water—the well had to be cleaned out before they could use it—and Jane set the table with a red and white cloth like Mrs Meade's and the dishes dad had got at the five-and-ten. She went out to the neglected garden and picked a bouquet of bleeding-heart and June lilies for the centre. There was nothing, to hold them but Jane found a rusty old tin can somewhere, swathed it in a green silk scarf she had dug out of her trunk—it was an expensive silk scarf Aunt Minnie had given her—and arranged her flowers in it. She cut and buttered bread, she made tea and fried the sausages. She had never done anything of the kind before but she had not watched Mary for nothing.

"It's good to get my legs under my own table again," said dad, as they sat down to supper.

"I suppose," thought Jane wickedly, "if grandmother could see me eating in the kitchen—and liking it—she would say it was just my low tastes."

Aloud all she said was . . . but she nearly burst with pride as she said it . . . "How do you take your tea, dad?"

There was a tangle of sunbeams on the bare white floor. They could see the maple wood through the east window, the gulf and the pond and the dunes through the north, the harbour through the west. Winds of the salt seas were blowing in. Swallows were swooping through the evening air. Everything she looked at belonged to dad and her. She was mistress of this house—her right there was none to dispute. She could do just as she wanted to without making excuses for anything. The memory of that first meal together with dad in Aunt Matilda Jollie's house was to be "a thing of beauty and a joy for ever." Dad was so jolly. He talked to her just as if she were grown up. Jane felt sorry for any one who didn't have her father.

Dad wanted to help her wash the dishes but Jane would none of it. Wasn't she to be the housekeeper? She knew how Mary washed dishes. She had always wanted to wash dishes . . . it must be such fun to make dirty plates clean. Dad had bought a dish-pan that day, but neither of them had thought about a dish-cloth or dish-towels. Jane got two new undervests out of her trunk and slit them open.

At sunset Jane and dad went down to the outside shore . . . as they were to do almost every night of that enchanted summer. All along the silvery curving sand ran a silvery curving wave. A dim, white-sailed vessel drifted past the bar of the shadowy dunes. The revolving light across the channel was winking at them. A great headland of gold and purple ran out behind it. At sunset that cape became a place of mystery to Jane. What lay beyond it? "Magic seas in fairylands forlorn?" Jane couldn't remember where she had heard or read that phrase but it suddenly came alive for her.

Dad smoked a pipe . . . which he called his "Old Contemptible" . . . and said nothing. Jane sat beside him in the shadow of the bones of an old vessel and said nothing. There was no need to say anything.

When they went back to the house they discovered that though dad had gotten three lamps he had forgotten to get any coal-oil for them or any petrol for his study lamp.

"Well, I suppose we can go to bed in the dark for once."

No need of that. Indefatigable Jane remembered she had seen a piece of an old tallow candle in the cupboard drawer. She cut it in two, stuck the pieces in the necks of two old glass bottles, likewise salvaged from the cupboard, and what would you ask more?

Jane looked about her tiny room, her heart swelling with satisfaction. There were as yet only the spool bed and a little table in it; the ceiling was stained with old leaks and the floor was slightly uneven. But this was the first room to be her very own, where she need never feel that someone was peeping at her through the key-hole. She undressed, blew out her candle and looked out of the window from which she could almost have touched the top of the steep little hill. The moon was up and had already worked its magic with the landscape. A mile away the lights of the little village at Lantern Corners shone. To the right of the window a young birch-tree seemed a-tiptoe trying to peer over the hill. Soft, velvety shadows moved among the bracken.

"I am going to pretend this is a magic window," thought Jane, "and sometime when I look out of it I shall see a wonderful sight. I shall see mother coming up that road looking for the lights of Lantern Hill."

Dad had picked a good mattress, and Jane was bone-tired after her strenuous day. But how lovely it was to lie in this comfortable little spool bed—neither Jane nor the Jimmy Johns knew that Aunt Matilda Jollie had been offered fifty dollars by a collector for that bed—and watch the moonlight patterning the walls with birch-leaves and know that dad was just across the little "landing" from you, and that outside were free hills and wide, open fields where you could run wherever you liked, none daring to make you afraid, spruce barrens and shadowy sand-dunes, instead of an iron fence and locked gates. And how quiet it all was—no honking, no glaring lights. Jane had pushed the window open and the scent of fern came in. Also a strange, soft far-away sound—the moaning call of the sea. The night seemed to be filled with it. Jane heard it and something deep down in her responded to it with a thrill that was between anguish and rapture. Why was the sea calling? What was its secret sorrow?

Jane was just dropping off to sleep when a terrible remembrance tore through her mind. She had forgotten to put the codfish to soak.

Two minutes later the codfish was soaking.

18

Jane, to her horror, slept in next morning, and when she rushed downstairs she saw an extraordinary sight . . . dad coming over from the Jimmy Johns' with a rocking-chair on his head. He also had a gridiron in his hand.

"Had to borrow one to broil the codfish on, Jane. And Mrs Jimmy John made me take the chair. She said it belonged to Aunt Matilda Jollie and they had more rocking-chairs than they had time to sit in. I made the porridge and it's up to you to broil the codfish."

Jane broiled it and her face as well, and it was delicious. The porridge was a bit lumpy.

"Dad isn't a very good cook, I guess," thought Jane affectionately. But she did not say so and she heroically swallowed all the lumps. Dad didn't; he ranged them along the edge of his plate and looked at her quizzically.

"I can write, my Jane, but I can't make porridgeable porridge."

"You won't have to make it after this. I'll never sleep in again," said Jane.

There is no pleasure in life like the joy of achievement. Jane realized that in the weeks that followed, if she did not put it in just those words. Old Uncle Tombstone, the general handy man of the Queen's Shore district, whose name was really Tunstone and who hadn't a niece or nephew in the world, papered all the rooms for them, patched the roof and mended the shutters, painted the house white with green trim and taught Jane how, when and where to dig for clams. He had a nice old rosy face with a fringe of white whisker under his chin.

Jane, bubbling over with energy, worked like a beaver, cleaning up after Uncle Tombstone, arranging the bits of furniture as dad brought them home, and getting curtains up all over the house.

"That girl can be in three places at once," said dad. "I don't know how she manages it. . . . I suppose there really is such a thing as witchcraft."

Jane was very capable and could do almost anything she tried to do. It was nice to live where you could show how capable you were. This was her own world and she was a person of importance in it. There was joy in her heart the clock round. Life here was one endless adventure.

When Jane was not cleaning up she was getting the meals. She studied her *Cookery for Beginners* every spare moment and went about muttering, "All measurements are level," and things like that. Because she had watched Mary and because it was born in her to be a cook, she got on amazingly well. From the very first her biscuits were never soggy or her roast underdone. But one day she flew too high and produced for dessert something that a charitable person might have called a plum pudding. Uncle Tombstone ate some of it and had to have the doctor that night— or so he said. He brought his own dinner the next day—cold bacon and cold pancakes tied up in a red handkerchief, and told Jane he was on a diet.

"That pudding of yours yesterday, miss, it was a mite too rich. My stomach ain't used to Toronto cookery. Them there vitamins now. . . . I reckon you have to be brought up on them for them to agree with you."

To his cronies he averred that the pudding would have given the rats indigestion. But he liked Jane.

"Your daughter is a very superior person," he told dad. "Most of the girls nowadays are all tops and no taters. But she's superior— yes, sir, she's superior." How dad and Jane laughed over that. Dad called her "Superior Jane" in a tone of mock awe till the joke wore out.

Jane liked Uncle Tombstone, too. In fact, nothing in her new life amazed her more than the ease with which she liked people. It seemed as if every one she met was sealed of her tribe.

She thought it must be that the P. E. Islanders were nicer, or at least more neighbourly, than the Toronto people. She did not realize that the change was in herself. She was no longer rebuffed, frightened, awkward because she was frightened. Her foot was on her native heath and her name was Jane. She felt friendly towards all the world and all the world responded. She could love all she wanted to . . . everybody she wanted to . . . without being accused of low tastes. Probably grandmother would not have recognized Uncle Tombstone socially; but the standards of 60 Gay were not the standards of Lantern Hill.

As for the Jimmy Johns, Jane felt as if she must have known them all her life. They were so called, she discovered, because Mr James John Garland had a James Garland to the north-east of him and a John Garland to the south-west of him, and so had to be distinguished in some way. Her first forenoon at Lantern Hill all the Jimmy Johns came galloping over in a body. At least, the young fry galloped with the three dogs . . . a brindled bull-terrier, a golden collie and a long brown dog who was just a dog. Mrs Jimmy John, who was as tall and thin as her Jimmy John was short and fat, with very wise, gentle grey eyes, walked briskly, carrying in her arms a baby as fat as a sausage. Miranda Jimmy John, who was sixteen, was as tall as her mother and as fat as her father. She had had a double chin at ten and nobody would ever believe that she was secretly overflowing with romance. Polly Jimmy John was Jane's age but looked younger because she was short and thin. "Punch" Jimmy John who had brought the key was thirteen. There were the eight-year-old twins . . . the George twin and the Ella twin . . . their bare chubby legs all spotted with mosquito bites. And every one of them had a pleasant smile.

"Jane Victoria Stuart?" said Mrs Jimmy John with a questioning smile.

"Jane!" said Jane, with such an intonation of triumph that the Jimmy Johns all stared at her.

"Jane, of course," smiled Mrs Jimmy John. Jane knew she was going to like Mrs Jimmy John.

Everybody except the baby had brought a present for Jane. Mrs Jimmy John gave her a lamb skin dyed red for a bedside rug. Miranda brought her a little fat white jug with pink roses on its sides, Punch brought her some early radishes, Polly brought her a rooted geranium slip and the twins brought a toad apiece "for her garden."

"You have to have toads in your garden for luck," explained Punch.

Jane felt it would never do to let her first callers go home without something to eat, especially when they had come bearing gifts.

"Mrs Meade's pie will go round if I don't take a piece," she thought. "The baby won't want any."

The baby *did* want some but Mrs Jimmy John shared hers with him. They sat around in the kitchen on the chairs and on the sandstone doorstep and ate the pie while Jane radiated hospitality.

"Come over whenever you can, dear," Mrs Jimmy John told her. Mrs Jimmy John thought Jane pretty young to be keeping house for anybody. "If there's any way we can help you, we'll be glad to."

"Will you teach me how to make bread?" said Jane coolly. "We can get it at the Corners of course but dad likes home-made bread. And what kind of cake flour would you recommend?"

Jane got acquainted with the Snowbeams also that week. The Solomon Snowbeams were a rather neglected rapscallion family who lived in a ramshackle house where the spruce barrens ran down to a curve of the harbour shore known as Hungry Cove. Nobody knew how Solomon Snowbeam contrived to feed his family . . . he fished a little and "worked out" a little and shot a little. Mrs Snowbeam was a big, pink, overblown woman and Caraway Snowbeam, "Shingle" Snowbeam, Penny Snowbeam and "Young John" Snowbeam were impudent, friendly little creatures who certainly did not looked starved. Millicent Mary Snowbeam, aged six, was neither impudent nor friendly. Millicent Mary was, so Polly Garland told Jane, not all there. She had blank, velvety nut-brown eyes . . . all the Snowbeams had beautiful eyes . . . reddish golden hair and a dazzling complexion. She could sit for hours without speaking—perhaps that was why the chattering Jimmy Johns thought her not all there—with her fat arms clasped around her fat knees. She seemed to be possessed of a dumb admiration for Jane and haunted Lantern Hill all that summer, gazing at her. Jane did not mind her.

If Millicent Mary did not talk, the rest of the Snowbeams made up for it. At first they were inclined to resent Jane a bit, thinking she must know everything because she came from Toronto and would be putting on airs about it. But when they discovered she hardly knew anything . . . except the little Uncle Tombstone had taught her about clams . . . they became very friendly. That is to say, they asked innumerable questions. There was no false delicacy about any of the Snowbeams.

"Does your pa put live people in his stories?" asked Penny.

"No," said Jane.

"Everybody round here says he does. Everybody's scared he'll put them in. He'd better not put *us* in if he doesn't want his snoot busted. I'm the toughest boy in Lantern Hill."

"Do you think you are interesting enough to put in a story?" asked Jane.

Penny was a little scared of her after that.

"We've been wanting to see what you looked like," said Shingle, who wore overalls and looked like a boy but wasn't, "because your pa and ma are divorced, ain't they?"

"No," said Jane.

"Is your pa a widow then?" persisted Shingle.

"No."

"Does your ma live in Toronto?"

"Yes."

"Why doesn't she live here with your pa?"

"If you ask me any more questions about my parents," said Jane, "I'll get dad to put you into one of his stories—every one of you."

Shingle was cowed but Caraway took up the tale.

"Do you look like your mother?"

"No. My mother is the most beautiful woman in Toronto," said Jane proudly.

"Do you live in a white marble house at home?"

"No."

"Ding-dong Bell said you did," said Caraway in disgust. "Ain't he the awful liar? And I s'pose you don't have satin bedspreads either?"

"We have silk ones," said Jane.

"Ding-dong said you had satin."

"I see the butcher bringing your dinner up the lane," said Young John. "What are you having?"

"Steak."

"My stars! We never have steak . . . nothing but bread and molasses and fried salt pork. Dad says he can't look a pig in the face 'thout grunting and mam says let him bring her home something else and she'll be mighty glad to cook it. Is that a cake you're making? Say, will you let me lick out the pan?"

"Yes, but stand back from the table. Your shirt is all over chaff," ordered Jane.

"Ain't you the bossy snip?" said Young John.

"Foxy-head," said Penny.

They all went home mad because Jane Stuart had insulted Young John. But they all came back next day and forgivingly helped her weed and clean up her garden. It was hard work and it was a hot day so that their brows were wet with honest sweat long before they had done it to Jane's taste. If anybody had made them work as hard as that they would have howled to high heaven; but when it was for fun . . . why, it *was* fun.

Jane gave them the last of Mrs Meade's cookies. She meant to try a batch of her own next day anyhow.

Jane had already decided that there was never a garden in the world like hers. She was crazy about it. An early, old-fashioned yellow rose-bush was already in bloom. Shadows of poppies danced here and there. The stone dike was smothered in wild rose-bushes starred with crimson bud-sheaths. Pale lemon lilies and creamy June lilies grew in the corners. There were ribbon-grass and mint, bleeding-heart, prince's feather, southernwood, peonies, sweet balm, sweet may, sweet-william, all with sated velvet bees humming over them. Aunt Matilda Jollie had been content with old-fashioned perennials and Jane loved them too, but she made up her mind that by hook or crook she would have some annuals next summer. Jane, at the beginning of this summer, was already planning for next.

In a very short time she was to be full of garden lore and was always trying to extract information about fertilizers from anybody who knew. Mr Jimmy John gravely advised well-rotted cow manure and Jane dragged basketfuls of it home from his barnyard. She loved to water the flowers . . . especially when the earth was a little dry and they drooped pleadingly. The garden rewarded her . . . she was one of those people at whose touch things grow. No weed was ever allowed to show its face. Jane got up early every morning to weed. It was wonderful to wake as the sun came over the sea.

The mornings at Lantern Hill seemed different from the mornings anywhere else—more morningish. Jane's heart sang as she weeded and raked and hoed and pruned and thinned out.

"Who taught you these things, woman?" asked dad.

"I think I've always known them," said Jane dreamily.

The Snowbeams told Jane their cat had kittens and she could have one. Jane went down to choose. There were four and the poor lean old mother cat was so proud and happy. Jane picked a black one with a pansy face—a really pansy face, so dark and velvety, with round golden eyes. She named it Peter on the spot. Then the Jimmy Johns, not to be outdone, brought over a kitten also. But this kitten was already named Peter and the Ella twin wept frantically over the idea of anybody changing it. So dad suggested calling them First Peter and Second Peter—which Mrs Snowbeam thought was sacrilegious. Second Peter was a dainty thing in black and silver, with a soft white breast. Both Peters slept at the foot of Jane's bed and swarmed over dad the minute he sat down.

"What is home without a dog?" said dad, and got one from old Timothy Salt at the harbour mouth. They named him Happy. He was a slim white dog with a round brown spot at the root of his tail, a brown collar and brown ears. He kept the Peters in their place and Jane loved him so much it hurt her.

"I like living things around me, dad."

Dad brought home the ship clock with the dog. Jane found it useful to time meals by, but as far as anything else was concerned there was really no such thing as time at Lantern Hill.

By the end of a week Jane knew the geography and people of Lantern Hill and Lantern Corners perfectly. Every hill seemed to belong to somebody . . . Big Donald's hill . . . Little Donald's hill . . . Old Man Cooper's hill. She could pick out Big Donald Martin's farm and Little Donald Martin's farm. Every household light she could see from the hill-top had its own special significance. She knew just where to look to see Min's ma's light sparkle out every night from the little white house in a misty fold of the hills. Min herself, an owl-eyed gipsy scrap, full of ginger, was already a bosom friend of Jane's. Jane knew that Min's colourless ma was entirely unimportant except as a background for Min. Min never would wear shoes or stockings in summer and her bare feet twinkled over the red roads to Lantern Hill every day. Sometimes Elmer Bell, better known as Ding-dong, came with her. Ding-dong was freckled and his ears stuck out but he was popular, though pursued through life by some scandalous tale of having sat in his porridge when he was an infant. When Young John wanted to be especially annoying he yelled at Ding-dong, "Sot in your porridge, you did—sot in your porridge!"

Elmer and Min and Polly Garland and Shingle and Jane were all children of the same year and they all liked each other and snubbed each other and offended each other and stood up for each other against the older and younger fry. Jane gave up trying to believe she hadn't always been friends with them. She remembered the woman who had called Gay Street dead. Well, Aunt Matilda Jollie's house wasn't dead. It was alive, every inch of it. Jane's friends swarmed all over it.

"You're so nice you ought to have been born in P. E. Island," Ding-dong told her.

"I was," said Jane triumphantly.

19

One day a blue two-wheeled cart lumbered up the lane and left a big packing-box in the yard.

"A lot of my mother's china and silver are in that, Jane," said dad. "I thought you might like to have them. You were named after her. They've been packed up ever since . . ."

Dad suddenly stopped and the frown that Jane always wanted to smooth out came over his brow.

"They've been packed up for years."

Jane knew perfectly well that he had started to say, "ever since your mother went away," or words to that effect. She had a sudden realization of the fact that this was not the first time dad had helped fix up a home . . . not the first time he had been nicely excited over choosing wallpaper and curtains and rugs. He must have had it all before with mother. Perhaps they had had just as much fun over it as dad and she were having now . . . more. Mother must have been sweet over fixing up her own home. She never had anything to say over the arrangements at 60 Gay. Jane wondered where the house dad and mother had lived in was . . . the house where she had been born. There were so many things she would have liked to ask dad if she had dared. But he was so nice. How could mother ever have left him?

It was great fun unpacking Grandmother Stuart's box. There were lovely bits of glass and china in it . . . Grandmother Stuart's dinner-set of white and gold . . . slender-stemmed glass goblets . . . quaint pretty dishes of all kinds. And silver! A tea-set, forks, spoons—"Apostle" spoons—salt-cellars.

"That silver does need cleaning," said Jane in rapture. What fun she would have cleaning it and washing up all those dainty and delicate dishes. Polishing up the moon was nothing to this.

In fact, the moon life had lost its old charm. Jane had enough to do keeping her house spotless without going on moon sprees. Anyhow, the Island moons never seemed to need polishing.

There were other things in the box . . . pictures and a delightful old framed motto worked in blue and crimson wool. "May the peace of God abide in this house." Jane thought this was lovely. She and dad had endless palavers as to where the pictures should go, but eventually they were all hung and made such a difference.

"As soon as you hang a picture on a wall," said dad, "the wall becomes your friend. A blank wall is hostile."

They hung the motto in Jane's room and every night when she went to bed and every morning when she got up Jane read it over like a prayer.

The beds blossomed out in wonderful patchwork quilts after that box came home. There were three of them that Grandmother Stuart had pieced . . . an Irish Chain, a Blazing Star and a Wild Goose. Jane put the Wild Goose on dad's bed, the blue Irish Chain on her own, and the scarlet Blazing Star on the boot-shelf against the day when they would have a bed for the spare-room.

They found a bronze soldier on horseback in the box and a shiny brass dog. The soldier went up on the clock-shelf but dad said the dog must go on his desk to keep his china cat in order. Dad's desk had been brought from Mr Meade's and was set up in the "study" . . . an old shining mahogany desk with sliding shelves and secret drawers and pigeonholes. The cat sat on one corner . . . a white, green-spotted cat with a long snaky neck and gleaming diamond eyes. For some reason Jane could not fathom, dad seemed to prize the thing. He had carried it all the way from Brookview to Lantern Mill in his hand so that it shouldn't get broken.

Jane's own particular booty was a blue plate with a white bird flying across it. She would eat every meal off it after this. And the old hour-glass, with its golden sands, on its walnut base was charming.

"Early eighteenth century," said dad. "My great-grandfather

was a U. E. Loyalist and this hour-glass was about all he had when he came to Canada . . . that and an old copper kettle. I wonder . . . yes, here it is. More polishing for you, Jane. And here's an old bowl of blue and white striped china. Mother mixed her salads in it."

"I'll mix mine in it," said Jane.

There was a little box at the very bottom of the big box. Jane pounced on it.

"Dad, what's this?"

Dad took it from her. There was a strange look on his face.

"That? Oh, that's nothing."

"Dad, it's a Distinguished Service Medal! Miss Colwin had one in her room at St Agatha's . . . her brother won it in the Great War. Oh, dad, you . . . you . . ."

Jane was breathless with pride over her discovery.

Dad shrugged his shoulders.

"You can never deceive your faithful Jane, says she. I won it at Passchendaele. Once I was proud of it. It seemed to mean something when . . . throw it out."

Dad's voice was oddly savage but Jane was not afraid of it . . . any more than she was afraid of his quick brief spurts of temper. Just a flash and a snap like lightning from a summer cloud, then sunshine again. He had never been angry with her but he and Uncle Tombstone had had a spat or two.

"I won't throw it out. I'm going to keep it, dad."

Dad shrugged.

"Well, don't let me see it then."

Jane put it on her bureau and gloated over it every day. But she was so excited over the contents of the box that she put icing sugar instead of salt in the Irish stew she made for dinner and her humiliation robbed her for a time of her high delight in life. Happy liked the stew, though.

20

"Let's entertain, my Jane. A very old friend of mine, Dr Arnett, is in Charlottetown. I'd like to invite him out for supper and a night. Can we manage it?"

"Of course. But we must get a bed for the guestroom. We've got the chest of drawers and the looking-glass and the wash-stand, but no bed. You know we heard Little Donalds had a bed to sell."

"I'll see to all that. But about the supper, Jane? Shall we be extravagant? Shall we buy a chicken . . . two chickens . . . from Mrs Jimmy John? If we do, can you cook them?"

"Of course. Oh, let me plan it, dad! We'll have cold chicken and potato salad. I know exactly how Mary made potato salad . . . I've often helped her peel the potatoes . . . and hot biscuits . . . you must get me a can of Flewell's Baking Powder at the Corners, dad . . . Flewell's, mind . . . it's the only one you can rely on" . . . already Jane was an authority on baking powders . . . "and wild strawberries and cream. Min and I found a bed of wild strawberries down the hill yesterday. We ate a lot but we left plenty."

Unluckily Aunt Irene came the very afternoon they were expecting Dr Arnett. She passed them in her car as Jane and her father were carrying an iron bedstead up the lane. Dad had bought it from Little Donald and Little Donald had left it at the end of the lane because he was in too much of a hurry to bring it all the way. It was a windy day, and Jane had her head tied up in an old shawl of Aunt Matilda Jollie's because she had had a slight toothache the night before. Aunt Irene looked quite horrified but kissed them both as they came into the yard.

"So you've bought old Tillie Jollie's house, 'Drew? What a funny little place! Well, I think you might have spoken to me about it first."

"Jane wanted it kept a secret . . . Jane loves secrets," dad explained lightly.

"Oh, Jane's secretive enough," said Aunt Irene, shaking a finger tenderly at Jane. "I hope it's only 'secretive' . . . but I do think you're a little inclined to be sly."

Aunt Irene was smiling, but there was an edge to her voice. Jane thought she would almost prefer grandmother's venom. You didn't have to look as if you liked that.

"If I had known I would have advised against it strongly, Andrew. I hear you paid four hundred for it. Jimmy John simply cheated you. Four hundred for a little old shack like this! Three would have been enough."

"But the view, Irene . . . the view. The extra hundred was for the view."

"You're so impractical, Andrew," shaking a laughing finger at him in his turn. At least, you felt the finger laughed. "Jane, you'll have to hold the purse-strings. If you don't, your father will be penniless by the fall."

"Oh, I think we'll be able to make both ends meet, Irene. If not, we'll pull them as close together as possible. Jane's a famous little manager. She looketh well to the ways of her household and eateth not the bread of idleness."

"Oh, Jane!" Aunt Irene was kindly amused over Jane. "If you had to have a house, 'Drew, why didn't you get one near town? There's a lovely bungalow out at Keppock . . . you could have rented it for the summer. I could have been near you then to help . . . and advise. . . ."

"We like the north shore best. Jane and I are both owls of the desert and pelicans of the wilderness. But we both like onions so we hit it off together. Why, we've even hung the pictures without quarrelling. That's phenomenal, you know."

"It isn't any joking matter, Andrew." Aunt Irene was almost plaintive. "How about your food supplies?"

"Jane digs clams," said dad solemnly.

"Clams! Do you expect to live on clams?"

"Why, Aunt Irene, the fishman calls every week and the butcher from the Corners comes twice a week," said Jane indignantly.

"Darrrling!" Aunt Irene became patronizing in an instant. She patronized everything ... the guest-room and the ruffled curtains of yellow net Jane was so proud of ... "a dear little closet," she called it sweetly. ... She patronized the garden ... "such a darling old-fashioned spot, isn't it, Jane?" ... She patronized the boot-shelf. ... "Really, Aunt Matilda Jollie had all the conveniences, hadn't she, lovey?"

The only thing she didn't patronize was the Apostle spoons. There was something acid in her sweetness when she spoke of them.

"I always think mother intended *I* should have them, 'Drew."

"She gave them to Robin," said 'Drew quietly.

Jane felt a tingle go over her. This was the first time she had heard dad mention mother's name.

"But when she left ..."

"We won't discuss it, Irene, if you please."

"Of course not, dear one. I understand. Forgive me. And now, Jane lovey, I'll borrow an apron and help you get ready for Dr Arnett. Bless her little heart, trying to get ready for company all by herself."

Aunt Irene was amused at her ... Aunt Irene was laughing at her. Jane was furious and helpless. Aunt Irene took smiling charge. The chickens were already cooked and the salad was already made but she insisted on making the biscuits and slicing the chickens and she would not hear of Jane going for wild strawberries.

"Luckily I brought a pie with me. I knew Andrew would like it. Men like something substantial, you know, lovey."

This maddened Jane. She vowed in her heart that she would learn pie-making in a week's time. Meanwhile she could only submit. When Dr Arnett came, Aunt Irene, a smiling and gracious hostess, made him welcome. Aunt Irene, still more smiling and gracious, sat at the head of the table and poured the tea and was charmed because Dr Arnett took a second helping of potato salad. Both men enjoyed the pie. Dad told Aunt Irene she was the best pie-maker in Canada.

"Eating is not such bad fun after all," said dad, with a faint air of surprise, as if he had just discovered the fact, thanks to the pie. Bitterness overflowed the heart of Jane. At that moment she could cheerfully have torn everybody in pieces.

Aunt Irene helped Jane wash the dishes before she went away. Jane thanked her stars that she and Min had walked to Lantern Corners three days before and bought towels. What would Aunt Irene have said if she had had to wipe dishes with an undervest?

"I have to go now, lovey ... I want to get home before dark. I do wish you were nearer me ... but I'll come out as often as I can. I don't know what your mother would have done without me many a time, poor child. 'Drew and Dr Arnett are off to the shore. ... I daresay they'll argue and shout at each other there most of the night. Andrew shouldn't leave you here alone like this. But men are like that ... so thoughtless."

And Jane adored being left alone. It was so lovely to have a chance to talk to yourself.

"I don't mind it, Aunt Irene. And I *love* Lantern Hill."

"You're easily pleased" ... as if she were a dear little fool to be so easily pleased. Somehow Aunt Irene had the most extraordinary knack of making you feel that what you liked or thought or did was of small account. And how Jane did resent her airs of authority in dad's house! Had she acted that way when mother was with dad? If she had ...

"I've brought you a cushion for your living-room, lovey. ..."

"It's a kitchen," said Jane.

... "And I'll bring my old chintz chair the next time I come—for the spare-room."

Jane, remembering the "dear little closet," permitted herself one satisfaction.

"I think there'll hardly be room for it," she said.

She eyed the cushion malevolently when Aunt Irene had gone. It was so new and gorgeous it made everything look faded and countrified.

"I think I'll stow it away on the boot-shelf," said Jane with a relish.

21

It was a sultry night and Jane went out and up and sat on the hill . . . "to get back into herself," as she expressed it. She had really been out of herself ever since the morning, more or less, because she had burned the toast for breakfast and walked in the humiliation of it all day. Cooking the chickens had been a bit of a strain . . . the wood-stove oven was not like that of Mary's electric range . . . and making up the guest-room bed under Aunt Irene's amused eyes—"fancy this baby having a spare-room," they seemed to say—had been worse. But now she was blessedly alone again and there was nothing to prevent her sitting on the hill in the cool velvet night as long as she wanted to. The wind was blowing from the south-west and brought with it the scent of Big Donald's clover field. All the Jimmy Johns' dogs were barking together. The great dune that they called the Watch Tower was scalloping up against the empty north sky. Beyond it sounded the long, low thunder of the surf. A silver moth of dusk flew by, almost brushing her face. Happy had gone with dad and Dr Arnett but the Peters came skittering up the hill and played about her. She held their purring silken flanks against her face and let them bite her cheeks delicately. It was all like a fairytale come true.

When she went back into the house Jane was her own woman again. Who cared for smooth, smiling Aunt Irene? She, Jane Stuart, was mistress at Lantern Hill; and she would learn to make pie-crust, that she would, by the three wise monkeys, as dad was so fond of saying.

Since dad was out, Jane sat down at his desk and wrote a page or two of her letter to mother. At first she hadn't known how she could live if she could write to mother only once a month. Then it occurred to her that though she could mail a letter only once a month, she could write a little of it every day.

"We had company for supper," wrote Jane. Being forbidden to mention dad she got around it by adopting the style royal. "Dr Arnett and Aunt Irene. Did you like Aunt Irene, mummy? Did she make you feel stupid? I cooked the chickens but Aunt Irene thought pie was better than strawberries. Don't you think wild strawberries would be more elegant than pie, mummy? I never tasted wild strawberries before. They are delicious. Min and I know where there is a bed of them. I'm going to get up early to-morrow morning and pick some for breakfast. Min's ma says if I can pick enough of them she will show me how to make them up into jam. I like Min's ma. Min likes her, too. Min only weighed three and a half pounds when she was born. Nobody thought she'd live. Min's ma has a pig she is feeding for their winter pork. She let me feed it yesterday. I like feeding things, mummy. It makes you important to feed things. Pigs have great appetities. So have I. There's something in the Island air, I guess.

"Miranda Jimmy John can't bear to be joked about being fat. Miranda milks four of the cows every night. The Jimmy Johns have fifteen cows. I haven't got acquainted with them yet. I don't know whether I'll like cows or not. I think they have an unfriendly look.

"The Jimmy Johns have big hooks in the kitchen rafters to hang hams on.

"The Jimmy John baby is so funny and solemn. It has never laughed yet although it is nine months old. They are worried about it. It has long curly black eyelashes. I didn't know babies were so sweet, mummy.

"Shingle Snowbeam and I have found a robin's nest in one of the little spruce-trees behind the house. There are four blue eggs in it. Shingle says we must keep it a secret from Penny and Young John or they would blow the eggs. Some secrets are nice things.

"I like Shingle now. Her real name is Marilyn Florence Isabel. Mrs Snowbeam says the only thing she could give her children was real fancy names.

"Shingle's hair is almost white but her eyes are just the right kind of blue, something like yours, mummy. But nobody could have quite such nice eyes as you.

"Shingle is ambishus. She is the only one of the Snowbeams that has any ambishun. She says she is going to make a lady of herself or die in the attempt. I told her if she wanted to be a lady she must never ask personal questions and she is not going to do it any more. But Caraway isn't particular whether she is a lady or not so she asks them and Shingle hears the answers. I don't like Young John Snowbeam much. He makes snoots. But he can pick up sticks with his toes.

"I like the sound of the wind here at night, mummy. I like to lie awake just to listen to it.

"I made a plum pudding one day last week. It would have been very successful if it had succeeded. Mrs Jimmy John says I should have steamed it, not boiled it. I don't mind Mrs Jimmy John knowing about my mistakes. She has such sweet eyes.

"It's such fun to boil potatoes in a three-legged iron pot, mummy.

"The Jimmy Johns have four dogs. Three who go everywhere with them and one who stays home. We have one dog. Dogs are very nice, mummy.

"Step-a-yard is the name of the Jimmy Johns' hired man. Not his real name of course. Miranda says he has been in love all his life with Miss Justina Titus and knows it's quite hopeless because Miss Justina is faithful to the memory of Alec Jacks who was killed in the Great War. She still wears her hair pompadore, Miranda says, because that is how she wore it when she said good-bye to Alec. I think that is touching, mummy.

"Mummy darling, I love to think you'll read this letter and hold it in your hands."

It did not give Jane so much pleasure to reflect that grandmother would read it, too. Jane could just see grandmother's thin-lipped smile over parts of it. "Well, like takes to like, you know, Robin. Your daughter has always had the knack of making friends with

417

the wrong people. Snoots!"

"How nice it would be," thought Jane, as she took a flying leap into bed for the fun of it, "if mummy was down there with dad instead of Dr Arnett and they would be coming back to me soon. It must have been that way once."

It was in the wee sma's that Andrew Stuart showed his guest to the neat guest-room where Jane had set Grandmother Stuart's blue and white bowl full of crimson peonies on the little table. Then he tiptoed into Jane's room. Jane was sound asleep. He bent over her with such love radiating from him that Jane felt it and smiled in her sleep. He touched one tumbled lock of russet-brown hair.

"It is well with the child," said Andrew Stuart.

22

With the help of *Cookery for Beginners,* Mrs Jimmy John's advice and her own "gumption," Jane learned to make pie-crust surprisingly soon and surprisingly well. She did not mind asking Mrs Jimmy John for advice, whereas she would have died before she would have asked Aunt Irene. Mrs Jimmy John was a wise, serene creature, with a face full of kindliness and wisdom. She had the reputation in Lantern Hill of never getting upset over anything, even church suppers. She did not laugh when Jane come over, white with despair, because a cake had fallen or a lemon filling had run all over the plate and dad had quirked a humorous eyebrow over it. In truth, Jane, for all her natural flair for cooking, would have made a good many muddles if it had not been for Mrs Jimmy John.

"I'd use a heaping tablespoon of cornstarch instead of a level one, Jane."

"It says all measurements are level," said Jane doubtfully.

"You can't always go by what the books say," said Step-a-yard, who was as much interested in Jane's progress as any one. "Just use gumption. Cooks are born, not made, I've always said, and you're a born one or I miss my guess. Them codfish balls you made the other day were the owl's whiskers."

The day Jane achieved unaided a dinner of roast lamb with dressing, creamed peas and a plum pudding that even Uncle Tombstone could have eaten was the proudest day of her life. What bliss to have dad pass his plate with "A little more of the same, Jane. What matter the planetesimal hypothesis or the quantum theory compared to such a dinner? Come, Jane, don't tell me you're ignorant of the quantum theory. A woman may get by without knowing about the planetesimal hypothesis but the quantum theory, Jane, is a necessity in any well-regulated household."

Jane didn't mind when dad ragged her. If she didn't know what the quantum theory was, she did know the plum pudding was good. She had got the recipe from Mrs Big Donald. Jane was a great forager for recipes, and counted that day lost whose low-descending sun didn't see her copying a new one on the blank leaves at the back of *Cookery for Beginners*. Even Mrs Snowbeam contributed one for rice pudding.

"Only kind we ever get," said Young John. "It's cheap."

Young John always came in for the "scrapings." He had some sixth sense whereby he always knew when Jane was going to make a cake. The Snowbeams thought it was great fun when Jane named all her cooking utensils. The tea-kettle that always danced on the stove when it was coming to a boil was Tipsy, the frying-pan was Mr Muffet, the dish-pan was Polly, the stew-pan was Timothy, the double boiler was Booties, the rolling-pin was Tillie Tid.

But Jane met her Waterloo when she tried to make doughnuts. It sounded so easy . . . but even the Snowbeams couldn't eat the result. Jane, determined not to be defeated, tried again and again. Everybody took an interest in her tribulations over the doughnuts. Mrs Jimmy John suggested and Min's ma gave hints. The storekeeper at the Corners sent her a new brand of lard. Jane had begun by frying them in Timothy, then she tried Mr Muffet. No use. The perverse doughnuts soaked fat every time. Jane woke up in the lone of the night and worried about it.

"This won't do, my adored Jane," said dad. "Don't you know that worry killed the widow's cat? Besides, people are telling me that you are old for your years. Just turn yourself into a wind-song, my Jane, and think no more on doughnuts."

In fact, Jane never did learn to make really good doughnuts . . . which kept her humble and prevented her showing off when Aunt Irene came. Aunt Irene came quite often. Sometimes she stayed all night. Jane hated to put her in the beloved guest-room.

Aunt Irene was always so delicately amused over Jane's having a guest-room. And Aunt Irene thought it just too funny to find Jane splitting kindlings.

"Dad mostly does it but he's been busy writing all day and I wouldn't disturb him," said Jane. "Besides, I like to split kindling."

"What a little philosopher it is!" said Aunt Irene, trying to kiss her.

Jane went crimson to the ears.

"Please, Aunt Irene, I don't like to be kissed."

"A nice thing to say to your own aunt, lovey" . . . speaking volumes by an amused lift of her fair eyebrows. Smooth, smiling Aunt Irene would never get angry. Jane thought she might have liked her better after a good fight with her. She knew dad was a little annoyed with her because she and Aunt Irene didn't click better and that he thought it must be her fault. Perhaps it was. Perhaps it was very naughty of her not to like Aunt Irene. "Trying to patronize us," Jane thought indignantly. It was not so much what she said as the way she said it . . . as if you were just playing at being a house-keeper for dad.

Sometimes they went to town and had dinner with Aunt Irene . . . gorgeous dinners certainly. At first Jane writhed over them. But as the weeks went on, she began to feel she could hold her own even with Aunt Irene when it came to getting up a meal.

"You're wonderful, lovey, but you have too much responsibility. I keep telling your father that."

"I like responsibility," said Jane huffily.

"Don't be so sensitive, lovey" . . . as if it were a crime.

If Jane couldn't learn to make doughnuts she had no trouble learning to make jam.

"I love making jam," she said, when dad asked her why she bothered. Just to go into the pantry and look at shelf after shelf of ruby and amber jams and jellies gave her the deep satisfaction of a job well done. Morning after morning she got up early to go raspberrying with Min or the Snowbeams. Later on, Lantern Hill reeked with the spicy smells of pickles. When Jennie Lister at the

Corners was given a jam and pickle shower before her wedding, Jane went proudly with the others and took a basket full of jellies and pickles. She had great fun at the shower, for by this time she knew everybody and everybody knew her. A walk to the village was a joy . . . she could stop to chat now with every one she met and every dog would pass the time of day with her. Jane thought almost everybody was nice in a way. There were so many different kinds of niceness.

She found no difficulty in talking to anybody on any subject. She liked to play with the young fry but she liked to talk to the older people. She could hold the most enthralling discussions with Step-a-yard on green feed and the price of pork and what made cows chew wood. She walked round Jimmy John's farm with him every Sunday morning and judged the crops. Uncle Tombstone taught her how to drive a horse and buggy.

"She could cramp a wheel after one showing," he told the Jimmy Johns.

Step-a-yard, not to be outdone, let her drive a load of hay into Jimmy John's big barn one day.

"Couldn't 'a' done it better myself. You've got a feeling for horses, Jane."

But Jane's favourite boy friend was old Timothy Salt who lived down near the harbour's mouth in a low-eaved house under dark spruces. He had the jolliest, shrewdest old face of wrinkled leather that Jane had ever seen, with deep-sunk eyes that were like wells of laughter. Jane would sit with him for hours while he opened quahaugs and told her tales of old disaster on the sea, fading old legends of dune and headland, old romances of the north shore that were like misty wraiths. Sometimes other old fishermen and sailors were there swapping yarns. Jane sat and listened and shooed Timothy's tame pig away when it came too near. The salt winds blew around her. The little waves on the harbour would run so fleetly from the sunset and later on the fishing boats would be bobbing to the moon. Sometimes a ghostly white fog would come creeping up from the dunes, the hills across the harbour would be phantom hills in the mist, and even ugly things would be lovely and mysterious.

"How's life with ye?" Timothy would say gravely and Jane would tell him just as gravely that life was very well with her.

Timothy gave her a glass box full of corals and sea-shells from the West and the East Indies. He helped her drag up flat stones from the shore to make paths in her garden. He taught her to saw and hammer in nails and swim. Jane swallowed most of the Atlantic Ocean learning to swim or thought she did, but she learned, and ran home, a wet delighted creature, to brag to dad. And she made a hammock out of barrel staves that was the talk of Lantern Hill.

"That child will stick at nothing," said Mrs Snowbeam.

Timothy swung it between two of the spruces for her . . . dad wasn't much good at doing things like that, though he told her he would do it if she would get him a rhyme for silver.

Timothy taught her to discern the signs of the sky. Jane had never felt acquainted with the sky before. To stand on Lantern Hill and see the whole sky around you was wonderful. Jane could sit for hours at the roots of the spruces gazing at sky and sea, or in some happy golden hollow among the dunes. She learned that a mackerel sky was a sign of fine weather and mare's tails meant wind. She learned that red sky at morning foretokened rain, as did the dark firs on Little Donald's hill when they looked so near and clear. Jane welcomed rain at Lantern Hill. She had never liked rain in the city but here by the sea she loved it. She loved to listen to it coming down in the night on the ferns outside her window; she liked the sound and the scent and the freshness of it. She loved to get out in it . . . get sopping wet in it. She liked the showers that sometimes fell across the harbour, misty and purple, when it was quite fine on the Lantern Hill side. She even liked thunderstorms, when they passed out to sea beyond the bar of the shadowy dunes, and didn't come too close. But one night there was a terrible one. Blue swords of lightning stabbed the darkness . . . thunder crackled all about Lantern Hill. Jane was crouching in bed, her head buried in a pillow, when she felt dad's arm go around her. He lifted her up and held her close to him, displacing an indignant pair of Peters.

"Frightened, my Jane?"

"No-o-o," lied Jane valiantly. "Only . . . it isn't decent."

Dad shouted with laughter.

"You've got the word. Thunder like that is an insult to decency. But it will soon pass . . . it is passing now. 'The pillars of heaven tremble and are astonished at His reproof.' Do you know where that is found, Jane?"

"It sounds like the Bible," said Jane, as soon as she got her breath after a crash that must have split the hill in two. "I don't like the Bible."

"Not like the Bible? Jane, Jane, this will never do. If any one doesn't like the Bible there's something wrong either with him or with the way he was introduced to it. We must do something about it. The Bible is a wonderful book, my Jane. Full of corking good stories and the greatest poetry in the world. Full of the most amazingly human 'human nature.' Full of incredible, ageless wisdom and truth and beauty and common sense. Yes, yes, we'll see about it. I think the worst of the storm is over . . . and to-morrow morning we'll hear the little waves whispering to each other again in the sunlight and there'll be a magic of silver wings over the bar when the gulls go out. I shall begin the second canto of my epic on Methuselah's life and Jane will swither in delightful anguish trying to decide whether to have breakfast indoors or out. And all the hills will be joyful together . . . more of the Bible, Jane. You'll love it."

Perhaps so . . . though Jane thought it would really need a miracle. Anyhow, she loved dad. Mother still shone on her life, like a memory of the evening star. But dad was . . . dad!

Jane dropped asleep again and had a terrible dream that she couldn't find the onions and dad's socks with the blue toes that needed mending.

23

After all Jane found it did not require a miracle to make her like the Bible. She and dad went to the shore every Sunday afternoon and he read to her from it. Jane loved those Sunday afternoons. They took their suppers with them and ate them squatted on the sand. She had an inborn love of the sea and all pertaining to it. She loved the dunes . . . she loved the music of the winds that whistled along the silvery solitude of the sand-shore . . . she loved the far dim shores that would be jewelled with home-lights on fine blue evenings. And she loved dad's voice reading the Bible to her. He had a voice that would make anything sound beautiful. Jane thought if dad had had no other good quality at all, she must have loved him for his voice. And she loved the little comments he made as he read . . . things that made the verses come alive for her. She had never thought that there was anything like that in the Bible. But then, dad did not read about knops and taches.

"'When all the morning stars sang together' . . . the essence of creation's joy is in that, Jane. Can't you hear that immortal music of the spheres? 'Sun, stand thou still upon Gibeon and thou, moon, in the vale of Ajalon.' Such sublime arrogance, Jane . . . Mussolini himself couldn't rival that. 'Here shall thy proud waves be stayed' . . . look at them rolling in there, Jane . . . 'so far and no farther' . . . the majestic law to which they yield obedience never falters or fails. 'Give me neither poverty nor riches' . . . the prayer of Agar, son of Jakeh. A sensible man was Agar, my Jane. Didn't I tell you the Bible was full of common sense? 'A fool uttereth all his mind.' Proverbs is harder on the fool than on anybody else, Jane . . . and rightly. It's the fools that make all the trouble in the world, not the wicked. 'Whither thou goest I will go; and where thou lodgest I will lodge; thy people shall be my people and thy God my God; where thou diest will I die and there will I be buried; the Lord do so to me and more also if aught but death part thee and me.' The high-water mark of the expression of emotion in any language that I'm acquainted with, Jane . . . Ruth to Naomi . . . and all such simple words. Hardly any of more than one syllable . . . the writer of that verse knew how to marry words as no one else has ever done. And he knew enough not to use too many of them. Jane, the most awful as well as the most beautiful things in the world can be said in three words or less . . . 'I love you' . . . 'he is gone' . . . 'he is come' . . . 'she is dead' . . . 'too late' . . . and life is illumined or ruined. 'All the daughters of music shall be brought low' . . . aren't you a little sorry for them, Jane . . . those foolish, light-footed daughters of music? Do you think they quite deserved such a humiliation? 'They have taken away my lord and I know not where they have laid him' . . . that supreme cry of desolation! 'Ask for the old paths and walk therein and ye shall find rest.' Ah, Jane, the feet of some of us have strayed far from the old paths . . . we can't find our way back to them, much as we may long to. 'As cold water to a thirsty soul so is good news from a far country.' Were you ever thirsty, Jane . . . really thirsty . . . burning with fever . . . thinking of heaven in terms of cold water? I was, more than once. 'A thousand years in thy sight is but as yesterday when it is past and as a watch in the night.' Think of a Being like that, Jane, when the little moments torture you. 'Ye shall know the truth and the truth shall make you free.' The most terrible and tremendous saying in the world, Jane . . . because we are all afraid of truth and afraid of freedom . . . that's why we murdered Jesus."

Jane did not understand all dad said but she put it all away in her mind to grow up to. All her life she was to have recurring flashes of insight when she recalled something dad had said. Not only of the Bible but of all the poetry he read to her that summer. He taught her the loveliness of words . . . dad read words as if he tasted them.

"'Glimpses of the moon' . . . one of the immortal phrases of literature, Jane. There are phrases with sheer magic in them. . . ."

"I know," said Jane. "'On the road to Mandalay' . . . I read that in one of Miss Colwin's books . . . and 'horns of elfland faintly blowing.' That gives me a beautiful ache."

"You have the root of the matter in you, Jane. But, oh, my Jane, why . . . why . . . did Shakespeare leave his wife his second best bed?"

"Perhaps because she liked it best," said Jane practically.

"'Out of the mouths of babes and sucklings' . . . to be sure. I wonder if that eminently sane suggestion has ever occurred to the commentators who have agonized over it. Can you guess who the dark lady was, Jane? You know when a poet praises a woman she is immortal . . . witness Beatrice . . . Laura . . . Lucasta . . . Highland Mary. All talked about hundreds of years after they are dead because great poets loved them. The weeds are growing over Troy but we remember Helen."

"I suppose she didn't have a big mouth," said Jane wistfully.

Dad kept a straight face.

"Not too small a one, Jane. You couldn't imagine goddess Helen with a rosebud mouth, could you?"

"*Is* my mouth too big, dad?" implored Jane. "The girls at St Agatha's said it was."

"Not too big, Jane. A generous mouth . . . the mouth of a giver, not a taker . . . a frank, friendly mouth . . . with very well-cut corners, Jane. No weakness about them . . . you wouldn't have eloped with Paris, Jane, and made all that unholy mess. You would have been true to your vows, Jane . . . in spirit as well as in letter, even in this upside-down world."

Jane had the oddest feeling that dad was thinking of mother, not of Argive Helen. But she was comforted by what he said about her mouth.

Dad did not always read from the masters. One day he took to the shore a thin little volume of poems by Bernard Freeman Trotter.

"I knew him overseas . . . he was killed . . . listen to his song about the poplars, Jane.

> "And so I sing the poplars and when I come to die
> I will not look for jasper walls but cast about my eye
> For a row of wind-blown poplars against an English sky.
> "What will you want to see when you get to heaven,

Jane?"

"Lantern Hill," said Jane.

Dad laughed. It was so delightful to make dad laugh . . . and so easy. Though a good many times Jane didn't know exactly what he was laughing at. Jane didn't mind that a bit . . . but sometimes she wondered if mother had minded it.

One evening after dad had been spouting poetry until he was tired Jane said timidly, "Would you like to hear me recite, dad?"

She recited "The Little Baby of Mathieu." It was easy . . . dad made such a good audience.

"You can do it, Jane. That was good. I must give you a bit of training along that line, too. I used to be rather good at interpreting the *habitant* myself."

"Someone she did not like used to be rather good at reading *habitant* poetry" . . . Jane remembered who had said that. She understood another thing now.

Dad had rolled over to where he could see their house in a gap in the twilit dunes.

"I see the Jimmy Johns' light . . . and the Snowbeam light at Hungry Cove . . . but our house is dark. Let's go home and light it up, Jane. And is there any of that apple-sauce you made for supper left?"

So they went home together and dad lighted his petrol lamp and sat down at his desk to work on his epic of Methuselah . . . or something else . . . and Jane got a candle to light her to bed. She liked a candle better than a lamp. It went out so graciously . . . the thin trail of smoke . . . the smouldering wick, giving one wild little wink at you before it left you in the dark.

When dad had converted Jane to the Bible, he set about making history and geography come alive for her. She had told him she always found those subjects hard. But soon history no longer seemed a clutter of dates and names in some dim, cold antiquity but became a storied road of time when dad told her old tales of wonder and the pride of kings. When he told the simplest incident with the sound of the sea in his voice, it seemed to take on such a colouring of romance and mystery that Jane knew she could never forget it. Thebes . . . Babylon . . . Tyre . . . Athens . . . Galilee . . . were places where real folks lived . . . folks she knew. And, knowing them, it was easy to be interested in everything pertaining to them. Geography, which had once meant merely a map of the world, was just as fascinating.

"Let's go to India," dad would say . . . and they went . . . though Jane would sew buttons on dad's shirts all the way. Min's ma was hard on buttons. Soon Jane knew all the fair lands far, far away as she knew Lantern Hill . . . or so it seemed to her after she had journeyed through them with father.

"Some day, Jane, you and I will really go and see them. The Land of the Midnight Sun . . . doesn't that phrase fascinate you, Jane? . . . far Cathay . . . Damascus . . . Samarkand . . . Japan in cherry blossom time . . . Euphrates among its dead empires . . . moonrise over Karnak . . . lotus vales in Kashmir . . . castles on the banks of the Rhine. There's a villa in the Apennines . . . 'the cloudy Apennines' . . . I want you to see, my Jane. Meanwhile, let's draw a chart of Lost Atlantis."

"Next year I'll be beginning French," said Jane. "I think I'll like that."

"You will. You'll wake up to the fascination of languages. Think of them as doors opening into a stately palace for you. You'll even like Latin, dead and all as it is. Isn't a dead language rather a sad thing, Janet? Once it lived and burned and glowed. People said loving things in it . . . bitter things . . . wise and silly things in it. I wonder who was the very last person to utter a sentence in living Latin. Jane, how many boots would a centipede need if a centipede needed boots?"

That was dad all over. Tender ... serious ... dreamy ... and then a tag of some delightful nonsense. But Jane knew just how grandmother would have liked that.

Sundays were interesting at Lantern Hill not only because of the Bible readings with dad but because she went to the Queen's Shore church with the Jimmy Johns in the mornings. Jane liked it tremendously. She put on the little green linen jumper dress grandmother had bought her and carried a hymn-book proudly. They went across the fields by a path that wound around the edge of Big Donald's woods, through a cool back pasture where sheep grazed, down the road past Min's ma's house, where Min joined them, and finally along a grassy lane to what was called "the little south church" ... a small white building set in a grove of beech and spruce where lovable winds seemed always purring. Anything less like St Barnabas's could hardly be imagined but Jane liked it. The windows were plain glass and you could see out of them right into the woods and past the big wild cherry-tree that grew close up to the church. Jane wished she could have seen it in blossom time. All the people had what Step-a-yard called their Sunday faces on and Elder Tommy Perkins looked so solemn and other-worldly that Jane found it almost impossible to believe that he was the same man as the jolly Tommy Perkins of weekdays. Mrs Little Donald always passed her a peppermint over the top of the pew and though Jane didn't like peppermints she seemed to like that one. There was, she reflected, something so nice and religious about its flavour.

For the first time Jane could join in the singing of the hymns and she did it lustily. Nobody at 60 Gay had ever supposed Jane could sing; but she found that she could at least follow a tune and was duly thankful therefor, as otherwise she would have felt like an outsider at the Jimmy Johns' "sing-songs" in their old orchard on Sunday evenings. In a way Jane thought the sing-songs the best part of Sunday. All the Jimmy Johns sang like linnets and everybody could have his or her favourite hymn in turn. They sang what Step-a-yard, who carried a tremendous bass, called "giddier" hymns than were sung in church, out of little dog-eared, limp-covered hymn-books. Sometimes the stay-at-home dog tried to sing, too. Beyond them was the beauty of a moonlit sea.

They always ended up with "God Save the King" and Jane went home, escorted to the door of Lantern Hill by all the Jimmy Johns and the three dogs who didn't stay at home. Once dad was sitting in the garden, on the stone seat Timothy Salt had built for her, smoking his Old Contemptible and "enjoying the beauty of the darkness," as he said. Jane sat down beside him and he put his arm around her. First Peter prowled darkly around them. It was so still they could hear the cows grazing in Jimmy John's field and so cool that Jane was glad of the warmth of father's tweed arm across her shoulders. Still and cool and sweet . . . and in Toronto at that moment every one was gasping in a stifling heat wave, so the Charlottetown paper had said yesterday. But mother was with friends in Muskoka. It was poor Jody who would be smothering in that hot little attic room. If only Jody were here!

"Jane," dad was saying, "should I have sent for you last spring?"

"Of course," said Jane.

"But should I? Did it hurt . . . anybody?"

Jane's heart beat more quickly. It was the first time dad had ever come so near to mentioning mother.

"Not very much . . . because I would be home in September."

"Ah, yes. Yes, you will go back in September."

Jane waited for something more but it did not come.

24

"Do you ever see anything of Jody?" wrote Jane to mother. "I wonder if she is getting enough to eat. She never says she isn't in her letters . . . I've had three . . . but sometimes they sound hungry to me. I still love her best of all my friends but Shingle Snowbeam and Polly Garland and Min are very nice. Shingle is making great progress. She always washes behind her ears now and keeps her nails clean. And she never throws spit balls though she thinks it was great fun. Young John throws them. Young John is collecting bottle caps and wears them on his shirt. We are all saving bottle caps for him.

"Miranda and I decorate the church every Saturday night with flowers. We have a good many of our own and we get some from the Titus ladies. We go over on Ding-dong's brother's truck to get them. They live at a place called Brook Valley. Isn't that a nice name? Miss Justina is the oldest and Miss Violet the youngest. They are both tall and thin and very ladylike. They have a lovely garden, and if you want to stand in well with them, Miranda says you must compliment them on their garden. Then they will do anything for you. They have a cherry walk which is wonderful in spring, Miranda says. They are both pillows in the church and every one respects them highly, but Miss Justina has never forgiven Mr Snowbeam because he once called her 'Mrs' when he was absent-minded. He said he would have thought she'd be pleased.

"Miss Violet is going to teach me hemstitching. She says every lady ought to know how to sew. Her face is old but her eyes are young. I am very fond of them both.

"Sometimes they quarrel. They have had a bad time this summer over a rubber plant that was their mother's who died last year. They both think it ugly but sacred and would never dream of throwing it away, but Miss Violet thinks that now their mother is gone they could keep it in the back hall, but Miss Justina said, no, it must stay in the parlour. Sometimes they would not speak to each other on account of it. I told them I thought they might keep it in the parlour one week and in the back hall one week, turn about. They were very much struck with the idea and adopted it and now everything is smooth at Brook Valley.

"Miranda sang 'Abide with Me' in church last Sunday night. (They have preaching at night once a month.) She says she loves to sing because she always feels thin when she sings. She is so fat she is afraid she will never have any beaus but Step-a-yard says no fear, the men like a good armful. Was that coarse, mummy? Mrs Snowbeam says it was.

"We sing every Sunday night in the Jimmy Johns' orchard— all sacred songs of course. I like the Jimmy Johns' orchard. The grass is so nice and long there and the trees grow just as they like. The Jimmy Johns have such fun together. I think a big family is splendid.

"Punch Jimmy John is teaching me how to run across a stubble-field on bare feet so it won't hurt. I go barefoot sometimes here. The Jimmy Johns and Snowbeams all do. It's so nice to run through the cool wet grass and wriggle your toes in the sand and feel wet mud squashing up between them. You don't mind, do you, mother?

"Min's ma does our washing for us. I'm sure I could do it but I am not allowed to. Min's ma does washing for all the summer boarders at the Harbour Head, too. Min's ma's pig was very sick but Uncle Tombstone doctored it up and cured it. I'm so glad it got well, for if it had died I don't know what Min and her ma would have to live on next winter. Min's ma is noted for her clam chowder. She is teaching me how to make it. Shingle and I dig the clams.

"I made a cake yesterday and ants got in the icing. I was so mortyfied because we had company for supper. I wish I knew how to keep ants in their place. But Uncle Tombstone says I can make soup that *is* soup. We are going to have chicken for dinner to-morrow. I've promised to save the neck for Young John and a drumstick for Shingle. And oh, mother, the pond is full of trout. We catch them and eat them. Just fancy catching fish in your own pond and frying them for supper.

"Step-a-yard has false teeth. He always takes them out and puts them in his pocket when he eats. When he is out of an evening and they give him lunch, he always says, 'Thanks, I'll call again,' but if they don't, he never goes back. He says he has to be self-respecting.

"Timothy Salt lets me look through his spy-glass. It's such fun looking at things through the wrong end. They seem so small and far away as if you were in another world.

"Polly and I found a bed of sweet grass on the sandhills yesterday. I've picked a bunch to take back for you, mother. It's nice to put among handkerchiefs, Miss Violet Titus says.

"We named the Jimmy Johns' calves to-day. We called the pretty ones after people we like and the ugly ones after people we don't like.

"Shingle and Polly and I are to sell candy at the ice-cream social in the Corners hall next week.

"We all made a fire of driftwood on the shore the other night and danced about it.

"Penny Snowbeam and Punch Jimmy John are very busy now bugging potatoes. I don't like potato bugs. When Punch Jimmy John said I was a brave girl because I wasn't afraid of mice, Penny said, 'Oh ho, put a bug on her and see how brave she'll be.' I am glad Punch did not put me to the test because I am afraid I could not have stood it.

"The front door had got sticky so I borrowed Step-a-yard's plane and fixed it. I also patched Young John's trousers. Mrs Snowbeam said she'd run out of patches and his little bottom was almost bare.

"Mrs Little Donald is going to show me how to make

marmalade. She puts hers up in such dinky little stone jars her aunt left her, but I'll have to put mine in sealers.

"Uncle Tombstone got me to write a letter to his wife who is visiting in Halifax. I started it 'My dear wife' but he said he never called her that and it might give her a turn and I'd better put 'Dear Ma.' He says he can write himself but it is the spelling sticks him.

"Mummy, I love you, love you, love you."

Jane laid her head down on the letter and swallowed a lump in her throat. If only mother were here . . . with her and daddy . . . going swimming with them . . . lying on the sand with them . . . eating fresh trout out of the pond with them . . . laughing with them over the little household jokes that were always coming up . . . running with them under the moon . . . how beautiful everything would be!

25

Little Aunt Em had sent word to Lantern Hill that Jane Stuart was to come and see her.

"You must go," said dad. "Little Aunt Em's invitations are like those of royalty in this neck of the woods."

"Who is little Aunt Em?"

"Blest if I know exactly. She's either Mrs Bob Barker or Mrs Jim Gregory. I never can remember which of them was her last husband. Anyway, it doesn't matter . . . everybody calls her Little Aunt Em. She's about as high as my knee and so thin she once blew over the harbour and back. But she's a wise old goblin. She lives on that little side-road you were asking about the other day and does weaving and spinning and dyeing rug rags. Dyes them in the good old-fashioned way with herbs and barks and lichens. What Little Aunt Em doesn't know about the colours you can get that way isn't worth knowing. They never fade. Better go this evening, Jane. I've got to get the third canto of my Methuselah epic done this evening. I've only got the young chap along as far as his first three hundred years."

At first Jane had believed with a touching faith in that epic of Methuselah. But now it was just a standing joke at Lantern Hill. When dad said he must knock off another canto, Jane knew he had to write some profound treatise for *Saturday Evening* and must not be disturbed. He did not mind having her around when he wrote poetry—love lyrics, idylls, golden sonnets—but poetry did not pay very well and *Saturday Evening* did.

Jane set out after supper for Little Aunt Em's. The Snowbeams, who had already missed one excitement that afternoon, wanted to go with her in a body, but Jane refused their company. Then they were all mad and—with the exception of Shingle who decided it wasn't ladylike to push yourself in where you weren't wanted and went home to Hungry Cove—persisted in accompanying Jane for quite a distance, walking close to the fence in exaggerated awe and calling out taunts as she marched disdainfully down the middle of the road.

"Ain't it a pity her ears stick out?" said Penny.

Jane knew her ears didn't stick out so this didn't worry her. But the next thing did.

"S'posen you meet a crocodile on the side-road?" called Caraway. "That'd be worse than a cow."

Jane winced. How in the world did the Snowbeams know she was afraid of cows? She thought she had hidden that very cleverly.

The Snowbeams had got their tongues loosened up now and peppered Jane with a perfect barrage of insults.

"Did you ever see such a high-and-lofty, stuck-up minx?"

"Proud as a cat driving a buggy, ain't you?"

"Too grand for the likes of us."

"I always said you'd a proud mouth."

"Do you think Little Aunt Em will give you any lunch?"

"If she does I know what it will be," yelled Penny. "Raspberry vinegar and two cookies and a sliver of cheese. Yah! Who'd eat that? Yah!"

"I'll bet you're afraid of the dark."

Jane, who was not in the least afraid of the dark, still preserved a withering silence.

"You're a foreigner," said Penny.

Nothing else they had said mattered. Jane knew her Snowbeams. But this infuriated her. She—a foreigner! In her own darling Island where she had been born! She stopped short at Penny.

"Just you wait," she said with concentrated venom, "till the next time any of you want to scrape a bowl."

The Snowbeams all stopped short. They had not thought of this. Better not rile Jane Stuart any more.

"Aw, we didn't mean to hurt your feelings . . . honest," protested

Caraway. They promptly started homeward but the irrepressible Young John yelled, "Good-bye, Collarbones," as he turned.

Jane, after she had shrugged off the Snowbeams, had a good time with herself on that walk. That she could go where she liked over the countryside, unhindered, uncriticized, was one of the most delightful things about her life at Lantern Hill. She was glad of an excuse to explore the side-road where Little Aunt Em lived. She had often wondered where it went to—that timid little red road, laced with firs and spruces, that tried to hide itself by twisting and turning. The air was full of the scent of sun-warmed grasses gone to seed, the trees talked all about her in some lost sweet language of elder days, rabbits hopped out of the ferns and into them. In a little hollow she saw a faded sign by the side of the road . . . straggling black letters on a white board, put up years agone by an old man, long since dead. "Ho, every one that thirsteth come ye to the waters." Jane followed the pointing finger down a fairy path between the trees and found a deep clear spring, rimmed in by mossy stones. She stooped and drank, cupping the water in her brown palm. A squirrel was impudent to her from an old beech and Jane sassed him back. She would have liked to linger there but the western sky above the tree-tops was already filled with golden rays, and she must hasten. When she passed up out of the brook hollow, she saw Little Aunt Em's house curled up like a cat on the hillside. A long lane led up to it, edged with clumps of white and gold life-everlasting. When Jane reached the house she found Little Aunt Em spinning on a little wheel set before her kitchen door, with a fascinating pile of silvery wool rolls lying on the bench beside her. She stood up when Jane opened the gate—she was really a little higher than dad's knee but she was not so tall as Jane. She wore an old felt hat that had belonged to one of her husbands on her rough, curly grey head, and her little black eyes twinkled in a friendly fashion in spite of her blunt question.

"Who are you?"

"I'm Jane Stuart."

"I knew it," said Aunt Em in a tone of triumph. "I knew it the minute I saw you walking up the lane. You can always tell a Stuart anywhere you see him by his walk."

Jane had her own way of walking . . . quickly but not jerkily, lightly but firmly. The Snowbeams said she strutted but Jane did not strut. She felt very glad that Little Aunt Em thought she walked like the Stuarts. And she liked Little Aunt Em at first sight.

"You might come and sit down a spell if you've a mind to," said Little Aunt Em, offering a wrinkled brown hand. "I've finished this lick of work I was doing for Mrs Big Donald. Ah, I'm not up to much now but I was a smart woman in my day, Jane Stuart."

Not a floor in Aunt Em's house was level. Each one sloped in a different direction. It was not notoriously tidy but there was a certain hominess about it that Jane liked. The old chair she sat down in was a friend.

"Now we can have a talk," said Little Aunt Em. "I'm in the humour for it to-day. When I'm not, nobody can get a word out of me. Let me get my knitting. I neither tat, sew, embroider nor crochet, but the hull Maritimes can't beat me knitting. I've been wanting to see you for some time . . . everybody's talking about you. I'm hearing you're smart. Mrs Big Donald says you can cook like a blue streak. Where did you learn it?"

"Oh, I guess I've always known how," said Jane airily. Not under torture would she have revealed to Little Aunt Em that she had never done any cooking before she came to the Island. That might reflect on mother.

"I didn't know you and your dad was at Lantern Hill till Mrs Big Donald told me last week at Mary Howe's funeral. I don't get anywhere much now 'cept to funerals. I always make out to get to them. You see everybody and hear all the news. Soon as Mrs Big Donald told me I made up my mind I'd see you. What thick hair you've got! And what nice little ears! You have a mole on your neck . . . that's money by the peck. You don't look like your ma, Jane Stuart. I knew her well."

Jane's spine felt tickly.

"Oh, did you?" breathlessly.

"I did. They lived in a house at the Harbour Head, and I was living there too, on a bit of a farm, beyant the barrens. It was just after I'd married my second, worse luck. The way the men get round you! I used to take butter and eggs to your ma and I was in the house the night you were born . . . a wonderful fine night it was. How is your ma? Pretty and silly as ever?"

Jane tried to resent mother being called silly but couldn't manage it. Somehow, you couldn't resent anything Little Aunt Em said. She twinkled at you so. Jane suddenly felt that she could talk to Little Aunt Em about mother . . . ask her things she had never been able to ask any one.

"Mother is well . . . oh, Aunt Em, can you tell me . . . I *must* find out . . . why didn't father and mother go on living together?"

"Now you're asking, Jane Stuart!" Aunt Em scratched her head with a knitting-needle. "Nobody ever knew rightly. Every one had a different guess."

"Did they . . . were they . . . did they really love each other to begin with, Aunt Em?"

"They did. Make no mistake about that, Jane Stuart. They hadn't a lick of sense between them but they were crazy about each other. Will you have an apple?"

"And why didn't it last? Was it me? They didn't want me?"

"Who said so? I know your ma was wild with joy when you was born. Wasn't I there? And I always thought your pa uncommon fond of you, though he had his own way of showing it."

"Then why . . . why . . . ?"

"Lots of people thought your Grandmother Kennedy was at the bottom of it. She was dead against them marrying, you know. They were staying at the big hotel on the south shore that summer after the war. Your dad was just home. It was love at first sight with him. I dunno's I blamed him. Your ma was the prettiest thing I ever did see . . . like a little gold butterfly she was. That little head of hers sorter shone like."

Oh, didn't Jane know it! She was seeing that wonderful knot of pale luminous gold at the nape of mother's white neck.

"And her laugh . . . it was a little tinkling, sparkling, young laugh. Does she laugh like that yet, Jane Stuart?"

Jane didn't know what to say. Mother laughed a great deal . . . very tinkly . . . very sparkly . . . but was it young?

"Mother laughs a good deal," she said carefully.

"She was spoiled of course. She'd always had everything she wanted. And when she wanted your pa . . . well, she had to have him too. For the first time in her life, I'm guessing, she wanted something her mother wouldn't get for her. The old madam was dead against it. Your ma couldn't stand up to her but she ran away with your pa. Old Mrs Kennedy went back to Toronto in a towering rage. But she kept writing to your ma and sending her presents and coaxing her to go for visits. Your pa's folks weren't any more in favour of the match than your ma's. He could have had any Island girl he liked. One in particular . . . Lilian Morrow. She was yaller and spindling then but she's grown into a handsome woman. Never married. Your Aunt Irene favoured her. I've always said it was that two-faced Irene made more trouble than your grandmother. She's poison, that woman, just sweet poison. Even when she was a girl she could say the most p'isonous things in the sweetest way. But she had your pa roped and tied . . . she'd always petted and pampered him . . . men are like that, Jane Stuart, every one of them, clever or stupid. He thought Irene was perfection and he'd never believe she was a mischief-maker. Your pa and ma had their ups and downs, of course, but it was Irene put the sting into them, wagging that smooth tongue of hers . . . 'She's only a child, 'Drew' . . . when your dad was wanting to believe he'd married a woman, not a child. 'You're so young, lovey' . . . when your ma was feeling scared she'd never be old and wise enough for your pa. And patronizing her . . . she'd patronize God, that one . . . running her house for her . . . not that your ma knew much about it . . . that was one of her troubles, I guess . . . she'd never been taught how to manage or connive . . . but a woman don't like another woman sailing in putting things to rights. I'd have sent her off with a flea in her ear . . . but your ma had darn too little spunk . . . she couldn't stand up to Irene."

Of course, mother couldn't stand up to Aunt Irene . . . mother couldn't stand up to any one. Jane bit deep into a juicy apple rather savagely.

"I wonder," she said, as if more to herself than to Little Aunt Em, "if father and mother would have been happier if they had married other people."

"No, they wouldn't," said Aunt Em sharply. "They was meant for each other, whatever spoiled it. Don't you go thinking different, Jane Stuart. 'Course they fought! Who don't? The times I've had with my first and second! If they'd been let alone they'd likely have worked it out sooner or later. At the last, when you was rising three, your ma went to Toronto to visit the old madam and never come back. That's all anybody knows about it, Jane Stuart. Your pa sold the house and went for a trip round the world. Leastwise, that's what they said but I ain't believing the world is round. If it was, when it turned round all the water would fall out of the pond, wouldn't it? Now, I'm going to get you a bite to eat. I've got some cold ham and pickled beets and there's red currants in the garden."

They ate the ham and beets and then went out to the garden for the currants. The garden was an untidy little place, sloping to the south, which somehow contrived to be pleasant. There was honeysuckle over the paling . . . "to bring the humming-birds," said Little Aunt Em and white and red hollyhocks against the dark green of a fir coppice and rampant tiger-lilies along the walk. And one corner was rich in pinks.

"Nice out here, ain't it?" said Little Aunt Em. "It's a fine, marvellous world . . . oh, it's a very fine, marvellous world. Don't you like life, Jane Stuart?"

"Yes," agreed Jane heartily.

"I do. I smack my lips over life. I'd like to go on living for ever and hearing the news. Always a tang to the news. Some of these days I'm going to scrape up enough spunk to go in a car. I've never done it yet, but I will. Mrs Big Donald says it's the dream of her life to go up in an airy-plane but I draw the line at sky-hooting. What if the engine stopped going while you was up there? How are you going to get down? Well, I'm glad you come, Jane Stuart. We're both wove out of the same yarn."

Little Aunt Em gave Jane a bunch of pansies and a handful of geranium slips when she went away.

"It's the right time of the moon to plant them," she said. "Good-bye, Jane Stuart. May you never drink out of an empty cup."

Jane walked home slowly, thinking over several things. She loved being out alone at night. She liked the great white clouds that occasionally sailed over the stars. She felt, as she always felt when alone with the night, that she shared some lovely secret with the darkness.

Then the moon rose . . . a great honey-hued moon. The fields all about were touched with her light. The grove of pointed firs on an eastern hill was like a magic town of slender steeples. Jane tripped along gaily, singing to herself, while her black shadow ran before her on the moonlit road. And then, just around a turn, she saw cows before her. One of them, a big black one with a strange white face, was standing squarely in the middle of the road.

Jane came out in gooseflesh. She could not try to pass those cows . . . she could not. The only thing to do was to execute a flanking movement by climbing the fence into Big Donald's pasture and going through it until she was past the cows. Ingloriously Jane did so. But half-way along the field she suddenly stopped.

"How can I blame mother for not standing up to grandmother when I can't stand up to a few cows?" she thought.

She turned and went back. She climbed the fence into the road. The cows were still there. The white-faced one had not moved. Jane set her teeth and walked on with steady, gallant eyes. The cow did not budge. Jane went past it, head in air. When she was beyond the last cow, she turned and looked back. Not a cow of them had paid her the slightest attention.

"To think I was afraid of you," said Jane contemptuously.

And there was Lantern Hill and the silver laughter of the harbour underneath the moon. Jimmy John's little red heifer was in the yard and Jane drove it out fearlessly.

Dad was scribbling furiously when she peeped into the study. Ordinarily Jane would not have interrupted him but she remembered that there was something she ought to tell him.

"Dad, I forgot to tell you the house caught fire this afternoon."

Dad dropped his pen and stared at her.

"Caught fire?"

"Yes, from a spark that fell on the roof. But I went up with a pail of water and put it out. It only burned a little hole. Uncle Tombstone will soon fix it. The Snowbeams were awful mad they missed it."

Dad shook his head helplessly.

"What a Jane!" he said.

Jane, having discharged her conscience and being hungry again after her walk, made a meal off a cold fried trout and went to bed.

26

"I like a patch of excitement about once a week," dad would say and then they would get into the old car, taking Happy with them and leaving milk for the Peters, travelling east, west and sideways, as the road took them. Monday was generally the day for these gaddings. Every day meant something at Lantern Hill. Tuesday Jane mended, Wednesday she polished the silver, Thursday she swept and dusted downstairs, Friday upstairs, Saturday she scrubbed the floor and did extra baking for Sunday. On Monday, as dad said, they just did fool things.

They explored most of the Island that way, eating their meals by the side of the road whenever they felt hungry. "For all the world like a pair of gipsies," condescended Aunt Irene smilingly. Jane knew Aunt Irene held her responsible for the vagabondish ways dad was getting into now. But Jane was beginning to fence herself against Aunt Irene by a sturdy little philosophy of her own. Aunt Irene felt it, though she couldn't put it into words. If she could have, she would have said that Jane looked at her and then, quietly and politely, shut some door of her soul in her face.

"I can't get near to her, Andrew," she complained.

Dad laughed.

"Jane likes a clear space round her . . . as I do."

They did not often include Charlottetown in their Mondays, but one day in late August they pacified Aunt Irene by having supper with her. Another lady was there . . . a Miss Morrow to whom Jane took no great fancy . . . perhaps because when she smiled at Jane she looked too much like a toothpaste advertisement. Perhaps because dad seemed to like her. He and she laughed and chaffed a great deal. She was tall and dark and handsome, with rather prominent brown eyes. And she tried so hard to be nice to

Jane that it was almost painful.

"Your father and I have always been great friends. So we should be friends, too."

"An old sweetheart of your father's, lovey," Aunt Irene whispered to Jane when Miss Morrow had gone, attended to the gate by father. "If your mother hadn't come along . . . who knows? Even yet . . . but I don't know if a United States divorce would be legal in P. E. Island."

They stayed in to see a picture and it was late when they left for home. Not that that mattered. The Peters wouldn't care.

"We'll take the Mercer road home," said dad. "It's a base-line road and not many houses along it but I'm told it's simply lousy with leprechauns. Perhaps we'll manage to see one, skipping madly out of reach of the car lights. Keep your eyes peeled, Jane."

Leprechauns or no leprechauns, the Mercer road was not a very good place to be cast away in. As they were rocking joyously down a dark narrow hill, shadowy with tall firs and spruces, the car stopped short, never to go again . . . at least, not until something decisive had been done to its innards. So dad decided after much fruitless poking and probing.

"We're ten miles from a garage and one from the nearest house where every one will be asleep, Jane. It's after twelve. What shall we do?"

"Sleep in the car," said Jane coolly.

"I know a better plan. See that old barn over there? It's Jake Mallory's back barn and full of hay. I've a yen for sleeping in a hay loft, Jane."

"I think that will be fun," agreed Jane.

The barn was in a pasture field that had "gone spruce." Tiny trees were feathering up all over it . . . at least, they looked like trees in the soft darkness. Maybe they were really leprechauns, squatting there. There was a loft filled with clover hay and they lay down on it before the open window where they could watch the stars blazing down. Happy lay cuddled up to Jane and was soon dreaming blissfully of rabbits.

Jane thought father had gone to sleep, too. Somehow, she couldn't sleep; she didn't especially want to. She was at one and the same time very happy and a little miserable. Happy because she was there with dad under the spell of the moonless night. Jane rather liked a night with no moon. You got closer to the secret moods of the fields then; and there were such beautiful mysterious sounds on a dark night. They were too far inland to hear the haunting rhythm of the sea, but there were whispers and rustles in the poplars behind the barn . . . "there's magic in the poplars when the wind goes through," remembered Jane . . . and sounds like fairy footsteps pattering by. Who knew but that the elves were really out in the fern? And each far wooded hill with a star for its friend seemed listening . . . listening . . . couldn't you hear it, too, if you listened? Jane had never, before she came to the Island, known how beautiful night could be.

But along with all this she was thinking of what Aunt Irene had said about Miss Morrow and a United States divorce. Jane felt that she was haunted by those mysterious United States divorces. Hadn't Phyllis talked of them? Jane wished peevishly that the United States would keep their divorces at home.

Little Aunt Em had told her that father could have had lots of girls. Jane rather liked to speculate on those girls father might have had, secure in the knowledge that he could never have them now. But Miss Morrow made them seem disagreeably real. Had dad held her hand a shade too long when he said good-bye? Somehow, life was all snarled up.

Jane suppressed several sighs and then allowed one to escape her. Instantly dad turned over and a lean, strong hand touched hers.

"It seems impossible to avoid the conclusion that something is bothering my Superior Jane. Tell Happy about it and I'll listen in."

Jane lay very still and silent. Oh, if she could only tell him everything—find out everything she wanted so much to know! But she couldn't. There was a barrier between them.

"Did your mother teach you to hate me, Jane?"

Jane's heart gave a bound that almost choked her. She had promised mother that *she* wouldn't mention her name to dad and she had kept that promise. It was dad who had done the mentioning. Would it be wrong to allow him?

Jane decided then and there to take a chance on it.

"No, oh, no, dad. I didn't even know you were alive until about a year and a half ago."

"You didn't! Ah, that would be your grandmother's doings. And who told you then that I was?"

"A girl in school. And I thought you couldn't have been good to mother or she wouldn't have . . . left . . . you and I did hate you then for that. But nobody ever told me to hate you . . . only grandmother said you had sent for me just to annoy mother. You didn't . . . did you, dad?"

"No. I may be selfish, Jane, no doubt I am . . . I was told so more than once . . . but I'm not so selfish as that. I thought you were being brought up to hate me and I didn't think that fair. I thought you ought to have a chance to like me if you could. That was why I sent for you. Your mother and I made a failure of our marriage, Jane, as many other young fools have done. That is the bare bones of it."

"But why . . . why . . . mother is so sweet. . . ."

"You don't need to tell me how sweet she is, Jane. When I first saw her, I was just out of the mud and stench and obscenity of the trenches and I thought she was a creature from another star. I had never been able to understand the Trojan War before that. Then I realized that Helen of Troy might have been worth fighting for if she were like my Robin of the golden hair. And her eyes. All blue eyes are not beautiful, but hers were so lovely that they made you feel that no eyes other than blue were worth looking at. Her lashes did things to me you wouldn't believe. She wore a green dress the first time I saw her . . . well, if any other girl had worn the dress, it would have been a green dress and nothing more. On Robin it was magic . . . mystery . . . the robe of Titania. I would have kissed the hem of it."

"And did she fall in love with you, dad?"

"Something like that. Yes, she must have loved me for a while. We ran away, you know . . . her mother had no use for me. I don't think she'd have liked any man who took Robin from her . . . but I was poor and a nobody so I was quite impossible.

"I asked Robin one moonlight night to come away with me. The old moonlight enchantment did not fail. Never trust yourself in moonlight, Superior Jane. If I'd my way I'd lock everybody up on moonlight nights. We went to live at the Harbour Head and we were happy . . . why, I found a new word for sweetheart every day . . . I discovered I was a poet . . . I babbled of pools and grots, Jane . . . yes, we were happy that first year. I've always got that . . . the gods themselves can't take *that* from me."

Dad's voice was almost savage.

"And then," said Jane bitterly, "I came . . . and neither of you wanted me . . . and you were never happy again."

"Never let any one tell you that, Jane. I admit I didn't want you terribly . . . I was so happy I didn't want any third party around. But I remember when I saw your big round eyes brighten the first time you picked me out in a roomful of other men. Then I knew how much I wanted you. Perhaps your mother wanted you too much . . . at any rate she didn't seem to want any one else to love you. You wouldn't have thought I had any rights in you at all. She was so wrapped up in you that she hadn't any time or love left for me. If you sneezed she was sure you were taking pneumonia and thought me heartless because I wouldn't go off the deep end about it. She seemed afraid even to let me hold you for fear I'd drop you. Oh well, it wasn't all you. I suppose by that time she had found she had married some mythical John Doe of her imagination and that he had turned out to be no dashing hero but just a very ordinary Richard Roe. There were so many things . . . I was poor and we had to live by my budget. . . . I wasn't going to have my wife live on money her mother sent her. . . . I made her send it back. I will say she was quite willing to. But we began quarrelling over trifles . . . oh, you know I've a temper, Jane. I remember once I told her to shut her head . . . but every normal husband says that to his wife at least once in his life, Jane. I don't wonder that hurt her . . . but she was hurt by so many things I never thought would hurt her. Perhaps I don't understand women, Jane."

"No, you don't," agreed Jane.

"Eh! What!" Dad seemed a bit startled and only half pleased over Jane's candid agreement with him. "Well, upon my word . . . well, we won't argue it. But Robin didn't understand me either. She was jealous of my work . . . she thought I put it before her. . . . I know she was secretly glad when my book was rejected."

Jane remembered that mother had thought dad was jealous, too.

"Don't you think Aunt Irene had something to do with it, dad?"

"Irene? Nonsense! Irene was her best friend. And your mother was jealous of my love for Irene. Your mother couldn't help being a little jealous . . . *her* mother was the most jealous creature that ever breathed. It was a disease with her. In the end Robin went back to Toronto for a visit . . . and when she got there, she wrote me that she was not coming back."

"Oh, dad!"

"Well, I suppose her mother got round her. But she had stopped loving me. I knew that. I didn't want to see hate growing in the eyes where I had seen love. That is a terrible thing, Jane. So I didn't answer the letter."

"Oh, dad . . . if you had . . . if you had asked her . . ."

"I agree with Emerson that the highest price you can pay for a thing is to ask for it. Too high sometimes. A year later I weakened . . . I did write and ask her to come back. I knew it had been as much my fault as hers . . . I'd teased her . . . once I said you had a face like a monkey . . . well, you had, Jane, at that time. . . . I'll swear you had. I never got any answer. So I knew it was no use."

A question came into Jane's head. *Had mother ever seen that letter?*

"It's all best as it is, Jane. We weren't suited to each other. . . . I was ten years her senior and the war had made me twenty. I couldn't give her the luxuries and good times she craved. She was very . . . wise . . . to discard me. Let's not discuss it further, Jane. I merely wanted you to know the rights of it. And you must not mention anything I've said to your mother. Promise me that, Jane."

Jane promised dismally. There were so many things she wanted to say and she couldn't say them. It mightn't be fair to mother.

But she had to falter, "Perhaps . . . it isn't too late yet, dad."

"Don't get any foolish notions like that into your russet head, my Jane. It *is* too late. I shall never again ask Mrs Robert Kennedy's daughter to come back to me. We must make the best of things as they are. You and I love each other . . . I am to be congratulated on that."

For a moment Jane was perfectly happy. Dad loved her . . . she was sure of it at last.

"Oh, dad, can't I come back next summer . . . every summer?" she burst out eagerly.

"Do you really want to, Jane?"

"Yes," said Jane eloquently.

"Then we'll have it so. After all, if Robin has you in the winter, I should have you in the summer. She needn't grudge me that. And you're a good little egg, Jane. In fact, I think we're both rather nice."

"Dad" . . . Jane had to ask the question . . . she had to go right to the root of the matter . . . "do you . . . love . . . mother still?"

There was a moment of silence during which Jane quaked. Then she heard dad shrug his shoulders in the hay.

"'The rose that once has blown for ever dies,'" he said.

Jane did not think that was an answer at all but she knew it was all she was going to get.

She turned things over in her mind before she went to sleep. So dad hadn't sent for her just to annoy mother. But he didn't understand mother. That habit of his . . . ragging you . . . she,

Jane, liked it but perhaps mother hadn't understood. And father hadn't liked it because he thought mother neglected him for her baby. And he couldn't see through Aunt Irene. And was this what mother had cried about that night in the darkness? Jane couldn't bear to think of mother crying in the dark.

Between Little Aunt Em and dad she now knew a good deal she had not known before but . . .

"I'd like to hear mummy's side of it," was Jane's last thought as she finally fell asleep.

There was a pearl-like radiance of dawn over the eastern hills when she awoke . . . awoke knowing something she had not known when she went to sleep. Dad still loved mother. There was no further question in Jane's mind about that.

Dad was still asleep but she and Happy slipped down the ladder and out. Surely there had never before been a day that dawned so beautifully. The old pasture around the barn was the quietest place Jane had ever seen, and on the grass between the little spruces . . . spruces by day all right whatever they were by night . . . were gossamers woven on who knew what fairy loom. Jane was washing her face in morning dew when dad appeared.

"It is the essence of adventure to see the break of a new day, Jane. What may it not be ushering in? An empire may fall to-day . . . a baby may be born who will discover a cure for cancer . . . a wonderful poem may be written. . . ."

"Our car will have to be fixed," reminded Jane.

They walked a mile to a house and telephoned a garage. Some time before noon the car was on its legs again.

"Watch our smoke," said dad.

Home . . . and the Peters welcoming them back . . . the gulf singing . . . Millicent Mary toddling adoringly in at the gate. It was a lovely August day but the Jimmy John wheat-field was tawny gold and September was waiting behind the hills . . . and September meant Toronto and grandmother and St Agatha's again where she would be on the edge of things instead of hunting with the pack as here. The ninety-five to-morrows had shrunk to only a few. Jane sighed . . . then shook herself. What was the matter with her? She loved mother . . . she longed to see her . . . but . . .

"I want to stay with dad," said Jane.

27

_____

August slipped into September. Jimmy John began to summer fallow the big pasture field below the pond. Jane liked the look of the fresh red furrows. And she liked Mrs Jimmy John's flock of white geese swimming about the pond. There had been a time when Jane had kept a flock of white swans on a purple lake in the moon, but now she preferred the geese. Day by day the wheat- and oat-fields became more golden. Then Step-a-yard mowed the Jimmy John wheat. The Peters grew so fat catching evicted field-mice that dad told Jane she would really have to put them on a slimming diet.

Summer was ended. A big storm marked the ending, preceded by a week of curiously still weather. Step-a-yard shook his head and didn't like it. Something uncommon was brewing, he said.

The weather all summer had behaved itself well . . . days of sun and days of friendly rain. Jane had heard of the north shore storms and wanted to see one. She got her wish with a vengeance.

One day the gulf changed sulkily from blue to grey. The hills were clear and sharp, foretelling rain. The sky to the north-east was black, the clouds were dark with bitter wind.

"Lots of int'resting weather coming . . . don't hold me responsible for it," warned Step-a-yard when Jane started home from the Jimmy Johns'. She literally blew along the path and felt that if Lantern Hill hadn't stood in the way she might have emulated Little Aunt Em's reputed exploit of blowing over the harbour. There was a wild, strange, hostile look all over the world. The very trees seemed strangers in the oncoming storm.

"Shut the doors and windows tight, Jane," said dad. "Our house will just laugh at the east wind."

The storm broke presently and lasted for two days. The wind

that night didn't sound like wind at all . . . it sounded like the roar of a wild beast. For two days you could see nothing but a swirl of grey rain over a greyer sea . . . hear nothing but the tremendous music of huge breakers booming against the stubborn rocks of lower Queen's Shore. Jane liked it all after she got used to it. Something in her thrilled to it. And they were very cosy, sitting before their fire of white birchwood those wild nights, while the rain poured against the window and the wind roared and the gulf thundered.

"This is something like, Jane," said dad puffing at the Old Contemptible with a Peter on either shoulder. "Mankind must have its hearth-fire after all. It's a cold life warming yourself before other people's stoves."

And then he told Jane that he had decided to keep on living at Lantern Hill.

Jane gave a gasp of joy and relief. At first it had been vaguely understood that when Jane went dad would shut up Lantern Hill and go to town for the winter; and Jane had consequently been cumbered with certain worries.

What would become of her windowful of geraniums? The Jimmy Johns had enough of their own to look after. Dad would take Happy with him but what about the Peters? And the house itself . . . the thought of its unlighted windows was unbearable. It would be so lonely . . . so deserted.

"Oh, dad, I'm so glad . . . I couldn't bear to think of it missing us. But won't you . . . how about your meals?"

"Oh, I can get up a bite for myself, I daresay."

"I'm going to teach you to fry a steak and boil potatoes before I go," said Jane resolutely. "You can't starve then."

"Jane, you'll beat your husband . . . I know you will. It is no use trying to teach me to cook. Remember our first porridge. I daresay the Jimmy Johns won't see me starve. I'll arrange for one good meal a day there. Yes, I'm staying on here, Jane. I'll keep the heart of Lantern Hill beating for you. I'll water the geraniums and see that the Peters don't get rheumatism in their legs. But I can't imagine what the place will be like without you. . . ."

"You *will* miss me a little, won't you, dad?"

"A little! My Jane is trying to be humorous. But one consolation is that I'll likely get a little real work done on my Methuselah epic. I won't have so many interruptions. And I'll be able to growl without getting dirty looks."

"You may just have one growl a day," grinned Jane. "Oh, I'm so glad I made lots of jam. The pantry is full of it."

It was the next night dad showed her the letters. He was at his desk with Second Peter snoozing at his feet when Jane went in after washing the supper dishes. He was leaning his head on his hand and Jane thought with a sudden pang that he looked old and tired. The cat with the green spots and the diamond eyes was winking at him.

"Where did you get that cat, dad?"

"Your mother gave it to me . . . for a joke . . . before we were married. We saw it in a shop-window and were taken by the weirdness of it. And here . . . here are some letters I wrote her, Jane . . . one week she and her mother went over to Halifax. I found them to-night when I was cleaning out a drawer. I've been laughing at myself . . . the bitterest kind of laughter in the world. You'll laugh, too, Jane. Listen . . . 'To-day I tried to write a poem to you, Robin, but it is not finished because I could not find words fine enough, as a lover could not find raiment dainty enough for his bride. The old words that other men have used in singing to their loves seemed too worn and common for you. I wanted new words, crystal clear or coloured only by the iris of light. Not words that have been stamped and stained with all the hues of other men's thoughts' . . . wasn't I a sentimental fool, Jane? . . . 'I watched the new moon to-night, Robin. You told me you always watched the new moon set. It has been a bond between us ever since. . . . Oh, how dear and human and girlish and queenly you are . . . half saint and half very womanly woman. . . . It is so sweet to do something for one we love, even if it be only opening a door for her to pass through or handing her a book. . . . You are like a rose, my Robin . . . like a white tea-rose by moonlight. . . ."

"I wonder if any one will ever compare me to a rose," thought Jane. It didn't seem likely. She couldn't think of any flower she resembled.

"She didn't care enough about those letters to take them with her, Jane. After she went away I found them in the drawer of the little desk I had given her."

"But she didn't know she wasn't coming back then, dad."

Second Peter snarled as if he had been pushed aside by a foot.

"Didn't she? I think she did."

"I'm sure she didn't." Jane was sure, though she couldn't have given any reason for her sureness. "Let me take them back to her."

"No!" Dad brought his hand down so heavily on his desk that he hurt himself and winced. "I'm going to burn them."

"Oh, no, no." Somehow Jane couldn't bear to think of those letters being burned. "Give them to me, dad. I won't take them to Toronto . . . I'll leave them in my table drawer . . . but please don't burn them."

"Well!" Dad pushed the letters over to her and picked up a pen, as if dismissing the subject of the letters and her at the same time. Jane went out slowly, looking back at him. How she loved him . . . she loved even his shadow on the wall . . . his lovely clear-cut shadow. How could mother ever have left him?

The storm spent itself that night with a wild red sunset and a still wilder north-west wind . . . the wind of fine weather. The beach was still a maelstrom of foam the next day and the shadows of wild black clouds kept tearing over the sands, but the rain had ceased and the sun shone between the clouds. The harvest fields were drenched and tangled, the ground in the Jimmy John orchard was covered with apples . . . and the summer was ended. There was an indefinable change over everything that meant autumn.

28

Those last few days were compounded of happiness and misery for Jane. She did so many things she loved to do and would not do again until next summer . . . and next summer seemed a hundred years away. It was funny. She hadn't wanted to come and now she didn't want to go. She cleaned everything up and washed every dish in the house and polished all the silver and scoured Mr Muffet and Company till their faces shone. She felt lonely and left out when she heard the Jimmy Johns and the Snowbeams talking about the cranberrying in October, and when dad said, "I wish you could see those maples over yonder against that spruce hill in two weeks' time," and she realized that in two weeks' time there would be a thousand miles between them . . . well, it seemed to her that she just couldn't bear it.

Aunt Irene came out one day when Jane was house-cleaning furiously.

"Aren't you tired of playing at housekeeping yet, lovey?"

But that true Aunt Irenian touch could not disturb Jane.

"I'm coming back next summer," said Jane triumphantly.

Aunt Irene sighed.

"I suppose that would be nice . . . in some ways. But so many things may happen before then. It's a whim of your father's to live here now, but we don't know when he'll take another. Still, we can always hope for the best, can't we, lovey?"

The last day came. Jane packed her trunk, not forgetting a jar of very special wild-strawberry jam she was taking home to mother and two dozen russet apples Polly Snowbeam had given her for her own and Jody's consumption. Polly knew all about Jody and sent her her love.

They had a chicken dinner—the Ella twin and the George twin

had brought the birds over with Miranda's compliments, and Jane wondered when she would have a slice off the breast again. In the afternoon she went down alone to say good-bye to the shore. She could hardly bear the loneliness of the waves lapping on the beach. The sound and the tang and the sweep of the sea would not let her go. She knew the fields and the windy golden shore were a part of her. She and her Island understood each other.

"I belong here," said Jane.

"Come back soon. P. E. Island needs you," said Timothy Salt, offering her the quarter of an apple on the point of his knife. "You will," he added. "The Island's got into your blood. It does that to some folks."

Jane and dad had expected a last quiet evening together but instead there was a surprise party. All Jane's particular friends, old and young, came, even Mary Millicent who sat in a corner all the evening, staring at Jane, and never spoke a word. Step-a-yard came and Timothy Salt and Min and Min's ma and Ding-dong Bell and the Big Donalds and the Little Donalds and people from the Corners that Jane didn't know knew her.

Every one brought her a farewell gift. The Snowbeams clubbed together and brought her a white plaster of Paris plaque to hang on her bedroom wall. It cost twenty-five cents and had a picture of Moses and Aaron on it in blue turbans and red gowns . . . and Jane saw grandmother looking at it! Little Aunt Em could not come but she sent word to Jane Stuart that she would save some hollyhock seeds for her. They had a very gay evening, although all the girls cried after they had sung, "For she's a jolly good fellow." Shingle Snowbeam cried so much into the tea towel with which she was helping Polly to dry the dishes that Jane had to get a dry one out.

Jane did not cry but she was thinking, "It's the last good time I'll have for ages. And everybody has been so lovely to me."

"You don't know how much I'm feeling this, Jane, right here in my heart," said Step-a-yard patting his stomach.

Dad and Jane sat up a little while after the folks had gone.

"They love you here, Jane."

"Polly and Shingle and Min are going to write to me every week," said Jane.

"You'll get the news of the Hill and the Corners then," said dad gently. "You know I can't write to you, Jane . . . not while you're living in that house."

"And grandmother won't let me write to you," said Jane sadly.

"But as long as you know there's a dad and I know there's a Jane, it won't matter too much, will it? I'll keep a diary, Jane, and you can read it when you come next summer. It will be like getting a bundle of letters all at once. And while we'll think of each other in general quite often, let's arrange one particular time for it. Seven o'clock in the evening here is six in Toronto. At seven o'clock every Saturday night I'll think of you and at six you think of me."

It was like dad to plan something like that.

"And, dad, will you sow some flower seeds for me next spring? I won't be here in time to do it. Nasturtiums and cosmos and phlox and marigolds . . . oh, Mrs Jimmy John will tell you what to get, and I'd like a little patch of vegetables, too."

"Consider it done, Queen Jane."

"And can I have a few hens next summer, dad?"

"Those hens are hatched already," said dad.

He squeezed her hand.

"We've had a good time, haven't we, Jane?"

"We've *laughed* so much together," said Jane, thinking of 60 Gay where there was no laughter. "You won't forget to send for me next spring, will you, dad?"

"No," was all dad said. "No" is sometimes a horrible word but there are times when it is beautiful.

They had to get up early the next morning because dad was going to drive Jane to town to catch the boat train and meet a certain Mrs Wesley who was going to Toronto. Jane thought she could travel very well by herself, but for once dad was adamant.

The morning sky was red with trees growing black against it.

The old moon was visible, like a new moon turned the wrong way, above the birches on Big Donald's hill. It was still misty in the hollows. Jane bade every room farewell and just before they left dad stopped the clock.

"We'll start it again when you come back, Janekin. My watch will do me for the winter."

The purring Peters had to be said good-bye to but Happy went to town with them. Aunt Irene was at the station and so was Lilian Morrow, the latter all perfume and waved hair. Dad seemed glad to see her; he walked up and down the platform with her. She called him "'Drew." You could hear the apostrophe before it like a coo or a kiss. Jane could have done very well without Miss Morrow to see her off.

Aunt Irene kissed her twice and cried.

"Remember you always have a friend in *me*, lovey" . . . as if she thought Jane had no other.

"Don't look so woebegone, dear," smiled Lilian Morrow. "Remember you're going home."

Home! "Home is where the heart is." Jane had heard or read that. And she knew she was leaving her heart on the Island with dad, to whom she presently said goodbye with all the anguish of all the good-byes that have ever been said in her voice.

Jane watched the red shores of the Island from the boat until they were only a dim blue line against the sky. And now to be Victoria again!

When Jane went through the gates of the Toronto station, she heard a laugh she would have known anywhere. There was only one such laugh in the world. And there was mother, in a lovely new crimson velvet wrap with a white fur collar and underneath a dress of white chiffon embroidered with brilliants. Jane knew this meant that mother was going out to dinner . . . and she knew grandmother had not allowed mother to break her engagement for the sake of spending Jane's first evening home with her. But mother, smelling of violets, was holding her tight, laughing and crying.

"My dearest . . . my very own little girl. You're home again. Oh, darling, I've missed you so. . . . I've missed you so."

Jane hugged mother fiercely . . . mother as beautiful as ever, her eyes as blue as ever, though, as Jane saw instantly, a little thinner than she had been in June.

"Are you glad to be back, darling?"

"So glad to be with you again, mummy," said Jane.

"You've grown . . . why, darling, you're up to my shoulder . . . and such a lovely tan. But I can never let you go away again . . . never."

Jane kept her own counsel about that. She felt curiously changed and grown-uppish as she went through the big lighted station with mother. Frank was waiting with the limousine and they went home through the busy, crowded streets to 60 Gay. 60 Gay was neither busy nor crowded. The clang of the iron gates behind her seemed a knell of doom. She was re-entering prison. The great, cold, still house struck a chill to her spirit. Mother had gone on to the dinner and grandmother and Aunt Gertrude were meeting her. She kissed Aunt Gertrude's narrow white face and grandmother's soft wrinkled one.

"You've grown, Victoria," said grandmother icily. She did not like Jane looking into her eyes on the level. And grandmother saw at a glance that Jane had somehow learned what to do with her arms and legs and was looking entirely too much mistress of herself. "Don't smile with your lips closed, if you please. I've never really been able to see the charm of 'La Gioconda.'"

They had dinner. It was six o'clock. Down home it would be seven. Dad would be . . . Jane felt she could not swallow a mouthful.

"Will you be good enough to pay attention when I am speaking to you, Victoria?"

"I beg your pardon, grandmother."

"I am asking you what you wore this summer. I have looked into your trunk and the clothes you took with you don't seem to have been worn at all."

"Only the green linen jumper suit," said Jane. "I wore it to church and the ice-cream social. I had gingham dresses to wear at home. I kept house for father, you know."

Grandmother wiped her lips daintily with her napkin. It seemed as if she were wiping some disagreeable flavour off them.

"I am not inquiring about your rural activities" . . . Jane saw grandmother looking at her hands. . . . "It will be wise for you to forget them. . . ."

"But I'm going back next summer, grandmother. . . ."

"Be kind enough not to interrupt me, Victoria. And as you must be tired after your journey, I would advise you to go to bed at once. Mary has prepared a bath for you. I suppose you will be rather glad to get into a real bath-tub once more."

When she had had the whole gulf for a bath-tub all summer!

"I must run over and see Jody first," said Jane . . . and went. She could not forget her new freedom so quickly. Grandmother watched her go with tightening lips. Perhaps she realized that never again would Jane be quite the meek, overawed Victoria of the old days. She had grown in mind as well as in body.

Jane and Jody had a rapturous reunion. Jody had grown too. She was thinner and taller and her eyes were sadder than ever.

"Oh, Jane, I'm so glad you're back. It's been so long."

"I'm so glad you're still here, Jody. I was afraid Miss West might have sent you to the orphanage."

"She's always saying she will . . . I guess she will yet. Did you really like the Island so much, Jane?"

"I just loved it," said Jane, glad that here was at least one person to whom she could talk freely about her Island and her father.

Jane was horribly homesick as she climbed the soft-carpeted stairway to bed. If she were only skipping up the bare, painted steps at Lantern Hill! Her old room had not grown any friendlier. She ran to the window, opened it and gazed out . . . but not on starry hills and the moon shining on woodland fields. The clamour of Bloor Street assailed her ears. The huge old trees about 60 Gay were sufficient unto themselves . . . they were not

463

her friendly birches and spruces. A wind was trying to blow . . . Jane felt sorry for it . . . checked here, thwarted there. But it was blowing from the west. Would it blow right down to the Island . . . to the velvety black night starred with harbour lights beyond Lantern Hill? Jane leaned out of the window and sent a kiss to dad on it.

"And now," remarked Jane to Victoria, "there will be only nine months to put in."

29

"She will soon forget everything about Lantern Hill," said grandmother.

Mother wasn't so sure. She felt the change in Jane as did everybody. Uncle David's family thought Jane "much improved." Aunt Sylvia said Victoria had actually become able to get through a room without danger to the furniture. And Phyllis was a shade less patronizing, though with plenty of room for improvement yet.

"I heard you went barefoot down there," she said curiously.

"Of course," said Jane. "All the children do in summer."

"Victoria has gone quite P. E. Island," said grandmother with her bitter little smile, much as if she had said, "Victoria has gone quite savage." Grandmother had already learned a new way to get under Jane's skin. It was to say little biting things about the Island. Grandmother employed it quite mercilessly. She felt that Jane, in so many respects, had somehow slipped beyond her power to hurt. All the colour still went out of Jane in grandmother's presence but she was not thereby reduced to the old flabbiness. Jane had not been chatelaine of Lantern Hill and the companion of a keen, mature intellect all summer for nothing. A new spirit looked out of her hazel eyes . . . something that was free and aloof . . . something that was almost beyond grandmother's power to tame or hurt. All the venom of her stings seemed unable to touch this new Jane . . . except when she sneered at the Island.

Because in a very real sense Jane was still living on the Island. This helped to take the edge off her first two weeks of unbearable homesickness. While she was practising her scales she was listening for the thunder of the breakers on Queen's Shore; while she ate her meals she was waiting for dad to come in from one of his long hikes with Happy trotting at his heels; when she was alone in the big gloomy house she was companioned by the Peters . . . who could have imagined that a couple of cat's a thousand miles away could be such comforts? . . . When she lay awake at night she was hearing all the sounds of her Island home. And while she was reading the Bible chapter to grandmother and Aunt Gertrude in that terrible, unchanged drawing-room, she was reading it to dad on the old Watch Tower.

"I should prefer a little more *reverence* in reading the Bible, Victoria," said grandmother. Jane had been reading an old Hebrew war tale as father would have read it, with a trumpet clang of victory in her voice. Grandmother looked at her vindictively. It was plain that reading the Bible was no longer a penance to Jane. She seemed positively to enjoy it. And what could grandmother do about it?

Jane had made a list on the back of her arithmetic notebook of the months that must pass before her return to the Island, and smiled when she ticked off September.

She had felt very reluctant to go back to St Agatha's. But in a short time she found herself saying one day in amazement, "I like going to school."

She had always felt vaguely left out . . . excluded at St Agatha's. Now, for some reason unknown to her, she no longer felt so. It was as if she had become a comrade and a leader overnight. The girls of her class looked up to her. The teachers began to wonder why they had never before suspected what a remarkable child Victoria Stuart was. Why, she was simply full of executive ability.

And her studies were no longer a tribulation. They had become a pleasure. She wanted to study as hard as she could, to catch up with dad. Dim ghosts of history . . . exquisite, unhappy queens . . . grim old tyrants . . . had become real . . . marked poems in the reader she and dad had read together were full of meaning for her . . . the ancient lands where they had roamed in fancy were places she knew and loved. It was so easy to learn about them. Jane brought home no more bad reports. Mother was delighted but grandmother did not seem overly pleased. She picked up a letter one day which Jane was writing to Polly Jimmy John, glanced over it, dropped it with disdain:

"Phlox is not spelled f-l-o-x, Victoria. But I suppose it does not matter to your haphazard friends how you spell."

Jane blushed. She knew perfectly well how to spell phlox but there was so much to tell Polly . . . to ask Polly . . . so many messages to send to the people in that far, dear Island by the sea . . . she just scribbled away furiously without thinking.

"Polly Garland is the best speller at Lantern Corners school," said Jane.

"Oh, I have no doubt . . . no doubt whatever . . . that she has all the backwoods virtues," said grandmother.

Grandmother's sneers could not poison Jane's delight in the letters she got from the Island. They came as thick as autumn leaves in Vallambroso. Somebody at Lantern Hill or Hungry Cove or the Corners was always writing to Jane. The Snowbeams sent composite letters, dreadfully spelled and blotted, written paragraph about. They possessed the knack of writing the most amusing things, illustrated along the edges with surprisingly well-done thumb-nail sketches by Shingle. Jane always wanted to shriek with laughter over the Snowbeam letters.

Elder Tommy had the mumps . . . fancy Elder Tommy with the mumps . . . Shingle had fancied it in a few sidesplitting curves. . . . The tail-board of Big Donald's cart had come out when he was going up Little Donald's hill and all his turnips had rolled out and down the hill and was he mad! The pigs had got into the Corners graveyard; Min's ma was making a silk quilt . . . Jane immediately began saving patches for Min's ma's quilt. . . . Ding-dong's dog had torn the whole seat out of Andy Pearson's second best trousers, the frost had killed all the dahlias, Step-a-yard was having boils, there had been a lovely lot of funerals this fall, old Mrs Dougald MacKay had died and people who were at the funeral said she looked perfectly gorgeous, the Jimmy Johns' baby had laughed at last, the big tree on Big Donald's hill had

blown down . . . Jane was sorry for that, she had loved that tree. .
. . "We miss you just awful, Jane. . . . Oh, Jane, we wish you could
be here for Hallowe'en night."

Jane wished it, too. If one could but fly in the darkness over
rivers and mountains and forests to the Island for just that one
night! What fun they would have running round putting turnip
and pumpkin Jack-o'-lanterns on gate-posts and perhaps helping
to carry off somebody's gate.

"What are you laughing at, darling?" asked mother.

"A letter from home," said Jane thoughtlessly.

"Oh, Jane Victoria, isn't this your home?" cried mother
piteously.

Jane was sorry she had spoken. But she had to be honest. Home!
A little house looking seaward . . . a white gull . . . ships going up
and down . . . spruce woods . . . misty barrens . . . salt air cold from
leagues of gulf . . . quiet . . . silence. *That* was home . . . the only
home she knew. But she hated to hurt mother. Jane had begun
to feel curiously protective about mother . . . as if, somehow, she
must be shielded and guarded. Oh, if she could only talk things
over with mother . . . tell her everything about dad . . . find out
everything. What fun it would be to read those letters to mother!
She did read them to Jody. Jody was as much interested in the
Lantern Hill folks as Jane herself. She began sending messages to
Polly and Shingle and Min.

The elms around 60 Gay turned a rusty yellow. Far away the
red leaves would be falling from the maples . . . the autumn mists
would be coming in from the sea. Jane opened her notebook and
ticked off October.

November was a dark, dry, windy month. Jane scored a secret
triumph over grandmother one week of it.

"Let me make the croquettes for lunch, Mary," she begged one
day. Mary consented very sceptically, remembering that there was
plenty of chicken salad in the refrigerator if the croquettes were
ruined. They were not. They were everything croquettes should
be. Nobody knew who had made them, but Jane had the fun of

watching folks eat them. Grandmother took a second helping.

"Mary seems to have learned how to make croquettes properly at last," she said.

Jane wore a poppy on Armistice Day because dad was a D.S. She was hungry to hear about him but she would not ask her Island correspondents. They must not know she and dad did not exchange letters. But sometimes there was a bit about him in some of the letters . . . perhaps only a sentence or two. She lived for and by them. She got up in the night to re-read the letters they were in. And every Saturday afternoon she shut herself up in her room and wrote him a letter which she sealed up and asked Mary to hide in her trunk. She would take them all to dad next summer and let him read them while she read his diary. She made a little ritual of dressing up to write to dad. It was delightful to be writing to him, while the wind howled outside, to father so far away and yet so near, telling him everything you had done that week, all the little intimate things you loved.

The first snow came one afternoon as she wrote, in flakes as large as butterflies. Would it be snowing on the Island? Jane hunted up the morning paper and looked to see what the weather report in the Maritimes was. Yes . . . cold, with showers of snow . . . clearing and cold at night. Jane shut her eyes and saw it. Great soft flakes falling over the grey landscape against the dark spruces . . . her little garden a thing of fairy beauty . . . egg flakes in the empty robin's nest she and Shingle knew of . . . the dark sea around the white land. "Clearing and cold at night." Frosty stars gleaming out in still frostier evening blue over quiet fields thinly white with snow. Would dad remember to let the Peters in?

Jane ticked off November.

30

Christmas had never meant a great deal to Jane. They always did the same things in the same way. There were neither tree nor stockings at 60 Gay and no morning celebration because grandmother so decreed. She said she liked a quiet forenoon and she always went to the service in St Barnabas's, though, for some queer reason of her own, she always wanted to go alone that day. Then they all went for lunch to Uncle William's or Uncle David's and there was a big family dinner at night at 60 Gay, with the presents in display. Jane always got a good many things she didn't want especially and one or two she did. Mother always seemed even a little gayer on Christmas than on any other day . . . too gay, as if, Jane in her new wisdom felt, she were afraid of remembering something if she stopped being gay for a moment.

But the Christmas season this year had a subtle meaning for Jane it had never possessed before. There was the concert at St Agatha's for one thing, in which Jane was one of the star performers. She recited another *habitant* poem and did it capitally . . . because she was reciting to an audience of one a thousand miles away and didn't care a hoot for grandmother's scornful face and compressed lips. The last number was a tableau in which four girls represented the spirits of the four seasons kneeling around the Christmas spirit. Jane was the spirit of autumn with maple-leaves in her russet hair.

"Your granddaughter is going to be a very handsome girl," a lady told grandmother. "She doesn't resemble her lovely mother, of course, but there is something very striking about her face."

"Handsome is as handsome does," said grandmother in a tone which implied that, judged by that standard, Jane hadn't the remotest chance of good looks. But Jane didn't hear it and wouldn't have cared if she had. She knew what dad thought about her bones.

Jane could not send presents to the Island . . . she had no money to buy them. An allowance was something Jane had never had. So she wrote a special letter to all her friends instead. They sent her little gifts which gave her far more delight than the fine ones she got in Toronto.

Min's ma sent her a packet of summer savoury.

"Nobody here cares for summer savoury," said grandmother, meaning that she didn't. "We prefer sage."

"Mrs Jimmy John always uses savoury in her stuffing and so do Min's ma and Mrs Big Donald," said Jane.

"Oh, no doubt we are sadly behind the times," said grandmother, and when Jane opened the packet of spruce-gum Young John had sent her grandmother said, "Well, well, so *ladies* chew gum nowadays. Other times, other manners."

She picked up the card Ding-dong had sent Jane. It had on it the picture of a blue and gold angel under which Ding-dong had written, "This looks like you."

"I have always heard," said grandmother, "that love is blind."

Grandmother certainly had the knack of making you feel ridiculous.

But even grandmother did not disdain the bundle of driftwood old Timothy Salt expressed up. She let Jane burn it in the fireplace on Christmas eve, and mother loved the blue and green and purple flames. Jane sat before it and dreamed. It was a very cold night . . . a night of frost and stars. Would it be as cold on the Island and would her geraniums freeze? Would there be a thick white fur on the windows at Lantern Hill? What kind of a Christmas would dad have? She knew he was going to Aunt Irene's for dinner. Aunt Irene had written Jane a note to accompany her gift of a pretty knitted sweater and told her so. "With a few of his old friends," said Aunt Irene.

Would Lilian Morrow be among the old friends? Somehow Jane hoped not. There was always a queer little formless, nameless fear in her heart when she thought of Lilian Morrow and her caressing "'Drew."

Lantern Hill would be empty on Christmas. Jane resented that. Dad would take Happy with him and the poor Peters would be all alone.

Jane had one thrill on Christmas Day nobody knew anything about. They went to lunch at Uncle David's and there was a copy of *Saturday Evening* in the library. Jane pounced on it. Would there be anything of dad's in it? Yes, there was. Another front page article on "The Consequences of Confederation in Regard to the Maritime Provinces." Jane was totally out of her depth in it, but she read every word of it with pride and delight.

Then came the cat.

31

They had had dinner at 60 Gay and were all in the big drawing-room, which even with a fire blazing on the hearth still seemed cold and grim. Frank came in with a basket.

"It's come, Mrs Kennedy," he said.

Grandmother took the basket from Frank and opened it. A magnificent white Persian cat was revealed, blinking pale green eyes disdainfully and distrustfully at everybody. Mary and Frank had discussed that cat in the kitchen.

"Whatever has the old dame got into her noddle now?" said Frank. "I thought she hated cats and wouldn't let Miss Victoria have one on any consideration. And here she's giving her one . . . and it costing seventy-five dollars. Seventy-five dollars for a cat!"

"Money's no object to her," said Mary. "And I'll tell you what's in her noddle. I haven't cooked for her for twenty years without learning to read her mind. Miss Victoria has a cat on that Island of hers. Her grandmother wants to cut that cat out. She isn't going to have Andrew Stuart letting Miss Victoria have cats when she isn't allowed to have them here. The old lady is at her wit's end how to wean Miss Victoria away from the Island and that's what this cat means. Thinks she—a real Persian, costing seventy-five dollars and looking like the King of All Cats, will soon put the child out of conceit with her miserable common kittens. Look at the presents she give Miss Victoria this Christmas. As if to say, 'You couldn't get anything like that from your father!' Oh, I'm knowing her. But she's met her match at last or I'm mistaken. She can't overcrow Miss Victoria any longer and she's just beginning to find it out."

"This is a Christmas present for you, Victoria," said grandmother. "It should have been here last night but there was some delay . . . somebody was ill."

Everybody looked at Jane as if they expected her to go into spasms of delight.

"Thank you, grandmother," said Jane flatly.

She didn't like Persian cats. Aunt Minnie had one . . . a pedigreed smoke-blue . . . and Jane had never liked it. Persian cats were so deceptive. They looked so fat and fluffy, and then when you picked them up, expecting to enjoy a good satisfying squeeze, there was nothing to them but bones. Anybody was welcome to their Persian cat for all of Jane.

"Its name is Snowball," said Grandmother.

So she couldn't even name her own cat. But grandmother expected her to like the cat and Jane went to work heroically in the following days trying to like it. The trouble was, the cat didn't want to be liked. No friendliness ever warmed the pale green fire of its eyes. It did not want to be petted or caressed. The Peters had been lapsters, with eyes of amber, and Jane from the first had been able to talk to them in their own language. But Snowball refused to understand a word she said.

"I thought . . . correct me if I'm wrong . . . that you professed to be fond of cats," said grandmother.

"Snowball doesn't like me," said Jane.

"Oh!" said grandmother. "Well, I suppose your taste in cats is on a par with your taste in friends. And I don't suppose there is very much that can be done about it."

"Darling, *couldn't* you like Snowball a little more?" pleaded mother, as soon as they were alone. "Just to please your grandmother. She thought you would be delighted. Can't you pretend to like it?"

Jane was not very good at pretending. She looked after Snowball faithfully, combed and brushed him every day, saw that he had the right kind of food and plenty of it, saw that he did not get out in the cold and take pneumonia . . . would not have cared in the least if he had. She liked pussies who went out boldly on their own mysterious errands and later appeared on the doorstep pleading to get in where there was a warm cushion and a drop of cream. Snowball took all her attention as a matter of course, paraded about 60 Gay, waving a plumy tail and was rapturously adored by all callers.

"Poor Snowball," said grandmother ironically.

At this unlucky point Jane giggled. She couldn't help it. Snowball looked so little desirous of pity. Sitting on the arm of the chesterfield, he was monarch of all he surveyed and quite happy about it.

"I like a cat I can hug," said Jane. "A cat that likes to be hugged."

"You forget you are talking to me, not to Jody," said grandmother.

After three weeks Snowball disappeared. Luckily Jane was at St Agatha's or grandmother might have suspected her of conniving at his disappearance. Everybody was away and Mary had left the front door open for a few moments. Snowball went out and apparently wandered into the fourth dimension. A lost-and-found ad. had no results.

"He's been stole," said Frank. "That's what comes of having them expensive cats."

"It's not me that's sorry. He had to be more pampered than a baby," said Mary. "And I'm not of the opinion Miss Victoria will break her heart about it either. She's still hankering after her Peters . . . she's not one to change and the old lady can put that in her pipe and smoke it."

Jane couldn't pretend any great grief and grandmother was very angry. She smouldered for days over it and Jane was uncomfortable. Perhaps she had been ungrateful . . . perhaps she hadn't tried hard enough to like Snowball. Anyhow, on the night the big white Persian suddenly materialized on the street corner, as she and mother were waiting for the Bloor car amid a swirl of snow, and wrapped itself around her legs in an apparent frenzy of recognition and hoarse miaows, Jane yelped with genuine delight.

"Mummy . . . mummy . . . here's Snowball."

That she and mother should be standing alone on a street corner, waiting for a car on a blustery January night was an unprecedented thing. There had been doings at St Agatha's that night . . . the senior girls had put on a play and mother had been invited. Frank was laid up with influenza and they had to go with Mrs Austen. Before the play was half through Mrs Austen had been summoned home because of sudden illness in her family and mother had said, "Don't think of us for a moment. Jane and I can go home perfectly well on the street-cars."

Jane always loved a ride on a street-car, and it was twice as much fun with mother. It was so seldom she and mother went anywhere alone. But when they did, mother was such a good companion. She saw the funny side of everything and her eyes laughed to Jane's when a joke popped its head up. Jane was sorry when they got off at Bloor for that meant they were comparatively near home.

"Darling, how can this be Snowball?" exclaimed mother. "It does look like him, I admit . . . but it's a mile from home. . . ."

"Frank always said he'd been stolen, mummy. It must be Snowball . . . a strange cat wouldn't make a fuss over me like this. . . ."

"I shouldn't have thought Snowball would either," laughed mother.

"I expect he's glad to see a friend," said Jane. "We don't know how he's been treated. He feels awfully thin. We must take him home."

"On the street-car. . . ."

"We can't leave him here. I'll hold him . . . he'll be quiet."

Snowball was quiet for a few moments after they entered the car. There were not many people on it. Three boys at the far end sniggered as Jane sat down with her armful of cat. A pudgy child edged away from her in terror. A man with a pimply face scowled at her as if he were personally insulted by the sight of a Persian cat.

Suddenly Snowball seemed to go quite mad. He made one wild

leap out of Jane's incautiously relaxed arms and went whizzing around the car, hurtling over the seats and hurling himself against the windows. Women shrieked. The pudgy child bounced up and screamed. The pimply-faced man's hat got knocked off by a wild Snowballian leap, and he swore. The conductor opened the door.

"Don't let the cat out," shrieked breathless, pursuing Jane. "Shut the door . . . shut it quick . . . it's my lost cat and I'm taking it home."

"You'd better keep hold of it then," said the conductor gruffly.

"Enough is as good as a feast," thought Snowball . . . evidently . . . for he allowed Jane to nab him. The boys all laughed insultingly as Jane walked back to her seat, looking neither to the right nor to the left. A button had burst off her slipper and she had stumbled and skinned her nose on the handle of a seat. But she was Jane victorious . . . as well as Victoria.

"Oh, darling . . . darling," said mother, in kinks of laughter . . . real laughter. When had mother laughed like that? If grandmother saw her!

"That's a dangerous animal," said the pimply-faced man warningly.

Jane looked at the boys. They made irresistibly comic faces at her and she made faces back. She liked Snowball better than she ever had before. But she did not relax her grip on him until she heard the door of 60 Gay clang behind her.

"We've found Snowball, grandmother," cried Jane triumphantly. "We've brought him home."

She released the cat who stood looking squiffily about.

"That is not Snowball," said grandmother. "That is a female cat."

Judging from grandmother's tone it was evident that there was something very disgraceful about a female cat!

The owner of the female cat was eventually discovered through another lost-and-found and no more Persians appeared at 60 Gay. Jane had ticked off December, and January was speeding away. The Lantern Hill news was still absorbing. Everybody was skating . . . on the pond or on the little round, tree-shadowed pool beyond the Corners. . . . Shingle Snowbeam had been queen in a Christmas concert and had worn a crown of scalloped tin; the new minister's wife could play the organ; the Jimmy John baby had eaten all the blooms off Mrs Jimmy John's Christmas cactus, every last one of them; Mrs Little Donald had had her gobbler for Christmas dinner . . . Jane remembered that magnificent white gobbler with the coral-red wattles and accorded him a meed of regret; Uncle Tombstone had butched Min's ma's pig and Min's ma had sent a roast to dad; Min's ma had got a new pig to bring up, a nice pink pig exactly like Elder Tommy; Mr Spragg's dog at the Corners had bit the eye out of Mr Loney's dog and Mr Loney was going to law about it; Mrs Angus Scatterby, whose husband had died in October, was disappointed over the result . . . "It's not so much fun being a widow as I expected," she was reported to have said; Sherwood Morton had gone into the choir and the managers had put a few more nails in the roof . . . Jane suspected Step-a-yard of that joke; there was wonderful coasting on Big Donald's hill; her dad had got a new dog, a fat white dog named Bubbles; her geraniums were blooming beautiful . . . "and me too far away to see them," thought Jane with a pang; William MacAllister had had a fight with Thomas Crowder because Thomas told William he didn't like the whiskers William would have had if he had had whiskers; they had had a silver thaw . . . Jane could see it . . . ice jewels . . . the maple wood a thing of unearthly splendour . . . every stalk sticking up from the crusted snow of the garden a spear of crystal; Step-a-yard was mudding . . . what on earth was mudding? . . . she must find out next summer; Mr Snowbeam's pig-house roof had blown off . . . "if he'd nailed the ridge-pole firmly on last summer when I advised him to, this wouldn't have happened," thought Jane virtuously; Bob Woods had fell on his dog and sprained his back . . . was it Bob's back or the dog's that was sprained? . . . Caraway Snowbeam had to have her tonsils out and was putting on such airs about it; Jabez Gibbs had set a trap for a skunk and caught his own cat; Uncle Tombstone had given all his friends an oyster supper; some said Mrs Alec Carson at the Corners had a new baby, some said she hadn't.

What had 60 Gay to offer against the colour and flavour of news like that? Jane ticked off January.

February was stormy. Jane spent many a blustery evening, while the wind howled up and down Gay Street, poring over seed catalogues, picking out things for dad to plant in the spring. She loved to read the description of the vegetables and imagine she saw rows of them at Lantern Hill. She copied down all Mary's best recipes to make them for dad next summer . . . dad who was likely at this very moment to be sitting cosily by their own fireside with two happy dogs curled up at his feet and outside a wild white night of drifting snow. Jane ticked off February.

32

When Jane ticked off March she whispered, "Just two and a half months more." Life went on outwardly the same at 60 Gay and St Agatha's. Easter came and Aunt Gertrude, who had refused sugar in her tea all through Lent, took it again. Grandmother was buying the loveliest spring clothes for mother who seemed rather indifferent to them. And Jane was beginning to hear her Island calling to her in the night.

On a wild wet morning in late April the letter came. Jane, who had been watching for it for weeks and was beginning to feel a bit worried, carried it in to mother with the face of

> One to whom glad news is sent
> From the far country of his home after long banishment.

Mother was pale as she took it and grandmother was suddenly flushed.

"Another letter from Andrew Stuart?" said grandmother, as if the name blistered her lips.

"Yes," said mother faintly. "He . . . he says Jane Victoria must go back to him for the summer . . . if she wants to go. She is to make her own choice."

"Then," said grandmother, "she will not go."

"Of course you won't go, darling?"

"Not go! But I must go! I promised I'd go back," cried Jane.

"Your . . . your father will not hold you to that promise. He says expressly that you can choose as you please."

"I *want* to go back," said Jane. "I'm going back."

"Darling," said mother imploringly, "don't go. You grew away from me last summer. If you go again I'll lose more of you. . . ."

Jane looked down at the carpet and her lips set in a line that had an odd resemblance to grandmother's.

Grandmother took the letter from mother, glanced at it and looked at Jane.

"Victoria," she said, quite pleasantly for her, "I think you have not given the matter sufficient thought. I say nothing for myself . . . I have never expected gratitude . . . but your mother's wishes ought to carry some weight with you. Victoria"—grandmother's voice grew sharper——"please do me the courtesy of looking at me while I am speaking to you."

Jane looked at grandmother . . . looked her straight in the eyes, unflinchingly, unyieldingly. Grandmother seemed to put a certain unusual restraint on herself. She still spoke pleasantly.

"I have not mentioned this before, Victoria, but I decided some time ago that I would take you and your mother for a trip to England this summer. We will spend July and August there. You will enjoy it, I know. I think that between a summer in England and a summer in a hut in a country settlement on P. E. Island even you could hardly hesitate."

Jane did not hesitate. "Thank you, grandmother. It is very kind of you to offer me such a lovely trip. I hope you and mother will enjoy it. But I would rather go to the Island."

Even Mrs Robert Kennedy knew when she was beaten. But she could not accept defeat gracefully.

"You get that stubborn will of yours from your father," she said, her face twisted with anger. For the moment she looked simply like a very shrewish old spitfire. "You grow more like him every day of your life . . . you've got his very chin."

Jane was thankful she had got a will from someone. She was glad she looked like dad . . . glad her chin was like his. But she wished mother were not crying.

"Don't waste your tears, Robin," said grandmother, turning scornfully from Jane. "It's the Stuart coming out in her . . . you could expect nothing else. If she prefers her trumpery friends down there to you, there is nothing you can do about it. *I* have said all I intend to say on the matter."

Mother stood up and dabbed her tears away with a cobwebby handkerchief.

"Very well, dear," she said brightly and hardly. "You have made your choice. I agree with your grandmother that there is nothing more to be said."

She went out, leaving Jane with a heart that was almost breaking. Never in her life had mother spoken to her in that hard, brittle tone. She felt as if she had been suddenly pushed far, far away from her. But she did not regret her choice. She had no choice really. She had to go back to dad. If it came to choosing between him and mother . . . Jane rushed to her room, flung herself down on the big white bearskin, and writhed in a tearless agony no child should ever have to suffer.

It was a week before Jane was herself again, although mother, after that bitter little outburst, had been as sweet and loving as ever. When she had come in to say good night she had held Jane very tightly and silently.

Jane hugged her mother closer to her.

"I have to go, mother . . . I have to go . . . but I *do* love you. . . ."

"Oh, Jane, I hope you do . . . but sometimes you seem so far away from me that you might as well be beyond Sirius. Don't . . . don't let any one ever come between us. That is all I ask."

"No one can . . . no one wants to, mother."

In one way, it occurred to Jane, that was not strictly true. She had known for a long while that grandmother would like very well to come between them if she could only bring it about. But Jane also knew that by "no one" mother meant dad, and so her answer was true.

There was a letter from Polly Garland the last day of April . . . a jubilant Polly.

"We're all so glad you're coming back this summer, Jane. Oh, Jane, I wish you could see the pussy-willows in our swamp."

Jane wished so, too. And there were other fascinating bits of news in Polly's letter. Min's ma's cow was worn out and Min's ma was going to get a new one. Polly had a hen setting on nine eggs . . . Jane could see nine real live wee baby chicks running round. Well, father had promised her some hens this summer . . . Step-a-yard had told Polly to tell her it was a great spring and even the roosters were laying; the baby had been christened William Charles and was toddling round everywhere and getting thin; Big Donald's dog had been poisoned, had had six convulsions, but had recovered.

"Only six more weeks." It was weeks now where it had been months. Down home the robins would be strutting round Lantern Hill and the mists would be coming in from the sea. Jane ticked off April.

33

It was the last week in May that Jane saw the house. Mother had gone one evening to visit a friend who had just moved into a new house in the new Lakeside development on the banks of the Humber. She took Jane with her and it was a revelation to Jane whose only goings and comings had been so circumscribed that she had never dreamed there were such lovely places in Toronto. Why, it was just like a pretty country village out here . . . hills and ravines with ferns and wild columbines growing in them and rivers and trees . . . the green fire of willows, the great clouds of oaks, the plumes of pines and, not far away, the blue mist that was Lake Ontario.

Mrs Townley lived on a street called Lakeside Gardens, and she showed them proudly over her new house. It was so big and splendid that Jane did not feel very much interested in it and after a while she slipped away in the dusk to explore the street itself, leaving mother and Mrs Townley talking cupboards and bathrooms.

Jane decided that she liked Lakeside Gardens. She liked it because it twisted and curved. It was a friendly street. The houses did not look at each other with their noses in the air. Even the big ones were not snooty. They sat among their gardens, with spireas afoam around them and tulips and daffodils all about their toes, and said, "We have lots of room . . . we don't have to push with our elbows . . . we can afford to be gracious."

Jane looked them over carefully as she went by but it was not until she was nearly at the end of the street, where it turned into a road winding down to the lake, that she saw *her* house. She had liked a great many of the houses she had passed but when she saw this house she knew at first sight that it belonged to her . . . just as

Lantern Hill did.

It was a small house for Lakeside Gardens but a great deal bigger than Lantern Hill. It was built of grey stone and had casement windows . . . some of them beautifully unexpected . . . and a roof of shingles stained a very dark brown. It was built right on the edge of the ravine overlooking the tree-tops, with five great pines just behind it.

"What a darling place!" breathed Jane.

It was a new house: it had just been built and there was a For Sale sign on the lawn. Jane went all around it and peered through every diamond-paned window. There was a living-room that would really *live* when it was furnished, a dining-room with a door that opened into a sun-room and the most delightful breakfast nook in pale yellow, with built-in china-closets. It should have chairs and table of yellow, too, and curtains at the recessed window between gold and green that would look like sunshine on the darkest day. Yes, this house belonged to her . . . she could see herself in it, hanging curtains, polishing the glass doors, making cookies in the kitchen. She hated the For Sale sign. To think that somebody would be buying that house . . . *her* house . . . was torture.

She prowled round and round it. At the back the ground was terraced right down to the floor of the ravine. There was a rock garden and a group of forsythia bushes that must have been fountains of pale gold in early spring. Three flights of stone steps went down the terraces, with the delicacy of birch shadows about them, and off to one side was a wild garden of slender young Lombardies. A robin winked at her; a nice chubby cat came over from the neighbouring rock garden. Jane tried to catch him, but . . . "Excuse me. This is my busy day," said the cat and pattered down the stone steps.

Jane finally sat down on the front steps and gave herself up to a secret joy. There was a gap in the trees on the opposite side of the street through which a far, purple-grey hill showed. There were misty, pale green woods over the river. The woods all around

Lantern Hill would be misty green, too. The banners of a city of night were being flaunted in the sunset sky behind the pines farther down. The gulls soared whitely up the river.

It grew darker. Lights bloomed out in the houses. Jane always felt the fascination of lighted houses in the night. There should be a light in the house behind her. She should be turning on the lights in it. She should be living here. She could be happy here. She could be friends with the wind and the rain here: she could love the lake even if it did not have the sparkle and boom of gulf seas; she could put out nuts for the saucy squirrels and hang up bird-houses for the feathered folk and feed the pheasants Mrs Townley said lived in the ravine.

Suddenly there was a slim, golden new moon over the oaks and the world was still . . . almost as still as Queen's Shore on a calm summer night and there was a sparkling of lights along the lake drive like a necklace of gems on some dark beauty's breast.

"Where were you all the evening, darling?" asked mother as they drove home.

"Picking out a house to buy," said Jane dreamily. "I wish we lived here instead of at 60 Gay, mummy."

Mother was silent for a moment.

"You don't like 60 Gay very well, do you, dearest?"

"No," said Jane. And then, to her own amazement, added, "Do you?"

She was still more amazed when mother said, quickly and vehemently, "I hate it!"

That night Jane ticked off May. Only ten days more. It was days now where it had been weeks. Oh, suppose she took ill and couldn't go! But no! God wouldn't . . . couldn't.

34

Grandmother coldly told mother to buy what clothes . . . *if any* . . . were necessary for Jane. Jane and mother had a happy afternoon's shopping. Jane picked her own things . . . things that would suit Lantern Hill and an Island summer. Mother insisted on some smart little knitted sweaters and one pretty dress of rose-pink organdie with delicious frills. Jane didn't know where she would ever wear it . . . it was too ornate for the little south church but she let mother buy it to please her. And mother got her the niftiest little green bathing-suit.

"Just think," reflected Jane happily, "in a week I'll be on Queen's Shore. I hope the water won't be too cold for swimming. . . ."

"We may be going to the Island in August," said Phyllis. "Dad says he hasn't been down for so long he'd like to spend another vacation there. If we do, we'll be stopping at the Harbour Head Hotel and it isn't very far from there to Queen's Shore. So we'll likely see you."

Jane didn't know whether she liked this idea or not. She didn't want Phyllis there, patronizing the Island . . . looking down her nose at Lantern Hill and the boot-shelf and the Snowbeams.

Jane went to the Maritimes with the Randolphs this year and they left on the morning train instead of the night. It was a dull, cloudy day but Jane was so happy she positively radiated happiness around her like sunshine. Mrs Randolph's opinion of Jane was the very opposite of what Mrs Stanley's had been. Mrs Randolph thought she had never met a more charming child, interested in everything, finding beauty everywhere, even in those interminable stretches of pulpwood lands and lumber forests in New Brunswick. Jane studied the time-table and hailed each station as a friend, especially the ones with quaint, delightful

names . . . Red Pine, Bartibog, Memramcook. And then Sackville
where they left the main line and got on the little branch train to
Cape Tormentine. How sorry Jane felt for any one who was not
going to the Island!

Cape Tormentine . . . the car ferry . . . watching for the red
cliffs of the Island . . . there they were . . . she had really forgotten
how red they were . . . and beyond them misty green hills. It was
raining again, but who cared? Everything the Island did was
right. If it wanted to rain . . . why, rain was Jane's choice.

Having left Toronto on the morning train, they were in
Charlottetown by mid-afternoon. Jane saw dad the moment she
stepped off the train . . . grinning and saying, "Excuse me, but
your face seems familiar. Are you by any chance . . ." but Jane had
hurled herself at him. They had never been parted . . . she had
never been away at all. The world was real again. She was Jane
again. Oh, dad, dad!

She had been afraid Aunt Irene would be there, too . . . possibly
Miss Lilian Morrow as well. But Aunt Irene, it transpired, was
away on a visit to Boston and had taken Miss Morrow with her.
Jane secretly hoped that Aunt Irene would be having such a fine
time in Boston that she wouldn't be able to tear herself away for
a long time.

"And the car has turned temperamental again," said dad. "I
had to leave it in the garage at the Corners and borrow Step-a-
yard's horse and buggy. You don't mind?"

Mind? Jane was delighted. She wanted that drive to Lantern
Hill to be so slow that she could drink the road in as she drove
along. And she liked to be behind a horse. You could talk to a
horse as you never could to a car. The fact was, if dad had said
they had to walk to Lantern Hill it wouldn't have mattered to
Jane.

Dad put lean strong hands under her arms and swung her up
to the buggy seat.

"Let's just go on from where we left off. You've grown since last
summer, my Jane."

"An inch," said Jane proudly.

It had stopped raining. The sun was coming out. Beyond, the white wave crests on the harbour were laughing at her . . . waving their hands at her.

"Let's go uptown and buy our house some presents. Jane."

"A double boiler that won't leak, dad. Booties always did, a little. And a potato-ricer . . . can we get a potato-ricer, dad?"

Dad thought the budget would stretch to a potato-ricer.

It was delightful, all of it. But Jane sparkled when they had left town behind them, going home to all the things they loved.

"Drive slow, dad. I don't want to miss *anything* on the road."

She was feasting her eyes on everything . . . spruce-clad hills, bits of gardens full of unsung beauty tucked away here and there, glimpses of sparkling sea, blue rivers . . . had those rivers really been so blue last summer? It had been an early spring and all the blossom show was over. Jane was sorry for that. She wondered if she would ever be able to get to the Island in time to see the Titus ladies' famous cherry walk in its spring-blow.

They called for a moment to see Mrs Meade, who kissed Jane and was sorry Mr Meade couldn't come out to see her, because he was in bed with an abyss in his ear. She gave them a packet of ham sandwiches and cheese to stay their stomachs if they were hungry on the road.

They heard the ocean before they saw it. Jane loved the sound. It was as if the spirit of the sea called to her. And then the first snuff of salt in the air . . . there was one particular hill where they always got the first tang. And from that same hill they caught their first far-away glimpse of Lantern Hill. It was wonderful to be able to see your own home so far off . . . to feel that every step the horse took was bringing you nearer to it.

From there on Jane was on her own stamping ground. It was so exciting to recognize all the spots along the road . . . green wood lanes, old beloved farms that held out their arms to her. The single row of spruces was still marching up Little Donald's hill. The dunes . . . and the fishing boats sailing in . . . and the little blue pond laughing at her . . . and Lantern Hill. Home after exile!

Somebody . . . Jane discovered later that it was the Snowbeams .
. . had made "Welcome" with white stones in the walk. Happy was
waiting for them in the yard and nearly ate Jane alive. Bubbles,
the new fat white dog, sat apart and looked at her, but he was so
cute that Jane forgave him on the spot for being Bubbles.

The first thing was to visit every room and every room
welcomed her back. Nothing was changed. She looked the house
over to make sure nothing was missing. The little bronze soldier
was still riding on his bronze horse and the green cat kept watch
and ward over dad's desk. But the silver needed polishing and the
geraniums needed pruning and when had the kitchen floor been
scrubbed?

She had been away from Lantern Hill for nine months, but
now it seemed to her that she had never been away at all. She had
really been living here all along. It was her spirit's home.

There was a bunch of little surprises . . . nice surprises. They
had six hens . . . there was a small henhouse built below the garden
. . . there was a peaked porch roof built over the glass-paned door
. . . and dad had got the telephone in.

First Peter was sitting on the doorstone when Jane came
downstairs, with a big mouse in his mouth, very proud of his
prowess as a hunter. Jane pounced on him, mouse and all, and
then looked around for Second Peter. Where was Second Peter?

Dad put his arm closely around Jane.

"Second Peter died last week, Jane. I don't know what happened
to him . . . he got sick. I had the vet for him but he could do
nothing."

Jane felt a stinging in her eyes. She would not cry but she
choked.

"I . . . I . . . didn't think anything I loved could die," she
whispered into dad's shoulder.

"Ah, Jane, love can't fence out death. He had a happy life if a
short one . . . and we buried him in the garden. Come out and see
the garden, Jane . . . it burst into bloom as soon as it heard you

were coming."

A wind ran through the garden as they entered it and it looked as if every flower and shrub were nodding a head or waving a hand at them. Dad had a corner where vegetables were all up in neat little rows and there were new beds of annuals.

"Miranda got what you wanted from the seedsman . . . I think you'll find everything, even the scabious. What do you want with scabious, Jane? It's an abominable name . . . sounds like a disease."

"Oh, the flowers are pretty, dad. And there are so many nicer names for them. . . . Lady's pincushion and Mourning Bride. Aren't the pansies lovely? I'm so glad I sowed them last August."

"You look like a pansy yourself, Jane . . . that red-brown one there with the golden eyes."

Jane remembered she had wondered if any one would ever compare her to a flower. In spite of the little pile of shore stones under the lilac . . . which Young John had piled over the grave of Second Peter . . . she was happy. Everything was so lovely. Even Mrs Big Donald's washing, streaming gallantly out against the blue sky on her hill-top, was charming. And away down by the Watch Tower the surf was breaking on the sand. Jane wanted to be out in that turmoil and smother of the waves. But that must wait till morning. Just now there was supper to be gotten.

"How jolly to be in a kitchen again," thought Jane, girding on an apron.

"I'm glad my cook is back," said dad. "I've practically lived on salt codfish all winter. It was the easiest thing to cook. But I don't deny the neighbours helped the commissariat out. And they've sent in no end of things for our supper."

Jane had found the pantry full of them. A cold chicken from the Jimmy Johns, a pat of butter from Mrs Big Donald, a jug of cream from Mrs Little Donald, some cheese from Mrs Snowbeam, some rose-red early radishes from Min's ma, a pie from Mrs Bell.

"She said she knew you could make as good pies as she can but she thought it would fill in till you'd have time to make some. There's a goodish bit of jam left yet and practically all the pickles."

Jane and dad talked as they ate supper. They had a whole winter of talk to catch up with. Had he missed her? Well, had he now? What did she think? They regarded each other with great content. Jane saw the new moon, over her right shoulder, through the open door. And dad got up and started the ship's clock. Time had begun once more.

Jane's friends, having considerately let her have her first rapture over, came to see her in the evening . . . the brown, rosy Jimmy Johns and the Snowbeams and Min and Ding-dong. They were all glad to see her. Queen's Shore had kept her in its heart. It was wonderful to be *somebody* again . . . wonderful to be able to laugh all you wanted to without any one resenting it . . . wonderful to be among happy people again. All at once Jane realized that nobody was happy at 60 Gay . . . except, perhaps, Mary and Frank. Grandmother wasn't . . . Aunt Gertrude wasn't . . . mother wasn't.

Step-a-yard whispered to her that he had brought over a wheelbarrow-load of sheep manure for her garden. "You'll find it by the gate . . . nothing like well-rotted sheep manure for a garden." Ding-dong had brought her a kitten to replace Second Peter . . . a scrap about as big as its mother's paw but which was destined to be a magnificent cat in black with four white paws. Jane and dad tried out all kinds of names on it before they went to bed and finally agreed on Silver Penny because of the round white spot between its ears.

To go to her own dear room where a young birch was fairly poking an arm in through the window from the steep hill-side . . . to hear the sound of the sea in the night . . . to waken in the morning and think she would be with dad all day! Jane sang the song of the morning stars as she dressed and got breakfast.

The first thing Jane did after breakfast was to run with the wind to the shore and take a wild exultant dip in the stormy waves. She fairly flung herself into the arms of the sea.

And what a forenoon it was, polishing silver and window-panes. Nothing had changed really, though there were surface changes. Step-a-yard had grown a beard because of throat trouble . . . Big Donald had repainted his house . . . the calves of last summer had grown up . . . Little Donald was letting his hill pasture go spruce. It was good to be home.

"Timothy Salt is going to take me codfishing next Saturday, dad."

35

Uncle David and Aunt Sylvia and Phyllis came in July to the Harbour Head Hotel but could stay only a week. They brought Phyllis over to Lantern Hill late one afternoon and left her there while they went to visit friends in town.

"We'll come back for her around nine," said Aunt Sylvia, looking in horror at Jane who had just got back from Queen's Creek where she had been writing a love letter for Joe Gautier to his lady friend in Boston. Evidently there was nothing Jane was afraid to tackle. She was still wearing the khaki overalls she had worn while driving loads of hay into the Jimmy John barn all the forenoon. The overalls were old and faded and were not improved by a huge splash of green paint on a certain portion of Jane's anatomy. Jane had painted the old garden seat green one day and sat down on it before it was dry.

Dad was away so there was nothing to take the edge off Phyllis who was more patronizing than ever.

"Your garden is *quite* nice," she said.

Jane made a sound remarkably like a snort. Quite nice! When everybody admitted that it was the prettiest garden in the Queen's Shore district, except the Titus ladies'. Couldn't Phyllis see the wonder of those gorgeous splashes of nasturtiums, than which there was nothing finer in the county? Didn't she realize that those tiny red beets and cunning gold carrots were two weeks ahead of anybody else's for miles around? Could she possibly be in ignorance of the fact that Jane's pink peonies, fertilized so richly by Step-a-yard's sheep manure, were the talk of the community? But Jane was a bit ruffled that day anyhow. Aunt Irene and Miss Morrow had been up the day before, having returned from Boston, and Aunt Irene as usual had been sweet and condescending and as usual had rubbed Jane the wrong way.

"I'm so glad your father put the telephone in for you . . . I hoped he would after the little hint I gave him."

"I never wanted a telephone," said Jane, rather sulkily.

"Oh, but, darling, you should have one, when you're so much alone here. If anything happened . . ."

"What could happen here, Aunt Irene?"

"The house might take fire. . . ."

"It took fire last year and I put it out."

"Or you might take cramps in swimming. I've never thought it . . ."

"But if I did I could hardly phone from there," said Jane.

"Or if tramps came . . ."

"There's been only one tramp here this summer and Happy bit a piece out of his leg. I was very sorry for the poor man. . . . I put iodine on the bite and gave him his dinner."

"Darling, you *will* have the last word, won't you? So like your Grandmother Kennedy."

Jane didn't like to be told she was like her Grandmother Kennedy. Still less did she like the fact that after supper dad and Miss Morrow had gone off by themselves for a walk to the shore. Aunt Irene looked after them speculatively.

"They have so much in common . . . it is a pity . . ."

Jane wouldn't ask what was a pity. But she lay awake for a long time that night and had not quite recovered her poise when Phyllis came, condescending to her garden. But a hostess has certain obligations and Jane was not going to let Lantern Hill down, even if she did make sundry faces at her pots and pans. The supper she got up for Phyllis made that damsel open her eyes.

"Victoria . . . you didn't cook all these things yourself!"

"Of course. It's easy as wink."

Some of the Jimmy Johns and Snowbeams turned up after supper and Phyllis, whose complacency had been somewhat jarred by that supper, was really quite decent to them. They all went to the shore for a dip but Phyllis was scared of the tumbling waves and would only sit on the sand and let them break over her while the others frolicked like mermaids.

"I didn't know you could swim like that, Victoria."

"You ought to see me when the water is calm," said Jane.

Still, Jane was rather relieved when it was time for Uncle David and Aunt Sylvia to come for Phyllis. Then the telephone rang and Uncle David was calling from town to say they were delayed by car trouble and wouldn't likely be able to come till late, so could the Lantern Hill folks see that Phyllis got to the hotel? Oh, yes, yes, indeed, Jane assured them.

"Dad can't be back till midnight so we'll have to walk," she told Phyllis. "I'll go with you. . . ."

"But it's four miles to the Harbour Head," gasped Phyllis.

"Only two by the short cut across the fields. I know it well."

"But it's dark."

"Well, you're not afraid of the dark, are you?"

Phyllis did not say whether she was afraid of the dark or not. She looked at Jane's overalls.

"Are you going in *them!*"

"No, I only wear these around home," explained Jane patiently. "I was driving in hay all the forenoon. Mr Jimmy John was away and Punch had a sore foot. I'll change in a jiffy and we'll start."

Jane slipped into a skirt and one of her pretty sweaters and fluffed a comb through her russet hair. People were beginning to look twice at Jane's hair. Phyllis looked more than twice at it. It was really wonderful hair. What had come over Victoria anyhow . . . Victoria whom she used to think so dumb? This tall, arms-and-legs girl, who somehow had ceased to be awkward in spite of arms and legs, was certainly not dumb. Phyllis gave a small sigh; and in that sigh, though neither of them was conscious of it, their former positions were totally reversed. Phyllis, instead of looking down on Jane, looked up to her.

The cool evening air was heavy with dew when they started. The winds were folded among the shadowy glens. The spice ferns were fragrant in the corners of the upland pastures. It was so calm and still you could hear all kinds of far-away sounds . . . a cart rattling down Old Man Cooper's hill . . . muted laughter from Hungry Cove . . . an owl on Big Donald's hill calling to an owl on Little Donald's hill. But it got darker and darker. Phyllis drew close to Jane.

"Oh, Victoria, isn't this the darkest night that ever was!"

"Not so very. I've been out when it was darker."

Jane was not in the least scared, and Phyllis was much impressed. Jane felt that she was impressed . . . Jane knew she was scared . . . Jane began to like Phyllis.

They had to climb a fence and Phyllis fell over it, tore her dress and skinned her knee. So Phyllis couldn't even climb a fence, thought Jane . . . but thought it kindly, protectively.

"Oh, what's that?" Phyllis clutched Jane.

"That? Only cows."

"Oh, Victoria, I'm so scared of cows. I can't pass them . . . I can't . . . suppose they think . . ."

"Who cares what a cow thinks?" said Jane superbly. She had forgotten that she had once been fussy about cows and their opinion of her.

And Phyllis was crying. From that moment Jane lost every shred of her dislike of Phyllis. Phyllis, patronizing and perfect in Toronto, was very different from a terrified Phyllis in a back pasture on an Island hill.

Jane put her arm around her. "Come on, honey. The cows won't even look at you. Little Donald's cows are all friends of mine. And then it's just a walk through that bit of woods and we'll be at the hotel."

"Will you . . . walk between me . . . and the cows?" sobbed Phyllis.

Phyllis, holding tightly to Jane, was safely convoyed past the cows. The little wood lane that followed was terribly dark but it was short, and at its end were the lights of the hotel.

"You're all right now. I won't go in," said Jane. "I must hurry home to get some supper ready for father. I always like to be there when he comes home."

"Victoria! Are you going back *alone?*"

"Of course. How else would I go?"

"If you'd wait . . . father would drive you home when he comes.
. . ."

Jane laughed.

"I'll be at Lantern Hill in half an hour. And I love walking."

"Victoria, you're the very bravest girl I ever saw in my life," said Phyllis earnestly. There wasn't a trace of patronage in her tone. There was never to be again.

Jane had a good time with herself on the walk back. The dear night brooded over her. Little wings were folded in nest homes, but there was wild life astir. She heard the distant bark of a fox . . . the sound of tiny feet in the fern . . . she saw the pale glimmer of night moths and took friendly counsel with the stars. Almost they sang, as if one star called to another in infinite harmony. Jane knew them all. Dad had given her lessons in astronomy all summer, having discovered that the only constellation she knew was the Big Dipper.

"This won't do, my Jane. You must know the stars. Not that I blame you for not being well acquainted with them. Humanity in its great lighted cities is shut out from the stars. And even the country folk are too used to them to realize their wonder. Emerson says something somewhere about how marvellous a spectacle we should deem them if we saw them only once in a thousand years."

So, with dad's field-glasses, they went star hunting on moonless nights and Jane became learned in lore of far-off suns.

"What star shall we visit to-night, Janelet? Antares . . . Fomalhaut . . . Sirius?"

Jane loved it. It was so wonderful to sit out on the hills with dad in the dark and the beautiful aloneness while the great worlds swung above them in their appointed courses. Polaris, Arcturus, Vega, Capella, Altair . . . she knew them all. She knew where to look for Cassiopeia enthroned on her jewelled chair, for the Milk

Dipper upside down in the clear south-west, for the great Eagle flying endlessly across the Milky Way, for the golden sickle that reaped some harvest of heaven.

"Watch the stars whenever you are worried, Jane," said dad. "They'll steady you . . . comfort you . . . balance you. I think if I had watched them . . . years ago . . . but I learned their lesson too late."

36

"Aunt Elmira is dying again," said Ding-dong cheerfully.

Jane was helping Ding-dong shingle his father's small barn. Doing it very well, too, and getting no end of a kick out of it. It was such fun to be away up in the air where you could see over the whole countryside under its gay and windy clouds, and keep easy tabs on what your neighbours were doing.

"Is she very bad this time?" asked Jane, hammering diligently.

Jane knew all about Aunt Elmira and her dying spells. She took one every once in so long and it had really become a nuisance. Aunt Elmira picked such inconvenient times for dying. Always when something special was in the offing Aunt Elmira decided to die and sometimes seemed so narrowly to escape doing it that the Bells held their breaths. Because Aunt Elmira did really have a heart condition that was not to be depended on, and who knew but that sometime she really would die?

"And the Bells don't want her to die," Step-a-yard had told Jane. "They need her board . . . her annuity dies with her. Besides, she's handy to look after things when the Bells want to go gadding. And I won't say but they're real fond of her, too. Elmira is a good old scout when she isn't dying."

Jane knew that. She and Aunt Elmira were excellent friends. But Jane had never seen her when she was dying. She was too weak to see people then, she averred, and the Bells were afraid to risk it. Jane, with her usual shattering insight, had her own opinion about these spells of Aunt Elmira's. She could not have expressed it in terms of psychology, but she once told dad that Aunt Elmira was just trying to get square with something and didn't know it. She felt rather than knew that Aunt Elmira liked pretty well to be in the limelight and, as she grew older, resented more and more the fact that she was gently but inexorably being elbowed out of it. Near dying was one way of regaining the centre of the stage for a time at least. Not that Aunt Elmira was a conscious pretender. She always honestly thought she was dying, and very melancholy she was about it. Aunt Elmira was not at all willing to give up the fascinating business of living.

"Awful," said Ding-dong. "Mother says she's worse than she's ever seen her. Dr Abbott says she's lost the will to live. Do you know what that means?"

"Sort of," admitted Jane cautiously.

"We try to keep her cheered up but she's awful blue. She won't eat and she doesn't want to take her medicine and ma's at her wit's end. We had everything planned for Brenda's wedding and now we don't know what to do."

"She hasn't died so often before," comforted Jane.

"But she's stayed in bed for weeks and weeks and said every day would be her last. Aunt Elmira," said Ding-dong reflectively, "has bid me a last good-bye seven times. Now, how can folks have a big wedding if their aunt is dying? And Brenda wants a splash. She's marrying into the Keyes and she says the Keyes expect it."

Mrs Bell asked Jane to have dinner with them, and Jane stayed because dad was away for the day. She watched Brenda arrange a tray for Aunt Elmira.

"I'm afraid she won't eat a bite of it," said Mrs Bell anxiously. She was a tired looking, pleasant-faced woman with kind, faded eyes, who worried a great deal over everything. "I don't know what she lives on. And she's so low in her spirits. That goes with the attacks, of course. She says she's too tired to make any effort to get better, poor thing. It's her heart, you know. We all try to keep her cheered up and never tell her anything to worry her. Brenda, mind you don't tell her the white cow choked to death this morning. And if she asks what the doctor said last night, tell her he thinks she's going to be all right soon. My father always said we should never tell sick people anything but the truth, but we must keep Aunt Elmira cheered up."

Jane did not join Ding-dong as soon as dinner was over. She hung about mysteriously till Brenda had come downstairs, reporting that Aunt Elmira couldn't touch a mouthful, and had taken her mother out to settle some question about the amount of wool to be sent to the carding mill. Then Jane sped upstairs.

Aunt Elmira was lying in bed, a tiny, shrunken creature with elf-locks of grey hair straggling about her wrinkled face. Her tray was on the table, untouched.

"If it isn't Jane Stuart!" said Aunt Elmira in a faint voice. "I'm glad someone hasn't forgotten me. So you've come to see the last of me, Jane?"

Jane did not contradict her. She sat down on a chair and looked very sadly at Aunt Elmira, who waved a claw-like hand at her tray.

"I haven't a speck of appetite, Jane. And it's just as well . . . ah me, it's just as well. I feel they begrudge me every bite I eat."

"Well," said Jane, "you know times are hard and prices low."

Aunt Elmira hadn't quite expected this. A spark came into her queer little amber eyes.

"I'm paying my board," she said, "and I earned my keep years before I started doing that. Ah well, I'm of no consequence to them now, Jane. We're not, after we get ill."

"No, I suppose not," agreed Jane.

"Oh, I know too well I'm a burden to every one. But it won't be for long, Jane, it won't be for long. The hand of death is on me, Jane. I realize that if nobody else does."

"Oh, I think they do," said Jane. "They're in a hurry to get the barn shingled before the funeral."

The spark in Aunt Elmira's eyes deepened.

"I s'pose they've got it all planned out, have they?" she said.

"Well, I did hear Mr Bell saying something about where he would dig the grave. But maybe he meant the white cow's. I think it was the cow's. It choked to death this morning, you know. And he said he must have the south gate painted white before . . . something . . . but I didn't just catch what."

"White? The idea! That gate has always been red. Well, why

502

should I worry? I'm done with it all. You don't worry over things when you're listening for the footfalls of death, Jane. Shingling the barn, are they? I thought I heard hammering. That barn didn't need shingling. But Silas was always extravagant when there's no one to check him up."

"It's only the shingles that cost. The work won't cost anything. Ding-dong and I are doing it."

"I s'pose that's why you've got your overalls on. Time was I couldn't abide a girl in overalls. But what does it matter now? Only you shouldn't go barefoot, Jane. You might get a rusty nail in your foot."

"It's easier getting round the roof with no shoes. And little Sid got a rusty nail in his foot yesterday although he had shoes on."

"They never told me! I daresay they'll let that child have blood-poisoning when I'm not round to look after him. He's my favourite, too. Ah well, it won't be long now . . . they know where I want to be buried . . . but they might have waited till I was dead to talk of grave-digging."

"Oh, I'm sure it was the cow," said Jane. "And I'm sure they'll give you a lovely funeral. I think dad would write a beautiful obituary for you if I asked him."

"Oh, all right, all right. That's enough about it anyway. I don't want to be buried till I *am* dead. Did they give you a decent bite of dinner? Nettie is kind-hearted but she ain't the best cook in the world. I was a good cook. Ah, the meals I've cooked in my time, Jane . . . the meals I've cooked!"

Jane missed an excellent opportunity to assure Aunt Elmira she would cook many more meals.

"The dinner was very nice, Aunt Elmira, and we had such fun at it. Ding-dong kept making speeches and we laughed and laughed."

"They can laugh and me dying!" said Aunt Elmira bitterly. "And pussy-footing round in here with faces as long as to-day and to-morrow, pretending to be sorry. What was them dragging noises I've been hearing all the forenoon?"

"Mrs Bell and Brenda were rearranging the furniture in the parlour. I expect they are getting it ready for the wedding."

"Wedding? Did you say wedding? Whose wedding?"

"Why, Brenda's. She's going to marry Jim Keyes. I thought you knew."

"'Course I knew they were going to be married sometime . . . but not with me dying. Do you mean to tell me they're going ahead with it right off?"

"Well, you know it's so unlucky to put a wedding off. It needn't disturb you at all, Aunt Elmira. You're up here in the ell all by yourself and . . ."

Aunt Elmira sat up in bed.

"You hand me my teeth," she ordered. "They're over there on the bureau. I'm going to eat my dinner and then I'm going to get up if it kills me. They needn't think they're going to sneak a wedding off me. I don't care what the doctor says. I've never believed I was half as sick as he made out I was anyhow. Half the valuable stock on the place dying and children having blood-poisoning and red gates being painted white! It's time somebody showed them!"

37

Hitherto Jane's career at Lantern Hill had been quite unspectacular. Even when she was seen barefooted, nailing shingles on a barn roof, it made only a local sensation, and nobody but Mrs Solomon Snowbeam said much about it. Mrs Snowbeam was shocked. There was nothing, she said again, that child would stick at.

And then, all at once, Jane made the headlines. The Charlottetown papers gave her the front page for two days, and even the Toronto dailies gave her a column, with a picture of Jane and the lion . . . some lion . . . thrown in. The sensation at 60 Gay must be imagined. Grandmother was very bitter . . . "just like a circus girl" . . . and said it was exactly what might have been expected. Mother thought, but did not say, that no one could really have expected to hear of Jane ambling about P. E. Island leading lions by the mane.

There had been rumours about the lion for a couple of days. A small circus had come to Charlottetown and a whisper got about that their lion had escaped. Certainly people who went to the circus saw no lion. There was a good deal of excitement. Once a monkey had escaped from a circus, but what was that to a lion? It did not seem certain that any one had actually seen the lion, but several were reported to have seen him . . . here, there and the other place, miles apart. Calves and young pigs were said to have disappeared. There was even a yarn that a short-sighted old lady in the Royalty had patted him on the head and said, "Nice dogglums." But that was never substantiated. The Royalty people indignantly denied that there were any lions at loose ends. Such yarns were bad for tourist traffic.

"I've no chance of seeing it," said Mrs Louisa Lyons mournfully.

"That's what comes of being bed-rid. You miss everything."

Mrs Louisa had been an invalid for three years and was reputed not to have put a foot under her without assistance in all that time, but it was not thought she missed much of what went on at the Corners and Queen's Shore and Harbour Head for all that.

"I don't believe there is any lion," said Jane, who had been shopping at the Corners and had dropped in to see Mrs Lyons. Mrs Lyons was very fond of Jane and had only one grudge against her. She could never pick anything out of her about her father and mother and Lilian Morrow. And not for any lack of trying.

"Closer than a clam, that girl is when she wants to be," complained Mrs Louisa.

"Then how did such a yarn start?" she demanded of Jane.

"Most people think the circus people never had a lion . . . or it died . . . and they want to cover it up because the people who came to see a lion would be disappointed and mad."

"But they've offered a reward for it."

"They've only offered twenty-five dollars. If they had really lost a lion, they'd offer more than that."

"But it's been *seen*."

"I think folks just imagined they saw it," said Jane.

"And I can't even imagine it," groaned Mrs Louisa. "And it's no use to *pretend* I imagined it. Every one knows a lion wouldn't come upstairs to my room. If I could see it, I'd likely have my name in the paper. Martha Tolling has had her name in the paper twice this year. Some people have all the luck."

"Martha Tolling's sister died in Summerside last week."

"What did I tell you?" said Mrs Louisa in an aggrieved tone. "Now she'll be wearing mourning. I never have a chanct to wear mourning. Nobody has died in our family for years. And black always did become me. Ah well, Jane, you have to take what you get in this world and that's what I've always said. Thank you for dropping in. I've always said to Mattie, 'There's something about Jane Stuart I like, say what you will. If her father is queer, it isn't her fault.' Mind that turn of the stairs, Jane. I haven't been down it for over a year but someone is going to break her neck there sometime."

It happened the next day . . . a golden August afternoon when Jane and Polly and Shingle and Caraway and Punch and Min and Ding-dong and Penny and Young John had gone in a body to pick blueberries in the barrens at Harbour Head and were returning by a short cut across the back pastures of the Corners farms. In a little wood glen, full of golden-rod, where Martin Robbin's old hay-barn stood, they met the lion face to face.

He was standing right before them among the golden-rod, in the shadows of the spruces. For one moment they all stood frozen in their tracks. Then, with a simultaneous yell of terror . . . Jane yelled with the best of them . . . they dropped their pails, bolted through the golden-rod and into the barn. The lion ambled after them. More yells. No time to close the ramshackle old door. They flew up a wobbly ladder which collapsed and fell as Young John scrambled to safety beside the others on the crossbeam, too much out of breath to yell again.

The lion came to the door, stood there a minute in the sunshine, slowly switching his tail back and forth. Jane, recovering her poise, noticed that he was somewhat mangy and lank, but he was imposing enough in the narrow doorway and nobody could reasonably deny that he was a lion.

"He's coming in," groaned Ding-dong.

"Can lions climb?" gasped Shingle.

"I . . . I . . . don't think so," said Polly, through her chattering teeth.

"Cats can . . . and lions are just big cats," said Punch.

"Oh, don't talk," whispered Min. "It may excite him. Perhaps if we keep perfectly quiet he will go away."

The lion did not seem to have any intention of going away. He came in, looked about him and lay down in a patch of sunshine with the air of a lion who had any amount of spare time.

"He don't seem cross," muttered Ding-dong.

"Maybe he isn't hungry," said Young John.

"Don't excite him," implored Min.

"He isn't paying any attention to us," said Jane. "We needn't have run. . . . I don't believe he'd have hurt us."

"You run as fast as us," said Penny Snowbeam. "I'll bet you was as scared as any of us."

"Of course I was. It was all so sudden. Young John, stop shaking like that. You'll fall off the beam."

"I'm . . . I'm . . . scared," blubbered Young John shamelessly.

"You laughed at me last night and said I'd be scared to pass a patch of cabbages," said Caraway venomously. "Now look at yourself."

"None of your lip. A lion isn't a cabbage," whimpered Young John.

"Oh, you *will* excite him," wailed Min in despair.

The lion suddenly yawned. Why, thought Jane, he looks exactly like that jolly old lion in the movie news. Jane shut her eyes.

"Is she praying?" whispered Ding-dong.

Jane was thinking. It was absolutely necessary for her to get home soon if she were going to have dad's favourite scalloped potatoes for his supper. Young John was looking absolutely green. Suppose he got sick? She believed the lion was only a tired, harmless old animal. The circus people had said he was gentle as a lamb. Jane opened her eyes.

"I am going down to take that lion up to the Corners and shut him up in George Tanner's empty barn," she said. "That is, unless you'll all come down with me and slip out and shut him up here."

"Oh, Jane . . . you wouldn't . . . you couldn't . . ."

The lion gave a rap or two on the floor with his tail. . . . The protests died away in strangled yelps.

"I'm going," said Jane. "I tell you, he's tame as tame. But you stay here quietly till I get him well away. And don't yell, any of you."

With bulging eyes and bated breath the whole gang watched Jane slide along the beam to the wall where she climbed nimbly down to the floor. She marched up to the lion and said, "Come."

The lion came.

Five minutes later Jake MacLean looked out of the door of his blacksmith shop and saw Jane Stuart go past leading a lion by the mane . . . "within spitting distance," as he solemnly averred later. When Jane and the lion—who seemed to be getting on very well with each other—had disappeared around the back of the shop, Jake sat down on a block and wiped the perspiration from his brow with a bandanna.

"I know I'm not quite sane by times, but I didn't think I was that far gone," he said.

Julius Evans, looking out of his store-window, didn't believe what he saw either. It couldn't be . . . it simply wasn't happening. He was dreaming . . . or drunk . . . or crazy. Aye, that was it . . . crazy. Hadn't there been a year when his father's cousin was in the asylum? Those things ran in families . . . you couldn't deny it. Anything was easier than to believe that he had seen Jane Stuart go up the side-lane by his store towing a lion.

Mattie Lyons ran up to her mother's room, uttering piteous little gasps and cries.

"What's the matter?" demanded Mrs Louisa. "Screeching like you was demented!"

"Oh, ma, ma, Jane Stuart's bringing a lion here!"

Mrs Louisa got out of bed and got to the window just in time to see the lion's tail disappear with a switch around the back porch.

"I've got to see what she's up to!" Leaving the distracted Mattie wringing her hands by the bed, Mrs Louisa got herself out of the room and down the staircase with its dangerous turn as nimbly as she had ever done in her best days. Mrs Parker Crosby, who lived next door and had a weak heart, nearly died of shock when she saw Mrs Louisa skipping across her back yard.

Mrs Louisa was just in time to see Jane and the lion ambling up Mr Tanner's pasture on their way to the hay-barn. She stood there and watched Jane open the door . . . urge the lion in . . . shut it and bolt it. Then she sat down on the rhubarb patch, and Mattie had to get the neighbours to carry her back to bed.

Jane went into the store on her way back and asked Julius Evans, who was still leaning palely over the collection of fly-spotted jugs on his counter, to call Charlottetown and let the circus people know that their lion was safe in Mr Tanner's barn. She found her dad in the kitchen at Lantern Hill looking rather strange.

"Jane, it's the wreck of a fine man that you see before you," he said hollowly.

"Dad . . . what is the matter?"

"Matter, says she, with not a quiver in her voice. You don't know . . . I hope you never will know . . . what it is like to look casually out of a kitchen window, where you are discussing the shamefully low price of eggs with Mrs Davy Gardiner, and see your daughter . . . your only daughter . . . stepping high, wide and handsome through the landscape with a lion. You think you've suddenly gone mad . . . you wonder what was in that glass of raspberry shrub Mrs Gardiner gave you to drink. Poor Mrs Davy! As she remarked pathetically to me, the sight jarred her slats. She may get over it, Jane, but I fear she will never be the same woman again."

"He was only a tame old lion," said Jane impatiently. "I don't know why people are making such a fuss over it."

"Jane, my adored Jane, for the sake of your poor father's nerves, don't go leading any more lions about the country, tame or otherwise."

"But it's not a thing that's likely to happen again, dad," said Jane reasonably.

"No, that is so," said dad, in apparent great relief. "I perceive that it is not likely to become a habit. Only, Janelet, if you some day take a notion to acquire an ichthyosaurus for a family pet, give me a little warning, Jane. I'm not as young as I used to be."

Jane couldn't understand the sensation the affair made. She hadn't the least notion she was a heroine.

"I was frightened of him at first," she told the Jimmy Johns. "But not after he yawned."

"You'll be too proud to speak to us now, I s'pose," said Caraway

Snowbeam wistfully, when Jane's picture came out in the papers. Jane and the barn and the lion had all been photographed . . . separately. Everybody who had seen them became important. And Mrs Louisa Lyons was a rapturous woman. Her picture was in the paper, too, and also a picture of the rhubarb patch.

"Now I can die happy," she told Jane. "If Mrs Parker Crosby had got her picture in the paper and I hadn't, I couldn't have stood it. I'm sure I don't know what they did put her picture in for. She didn't see you and the lion . . . she only saw me. Well, there are some folks who are never contented unless they're in the limelight."

Jane was to go down in Queen's Shore history as the girl who thought nothing of roaming round the country with a lion or two for company.

"A girl absolutely without fear," said Step-a-yard, bragging everywhere of his acquaintance with her.

"I realized the first time I saw her that she was superior," said Uncle Tombstone. Mrs Snowbeam reminded everybody that she had always said that Jane Stuart was a child who would stick at nothing. When Ding-dong Bell and Punch Garland would be old men, they would be saying to each other, "Remember the time Jane Stuart and us drove that lion into the Tanner barn? Didn't we have a nerve?"

38

A letter from Jody, blotted with tears, gave Jane a bad night in late August. It was to the effect that she was really going to be sent to an orphanage at last.

"Miss West is going to sell her boarding-house in October and retire," wrote Jody. "I've cried and cried, Jane. I hate the idea of going into an orfanage and I'll never see you, Jane, and oh, Jane, it isn't fair. I don't mean Miss West isn't fair but something isn't."

Jane, too, felt that something wasn't being fair. And she felt that 60 Gay without her back yard confabs with Jody would be just a little more intolerable than it ever had been. But that didn't matter as much as poor Jody's unhappiness. Jane thought Jody might really have an easier time in an orphanage than she had as the little unpaid drudge at 58 Gay, but still she didn't like the idea any better than Jody did. She looked so downhearted that Step-a-yard noticed it when he came over with some fresh mackerel for her which he had brought from the harbour.

"Do for your dinner to-morrow, Jane."

"To-morrow is the day for corned beef and cabbage," said Jane in a scandalized voice. "But we'll have them the day after. That's Friday anyhow. Thank you, Step-a-yard."

"Anything troubling you, Miss Lion-tamer?"

Jane opened her heart to him.

"You just don't know what poor Jody's life's been," she concluded.

Step-a-yard nodded.

"Put upon and overworked and knocked about from pillar to post, I reckon. Poor kid."

"And nobody to love her but me. If she goes to an orphanage, I'll never see her."

"Well, now." Step-a-yard scratched his head reflectively. "We must put our heads together, Jane, and see what can be done about it. We must think hard, Jane, we must think hard."

Jane thought hard to no effect but Step-a-yard's meditations were more fruitful.

"I've been thinking," he told Jane next day, "what a pity it is the Titus ladies couldn't adopt Jody. They've been wanting to adopt a child for a year now but they can't agree on what kind of a child they want. Justina wants a girl and Violet wants a boy, though they'd both prefer twins of any sex. But suitable twins looking for parents are kind of scarce, so they've given up that idea. Violet wants a dark complected one with brown eyes and Justina wants a fair one with blue eyes. Violet wants one ten years old and Justina wants one about seven. How old is Jody?"

"Twelve, like me."

Step-a-yard looked gloomy.

"I dunno. That sounds too old for them. But it wouldn't do any harm to put it up to them. You never can tell what them two girls will do."

"I'll see them to-night right after supper," resolved Jane.

She was so excited that she salted the apple sauce and no one could eat it. As soon as the supper dishes were out of the way . . . and that night they were not proud of the way they were washed . . . Jane was off.

There was a wonderful sunset over the harbour, and Jane's cheeks were red from the stinging kisses of the wind by the time she reached the narrow perfumed Titus lane where the trees seemed trying to touch you. Beyond was the kind, old, welcoming house, mellowed in the sunshine of a hundred summers, and the Titus ladies were sitting before a beechwood fire in their kitchen. Justina was knitting and Violet was clipping creamy bits of toffee from a long, silvery twist, made from a recipe Jane had never yet been able to wheedle out of them.

"Come in, dear. We are glad to see you," said Justina, kindly and sincerely, though she looked a little apprehensively over

Jane's shoulder, as if she feared a lion might be skulking in the shadows. "It was such a cool evening we decided to have a fire. Sit down, dear. Violet, give her some toffee. She is growing very tall, isn't she?"

"And handsome," said Violet. "I like her eyes, don't you, sister?"

The Titus ladies had a curious habit of talking Jane over before her face as if she wasn't there. Jane didn't mind . . . though they were sometimes not so complimentary.

"I prefer blue eyes, as you know," said Justina, "but her hair is beautiful."

"Hardly dark enough for my taste," said Violet. "I have always admired black hair."

"The only kind of hair that is really beautiful is curling, red-gold hair," said Justina. "Her cheek-bones are rather high but her insteps are admirable."

"She is very brown," sighed Violet. "But they tell me that is fashionable now. We were very careful of our complexions when we were girls. Our mother, you remember, always made us wear sunbonnets when we went out of doors . . . pink sunbonnets."

"Pink sunbonnets! They were blue," said Justina.

"Pink," said Violet positively.

"Blue," said Justina, just as positively.

They argued for ten minutes over the colour of the sunbonnets. When Jane saw they were getting rather warm over it, she mentioned that Miranda Garland was going to be married in two weeks' time. The Titus ladies forgot the sunbonnets in their excitement.

"Two weeks? That's very sudden, isn't it? Of course, it is to Ned Mitchell. I heard they were engaged . . . even that seemed to me very precipitate when they had been keeping company only six months . . . but I had no idea they were to be married so soon," said Violet.

"She does not want to take a chance on his falling in love with a thinner girl," said Justina.

"They've hurried up the wedding so that I can be bridesmaid," explained Jane proudly.

"She is only seventeen," said Justina disapprovingly.

"Nineteen, sister," said Violet.

"Seventeen," said Justina.

"Nineteen," said Violet.

Jane cut short what seemed likely to be another ten minutes' argument over Miranda's age by saying she was eighteen.

"Oh, well, it's easy enough to get married," said Justina. "The trick nowadays seems to be to stay married."

Jane winced. She knew Justina hadn't meant to hurt her. But her father and mother hadn't stayed married.

"I think," said Violet, kindling, "that P. E. Island has a very good record in that respect. Only two divorces since Confederation . . . sixty-five years."

"Only two real ones," conceded Justina. "But quite a few . . . at least half a dozen . . . imitation ones . . . going to the States and getting a divorce there. And likely to be more from all accounts."

Violet sent Justina a warning glance which Jane, luckily for her peace of mind, did not intercept. Jane had come to the conclusion that she must mention the object of her call now if she were ever going to do it. No use waiting for a chance . . . you just had to make your chance.

"I hear you want to adopt a child," she said, with no beating round the bush.

Again the sisters interchanged glances.

"We've been talking of it off and on for a couple of years," acknowledged Justina.

"We've got along as far as both being willing for a little girl," said Violet with a sigh. "I would have liked a boy . . . but, as Justina pointed out, neither of us knows anything about dressing a boy. It would be more fun dressing a little girl."

"A little girl about seven, with blue eyes and fair curling hair and a rosebud mouth," said Justina firmly.

"A little girl of ten with sloe-black hair and eyes and a creamy skin," said Violet with equal firmness. "I have given in to you about the sex, sister. It is your turn to give in about the age and the complexion."

"The age possibly, but not the complexion."

"I know the very girl for you," said Jane brazenly. "She's my chum in Toronto, Jody Turner. I know you'll love her. Let me tell you about her."

Jane told them. She left nothing untold that might incline them in Jody's favour. When she had said what she wanted to say, she held her tongue. Jane always knew the right time to be silent.

The Titus ladies were silent also. Justina went on knitting and Violet, having finished snipping toffee, took up her crocheting. Now and then they lifted their eyes, looked at each other and dropped them again. The fire crackled companionably.

"Is she pretty?" said Justina at last. "We wouldn't want an ugly child."

"She will be very handsome when she grows up," said Jane gravely. "She has the loveliest eyes. Just now she is so thin . . . and never has any nice clothes."

"She hasn't too much bounce, has she?" said Violet. "I don't like bouncing girls."

"She doesn't bounce at all," said Jane. But this was a mistake because . . .

"I like a little bounce," said Justina.

"She wouldn't want to wear pants, would she?" said Violet. "So many girls do nowadays."

"I'm sure Jody wouldn't want to wear anything you didn't like," answered Jane.

"I wouldn't mind girls wearing pants so much if only they didn't call them pants," said Justina. "But not pyjamas . . . never, never pyjamas."

"Certainly not pyjamas," said Violet.

"Suppose we got her and couldn't love her?" said Justina.

"You couldn't help loving Jody," said Jane warmly. "She's sweet."

"I suppose," hesitated Justina, "she wouldn't . . . there wouldn't be any danger . . . of there being . . . of her having . . . unpleasant insects about her?"

"Certainly not," said Jane shocked. "Why, she lives on Gay Street." For the first time in her life Jane found herself standing up for Gay Street. But even Gay Street must have justice. Jane felt sure there were no unpleasant insects on Gay Street.

"If . . . if she had . . . there is such a thing as a fine-tooth comb," said Violet heroically.

Justina drew her black eyebrows together.

"There has never been any necessity for such an article in our family, Violet."

Again they knitted and crocheted and interchanged glances. Finally Justina said, "No."

"No," said Violet.

"She is too dark," said Justina.

"She is too old," said Violet.

"And now that is settled perhaps Jane would like to have some of that Devonshire cream I made to-day," said Justina.

In spite of the Devonshire cream and the huge bunch of pansies Violet insisted on giving her, Jane went home with a leaden weight of disappointment on her heart. She was surprised to find that Step-a-yard was quite satisfied.

"If they'd told you they'd take her, you'd likely get word to-morrow that they'd changed their minds. Now it'll be the other way round."

Still, Jane was very much amazed to get a note from the Titus ladies the next day, telling her that they had, on second thought, decided to adopt Jody and would she come down and help them settle the necessary arrangements.

"We have concluded she is not too old," said Violet.

"Or too dark," said Justina.

"You'll love her I know," said happy Jane.

"We shall endeavour to be to her as the best and kindest of parents," said Justina. "We must give her music lessons of course. Do you know if she is musical, Jane?"

"Very," said Jane, remembering Jody and the piano at 58.

"Think of filling her stocking at Christmas," said Violet.

"We must get a cow," said Justina. "She must have a glass of warm milk every night at bedtime."

"We must furnish the little south-west room for her," said Violet. "I think I should like a carpet of pale blue, sister."

"She must not expect to find here the excitements of the mad welter of modern life," said Justina solemnly, "but we shall try to remember that youth requires companionship and wholesome pleasures."

"Won't it be lovely to knit sweaters for her?" said Violet.

"We must get out those little wooden ducks our uncle whittled for us when we were small," said Justina.

"It will be nice to have something young to love," said Violet. "I'm only sorry she isn't twins."

"On mature reflection," said Justina, "I am sure you will agree that it is wise for us to find out how we get along with one child before we embark on twins."

"Will you let her keep a cat?" asked Jane. "She loves cats."

"I don't suppose we would object to a bachelor cat," said Justina cautiously.

It was eventually arranged that when Jane went back to Toronto she was to find someone coming to the Island who might bring Jody along with her, and Justina solemnly counted out and gave into Jane's keeping enough money for Jody's travelling expenses and clothes suitable for such travelling.

"I'll write to Miss West right away and tell her, but I'll ask her not to say anything about it to Jody till I get back. I want to tell her . . . I want to see her eyes."

"We are much obliged to you, Jane," said Justina, "you have fulfilled the dream of our lives."

"Completely," said Violet.

39

"If we could only make the summer last longer," sighed Jane.

But that was impossible. It was September now, and soon she must put off Jane and put on Victoria. But not before they got Miranda Jimmy John married off. Jane was so busy helping the Jimmy Johns get ready for the wedding that Lantern Hill hardly knew her except to get a bite for dad. And as bridesmaid she had a chance to wear the adorable dress of rose-pink organdie with its embroidered blue and white spots which mother had gotten her. But once the wedding was over, Jane had to say good-bye to Lantern Hill again . . . to the windy silver of the gulf . . . to the pond . . . to Big Donald's wood-lane . . . which, alas, was going to be cut down and ploughed up . . . to her garden which was to her a garden that never knew winter because she saw it only in summer . . . to the wind that sang in the spruces and the gulls that soared whitely over the harbour . . . to Bubbles and Happy and First Peter and Silver Penny. And dad. But though she felt sad over it, there was none of the despair that had filled her heart the year before. She would be back next summer . . . that was an understood thing now. She would be seeing mother again . . . she did not dislike the idea of going back to St Agatha's . . . there was Jody's delight to be looked forward to . . . and dad was going with her as far as Montreal.

Aunt Irene came to Lantern Hill the day before Jane left and seemed to want to say something she couldn't quite manage to say. When she went away, she held Jane's hand and looked at her very significantly.

"If you hear some news before next spring, lovey . . ."

"What news am I likely to hear?" said Jane with the terrible directness which Aunt Irene always found so trying.

"Oh . . . one can never tell . . . who knows what changes may come before then?"

Jane was uncomfortable for a few moments and then shrugged it away. Aunt Irene was always giving mysterious hints about something, throwing out wisps of insinuation that clung like cobwebs. Jane had learned not to mind Aunt Irene.

"I've never really been able to make as much of that child as I would like," mourned Aunt Irene to a friend. "She holds you at arms' length somehow. The Kennedys were all hard . . . her mother now . . . you'd think to look at her she was all rose and cream and sweetness. But underneath, my dear . . . hard as a rock. She ruined my brother's life and did everything . . . *everything*, I understand . . . to set his child against him."

"Jane seems very fond of her father now," said the friend.

"Oh, I'm sure she is . . . as fond as she can be of any one. But Andrew is a very lonely man. And I don't know if he will ever be anything else. Lately I've been wondering . . ."

"Wondering if he'll finally work himself up to getting a United States divorce and marrying Lilian Morrow," said the friend bluntly. She had had much experience in filling up Irene's blanks.

Aunt Irene looked quite shocked at such plain speaking.

"Oh, I wouldn't like to say that. . . . I don't really know . . . but of course Lilian is the girl he should have married instead of Robin Kennedy. They have so much in common. And though I don't approve of divorce ordinarily . . . I think it shocking . . . still . . . there are special circumstances. . . ."

Jane and dad had a delightful trip to Montreal.

"How nice to think we're an hour younger than we were," said dad, as he put his watch back at Campbellton. He said things like that all along the way about everything.

Jane clung to him very tightly in Montreal station.

"Dad darling . . . but I'll be back next summer, you know."

"Of course," said dad. Then he added:

"Jane, here's a spot of hard cash for you. I don't suppose you get a very huge allowance at 60 Gay."

"None at all. . . . But can you spare this, dad?" Jane was looking at the bills he had put into her hand. "Fifty dollars? That's an awful lot of money, dad."

"This has been a good year for me, Jane. Editors have been kind. And somehow . . . when you're about I write more . . . I've felt some of my old ambition stirring this past year."

Jane, who had spent all her lion-reward money on things for Lantern Hill and treats for the young fry who had been associated with her in the episode, tucked the money away in her bag, reflecting that it would come in handy at Christmas.

"Life, deal gently with her . . . love, never desert her," said Andrew Stuart, looking after the Toronto train as it steamed away.

Jane found that grandmother had had her room done over for her. When she went up to it, she discovered a wonderful splendour of rose and grey, instead of the old gloom. Silvery carpet . . . shimmering curtains . . . chintz chairs . . . cream-tinted furniture . . . pink silk bedspread. The old bearskin rug . . . the only thing she had really liked . . . was gone. So was the cradle. The big mirror had been replaced by a round rimless one.

"How do you like it?" asked grandmother watchfully.

Jane recalled her little room at Lantern Hill with its bare floor and sheepskin rug and white spool bed covered with its patchwork quilt.

"It is very beautiful, grandmother. Thank you very much."

"Fortunately," said grandmother, "I did not expect much enthusiasm."

After grandmother had gone out, Jane turned her back on the splendour and went to the window. The only things of home were the stars. She wondered if dad were looking at them . . . no, of course he wouldn't be home yet. But they would all be there in their proper places . . . the North Star over the Watch Tower, Orion sparkling over Big Donald's hill. And Jane knew that she would never be the least bit afraid of grandmother again.

"Oh, Jane," said Jody. "Oh, Jane!"

"I know you'll be happy with the Titus ladies, Jody. They're a little old-fashioned but they're so kind . . . and they have the loveliest garden. You won't have to make a garden by sticking faded flowers in a plot any more. You'll see the famous cherry walk in bloom . . . I've never seen that."

"It's like a beautiful dream," said Jody. "But oh, Jane, I hate to leave you."

"We'll be together in the summers instead of in the winters. That will be the only difference, Jody. And it will be ever so much nicer. We'll swim . . . I'll teach you the crawl. Mother says her friend, Mrs Newton, will take you as far as Sackville, and Miss Justina Titus will meet you there. And mother is going to get your clothes."

"I wonder if it will be like this when I go to heaven," said Jody breathlessly.

Jane missed Jody when she went, but life was growing full. She loved St Agatha's now. She liked Phyllis quite well and Aunt Sylvia said she had really never seen a child blossom out socially as Victoria had done. Uncle William couldn't floor her when he asked about capitals now. Uncle William was beginning to think that Victoria had something in her, and Jane was finding that she liked Uncle William reasonably well. As for grandmother .. . well, Mary told Frank it did her heart good to see Miss Victoria standing up to the old lady.

"Not that stands up is just the right word either. But the madam can't put it over her like she used to. Nothing she says seems to get under Miss Victoria's skin any more. And does that make her mad! I've seen her turn white with rage when she'd said something real venomous and Miss Victoria just answering in that respectful tone of hers that's just as good as telling her she doesn't care a hoot about what any Kennedy of them all says any more."

"I wish Miss Robin would learn that trick," said Frank.

Mary shook her head.

"It's too late for her. She's been under the old lady's thumb too long. Never went against her in her life except for one thing and lived to repent that, so they say. And anyhow she's a cat of a different breed from Miss Victoria."

One November evening mother went again to Lakeside Gardens to see her friend and took Jane with her. Jane welcomed the chance to see her house again. Would it be sold? Unbelievably it wasn't. Jane's heart gave a bound of relief. She was so afraid it would be. She couldn't understand how it wasn't, it seemed so entirely desirable to her. She did not know that the builder had decided that he had made a mistake when he built a little house in Lakeside Gardens. People who could live in Lakeside Gardens wanted bigger houses.

Though Jane was glad to her toes that her house hadn't been sold, she was inconsistently resentful that it was unlighted and unwarmed. She hated the oncoming winter because of the house. Its heart must ache with the cold then. She sat on the steps and watched the lights blooming out along the Gardens and wished there was one in her house. How the dead brown leaves still clinging to the oaks rustled in the windy night! How the lights along the lake shore twinkled through the trees of the ravine! And how she hated, yes, positively hated, the man who would buy this house!

"It just isn't fair," said Jane. "Nobody will ever love it as I do. It really belongs to me."

The week before Christmas Jane bought the materials for a fruit-cake out of the money dad had given her and compounded it in the kitchen. Then she expressed it to dad. She did not ask any one's permission for all this . . . just went ahead and did it. Mary held her tongue and grandmother knew nothing about it. But Jane would have sent it just the same if she had.

One thing made Christmas Day memorable for Jane that year. Just after breakfast Frank came in to say that long distance was calling Miss Victoria. Jane went to the hall with a puzzled look . . . who on earth could be calling her on long distance? She lifted the receiver to her ear.

"Lantern Hill calling Superior Jane! Merry Christmas and thanks for that cake," said dad's voice as distinctly as if he were in the same room.

"Dad!" Jane gasped. "Where are you?"

"Here at Lantern Hill. This is my Christmas present to you, Janelet. Three minutes over a thousand miles."

Probably no two people ever crammed more into three minutes. When Jane went back to the dining-room, her cheeks were crimson and her eyes glowed like jewels.

"Who was calling you, Victoria?" asked grandmother.

"Dad," said Jane.

Mother gave a little choked cry. Grandmother wheeled on her furiously.

"Perhaps," she said icily, "you think he should have called you."

"He should," said Jane.

40

At the end of a blue and silver day in March, Jane was doing her lessons in her room and feeling reasonably happy. She had had a rapturous letter from Jody that morning . . . all Jody's letters were rapturous . . . giving her lots of interesting news from Queen's Shore . . . she had had a birthday the week before and was now in her leggy teens . . . and two bits of luck had come her way that afternoon. Aunt Sylvia had taken her and Phyllis with her on a shopping expedition, and Jane had picked up two delightful things for Lantern Hill . . . a lovely old copper bowl and a comical brass knocker for the glass-paned door. It was the head of a dog with his tongue hanging waggishly out and a real dog-laugh in his eyes.

The door opened and mother came in, ready dressed for a restaurant dinner party. She wore the most wonderful sheath dress of ivory taffeta, with a sapphire velvet bow at the back and a little blue velvet jacket over her lovely shoulders. Her slippers were blue, with slender golden heels and she had her hair done in a new way . . . a sleek flat top to her head and a row of tricksy little curls around her neck.

"Oh, mums, you are perfectly lovely," said Jane, looking at her with adoring eyes. And then she added something she had never intended to say . . . something that seemed to rush to her lips and say itself:

"I do wish dad could see you now."

Jane pulled herself up in dire dismay. She had been told never to mention dad to mother . . . and yet she had done it. And mother was looking as if she had been struck in the face.

"I do not suppose," said mother bitterly, "that he would be at all interested in the sight."

Jane said nothing. There seemed to be nothing she could say. How did she know whether dad would be interested or not? And yet . . . and yet . . . she was sure he still loved mother.

Mother sat down on one of the chintz chairs and looked at Jane.

"Jane," she said, "I am going to tell you something about my marriage. I don't know what you have heard about the other side of it . . . there was another side, of course . . . but I want you to hear my side. It is better you should know. I should have told you before . . . but . . . it hurt me so."

"Don't tell it now, if it hurts you, darling," said Jane earnestly. (Thinking—*I know more about it than you suppose already.*)

"I must. There are some things I want you to understand . . . I don't want you to blame me too much. . . ."

"I don't blame you at all, mother."

"Oh, I was to blame a great deal . . . I see that now when it is too late. I was so young and foolish . . . just a careless, happy little bride. I . . . I . . . ran away to be married to your father, Jane."

Jane nodded.

"How much do you know, Jane?"

"Just that you ran away and were very happy at first."

"Happy? Oh, Jane Victoria, I was . . . I was . . . so happy. But it really was . . . a very unfortunate marriage, dearest."

(That sounds like something grandmother said.)

"I shouldn't have treated mother so . . . I was all she had left after my father died. But she forgave me. . . ."

(And set herself to work to make trouble between you and dad.)

"But we were happy that first year, Jane Victoria. I worshipped Andrew . . . that smile of his . . . you know his smile. . . ."

(Do I know it?)

"We had such fun together . . . reading poetry by driftwood fires down at the harbour . . . we always made a rite of lighting those fires . . . life was wonderful. I used to welcome the days then as much as I shrink from them now. We had only one quarrel that first year . . . I forget what it was about . . . something silly . . .

I kissed the frown on his forehead and all was well again. I knew there was no woman in the world so happy as I was. If it could have lasted!"

"Why didn't it last, mother?"

"I . . . I hardly know. Of course I wasn't much of a housekeeper but I don't think it was that. I couldn't cook, but our maid didn't do so badly and Little Aunt Em used to come in and help. She was a darling. And I couldn't keep accounts straight ever . . . I would add up a column eight times and get a different answer every time. But Andrew just laughed over that. Then you were born. . . ."

"And that made all the trouble," cried Jane, in whom that bitter thought had persisted in rankling.

"Not at first . . . oh, Jane Victoria darling, not at first. But Andrew never seemed the same after. . . ."

(I wonder if it wasn't you who had changed, mother.)

"He was jealous of my love for you . . . he was, Jane Victoria. . . ."

(Not jealous . . . no, not jealous. A little hurt . . . he didn't like to be second with you after he had been first . . . he thought he came second then.)

"He used to say 'your child' . . . 'your daughter,' as if you weren't his. Why, he used to make fun of you. Once he said you had a face like a monkey."

(And no Kennedy can take a joke.)

"You hadn't . . . you were the cutest little thing. Why, Jane Victoria darling, you were just a daily miracle. It was such fun to tuck you in at night . . . to watch you when you were asleep."

(And you were just a darling big baby yourself, mother.)

"Andrew was angry because I couldn't go out with him as much as before. How could I? It would have been bad for you if I'd taken you and I couldn't leave you. But he didn't care really . . . he never did except for a little while at the first. He cared far more for that book of his than for me. He would shut himself up with it for days at a time and forget all about me."

(And yet you think he was the only jealous one.)

"I suppose I simply wasn't capable of living with a genius. Of course, I knew I wasn't clever enough for him. Irene let me see that she thought that. And he cared far more for her than for me. . . ."

(Oh, no, not that . . . never that!)

"She had far more influence over him than I had. He told her things before he told me. . . ."

(Because she was always trying to pick them out of him before he was ready to tell any one.)

"He thought me such a child that if he had a plan, he consulted her before he consulted me. Irene made me feel like a shadow in my own house. She liked to humiliate me, I think. She was always sweet and smiling . . ."

(She would be!)

". . . but she always blew my candles out. She patronized me. . . ."

(Do I know it!)

"'I've noticed,' she would say. That had such a sting as if she'd been spying on me right along. Andrew said I was unreasonable . . . I wasn't . . . but he always sided with her. Irene never liked me. She had wanted Andrew to marry another girl . . . I was told she had said from the first that she knew our marriage would be a failure. . . ."

(And did her best to make it one.)

"She kept pushing us apart . . . here a little . . . there a little. I was helpless."

(Not if you had had a wee bit of backbone, mummy.)

"Andrew was annoyed because I didn't like her, and yet he hated my family. He couldn't speak of mother without insulting her . . . he didn't want me to visit her . . . get presents from her . . . money . . . oh, Jane Victoria, that last year was dreadful. Andrew never looked at me if he could help it."

(Because it hurt him too much.)

"It seemed as if I were married to a stranger. We were always saying bitter things to each other. . . ."

(That verse I read in the Bible last night, "Death and Life are in the power of the tongue" . . . it's true . . . it's true!)

"Then mother wrote and asked me to come home for a visit. Andrew said, 'Go if you want to' . . . just like that. Irene said it would give things a chance to heal up. . . ."

(I can see her smiling when she said it.)

"I went. And . . . and . . . mother wanted me to stay with her. She could see I was so unhappy. . . ."

(And took her chance.)

"I couldn't go on living with a person who hated me, Jane Victoria . . . I couldn't . . . so I . . . I wrote him and told him I thought it would be better for both of us if I didn't go back. I . . . I don't know . . . nothing seemed real someway . . . if he had written and asked me to go back . . . but he didn't. I never heard from him . . . till that letter came asking for you."

Jane had kept silence while mother talked, thinking things at intervals, but now she could keep silence no longer.

"He *did* write . . . he wrote and asked you to come back . . . and you never answered . . . you never answered, mother."

Mother and daughter looked at each other in the silence of the big, beautiful, unfriendly room.

After a little, mother whispered, "I never got it, Jane Victoria."

They said nothing more about it. Both of them knew quite well what had happened to the letter.

"Mother, it isn't too late yet. . . ."

"Yes, it is too late, dear. Too much has come between us. I can't break with mother again . . . she'd never forgive me again . . . and she loves me so. I'm all she has. . . ."

"Nonsense!" Jane was as brusque as any Stuart of them all. "She has got Aunt Gertrude and Uncle William and Aunt Sylvia."

"It's . . . it's not the same. She didn't love *their* father. And . . . I can't stand up to her. Besides, he doesn't want me any more. We're strangers. And oh, Jane Victoria, life's slipping away . . . like that . . . through my fingers. The harder I try to hold it, the faster it slips. I've lost you. . . ."

"Never, mother!"

"Yes, you belong more to him than to me now. I don't blame you . . . you can't help it. But you'll belong a little more to him every year . . . till there'll be nothing left for me."

Grandmother came in. She looked at them both suspiciously.

"Have you forgotten you are dining out, Robin?"

"Yes, I think I had," said mother strangely. "But never mind. . . . I've remembered now. I . . . I shan't forget again."

Grandmother lingered for a moment after mother had gone out.

"What have you been saying to upset your mother, Victoria?"

Jane looked levelly at grandmother.

"What happened to the letter father wrote mother long ago, asking her to go back to him, grandmother?"

Grandmother's cold cruel eyes suddenly blazed.

"So that's it? Do you think it any of your business exactly?"

"Yes, I think it is, since I am their child."

"I did what was right with it . . . I burned it. She had seen her mistake . . . she had come back to me, as I always knew she would . . . I was not going to have her misled again. Don't begin plotting, Victoria. I am a match for you all yet."

"No one is plotting," said Jane. "There is just one thing I want to tell you, grandmother. My father and mother love each other yet . . . I *know* it."

Grandmother's voice was ice.

"They do not. Your mother has been happy all these years till you began stirring up old memories. Leave her alone. She is my daughter . . . no outsider shall ever come between us again . . . neither Andrew Stuart nor you nor any one. And you will be good enough to remember that."

530

41

The letters came on the afternoon of the last day of March. Jane was not at St Agatha's . . . she had had a touch of sore throat the day before and mother thought it was wiser for her to stay home. But her throat was better now and Jane was reasonably happy. It was almost April . . . if not quite spring yet, at least the hope of spring. Just a little over two months and she would keep her tryst with June at Lantern Hill. Meanwhile, she was planning some additions to her garden . . . for one thing, a row of knightly hollyhocks along the dike at the bottom. She would plant the seeds in August and they would bloom the *next* summer.

Grandmother and Aunt Gertrude and mother had all gone to Mrs Morrison's bridge and tea, so Mary brought the afternoon mail to Jane who pounced joyfully on three letters for herself. One from Polly . . . one from Shingle . . . one . . . Jane recognized Aunt Irene's copper-plate writing.

She read Polly's first . . . a good letter, full of fun and Lantern Hill jokes. There was one bit of news about dad in it . . . he was planning a trip to the States very soon . . . Boston or New York or somewhere . . . Polly seemed rather vague. And Polly wound up with a paragraph that gave Jane a good laugh . . . her last laughter for some time . . . the last laughter of her childhood, it always seemed to Jane, looking back on it from later years.

Polly wrote: "Mr Julius Evans was awful mad last week, a rat got drowned in his cask of new maple syrup and he made a terrible fuss over such a waste. But dad says he isn't sure it was wasted, so we are getting our syrup from Joe Baldwin's to be on the safe side."

Jane was still laughing over this when she opened Shingle's letter. A paragraph on the second page leaped to her eye.

"Everybody is saying your dad is going to get a Yankee divorce and marry Lilian Morrow. Will she be your mother then? How do you like the idea? I guess she'll be your stepmother . . . only that sounds so funny when your own mother is still alive. Will your name be changed? Caraway says not . . . but they do such queer things in the States. Anyway, I hope it won't make any difference about you coming to Lantern Hill in the summer."

Jane felt literally sick and cold with agony as she dropped the letter and snatched up Aunt Irene's. She had been wondering what Aunt Irene could be writing to her about . . . she knew now.

The letter told Jane that Aunt Irene suspected that her brother Andrew intended going to the States and living there long enough to get a United States divorce.

"Of course, it may not be true, lovey. He hasn't told me. But it is all over the country, and where there is so much smoke there must be some fire, and I think you ought to be prepared, lovey. I know that several of his friends advised him long ago to get a divorce. But as he never discussed it with me, I have given no advice for or against. For some reason I am at a loss to understand, he has shut me out of his confidence these past two years. But I have felt that the state of his affairs has long been very unsatisfactory. I'm sure you won't worry over this. . . . I wouldn't have told you if I thought it would worry you. You have too much good sense . . . I've often remarked how old you are for your years. But of course, if it is true, it may make some difference to you. He might marry again."

If you have seen a candle-flame blown out, you will know what Jane looked like as she went blindly to the window. It was a dark day with occasional showers of driving rain. Jane looked at the cruel, repellent, merciless street but did not see it. She had never felt such dreadful shame . . . such dreadful misery. Yet it seemed to her she ought to have known what was coming. There had been a hint or two last summer . . . she remembered Lilian Morrow's caressing "'Drew" and dad's pleasure in her company. And now . . . if this hideous thing were true, she would never spend a summer at Lantern Hill again. Would *they* dare to live at Lantern Hill? Lilian Morrow her mother! Nonsense! Nobody could be her mother except mother. The thing was unthinkable. But Lilian Morrow would be father's wife.

This had all been going on in these past weeks when she had been so happy, looking forward to June.

"I don't suppose I'll ever feel glad again," thought Jane drearily. Everything was suddenly meaningless . . . she felt as if she were far removed from everything . . . as if she were looking at life and people and things through the big end of Timothy Salt's telescope. It seemed years since she had laughed over Polly's tale of Mr Evans's wasted—or unwasted—maple syrup.

Jane walked the floor of her room all the rest of that afternoon. She dared not sit down for a moment. It seemed that as long as she kept moving her pain marched with her and she could bear it. If she were to stop, it would crush her. But by dinner-time Jane's mind had begun to function again. She must know the truth and she knew what she must do to learn it. And it must be done at once.

She counted the money she had left from father's gift. Yes, there was just enough for a one-way ticket to the Island. Nothing left over for meals or a Pullman but that did not matter. Jane knew she would neither eat nor sleep until she knew. She went down to her dinner, which Mary had spread for her in the breakfast-room, and tried to eat something lest Mary should notice.

Mary did.

"Your throat worse, Miss Victoria?"

"No, my throat is all right," said Jane. Her voice sounded strange in her ears . . . as if it belonged to someone else. "Do you know what time mother and grandmother will be home, Mary?"

"Not till late, Miss Victoria. You know your grandmother and Aunt Gertrude are going to dinner at your Uncle William's, meeting some of your grandmother's old friends from the west, and your mother is going to a party. She won't be home till after midnight, but Frank goes for the old lady at eleven."

The International Limited left at ten. Jane had all the time she needed. She went upstairs and packed a small hand grip with some necessities and a box of gingersnaps that were on her bedroom table. The darkness outside the window seemed to look in at her menacingly. The rain spat against the panes. The wind was very lonely in the leafless elms. Once Jane had thought the rain and the wind were friends of hers, but they seemed enemies now. Everything hurt her. Everything in her life seemed uprooted and withered. She put on her hat and coat, picked up her bag, went to mother's room and pinned a little note on a pillow, and crept down the stairs. Mary and Frank were having their dinner in the kitchen and the door was shut. Very quietly Jane telephoned for a taxi; when it came, she was waiting outside for it. She went down the steps of 60 Gay and out of the grim iron gates for the last time.

"The Union Station," she told the taxi-driver. They moved swiftly away over the wet street that looked like a black river with drowned lights in it. Jane was going to ask for the truth from the only one who could tell it to her . . . her father.

42

Jane left Toronto Wednesday night. On Friday night she reached the Island. The train whirled over the sodden land. Her Island was not beautiful now. It was just like every other place in the ugliness of very early spring. The only beautiful things were the slim white birches on the dark hills. Jane had sat bolt upright all the time of her journey, night and day, subsisting on what ginger-snaps she could force herself to swallow. She hardly moved but she felt all the time as if she were running . . . running . . . trying to catch up with someone on a road . . . someone who was getting farther and farther ahead all the time.

She did not go on to Charlottetown. She got off at West Trent, a little siding where the train stopped when it was asked to. It was only five miles from there to Lantern Hill. Jane could hear plainly the roar of the distant ocean. Once she would have thrilled to it . . . that sonorous music coming through the windy, dark grey night on the old north shore. Now she did not notice it.

It had been raining but it was fine now. The road was hard and rough and dotted with pools of water. Jane walked through them unheedingly. Presently there were dark spires of fir-trees against a moonrise. The puddles on the road turned to pools of silver fire. The houses she passed seemed alien . . . remote . . . as if they had closed their doors to her. The spruces seemed to turn cold shoulders on her. Far away over the pale moonlit landscape was a wooded hill with the light of a house she knew on it. Would there be a light at Lantern Hill or would dad be gone?

A dog of her acquaintance stopped to speak to her, but Jane ignored him. Once a car bumped past her, picking her out with its lights and splashing her from head to foot with mud. It was Joe Weeks who, being a cousin of Mrs Meade, had the family trick of malapropisms and told his sceptical wife when he got home that he had met either Jane Stuart or her operation on the road. Jane felt like an apparition. It seemed to her that she had been walking for ever . . . must go on walking for ever . . . through this ghostly world of cold moonlight.

There was Little Donald's house with a light in the parlour. The curtains were red, and when they were drawn at night, the light shone rosily through them. Then Big Donald's light . . . and at last the lane to Lantern Hill.

There was a light in the kitchen!

Jane was trembling as she went up the rutted lane and across the yard, past the forlorn and muddy garden where the poppies had once trembled in silken delight, to the window. What a sadly different home-coming from what she had planned!

She looked in. Dad was reading by the table. He wore his shabby old tweed suit and the nice grey tie with tiny red flecks in it, which Jane had picked out for him last summer. The Old Contemptible was in his mouth and his legs were cocked up on the sofa where two dogs and First Peter were sleeping. Silver Penny was stretched out against the warm base of the petrol lamp on the table. In the corner was a sinkful of dirty dishes. Even at that moment a fresh pang tore Jane's heart at the sight.

A moment later an amazed Andrew Stuart looked up to see his daughter standing before him . . . wet-footed, mud-splashed, white-faced, with her eyes so terribly full of misery that a hideous fear flashed into his mind. Was her mother . . .?

"Good heavens, Jane!"

Literally sick from fear, Jane bluntly put the question she had come so far to ask.

"Father, are you going to get a divorce and marry Miss Morrow?"

Dad stared at her for a moment. Then, "No!" he shouted. And again, "No . . . no . . . no! Jane, who told you such a thing?"

Jane drew a deep breath, trying to realize that the long nightmare was over. She couldn't . . . not just at first.

"Aunt Irene wrote me. She said you were going to Boston. She said . . ."

"Irene! Irene is always getting silly notions in her head. She means well but . . . Jane, listen, once for all. I am the husband of one wife and I'll never be anything else."

Dad broke off and stared at Jane.

Jane, who never cried, was crying.

He swept her into his arms.

"Jane, you darling little idiot! How could you believe such stuff? I like Lilian Morrow . . . I've always liked her. And I could never love her in a thousand years. . . . Going to Boston? Of course, I'm going to Boston. I've great news for you, Jane. My book has been accepted after all. I'm going to Boston to arrange the details with my publishers. Darling, do you mean to tell me that you walked from West Trent? How lucky I hung a moon out! But you are just sopping. What you need is a brew of good hot cocoa, and I'm going to make it for you. Look pleasant, dogs. Purr, Peter. Jane has come home."

43

The next day Andrew Stuart sent for the doctor, and a few hours later the nurse came. The word went around Queen's Shore and the Corners that Jane Stuart was very ill with a dangerous type of pneumonia.

Jane could never remember anything of those first days very clearly. She was delirious almost from the beginning of her illness. Faces came and went dimly . . . dad's in anguish . . . a grave, troubled doctor . . . a white-capped nurse . . . finally another face . . . only *that* must be a dream . . . mother couldn't be there . . . not even if Jane could smell the faint perfume of her hair. Mother was in far-away Toronto.

As for her own whereabouts, Jane did not know where she was . . . she only knew that she was a lost wind seeking some lost word for ever. Not till she found that word could she stop being a wind and be Jane Stuart again. Once, it seemed to her, she heard a woman crying wildly and someone saying, "There is still hope, dearest, there is still a little hope." And again . . . long afterwards . . . "There will be a change, one way or another, to-night."

"And then," said Jane, so clearly and distinctly that she startled every one in the room, "I shall find my lost word."

Jane didn't know how long it was after that to the day when she understood that she was Jane again and no longer a lost wind.

"Am I dead?" she wondered. She lifted her arms feebly and looked at them. They had grown terribly thin, and she could hold them up only a second, but she concluded that she was alive.

She was alone . . . not in her own little room at Lantern Hill but in father's. She could see through the window the gulf sparkling and the sky so softly, so ethereally blue over the haunted dunes. Somebody . . . Jane found out later it had been Jody . . . had found the first mayflowers and put them in a vase on the table by her bed.

"I'm . . . sure . . . the house . . . is listening," thought Jane.

To what was it listening? To two people who seemed to be sitting on the stairs outside. Jane felt that she ought to know who they were, but the knowledge just escaped her. Fitful sentences came to her, though they were uttered in muted tones. At the time they meant nothing to Jane, but she remembered them . . . remembered them always.

"Darling, I didn't mean a word of those dreadful things I said. . . ." "If I had got your letter . . ." "My poor little love . . ." "Have you ever thought of me in all those years?" . . . "Have I thought of anything else, loveliest?" . . . "When your wire came . . . mother said I mustn't . . . she was terrible . . . as if anything could keep me from Jane. . . ." "We were just two very foolish people . . . is it too late to be wise, Robin?"

Jane wanted to hear the answer to that question . . . wanted to dreadfully . . . somehow she felt that it would be of tremendous importance to everybody in the world. But a wind came in from the sea and blew the door shut.

"I'll never know now," she whispered piteously to the nurse when she came in.

"Know what, dear?"

"What she said . . . the woman on the stairs . . . her voice was so like mother's. . . ."

"It was your mother, dear. Your father wired for her as soon as I came. She has been here right along . . . and if you're good and don't get excited, you can have just a peep at her this evening."

"So," said Jane feebly, "mother must have stood up to grandmother for once."

But it was several days before Jane was allowed to have her first real talk with father and mother. They came in together, hand in hand, and stood looking down at her. Jane knew that there were three tremendously happy people in the room. Never had she seen either of them looking like that. They seemed to have drunk from some deep well of life, and the draught had made them young lovers again.

"Jane," said dad, "two foolish people have learned a little wisdom."

"It was all my fault that we didn't learn it long ago," said mother. There was a sound of tears in her voice and a sound of laughter.

"Woman!" What a delightful way dad had of saying "woman"! And mother's laugh . . . was it a laugh or a chime of bells? "I will not have you casting slurs at my wife. Your fault indeed! I will not have one particle of the blame taken away from me. Look at her, Jane . . . look at my little golden love. How did you ever have the luck to pick such a mother, Jane? The moment I saw her I fell in love with her all over again. And now we will all go in search of ten lost years."

"And will we live here at Lantern Hill?" asked Jane.

"Always, when we're not living somewhere else. I'm afraid with two women on my hands I'll never get my epic on Methuselah's life finished now, Jane. But there will be compensations. I think a honeymoon is coming to us. As soon as you're on the hoof, Superior Jane, we'll all take a little run up to Boston. I have to see about that book of mine, you know. Then a summer here and in the fall . . . the truth is, Jane, I've been offered the assistant editorship of *Saturday Evening* with a healthy salary. I had meant to refuse, but I think I'll have to accept. What about it, Jane? The winters in Toronto . . . the summers at Lantern Hill?"

"And we'll never have to say good-bye again. Oh, dad! But . . ."

"But me no buts. What is troubling you, dearest dear?"

"We . . . we won't have to live at 60 Gay?"

"Not by a jugful! A house we must have, of course. How you live is much more important than where you live . . . but we must have a roof over us."

Jane thought of the little stone house in Lakeside Gardens. It had not been sold yet. They would buy it. It would live . . . they would give it life. Its cold windows would shine with welcoming lights. Grandmother, stalking about 60 Gay, like a bitter old queen, her eyes bright with venom, forgiving or unforgiving as she chose, could never make trouble for them again. There would be no more misunderstanding. She, Jane, understood them both and could interpret them to each other. And have an eye on the housekeeping as well. It all fitted in as if it had been planned ages ago.

"Oh, dad," cried this happiest of all Janes, "I know the very house."

"You would," said dad.

THE END

OTHER BOOKS TO EXPLORE BY
L. M. MONTGOMERY

OTHER BOOKS TO EXPLORE BY
L. M. MONTGOMERY

NOVELS
Kilmeny of the Orchard
The Blue Castle
A Tangled Web
Magic for Marigold
Jane of Lantern Hill

POETRY
The Watchman & Other Poems

AUTOBIOGRAPHY
The Alpine Path: The Story of My Career

COLLECTIONS
The Anne of Green Gables Collection - Volumes 1-3
   (Anne of Green Gables, Anne of Avonlea and Anne of the Island)
The Emily Starr Series
   (Emily of New Moon, Emily Climbs and Emily's Quest)
The Story Girl & The Golden Road
Pat of Silver Bush & Mistress Pat
The Blue Castle & A Tangled Web
Magic for Marigold & Jane of Lantern Hill
Lucy Maud Montgomery Short Stories, 1896 to 1901
Lucy Maud Montgomery Short Stories, 1902 to 1903
Lucy Maud Montgomery Short Stories, 1904
Lucy Maud Montgomery Short Stories, 1905 to 1906
Lucy Maud Montgomery Short Stories, 1907 to 1908
Lucy Maud Montgomery Short Stories, 1909 to 1922